Wakefield
& Informatic

This book should be returned by the last date stamped above. You may renew the loan personally, by post or telephone for a further period if the book is not required by another reader.

educational voice in contemporary British crime fiction, the utterly fabulous Christopher Fowler."

HOT WATER

CHRISTOPHER FOWLER

TITAN BOOKS

Hot Water
Print edition ISBN: 9781789099843
E-book edition ISBN: 9781789099850

Published by Titan Books
A division of Titan Publishing Group Ltd
144 Southwark Street, London SE1 0UP
www.titanbooks.com

First edition: March 2022
10 9 8 7 6 5 4 3 2 1

A CIP catalogue record for this title is available from the British Library.

Printed and bound in Great Britain by CPI Group Ltd.

For Pete

Yesterday, upon the stair
I met a girl who wasn't there
She wasn't there again today
Oh how I wish she'd go away.

(With apologies to William Hughes Mearns, 1899)

ONE:
THE GIRL

1.

'How do I know you're telling the truth?'

Julia Martinez tapped the reference letter with a glitter-tipped nail that belonged on a teenaged hand. *Tap tap tap* ticked the fingers as she thought it over.

Hannah could see that after three weeks of doing the rounds her letter was starting to look over-handled, but it was all she had.

Julia made a sour face and slid the recommendation back in Hannah's direction. 'This is from your tutor. No use. You have never been a maid before. Not with those hands.'

Hannah sat on the other side of the desk, her fingers laced in her lap. She had dressed conservatively in winter greys. She tried not to let her nervousness show. Without thinking, she pushed her blonde hair back from her face and tucked a stray strand behind her left ear. It had fallen down ever since she was little.

'You are too pretty for this work. Pretty always means trouble. This I know. Are you a sensible girl, Miss Carreras?'

Julia rolled her Rs spectacularly on the surname, turning it into something Venezuelan.

'I think so.' Hannah attempted to look trustworthy.

'So when the men play their little games you know what to do, yes?'

What did her employer want to hear? The plastic sign on the wall above Julia's enormous mass of coppery hair read: *Vacances Paradis*. Julia arranged stays at holiday villas and hired staff for them. The agency was situated at the wrong end of the Promenade des Anglais, its posters bleached to baby blue in the windows. Her office, dark and not much bigger than a *tabac*, was overfilled with boxes of undistributed brochures advertising the season just ending, a testament to the failing company.

Julia was the agency's manager, past her peak in property management, a living embodiment of what late nights, red wine and a lazy husband could do to an ambitious woman. She applied lipstick so thickly that cigarettes hung from her lip in a cheerfully slutty manner, so that she resembled the late-career Simone Signoret, which for some senior clients was no bad thing.

She tapped her nails again and jiggled a cheap-looking charm bracelet. 'We don't get many Englishes. You are very – how do you call this? English rose. Clients will like you. I can't employ African girls, it makes our nice liberal renters feel like slave-owners. Or Muslims: pity because they work hard, but people think *terrorists*. I state this purely as a fact. Why do you leave England?'

The air-conditioned office was freezing. Hannah discreetly rubbed her arms. She wanted to answer honestly. She longed to say, 'Because of Aidan and his mother and the police,' but instead she said, 'I speak French and know the region a little, so this seems the right choice for me.'

Julia was unimpressed. 'You have a useless degree and no skills. Is this why you want to clean toilets?'

'I need the money, Madame Martinez. And I work well alone.'

'Okay, the last part I like. How old are you?'

'Twenty-three next month.'

'You're staying in Nice, yes?'

'I'm sharing a flat in the Old Town. I have to leave it by Saturday –'

'Your problem, don't care.' Julia waved the information away with her polished claw. 'You must know this. It's not glamorous work. Changing beds is like lifting weights.' She tapped a lurid purple cigarette out of its shiny sarcophagus and lit it. 'The guests are pigs. They do drugs off the coffee tables and their children piss everywhere. The French are fussy. The Italians never shut up. The English drink like fish. The Russians, sometimes you have to call the police out. I pay over the going rate so you don't steal from me.'

'You mean I have the job?'

'Maybe I regret this later but yes, you have the job.' Julia raised her nicotined index finger, drawing a line in the smoky air. 'There is only one rule I insist upon. You do *not* make gossip with the guests. I keep them happy, you keep them clean. Do the bathrooms, bedrooms, kitchens. Make sure the stairs are dry before you leave so they can't slip and sue me. No extra ironing, no repairs. If a bulb goes they'll ask you to replace it; not your job. I can't afford accidents. If they want you to cook them breakfast or clear things away tell them you'll be happy to do so. When you finish your villa, help a co-worker with another property. Seven days a week, three hours per villa, just a tidy-up on Sunday because the guests always leave a mess Saturday night. You can move your times but put down your hours; I need to know for the chargings. There are gardeners and pool boys. Don't have funny business with them on my time.' When she touched her spray-stiff hair with her cigarette hand, Hannah thought the place might go up.

'I need a copy of your passport and a major credit card. Security because the girls steal things and run away. They never save and get into debt. I am not a bank. I can advance only two weeks. If you're in trouble maybe I can help, maybe not. I don't involve the police. I can handle most things. I have a gun.' Julia flashed a brisk smile. 'Maybe you could do better than this, but then you pay taxes.'

Hannah knew she was right. There was nothing else legal that paid as much. Cleaning didn't bother her. She had looked after her grandmother, wiping up after accidents, answering questions that made no sense, dealing with the old lady's constant shame. She tried not to sound desperate. 'When could I start?'

Julia did not need to check her screen but it looked more professional to do so. She pecked at the keyboard and squinted. 'The Villa Lavardin has just been rented for two weeks but maybe is only going to be occupied for one, I don't know, some confusion there, let me sort out. The client is English so it could be a good way to start.' She took up her ridiculously long cigarette and sat back. 'Do you drive?'

'I can, but I don't have a car.'

'I will arrange for you to get a lift with Daniela. She is very religious, good worker, bad driver, pray to Jesus before you get in the car with her. You wear our standard uniform, nylon, cheap so I don't make you buy it. It's so the guests don't mistake you for an intruder and shoot you. When you're inside your villa turn your phone off. I don't pay for talk.'

Julia leaned forward confidentially, shrouding them in smoke. 'I'll be honest with you, Hannah.' She pronounced it with a hard H. 'I don't have good experience with English girls. Too much learning, no initiative. They don't want to hold a toilet brush. Give me Slovakians, Romanians, Latvians. They know how to work.'

'I know how to work,' Hannah said defiantly.

Julia squinted at her through the smoke. 'So there's nothing I need to know about you that's going to come and bite me in the ass.'

Hannah widened her eyes.

Julia had seen that innocent look before. 'Nothing?'

'No.' She cleared her throat and tried again. 'No.'

'Hm.' She stared through the grey haze as if trying to pinpoint a fault. 'Just make sure you know how to keep your mouth shut. Some of the guests think they can do whatever they like.'

'What do I do if they try to make conversation?'

Julia shrugged. 'Act stupid. That way there will be no trouble. You can start on Monday. So… your first guest will be Steven Ells… berry, is that how you pronounce?'

Hannah took a look at the page on the desk. 'Elsbury. Steven Elsbury.'

'Englishes,' said Julia with a sigh. 'Always with the crazy names.'

2.

Summer was trouble. He'd known she would be from the moment he saw her. It was in the way she moved, the way she studied the room before moving in. It hadn't stopped him from becoming involved.

Steve had not planned to start seeing someone behind his wife's back. He and Jennifer had been together for seventeen years and married for twelve of those. Their son was now sixteen and had entered his morose period, but in every other way Jamie reminded Steve of himself. He couldn't remember the last time the three of them were away together as a family – maybe to that awful cat-filled villa in Tuscany when Jamie was twelve?

Setting up the company had consumed all of his energies since then. He was away two weeks in four. During that time he had not been faithful but he had been careful. He made sure that Jennifer never had cause to know and get upset. Nothing disturbed their orderly home life. Everything was neat and tidy.

So how had this happened? An eighteen-year-old had come

along with her cigarettes and gin and eye-watering perfume
and upset everything. She was the kind of girl his son would
fancy, which made her all kinds of wrong for him. First they
were chatting online, then they agreed to meet, which made
the fantasy real.

As far as he could tell Summer Farrow's parents were
divorced and she lived with her aunt – there was a frustrating
elusiveness in her details – and because he had nowhere to
take her they mainly sat in station bars and talked. It was silly,
flirtatious, inconsequential chatter. How could there be any
harm in that?

Sometimes their fingers interlocked across tables and
counters. On two occasions he had demurely kissed her in public.
Nothing was planned. She smoked and the smell transferred
to his shirt, so he kept aftershave in his bag. Whenever he met
up with her he switched his phone to airplane mode. Summer
insisted she was planning to study theatre design but who knew
what went on in the brains of girls? She had been privately
educated and was confident far beyond her years, but changed
her mind about everything every few minutes.

Jennifer did not have a suspicious nature because the idea of
cheating was as alien to her as learning to fly. After five weeks
his relationship with Summer, such as it was, became strained.
It needed to be taken to the next level or halted altogether.

He arranged to meet her in a Henrietta Street wine bar,
which in retrospect was always a risk given that his office was in
the same street. Even so, he did not expect his newest employee
to come wandering in and see them together.

Which he did.

Steve had made Giles his number two in a company of seven because he needed someone to accompany him around Europe. Giles spoke French and Spanish, albeit with a horrendous schoolboy accent, and was unambitious but naturally chatty, so he could deal with the vintners.

During their honeymoon period the pairing had worked well, so long as Giles's puppyish enthusiasm could be periodically dampened. The cracks began to appear on their first business trip abroad together, when Giles turned up drunk for their meeting in Lyon. It turned out he was terrified of flying and always went to the bar before a flight. People in the hospitality industry were notoriously heavy drinkers, but the wine trade considered itself a venerable and noble profession far above those who merely sold alcohol. Giles had been hired for his contacts, not his opinions, which was just as well, for he possessed no critical faculties whatsoever. So far, though, the yield from his supposedly famous address book had been of alarmingly low quality.

Steve was well aware that the wine trade had its shady side, especially when it came to the lax labelling laws that allowed regions and alcohol percentages to be fudged. Working these weaknesses had lately become his speciality, so he needed someone to give the company a sheen of class. Unfortunately, it was starting to look as if Giles was not the man to provide it.

When Giles entered the wine bar and saw the incongruous couple holding hands at the counter, Steve wondered how he would react. Summer was wearing a short white dress, something only a girl like her could get away with, so she was hard to miss. Typically Giles made an elaborate pretence of not having seen them before stumbling off to the other end of the room and theatrically looking for a friend who did not exist. He had been caught sneaking in alone for a drink, so at least they both had something to hide.

Summer was smart and cynical, far too knowing for someone born when he was twenty-four and on his third serious girlfriend, although she was not as clever as she thought she was. He knew he would have to talk to Giles about what just happened. Summer caught his furtive look and flicked a coaster at him. 'This bar is full of old drunks. What are you doing?'

'Someone from work just came in.'

'What, you want me to hide under a table or something?'

'No, but he saw you. He couldn't miss you in that dress.'

'I'm not sure I take that as a compliment. You know, it would be nice not to hide for once.'

'I've been thinking about that.' He looked back at her. 'We could go away somewhere for a weekend. I can get a good deal through the company.'

She hesitated, and for the first time he could see that he might soon lose her. 'I'm not sure I want to be seen going into a hotel with a much older man. It might not work out and I'd be stuck there with you.'

'If you knew me better, Summer, you'd know I'm not the kind of person who turns weird. I'm civilised and sensible. And I'm ruthlessly organised.'

She ran a coral nail through some spilled wine on the counter. 'I'd like to get a tan. I went to Ibiza last year: it was mad. I want to work at a club there next summer: not a superclub, just a beach bar with a good sound system. Or maybe Phraxos. There's a book called *The Magus* that was set there. Did you read it?'

'I don't read fiction,' he replied distractedly.

'I could go there and stay for the whole season.'

'Loud music and men pawing at you.'

'Men like you, you mean. Not such a bad prospect. Of course, they'd be a lot younger.'

He was starting to get fed up with her constant references to his age. 'What about your studies?'

She gave a carefree shrug. 'School of life, darling. Studies can wait until I'm ready. I could bum around the beach clubs for years until my looks start to go, then marry some horrible old man with a yacht and let him watch while I make love to beautiful girls. What do you think?'

'I never know when you're joking,' he said uneasily.

She had a way of looking that stripped him naked. 'It's very simple,' she told him. 'I'm never joking. If I say I've changed my mind about having sex with you and will burn your house down instead, you need to be scared.' She show perfect bright teeth when she smiled. 'Cheers.'

3.

Shortly after Giles Sutherland blundered into the bar and saw them together, Steve took his manager on a two-day trip to Spain. He hired a black A-Class Mercedes and drove them to Priorat, in the turquoise hills west of Tarragona, where the vista looked like a backdrop from an old spaghetti western.

He was hoping to strike a deal with the collective of local vineyards that sat on the sun-washed slopes, a small high-end appellation with 1,700 hectares of vines and just over sixty bodegas but growing fast. It was still largely undiscovered, so the prices were competitive.

At lunchtime they headed for a brightly painted village square devoid of tourists, and found a café that cooked for the vineyard workers. They sat outside and ordered the special, *conejo con ciruelas*, and sampled a 2013 Finca Dofi.

'That was a nice bit of theatre the other day,' Steve said as the wine arrived, 'you doing a double-take in the wine bar and walking into a pillar.'

'I was surprised to see you, that's all.'

Shame and apology were never far from Giles's features. He was a baby-faced man with thin sandy hair and an unset look, short and rotund, as pale as mist. On a hot bright day he was wearing cufflinks and a tie-pin because he thought they gave him an air of authority, but they made him look like a kitchen salesman. Giles was from an old-money Winchester family, high Church, high Tory, high command. Unfortunately, his mental fabric was not of the highest thread-count and his career choices had been limited to auction houses and property development. He was jovial, old-fashioned, grateful and pliable, and knew all the right people if only because he had once played rugby with them.

'You caught me in a bar with a young lady.' Steve mentioned it with studied lightness. 'Don't tell me it's never happened to you.'

'Actually it hasn't. And she was *very* young.' Giles snorted dubiously.

'In some countries girls can get married at fourteen. She's perfectly legal and very mature. Besides, I wasn't coercing her. She was totally in charge of the situation.'

'Well, it's nothing to do with me, obviously. Chatham House rules.' Giles laid his index finger along the side of his nose in what was intended to be a gesture of amiable conspiracy.

Pushing aside his luncheon plate, Steve leaned forward on his elbows, inducing confidentiality. 'It doesn't mean I don't love my wife, Giles. Jennifer is everything to me. She's a wonderful woman. There's no reason why it should put you in an uncomfortable situation. Recreational sex is the opening of a pressure valve, nothing more. Like a sport. I play squash; it's the same thing. We're all adults. I've been thinking, I have a lot of meetings in Europe. I could take Summer away somewhere –'

'Her name is Summer?' Giles stared at him in wonder.

'– take her somewhere, do the job and get it out of my system.' He spoke with clarity and confidence, even though he sounded like a foreman planning to unblock a drain. 'It's September, the month with the most travel because of the harvests. So, why not combine business with a little pleasure?'

'I don't think you should tell me anything more.' Giles placed his palm over his wineglass as Steve went to refill it, as if nobly refusing a bribe. 'I'm absolutely crap at keeping secrets. Melissa sees right through me. I'm an open book to her. She's not to be trifled with.'

Steve ran a nail idly across the tablecloth. 'It's just that I may need your help to cover for me at some point.'

Giles blinked. 'I can't do that, Steve. What you do is your own business.'

Steve had always made bold choices that frightened other people. An element of risk made life more interesting. 'I have to go to Nice to see the Bandol managers, and you'll need to come out at some point. I might take Summer with me.'

'No, no –' Giles actually raised his hands to his ears. 'Please don't say it.'

'It's just so you know I'll be out of the office a couple of days longer than I'm telling people, okay?'

'Okay.'

'I'm merely being practical.'

'I said okay.' Giles drank from necessity rather than pleasure, sipping continuously until his glass was empty.

'I'm not going to get you into any kind of trouble. If you follow my lead nothing will go wrong, I promise. This is just between you and me.'

Giles looked at him dubiously. 'Right ho,' he said, glancing anxiously at his empty wineglass.

4.

Daniela was small and dark and thirtyish but could have been any age really, with an odd skew to her ruddy face and hands as rough as a ropemaker's, but she was sweet and flustered and prepared to drive Hannah anywhere in her little silver Fiat with three missing hubcaps.

She displayed her devotion to Christ by pulling over when they passed the Church of Maria St Martin just outside the village so that she could whisper thanks, touch her rosary and genuflect before crunching gears and taking off again.

'I clean a villa called the Champs D'Or a kilometre past the Villa Lavardin so I can take you there in the mornings,' she explained, smashing another gear change and turning sharp right without looking. 'I have to pass right by you on my way.' Her English was surprisingly good although she had a habit of mixing it with idiomatic French. 'You also have the keys to Villa Caprice, which is a few hundred yards beyond Villa Lavardin. Nobody lives there so you can choose your own times to do that one.'

'Why does it need to be cleaned if no one's there?' Hannah asked.

'The owners are rich Russians, they like the place to be ready in case they decide to visit, but I've been here two years and they never come. They pay for a gardener and a pool girl every Saturday too.'

'Why would they do that?'

'It's a place to bury cash. They all do it up here. Form a company, build a villa, buy a boat, clean the dirty money. These are not nice people. It's best to, you know, *aller se faire cuire un oeuf.*'

Boil yourself an egg, that's got lost in translation, Hannah thought. She considered the Riviera towns. The peninsular of Cap Ferrat was expensive because it got two hours' more sunlight each day and was as dull as only a wealthy neighbourhood could be. Safe havens, financially sound, cunningly protected, reassuringly timeless. The Chinese had arrived to replace the Russians, who filled the hotels vacated by the Americans and the English. The French just shrugged; whoever came, it was all just money.

As Daniela dipped her head to read a road sign, Hannah realised that her co-worker was incredibly short-sighted, not a reassuring discovery when they were driving just a few feet from a sheer drop into the valley.

'Are there ever any road accidents up here?' she asked.

'Oh all the time, it's terrible, especially in bad weather. The Champs D'Or is a very grand house. It's further up the mountain. We should finish around the same time, so maybe we can take our lunch breaks together some days. I drive home to my mother's house in Fabron every night to collect Theo, my little boy, so I can drop you all the way.'

She explained to Hannah that Julia wanted her to go in a couple of times before the renters arrived. 'You could do today and tomorrow, then help me with the other villas. There's a maid's room in the pool house but don't be tempted to stay over, because Julia will find out if you do. There's a security camera in the porch, so they know when everyone comes and goes.'

'Don't worry, I'll stick to the schedule. And I'm not to gossip with the guests.'

'Oh, you had the talk. Obviously introduce yourself and answer their questions, just don't get involved. Think of them as troops of monkeys. Interfere with their social patterns and they will bite you. I hope you know how to cook breakfast. They'll ask you to help because when people go on holiday they –' she thinks for a moment '– *devenir chèvre*, you know this?'

Become goats, Hannah thought. *I get the gist.* 'How many other rentals do we have to cover?' Julia had been a little vague on the details, probably because she didn't want to put her off.

Daniela braked unnecessarily. 'There are four rental apartments on the Baie des Anges – two of those are occupied at the moment. Of course, it changes all the time but the properties are generally either waterside or mountainside. It's easy money. Although,' she gave Hannah an appraising look, 'you'll have to be careful.'

'Why?'

Daniela gestured vaguely. 'Oh, the men. They'll look at you and get the wrong idea.'

'In this?' She glanced down at her blue T-shirt and jeans. She was dressed as she would dress at home.

'It's better not to be provocative.'

'They won't think I'm provocative when they see me in Julia's uniform. I just want to be left alone.'

'They may not see it that way. You're the maid.'

'So what?'

'It means they are in charge.' Daniela drove her to the turning and stopped. 'Don't look so worried, you'll be fine. Before you, Julia had a girl from Kazakhstan, bad-tempered, face like a cow but a good worker. One day she cut off the top of her thumb and was only worried about bleeding on the carpet. You'll soon get the hang of it. Villa Lavardin is just down the path. After that, go across to the Caprice, call me when you've finished and I'll show you all the exciting things to do in the village. That'll take five minutes, even including the Spar grocery. If you don't want to get the bus there's a good taxi service nearby. Gerard robs the tourists blind but tell him you're working here and you'll get the local rate.'

Hannah took a deep breath. Monday morning, her first day. She thanked Daniela and headed for the Villa Lavardin.

She had trouble with the front door before realising that French keys needed to be turned several times in the lock before opening. Pushing her way inside, she peered around the corner and sniffed the air. A cloying floral perfume with bitter undertones, the smell of burnt toast coming from the kitchen.

There was no one around but nor was the place empty. Someone had certainly been here. She could see a coffee mug on a table, an opened magazine, a girl's sequined denim jacket hanging on the back of a chair, cigarette ends tossed in a saucer.

Following the page of instructions Daniela had given her, she hunted for her cleaning supplies. In a windowless room off one of the maze-like corridors she pulled the cord on a bare bulb and found everything neatly stacked on shelves.

She dragged out a new vacuum cleaner, cloths, a dustpan and brush, bleach, a mop bucket and several bottles marked *Alcool A Brüler*, which she had been instructed to use neat on the marble surfaces downstairs because it dried fast, so no one would slip over and sue the agency.

Heading upstairs, she found more signs of occupancy. The biggest bed had been explosively unmade and was surrounded by makeup, moisturizer, a T-shirt, hair gel and deodorant. A beer can and an empty cigarette packet lay on the floor.

Steven Elsbury was obviously here with his wife. No, his daughter. It was the kind of mess someone young would make.

Descending the curving staircase to the terrace, she headed down to the acre of terracotta tiles that made up the poolside patio, on a great stone ledge built out over the valley. At the bottom of the staircase she stopped and lowered her bucket.

The girl had white plastic buds in her ears and was asleep on a yellow striped sun lounger. She was impossibly slender and completely naked, save for a pair of huge black sunglasses with diamante rims.

5.

When Steve got home from work he shook out his umbrella and went straight to the tiny office he had installed next to their bedroom. Closing the door, he opened his laptop and looked for a property rental company based in Nice.

He had been recommended one called *Vacances Paradis*, a chi-chi little outfit that had villas in the Alps Maritimes priced at end-of-season rates. He bookmarked a villa with a pool, an open-air kitchen and no close neighbours, and called to enquire about dates.

'It is available, you have it, it is yours,' Julia Martinez told him. He heard the click of a cigarette lighter and a relieved exhalation.

'So, do I give you a deposit now?' he asked.

'You can pay up front in full if you like,' said Julia, pushing her luck.

'And I can give you a deposit now, over the phone,' he replied. He read her the number on his Mastercard.

After the charge had been approved she told him, 'One small point, Monsieur Else-barry, it is a two-week rental.'

'What do you mean? I only want it for one week.'

'Trust me, it works out cheaper than taking a small villa for one week. The owner is fussy, only accepts two-week bookings.'

'But why?'

'Because that is how it works here. It is a big villa, for families really.'

How very fucking French, he thought. 'Fine,' he said aloud, wondering if he should search for another property before deciding no, he liked the look of the place and had made up his mind. Besides, it was a company cost.

As Jennifer served dinner and Jamie sat with his headphones on, waiting to be passed a bowl, Steve worked on his plan.

'So, what's happening with Nice?' Jennifer asked, as if she could read his mind.

'We sell a lot of Provence rosés,' Steve said vaguely. 'It's really about next year's prices. It's going to be a problematic harvest this year, and late because of the changeable weather. Some chateaux lost most of their crops. Bordeaux is likely to be especially bad.'

'Jamie, headphones off. If it's climate change they'll have to get used to the different weather patterns, won't they?' She pushed a bowl of potatoes at him.

He tried to stop imagining Summer Farrow lying by the pool, tanned and naked. Jennifer was holding a serving spoon, waiting for his answer. 'Yes, I suppose they will,' he said absently.

'It's not climate change, it's the global heating emergency.' Jamie removed his headphones. 'People say "change" because it doesn't sound as bad.'

'Well some people say "change" because they missed the memo on revised terminology.' Jennifer caught her husband's eye, then continued serving.

'I'll be gone for a week or so,' Steve ventured.

'I haven't been to Nice in years.' His wife looked wistful.

'The world is shit,' said Jamie.

The next day, he called Summer Farrow from the Henrietta Street office. Whenever he spoke to her there always seemed to be loud music in the background.

'I have a surprise for you,' he said. 'How would you like a villa in the South of France, all to yourself? I have to go there on business.'

'What do you mean, all to myself?'

'I had to book it for a fortnight but I'm not due out until Thursday. You could get yourself a base tan, ready for when I arrive.'

Giles looked up from his screen at the opposite desk, a question on his lips. 'It's her, okay?' Steve whispered. 'Don't look so worried all the time.'

Giles had a way of shifting about in his chair that made it seem as if his clothes were too tight. 'I'm not sure you should bring her out on the Nice trip. There could be complications.'

'The booking is for two weeks so why waste the first one?' *It's like talking to a child,* Steve thought, turning back to the phone. 'Summer, stay a few days and I'll join you toward the end of the week,' he said.

It was a very simple plan, but then it got a little more complicated.

'I'm going to invite Jennifer out for the second week,' Steve announced. 'Summer and I will be able to spend some time together before my wife arrives.'

'But that's –'

'Crazy, I know.'

'You'd have to get her out before –' Giles stalled, suddenly unsure of himself.

'The young lady will have a return ticket, Giles, a flight back from Nice to Gatwick on Saturday night. What part of that is confusing you?' He could tell Giles was aching to say, *I think it's wrong*, but was too well bred to do so.

'A villa in the hills works out cheaper than a hotel,' Steve told his wife that night. He stood before the garden windows with his hands in his pockets, watching the rain patter into the laurel tree. 'I thought you might like to come out and join me.'

Jennifer dismissed the idea before thinking it through. 'I couldn't do that. I'm going out with the girls on Wednesday. I have all kinds of appointments.'

'I'm sure there's nothing that urgent. Move them.' He made it sound like the easiest thing in the world. Jennifer knew he had already won the argument, but hesitated.

'God, Jennifer, it's a free week in a villa in the South of France.

You won't even have me under your feet because I'll be working most of the time.'

She put down the plate she was holding. 'What about Jamie? I can't just leave him here.'

'Then bring him along. I'll clear it with his teachers.'

'They won't be happy about that. He's in enough trouble as it is. And he has a hygienist's appointment. Don't you have lots of meetings? We wouldn't see anything of you.'

'I'll be back and forth. I'll sort out the flights. Come for a week. The place is beautiful. Surely I don't have to sell it to you.'

'No, but —'

He kissed her on the forehead. 'I think it'll do you good to get some proper sun. Do you want to talk to Jamie or shall I?'

'Well, I suppose I can see if it's something he'd consider.'

'He hasn't got the vote yet, so he'll do what we tell him. Perhaps we can make him live a little.'

She frowned as she watched him pour soy milk onto his granola and carefully arrange slices of apricot on top. When he was this cheerful she couldn't help wondering what he was up to.

6.

Summer Farrow watched the black road, harsh rocks shimmering in the heat haze, a dense dry row of gnarled olive trees, a grasshopper flying past. There was nothing in the view that eased the eye. Around the next spur of land was a village, its houses built along the edge of the main road so that they hung precariously over the hillside in a series of grubby grey cliffs.

She asked the taxi driver to stop at a supermarket and bought six frozen pizzas, two family bags of Doritos, a dozen beers, tonics and a bottle of gin. He covertly watched her in his mirror as she walked back, so she slowed down for him. Men were so predictable.

When they reached the villa she sent the cab away, perched herself on a rock, popped a beer and waited for the agent to turn up.

An old white Mercedes SLK arrived at the foot of the path. The woman carefully uncreased herself as she climbed out. She was wearing a pink suit jacket with padded shoulders and a matching skirt too short at the knee, with pink patent leather heels and enormous sunglasses. She had sparkly nails and a foot of spray-stiffened hair like copper wire.

'*Disculpe*, sorry, *je suis désolée*. I am Julia Martinez.' She gave her client the once-over and switched from French with a Spanish accent to slow, exaggerated English. 'You are not Mister Elles-berry.'

'Well spotted. Steve will be here later. You can give me the keys.'

'He did not tell me –'

'He doesn't have to.' Summer folded her arms against this pink witch. Today she was wearing a tiny, floaty red dress designed to age any woman who looked at her.

'But I can't just give the keys to you, you could be anyone.' Nobody pulled a sour face quite like Julia.

'Yeah, and I could be the girlfriend of the guy who's paying you.' Summer turned her phone screen to Julia. On it was a shot she'd snuck of Steve in the Henrietta Street wine bar.

'Then I suppose is okay, I am not responsible. No problem, is a big house, very big, so there are some instructions. Maybe in English, maybe not, I don't know.' Dragging out an enormous bunch of keys she rotated them, rattling a gaudy charm bracelet. 'It is here, it is here, where is it?' She pursed her coral lips and shut one eye. Isolating a key, she unlocked the door, put her right knee against it and shoved hard.

Inside, she swept through the living room and kitchen, tutting and running an index finger over the counters. 'The last cleaner here, she was not so good. From the Ukraine. One of the poor ones.' She grimaced. 'There are many rich Russians in the hills all hiding away their money. Sometimes they just *disappear*. Bad things happen when they don't pay their bills. So you are waiting for your "gentleman friend", yes?'

'Yes,' said Summer flatly.

'That's what the men make us do, no? My husband is a lazy pig who won't get a job and still I wait around thinking he might change, but he won't. They never do.' She rested a hand on her hip. 'I tell you why,' she continued as if a question had been asked. 'Because they hate us for being so patient. Always we say we will leave them, and then we never go. We should say we will *never* leave them and then just go. My advice, free.' She snapped her fingers. 'There are not enough toilet brushes. I will speak to the maid. My card is on the table. Office hours only.' She considered a vase and turned it around proprietorially.

'So someone comes in to clean?'

'She comes early in the morning, if you can get up. How long are you going to be here?'

'For one week, until next Saturday.'

'I guess you will leave before the others arrive.'

Summer looked puzzled. 'What others?'

'His family and another couple, I think.'

She tried not to sound surprised. 'Yeah, I knew about them. Remind me what time they're coming?'

'Saturday night, he tells me. So you must be gone before then, yes?' Julia gave a tight smile, letting her know that she understood exactly what was going on. 'You go, the wife comes. It's very French, no?' She gave the place one last sweeping look. 'I will be back.' It sounded like a threat.

Summer waited impatiently for her to leave. She unpacked in the biggest bedroom and settled herself by the pool, then texted Jihane.

Check out this place fucken amazing you can stay here no one will ever find us pls pls pls come over!!!

Jihane was a French-Algerian boy she'd met in Ibiza last summer. He'd been working in a bar in Marseille but was now house-sitting in Nice. The job involved cooking and cleaning for a rich Chinese family who only visited for one month a year, so it was easy money. Jihane was cute and camp and rode a ridiculously macho motorbike, go figure, but she liked him.

Moments later he texted back.

Can't come tonight the family's in town
we can still do something this week don't know when yet
enjoy sun remember to moisturise!!! xxx

She dappled about in the bright blue pool, dried off and oiled herself, fell asleep, woke up and drank a beer, took another dip, read a magazine, and quickly grew bored. When her phone lit up she knew it was going to be Steve with bad news. She wasn't sure she wanted to talk to him, so she left it ringing and decided to call him back when she was ready. She would show him who was in control.

Steve looked at his watch. Roughly eight hundred miles away, there was a girl impatiently waiting for him to arrive, stretching in the sun, applying lotion to her legs on a lounger, and here he was, stuck in rainswept London. A woman had just passed their front garden with a scarf tied around her head, for God's sake.

Every wasted minute in this damp Victorian house was burned into him. He felt as if blank pages were being torn from the diary of his life, another day gone, then another. Sex always marked the passage of time and gave him something to remember, but lately the supply line had been severed. He had a nagging suspicion that his wife no longer idolised him.

When he pulled up the dates on his laptop he found another problem. Giles had moved their most important meeting to 3:00 p.m. on Friday. The client hated having her schedule rearranged and he couldn't send Giles to handle the presentation alone, so it looked as if he would have to catch a later flight.

He called the agent at *Vacances Paradis*. Julia confirmed that she gave the girl keys and showed her the layout of the villa. There was a hint of disapproval in her voice.

He tried calling Summer but there was no answer.

Jennifer pushed the study door open. 'Do you want coffee?'

He covered the phone. 'I'm on a work call. Maybe later.'

'Okay. I've already started to pack for Saturday. I'm actually excited. You're right, it's going to be good for me. And for Jamie.' She would have liked to say more but it was clear that he wanted her to go.

He was about to call Summer's number again when his phone vibrated. 'I need to talk to you,' Summer said.

'Why do you never answer? Is everything okay?' He moved away from the door, hoping that Jennifer couldn't hear.

'When exactly are you planning to arrive, Steve?'

'Something's come up. I may not be able to get there as early as I thought.'

'You're a bastard, you know that?' She said something else but the signal cut out.

'Summer?'

Her voice returned. 'You didn't tell me you're bringing your fucking wife out with you.'

He immediately thought of Giles. 'Who told you that?'

'The agent. You booked the villa for two weeks and invited her for the second week. I can't believe it. How could I have been so stupid? You thought you'd squeeze me in before she arrived?'

'It's not like that. Someone at work changed an important meeting. It's out of my hands. We'll still have time to spend together in an empty villa. After, I'll get you a car so you can catch your flight. Jennifer doesn't arrive until the evening.'

'So we can have a quick fuck and immediately afterwards you call me a taxi, kick me out the door and sit back to wait for the woman you married. Why not just buy a whore and book a hotel room? I'm sitting around here with nothing to do –'

'– on a free holiday,' he hissed. 'You've only just got there, you can't be bored already.'

'I don't want to do it this way. In fact, I don't want to do it at all. I don't know what I was thinking.'

'Wait, wait.' He saw the remains of his plan tearing apart. 'You wanted it as much as me. My wife found out about the booking so I had to invite her. You think I want her hanging around while I'm trying to arrange business meetings?'

'I have a friend here. I'll get him to pick me up.'

'What friend? Who do you know in the South of France?'

'I met him last summer, he's working in Nice. He's my own age and he's very cute. It'll be better for both of us.'

'I don't see how it will be better for me.'

'Then it's better for me, okay? I can change my plans too.'

'Look, let's compromise,' he suggested, not prepared to lose.

'I've made up my mind, Steve. I've been sitting here thinking what a terrible idea this is. I should never have let you talk me into it. I have to go now.'

She hung up on him.

The next morning he had just reached his office entrance when he got a call with a +33 prefix.

'Hello, Mr Else-barry? Is Julia from the agency. Your lady friend say she is leaving the villa, that there has been a change of plan. I need to know if you are still coming out? Because if it's a single occupant there may be a surcharge or something, I don't know. Wait, I have another call. Can you call me back?'

'*Me* call *you* back? I'm the one paying.' But she had gone. The agency could do what it liked, he decided, it was a company cost. But Summer Farrow playing hard to get and threatening to throw him over for some skinny barman she picked up last summer – more than anything else, his ego had been dented. Perhaps that had been her plan all along, to get a free holiday and swan off with her boyfriend. It crossed his mind that she might bring him back to the villa. Was that it? Were they planning to make love in his bed?

He was losing his touch. For the first time he felt his powers of persuasion failing. He called Summer back.

'Don't hang up,' he said hurriedly. 'Summer, I miss you.

I wanted you to be happy. I think about you all the time. I'll be out as soon as I can, I promise. At least we can spend a little time with each other, more than we've ever spent together in London. We can still make it work.'

He could feel her hesitation at the other end of the line. Summer loved hearing people say they needed her.

'We'll have some time alone together, I promise. I'll call you as soon as I've sorted it out, okay?'

Silence. He could hear her breathing.

'Please, Summer, stay.'

'Well —'

He rang off before she had time to answer. He was back in control.

Summer called Jihane, cutting across him when he tried to tell her that he was really *really* busy and had no time to talk.

'I can't believe I let him talk me into this, Jihane. He's put his arrival back because of a stupid meeting.'

'Wait, who has? You haven't told me what you're doing —'

'Because it's boring, I'm meeting this married man and he promised to get here on Thursday, then on Friday, and now he's saying Saturday so I'll be hanging around for the whole week waiting for him like some kind of fucking concubine. I can't stay here by myself that long. I'll just end up getting totally hammered every night, then I'll go mad and accidentally burn the house down or something. I'm going to leave and come to Nice. You'll be cool with that, won't you?'

'No, Summer, because the house won't be empty just yet.

As soon as it's free you can come and stay as long as you like, but not until then.' Jihane had to spell it out. He couldn't quite grasp what she was talking about, but that seemed fairly normal. She had a way of throwing out random information that didn't give you enough to work with.

'Okay, but will you be able to pick me up when I leave?'

Jihane groaned. 'It wouldn't kill you to book a cab.'

'Please baby, I just want to hang out with you and all your lovely friends.'

'I don't do friends, Summer, just hook-ups, you know that. Things should be easier in a couple of days. Can you at least wait until I call you?'

'Love you, I'll buy you drinks, you're adorable, so cute, hurry up and call me, bitch.' She hung up on him.

She had decided she wasn't going to wait around for Steve. She still had some money. She'd stay until Jihane came by. She could move her flight and leave whenever she wanted to, maybe after spending a few weeks in Nice. Or better yet, get a flight to Santorini and find a cool hostel, because she'd heard that all the waiting staff from hotels on other Greek islands went there for their final end-of-summer parties.

I'm free to do whatever I want, she told herself, not yet grasping that freedom was granted by others. Impatient and frustrated by life, she went to make herself a drink.

7.

Hannah stood frozen before the naked body.

She tried to move quietly around the edge of the deck but her shadow fell on the girl, who gave a little scream as she pulled the buds from her ears. She sat up, pushed away tumbles of hair and grabbed a shimmering butterfly-wing wrap. Her hair and skin were golden. She looked like a carefully retouched selfie.

'I'm sorry,' Hannah said without thinking, 'I didn't mean to disturb you.'

The girl pulled the gauzy shawl around her shoulders. It made no difference to her nakedness at all, but at least it matched her coral toenail polish.

Hannah was wearing a black-and-white nylon maid's uniform that looked as if it had been bought in a sex shop. She raised her yellow plastic bucket in one plastic gloved hand, but the girl still looked puzzled.

'I was having the oddest dream,' the girl said, as if picking up on an old conversation. 'One of those dreams where you're floating? You know that Salvador Dalí painting where the woman is floating with a swan? Something to do with Leda. They say you must never fall in a dream because it means that your heart has stopped. Isn't that weird? Are you the maid? There's not much that needs doing.' She waved a finger at the poolside room. 'I spilled a can of Coke on the rug and the microwave is a bit fucked because I left the pizza in too long and it kind of caught fire.'

Hannah nodded comprehension and made to leave.

'Hey, tell me what this is?' She held out a white plastic ear bud.

Hannah cautiously placed it in her ear and listened for a moment. 'It's "Heroes" by David Bowie.'

'Oh. I've not heard it before.'

'It's famous, except yours is in German for some reason.' She handed the ear bud back.

'Wait, what's your name?' the girl asked.

'I'm not allowed to talk to the guests,' Hannah said, mentally biting her tongue.

'Oh I'm not a guest, at least I'm not paying for it, someone else is.' She studied Hannah over the top of her sunglasses. 'So I guess that doesn't count. My name's Summer. Who are you?'

When Hannah hesitated, she pushed. 'There's no one else around. I promise I won't tell.' She held up two pairs of crossed fingers.

'Hannah.' She felt guilty giving her name. 'I thought the villa was empty this week.'

'Yeah, I bet. I didn't make the arrangements. I met the agent – Julia, is that her name? Huge shoulders, tons of orange makeup. She gave me the keys. I don't think she was too happy about it. Probably thought I was a tart, waiting for my *papa-sucre*. Where are you from?'

'London.'

Summer sat up, suddenly interested. She had eyes that matched the sky and a burnished sheen to her cheeks that Hannah's mother used to call 'high colour'. 'Me too. Just you, me and nine million others, right? How old are you?'

Having already broken the prime rule, there seemed little point in holding back now. 'I'm twenty-three,' she said, standing awkwardly with the bucket.

'God, you don't look it. Guess how old I am – no, don't. I'm eighteen. I'm not really supposed to be here.'

'Neither am I.'

'Why not?'

'It's complicated.' It was not something she was prepared to get into with a total stranger.

'I was meant to start uni,' Summer said airily. 'I wrote myself a note saying I couldn't come because I had to be my mother's carer. Which I would probably have been if she was alive.'

'So…' Hannah began.

'So why am I here, right?' Summer adopted a confidential look. 'I'm meeting a friend. He hasn't arrived yet. He's always working. I'm here until Saturday. It's deadly, deathly boring being in a place like this alone. The broadband totally sucks and my phone signal is all over the place. I'm out of cigs and it's like half a fucking mile to the nearest shop. I walked there yesterday but everyone had gone to church and there was nothing open.' The sunglasses irritated her for some reason, so she threw them off. 'Do you want a drink?'

Hannah was shocked by Summer's candour. She had assumed that all teenagers could only communicate via their phones now, but the girl was studying her with an unnerving frankness. Her breasts were small and china-white; it was hard not to look at them. 'Thanks for the offer, but I have to work. I've got to account for my hours when I finish.'

'Do you do this full-time?'

'I only just started. It's temporary. Cash in hand.'

'Broke, huh?' Summer looked her over. 'I bet you speak great French. I can't, not a word. I mean I try but it gets me into trouble. A waitress asked me if I wanted dessert and I meant to say *plus tard* but she thought I said *putain* and threw me out. It was my first night and I was a bit wasted. I found the most massive spliff in an old cigar box in the living room. I'm amazed it didn't make me throw up. Will you be coming back?'

'Not really,' Hannah said.

'Couldn't you come in a couple of times this week? Just to stop me from killing myself.'

'I would have to check.'

'Just tell your boss and she'll charge it.'

Summer rose from her sunbed by the leverage of one leg and looked around for her bikini, sparkling scraps of crimson material held together with white strings. She was shorter than Hannah expected but had the grace of an art deco figurine. 'Pity if you can't come back later. The sunsets are amazing because the sun goes down right over there.' She pointed to a line of black firs. 'It would be nice to share the moment with somebody.'

'It's my first day,' Hannah said apologetically.

'Then you'll *obviously* need a drink.' She slipped into her bikini and adjusted its straps.

Hannah hesitated. Would it be so very wrong, so long as she did the work? 'I've got to do another villa but I have to pass by at the end of the afternoon.'

'Great, so if you're passing come in. I'm learning how to make cocktails. I'm not very good at them yet. The one I made last night tasted of sausages, which was weird.'

Hannah thought for a moment. 'I know how to mix Aviations.'

'What are they?'

'They're like gin sours. Maraschino liqueur, *crème de violette* and lemon juice. You need the *violette* because of the colour. It matches the night sky.'

'I don't think there's anything like that here. I went through all the cupboards last night. I think the previous renters were more interested in weed. They certainly didn't leave any booze behind or if they did the cleaners stole it –' She suddenly realised what she had said. 'I didn't mean –'

'It doesn't matter, this is just temporary.' Hannah shrugged pleasantly.

Summer clasped her hands together. 'Please, *please* come and hang out. I'm going absolutely fucking insane without anyone to talk to. I'll tell you all my secrets.'

Hannah glanced back at the house, half-expecting to find herself being watched. 'I don't know how long the work will take.'

'You're making excuses. You'd better go to your other villa

before you get into trouble.' She pirouetted on the ball of one foot.

'I won't, there's nobody there at the moment.'

'Perfect, then you can see if they have any cocktail ingredients in their bar. If they do, you could steal some.'

'Let me see.' She tried to sound non-committal. 'Well, it was very nice meeting you.'

'See you this evening, then.' Summer climbed back onto the lounger and turned her face to the sun. 'Make sure you don't forget.'

8.

Hannah finished up and headed across to the deserted Villa Caprice, but there was nothing much for her to do. Everything there was gold and silver, marble and chrome, and all of it immaculately clean, if a little dusty. The bathroom taps were shaped like dolphins and large chunks of blue Venetian glass had been turned into extraordinarily ugly lamps with sharp edges.

Armed with spray polish and a cloth, she searched vainly for dirt. The rooms had the dead air of an unpopular provincial museum, so she opened the windows. A lap pool had a blue plastic cover. Some plants awaited repotting. The last maid had been so bored that she had alphabetised the spice rack and fanned all the magazines on coffee tables as if creating a show home. There was a shelf filled with murder mysteries, to which she was guiltily addicted, so she slipped a couple into her bag, planning to read them and bring them back.

The bar was a mahogany grotto with dried starfish and brass fittings that made it look cartoonishly nautical. She was just closing the windows when Daniela called her with instructions for another villa in the area. The work took them to 5:00 p.m., after which her companion returned her to the Villa Lavardin.

'Why do you need to go back?' Daniela asked as she pulled up outside, a thread of suspicion in her tone.

'I forgot a couple of things.' Hannah raised a plastic shopping bag. 'Don't wait for me. I need some air anyway. All I can smell is bleach. I'll catch the bus back.'

Daniela watched her with doubt in her eyes. 'Okay, but remember there's only one bus an hour.' She touched Hannah on the arm. 'You're not thinking of sleeping there, are you?'

'No, of course not.'

'Good. We had a girl who slept in the properties once. She got fired.'

'I wouldn't do that. Anyway, there's somebody staying here.'

'Are you sure? There's not supposed to be. I'm certain Julia said it was empty this week.'

'No, there's a girl. I'll see you tomorrow.'

'Do you want me to call Julia and check for you?'

Hannah wondered if Daniela was spying on her but felt rebellious. 'It's okay, I'm sure it's fine. I can call her if I have to.'

She waited until the Fiat had lurched away and then rang the front bell, but there was no answer. Guessing that Summer was still down by the pool, she tried the wooden side gate and found that she could easily reach the inside latch to open it.

Standing in the middle of the terrace, she took a panoramic shot of the villa on her phone.

The back of the main building was painted in pinkish apricot and sat half buried in red and purple bougainvillea. On either side two curving staircases swept down to a middle patio filled with palms in pots. Near the open kitchen, luxurious outdoor sofas were arranged in a conversation pit with a circular gas-operated fireplace at the centre.

A stone path led down to a separate little pool house with four rooms that ran end to end, with another kitchen and bedroom. An outdoor shower was finished in elegant grey slate. The wall beneath the pool patio was covered with a dense curtain of fire-red bougainvillea that looked beautiful but had pairs of razor-sharp thorns along every branch, as she discovered when she brushed past them.

As she looked back at the jumble of buildings connected with twisting stone staircases she was reminded of an M.C. Escher print. She imagined the guests scurrying past each other at different angles, defying gravity.

There was a cool edge to the air now.

Bats soared and dropped, gathering dusk insects. Goats clanked their bells in the distance, coming home. The hills were violet and indigo. Soon the mistral would be here, whipping pine needles and crimson petals into the air, ruffling the surface of the sapphire swimming pool.

Summer wandered out of the pool house dressed in her diaphanous butterfly wrap, her crimson bikini bottom and silver sandals. Her delight was palpable. She clapped her hands like a child.

'I knew it! I knew you'd come back!'

'How did you know?'

'My secret.' She touched the side of her tiny nose.

Hannah held up the shopping bag. 'Look what I found. Maraschino liqueur and *crème de violette*. The Russians in the other villa are never there but they're total lushes. They have this horrible *Titanic*-type bar with hundreds of bottles behind it. Nobody will miss a couple.'

'Fantastic. I have lovely, lovely gin here. How do you make a dirty martini? Do you have to use an unwashed glass? Hang on.' Summer climbed over the low staircase wall and shook a tree, stooping to pick up the fallen lemons. She rose with half a dozen in her arms. 'Will these be enough?'

'I'm sure we can think of a use for the rest.' She caught them as Summer threw. So what if she sat with this strange young guest on the upstairs balcony sipping violet cocktails, watching purple fire sweep the sky? The no-talking-to-guests rule was only there to protect Julia. It couldn't do any harm to have a drink.

'You looked so glamorous lying down there by the pool,' Hannah said. 'I like your neck chain.'

She pulled at the fine golden thread of the chain until it revealed an engraved nameplate reading *Summer* in elaborate script. 'My mother had it made for me in Paris for my fifth birthday. I've never taken it off since.'

'My mother was too practical to ever do something like that. She once bought me a blackboard.'

Summer laughed. 'Sounds like she wanted to give you an education.'

She gave me an education all right, Hannah thought. *I learned not to do anything she did.*

Summer turned up her phone and tried a few dance steps. 'It looks like I'm going to be here by myself for a few days. You can swim in the pool whenever you like.'

'Thanks, but I don't swim. I hate the smell of chlorine. And I don't want to get fired in my first week.'

'No one's spying on you.'

'You don't know my boss. I wouldn't be surprised if she found a way.'

'Well, I came out here for a fuck,' Summer suddenly announced. 'At eighteen I shouldn't have to travel *this* far, for Christ's sake.' She studied Hannah's features, waiting for a response, then burst out laughing, her hand flying to her mouth. 'I'm sorry,' she said, 'your face.'

'Did you have anyone specific in mind?' Hannah enquired.

'The guy who rented this place. I was quite excited by the idea but I've gone off it a bit now.'

'What's he like?'

'Very handsome for a senior gentleman of forty-two. I'm not attracted to boys my age. They're not ready to understand women.'

'So you prefer men who are more than twice your age?'

'Who said I prefer men?' She smiled back. Somewhere in the valley below, an animal burst out of bushes.

Oh, Hannah thought.

'I have the soul of an old warrior. Seriously, I was told by a spiritualist. The ancient Egyptians believed that you die twice, once when your soul leaves your body and again when the last person who remembers your name dies. Then you're gone forever.' She touched the gold chain at her breastbone. 'So you need to pass your name on to someone and keep passing it on until you find your harmony. It's like when you hit G Major and wait for the fifth to kick in and resolve it. I'll be waiting for that moment.'

'So you're musical.' Hannah was impressed.

'Piano, four years. I'm not sure that makes me musical but I don't trust anyone who can't hear music in their head. Have you seen my toe ring?' Summer tipped her tiny right foot this way and that. A silver ring covered in script gleamed on her third toe.

'What does it say?'

'It's Arabic. *Actions speak louder than words.* A friend gave it to me.'

'It's lovely. I have nothing like that.' Hannah's eye went to the treeline, where a bird with an immense wingspan was rising and dropping among the top branches. 'What do you think that is?'

'It's an eagle.' Summer sounded confident. 'There are vultures and kestrels up here. Not as many as there used to be, but you still see a few about.' She saw Hannah looking at her. 'I used to sit with my father watching the birds every evening. I adored him. He was a music teacher, a pianist, a lost heart. He's dead now. Cancer. Oddly enough *he* was forty-two.'

'That's awful.'

'When I was fifteen my mother got remarried to this super-rich creep I couldn't stand, then drank herself to death, so I take care of myself now. Sometimes I stay with my aunt, although she has her own shit going on so I'm usually alone. I'm fine. I have money. I know what I'm doing. Sometimes I get this weird sense of where my life is heading and how things are going to happen. Don't you ever get that?'

Hannah shook her head. 'No, I wish I did but I really don't.'

'Let's mix the cocktails and you can tell me about yourself, but only if you promise to tell the absolute truth.'

They ransacked the cupboards at the poolside kitchen, finding ice and tumblers and a silver cocktail shaker. Hannah took over because she knew how to balance the ingredients and Summer had clearly never mixed a proper cocktail in her young life. She didn't know which way to cut a lemon.

They swung around on stools at the counter like out-of-towners at an exclusive bar. Summer lit a black cigarette in order to strike a pose but couldn't control where the smoke went and ended up patting it away.

Hannah's throat closed and she coughed. 'What *are* those?'

'Black Devils. Tobacco mixed with vanilla caramel.' Summer examined the glowing tip. 'They're American. They have more tar than any other cigarette in the world. They're banned in France. I love them.'

Hannah zested the lemon peel for the glasses. 'So, what's his name?'

'Who?'

'Your putative deflowerer.'

'I love the way you talk. How do you know I'm a virgin? It's not just about penises in vaginas. If there's an orgasm without male penetration does that mean I'm still a virgin? In whose eyes? Anyway his name's Steve. He completely lacks a sense of irony. Oh, and he's happily married.'

Steve Elsberry, she thought. *This is why Julia doesn't want her*

staff talking to guests. They start to put two and two together. 'You
know what you're doing is incredibly irresponsible, don't you?
Dumping college and running away?' Hannah took a sip of her
mix, testing its sharpness. 'Are you sure you can handle it?'

'If you mean the married part, I've got him tied around
my little finger. It's perfect because he'll go back to his wife
like they always do and there'll be no strings. I wouldn't be
able to cope with some lovesick chimp in his forties lurking
outside my school. And I'm not running away, I'm choosing
a suitable location.'

'You're very relaxed about the whole thing. I'd be terrified.'

'How was your deflowering?'

Hannah was shocked by the question but tried not to show
it. She decided that Summer's honesty deserved a similar
response. 'I remember wishing it was over. I didn't particularly
like the boy, but I didn't like being a virgin either so I let him.'

'Why didn't you like being a virgin?'

'My mother said it was a girl's most precious gift. I wanted
to get back at her for leaving my dad.' *My God*, she thought,
did I ever acknowledge that before? Appalled, she shut up and
concentrated on the cocktails.

'How old were you?'

'Summer, I don't –'

'It's just between us.'

Hannah thought for a moment. 'Nineteen.'

'Really? I guess girls started later back in the olden days.'

'Thanks.'

'What happened?'

'I married him,' Hannah said.

9.

It had been the worst possible time to tell anyone bad news. The sky black, seven degrees outside and the rain so loud that it sounded like someone frying chips. Aidan could only leave his office for a few minutes, so he told her to meet him across the road by the playground. November in a London park, when even the swans lurking on the rain-battered lake looked inelegant and miserable.

She watched him walking toward her, one hand deep in his overcoat, the other holding a black umbrella. Aidan had a thin face and thinning mousey hair that made him appear vaguely ill, but his eyes were alert and calculating. Hannah was nineteen, Aidan twenty-seven. He was a teacher, and probably because her parents were academics she was drawn to intelligence in others. Aidan had an abrupt manner that made him respected rather than liked, and always carried a book in his coat pocket in case the company grew boring. When he reached her he showed no affection. Rather, he looked at her warily, the way a child would look at a dog.

Hannah tried to think of a way of breaking the news gently, but she could sense his impatience, so she simply said, 'I'm pregnant.'

She knew the first words from him would indicate how he felt, so she waited. He stole a furtive glance at her stomach. 'Are you sure?'

'Of course I'm sure.'

'No, I mean – are you sure it's mine?'

She was dumbfounded.

He told her he needed time to think and would call her in a day or so. She honestly wondered if he would ever call again because she didn't have much faith in his nature. However, two days later he asked her out to dinner, in the course of which he told her that he wanted to marry her.

Which was not what Hannah wanted at all. She did not love him and could never grow to love him. She certainly did not want to have his baby.

Her mother was furious but paid for a termination. Hannah told Aidan that she'd had a miscarriage. Her next step was inexplicable, because two months later she found herself marrying him. She left a domineering, unstable mother for a weak, stable man. A psychologist would have had a field day.

Just before the wedding, standing on the steps of the registry office, Hannah's mother caught her arm and said, 'I just need you to know this. You are making the worst mistake of your life.'

In the months that followed it became apparent that Aidan did not want a wife; he wanted a mother, a manager, a servant, an opinion-free mute whose only purpose was to smooth his path through life. He disapproved of her because she chose to read crime novels over literature, and clearly felt that he had married an intellectual inferior. Meanwhile, Hannah discovered what she did not want. Top of the list was any more fast, selfish, dreadful sex with Aidan. She stayed because she was scared of what she really wanted.

'Holy shit, you are *way* crazier than you look.' Summer swung her stool around and raised her glass. 'You married him? I thought I was the one who made all the bad decisions. Cheers.'

They raised their glasses. Summer took a selfie of their toast. Hannah studied her new companion. She seemed so confident and self-assured, as if nothing had ever gone wrong in her young life.

'It's my turn to ask a question,' she said. 'Whose idea was this… liaison?'

Summer shrieked with delight. '*Liaison, putative*, I love it. Whose idea? His, out of desperation. And mine, out of curiosity.' She sipped the wincingly sharp drink without a flinch. 'I thought I should try it once. I think you should try everything once, don't you?'

'Not quite everything.'

'Really? That's unadventurous of you. My turn. I'm guessing you didn't stay with your husband. What happened?'

'Can we just… not talk about it anymore tonight?' she asked, a shiver running down her arms. 'Can we just enjoy the sunset?'

'Only if you come here.'

Summer moved her stool closer. Her lips shone red.

Everywhere, the light was violet. Their arms were violet. Summer's coral wrap slid from her shoulders. Hannah felt the hairs on her arms lifting. She smelled jasmine and sun-oil and sweat.

Summer's lips brushed hers so lightly that it felt as if a small bird was passing by. Summer's tongue flickered into her mouth and she found herself pushing back. She felt Summer's fingers, orientally delicate, touching her bare thigh. She pressed her hand on Summer's shoulder in modest protest but it slipped to her back and urged her forward.

The stools went over with a crash.

From this point on elegance was sacrificed, then dignity. Clothing was torn in a chaotic struggle, each one helping and hindering the other. They moved across the tiled floor bruising themselves in the violet light, elbows and ankles, mouths connected, hips touching, joined together by hands and heat and hair, a glass toppling and smashing somewhere, and the violet warmth spread from Hannah's gut down between her legs, and Summer's hand was there, and soon the violet turned to crimson and gold.

10.

Hannah found a dustpan and brush for the glass, then forensically searched out every hidden sliver around the base of the kitchen counter. In a state of shock, she forced herself to concentrate on the task at hand.

Summer walked over the tiles with bare feet, unconcerned. It was dark outside so she turned the pool lights on from a remote. 'It's the curse of living in a patriarchy.' She waved her black cigarette around and left a trail of ash. 'We have to hold a conversation about our relationships with men before we can talk about ourselves. How long ago did you divorce your husband?'

'I didn't.'

Hannah concentrated on locating the shards of glass. A large curved spike winked back at her from under a wicker chair.

'Then what the hell happened?'

I am not going to answer any more questions, Hannah told herself, emptying the dustpan into a cardboard carton and sealing the lid. *I've said too much already.*

'I love this song.' Summer ran behind the kitchen counter, turned up the music and started moving to it, turning to watch her reflection in the glass doors.

Hannah tried to concentrate on the task she had set herself – checking the counter top for stray fragments of glass – but her eyes strayed across the room. Summer was backlit by sunset like a tropical palm, a heat-mirage, a ghost image, something that shouldn't exist but miraculously did.

'Can you stop fucking cleaning for a moment?' Summer came over and took the dustpan away from her.

She led her to the sofa in the living room. 'You know what they say about women who clean up all the time? They're frustrated. I can still taste you. I want to talk about everything, you being here with me, what you're thinking, how you deal with it. Do you even know who you are?'

It was not a conversation Hannah wanted to have. She turned to face Summer. 'I don't understand.'

'You don't understand?'

'Why me?'

'What do you mean?'

She had been holding everything back for so long that now she found herself hopelessly tongue-tied. 'I'm nobody. It's just – you're so – you're *golden* –'

'Yeah, that's from my Mac makeup brush. It's called Mineralise Skinfinish. It's just a surface sheen. This is me.' Summer stopped her confusion with a kiss. 'And nothing ever happened to you before? Well, I guess it has now.' She tore the wrapper off a fresh pack of cigarettes and tossed the cellophane on the floor. 'Don't judge me, I'm giving up next month.'

'I'm not judging,' Hannah whispered, watching her.

Summer smiled slyly. 'Oh yes you are. You're looking at me like, *she's trouble*. Like I'm one big bad habit. Maybe that's what I am.'

'Why did you dump college?'

Summer shrugged. 'I've always been a little rebel.'

'That usually just means skipping a few classes, dyeing your hair black and hanging out with the art crowd.'

'I couldn't see the point.'

'And your father didn't kill you?'

A white cat slunk across the terrace as if trying to avoid a beating. Summer threw a walnut at it. 'My father lives in a gated community in Almeria. He sends me money so that I won't visit. I call it my Keep Away Cash. I stash it all away for a rainy day. I prefer staying with my aunt. She spends all her time organising charity luncheons and never listens to a word anyone says.'

'It sounds perfect,' she said but thought, *It sounds like you're skipping over the bad stuff.*

Summer stroked her face. 'I'm here all week by myself and I have no plans beyond waiting for this big stupid married monkey. I'm sitting by a pool looking fabulous and eighteen for Christ's sake and I'm reading a magazine that's two years out of date and it's telling me how to decorate a dining room with beige fucking cushions. I could very easily go mad. I need supervision. It's practically a legal requirement that you're here, so come whenever you want. Will you visit again?'

'I have to be here to do the cleaning,' said Hannah, careful not to commit herself.

Summer took her right hand in both of hers. 'I mean in the evenings. We can make this a ritual.'

She felt the hot flush of embarrassment returning. 'You mean –'

'Our own secret cocktail party.' She looked down at Hannah's hand. 'I can feel the tension inside you. Everything is tightly wound.' She pressed her wrist to her face. 'I still smell of you. You linger. Do you have any idea how exciting that is? To linger? That's what I should like to do, linger on long after I've gone.'

Hannah had no idea how she managed to get home. She forced herself to move in a deliberate stately fashion, like someone stepping off a roller coaster.

At her dank third-floor flatshare in Nice's *Vieux Carré*, she perched on her tiny wrought-iron balcony with a bowl of coffee. Above her, the hillside villas were being locked up for autumn. Soon the temperature would sink and whole neighbourhoods would fall asleep beneath the protecting fold of amber rock known as the Massif Central.

She tried to ignore the squawk of the saxophone in the next room. Her flatmate would probably have been a beatnik in the 1950s, but now he was just another burned-out old jazz-dude who couldn't remember why he came to France, and she was stuck outside during his interminable practice sessions.

She wondered what had just happened to her at the Villa Lavardin.

Summer had happened.

Tonight she knew she would not sleep. Untangling herself from the balcony railings, she headed down into the market. By day it was lined with stalls selling flowers, yet it always smelled of fried fish. Tourists were still ambling sluggishly through the narrow backstreets, examining key rings and fridge magnets produced in Chinese factories. As they photographed each other in graffiti-covered doorways she felt herself drifting above them all, because she had a secret that none of them knew. Summer felt like her future.

She wanted to spend every night at the villa, drinking, talking, weather-watching. She wanted Summer to restore and heal her with her golden health-giving youth. She was only five years younger but might have descended from another planet.

Hannah wanted to be as confident and self-aware as the girl in the villa. She knew how important it was to seize this shining moment before it dissolved, leaving only radiant golden dust and the trace of bitter jasmine.

It meant she would have to stop Summer from meeting this ridiculous middle-aged married man, who would only try to seduce her and ruin everything for both of them. She knew all too well how such men operated, lying with their eyes and smiles, slipping through closed doors as they uttered nonsense promises. Summer deserved better. She might have the soul of an old warrior but there was also a naivety to her that could be exploited by a forty-two-year-old lothario. *Lothario.* Summer would laugh and add that word to her list.

Summer had sent her contact details, so she called.

'I don't think you should go through with this,' she said.

'You're old enough to decide what you want. Don't make the same mistake I made.'

'I'm sleeping, I'm like *actually* asleep.' Summer fought off a yawn. 'Why can't you just text? You worry too much. I'm not you, Hannah. I don't have your issues, okay? Nothing bad is going to happen. Everything's lovely. Call me tomorrow. Not early though.'

She hung up.

11.

Summer stretched like a cat on the striped yellow lounger. Removing her sunglasses, she gingerly touched her eye and checked it in the mirrored lens. It had probably blackened as far as it would go, so the bruise could be hidden with a little more makeup.

Her phone lay in the shadow underneath the lounger. She checked the time. Almost 5:00 p.m. Hannah would be here any minute.

She heard the car door shut just as she was heading up toward the kitchen, where Hannah had left the liqueur bottles. It was Thursday, and their evening cocktails had become a ritual.

'Hey.' Hannah came around the side of the house, bouncing into the kitchen. 'I told Daniela you asked me to prepare a meal for extra money. But I think she's getting suspicious. She pulls a pinched little face when she drops me off.' She sniffed the air. 'I always know where you are because of that scent you wear. What is it?'

'Weird, eh? Sort of bitter. I love it, it's called "Dangerous" and comes in these huge cheap-looking bottles. You could use it to track people.'

Hannah was conscious of her black-and-white maid's outfit. She had tied back her hair and was wearing minimal makeup. She needed a shower. 'I have to get changed.'

Summer jumped at her, kissing her so violently that their teeth clashed. 'No, keep the uniform on, it's kind of sexy.'

'Then I'll serve,' Hannah said. 'Seeing as I'm literally your maid. And you look like you need a drink.' She pulled at her uniform and popped open its press-studs. 'I've been helping my teammate clean up after three Russian children who slowly and very deliberately poured blackberry jam all over a white shag carpet, knowing I'm not allowed to argue with them.' She touched Summer's cheek. 'What happened to your eye?'

Summer turned away to pour the gins. 'It doesn't hurt. It was stupid. After you went last night I walked into the village to meet Jihane.'

'You said you were going to sleep. You were pretty drunk.'

'Yeah, so there's that. I say a lot of things. Anyway, I went for a walk to clear my head, actually to get some less disgusting cigs because these things are giving me the lungs of a fucking eighty-year-old, and it turned out Jihane was nearby doing a favour for his boss so we met up in the main bar in the square…'

'Chez Dany, I've been there, awful place, stinks of ashtrays but the owner's friendly.'

'There are two other bars but they look worse.'

Hannah folded up her uniform and carefully placed it in her bag. 'Do you decide everything on the spur of the moment?'

'Pretty much. You should try it. Plans are for old people.

Jihane was supposed to be taking me back to Nice with him to some party.'

'On a Wednesday night.'

'You sound so prim. You told me last night I made you feel alive.'

'You do,' she said, 'but I have to work.'

'So anyway, Jihane's crazy Chinese family changed their minds about leaving so he couldn't be out late.'

'These are the people he works for?'

'He takes care of their house. They're hardly ever here so he basically gets free rent. But now they're staying on until the weekend because they want to buy some stupid art, which means he has to cook for them and I'm stuck here.'

'I'd offer you a bed at my place but I don't think it's up to your standards,' Hannah said.

'It's okay, this isn't exactly a dump. So we had a few drinks and one of the pissed locals decided to lift up the hem of my skirt and go for a selfie. Jihane saw it happen and it turned into a bit of a shoving fight. The locals finally noticed he's as gay as a flamingo and thought it would be fun to mimic him. In the process I managed to get my delicate features in the way.'

'You're not lying, this drunk guy didn't beat you up or anything?'

Summer looked hurt. 'No, of course not. It was a dumb accident. Really.'

Hannah examined her eye. 'I guess you won't be going back there in a hurry.'

'Seeing as the barman wanted us to pay for the table his drunk regular smashed, unlikely. Where's my drink?'

They took their Aviations out to the big wicker sofa on the upper terrace to watch the sun setting. Summer slid her head into Hannah's lap.

'When do you think you'll go home?' Hannah asked.

'Who says I'm going home? Maybe I'll stay here forever.'

'What will you do when the money runs out?'

'I have an allowance to keep me afloat. My dad's loaded, he just wants me to be happy wherever I am so long as it's not at his place, because his girlfriend hates me.'

'Does he know you're here?'

'I may have told him but I doubt he was sober enough to remember. I didn't clear the trip with my aunt. She's medicated the whole time but at some point even she's going to notice I'm not around.' When she looked up she seemed absurdly, dangerously young.

Hannah tasted her drink. 'How do you keep track of all the lies you tell everyone?'

Summer brightened up. 'I keep them in my phone. I keep my entire life on my phone. If I lost it I'd have to kill myself. Anyway, they're not lies if they don't hurt anyone.'

'Do you tell me the truth?'

'I told you, I'm honest with you. Do you tell the truth?'

'Unfortunately, yes.'

Except, of course, she didn't. Hannah had admitted to the marriage but not what happened after. She continued watching Summer over the rim of her glass, but Summer liked being watched, and slowly, languorously pulled off her T-shirt. Their hands touched.

Lovemaking was measured, deliberate and silent, their

breathing slow and rhythmic, their senses heightened and prolonged.

After, they watched as a bird with long brown feathers and a sinister beak hopped across the patio. It peered at them malevolently, as if preparing to file a report.

'This place is creepy late at night,' said Summer, stretching her arms. 'Too dark, too many weird noises. I have to go around putting all the lights on. There are funny little rooms all over the place. Someone else could be living here and I'd never know. Why can't you stay over?'

'Because I'm not allowed to,' Hannah reminded her. 'I keep thinking I'll look up and you'll be gone.'

She had seen Summer four nights in a row, but was still unable to predict her erratic moods. 'What are you going to do about your married man?' she asked again, kissing Summer's shoulder, savouring the sunset smoothness of her skin.

'He's flying out first thing the day after tomorrow. Which is also the day I leave. So now I know where I stand. When you strip it down to basics, he's not interested in having dinner somewhere romantic or listening to me prattle on by the pool. I'm just a fuck. I have to decide whether to be here or not.'

'Either way it's the end of our cocktail hour.' Hannah raised her glass.

'No, you don't get off that lightly.'

'What do you mean?'

'We can meet up at Jihane's for drinks. I'm going to move my flight back and stay with him. He lives in the old town, near you.'

'Sunset will be tricky. I'll only just be coming back from

the other villa. At least I won't be cleaning up after you. You're very messy, you know.'

Summer tipped her head coquettishly. 'Only because I know you'll be there to pick up after me every day.'

'Shall we have another drink?'

Summer turned to her. 'No, instruct me. Say, "Get me another drink."'

'I can't say that.'

'You have to assert yourself, Hannah. What would you do if I wasn't there? Let me see if I can make you one this time.'

They ran back to the kitchen. The silver-plated tray on the counter held a collection of bottles. Gin, cherries, violets, lemon; a unique flavour in the cocktail world. She uncapped the silver shaker and removed the glasses from the ice bucket.

'Always start with a fresh chilled glass,' Hannah reminded her. 'I'm going to have to clean up after your married man. Do you want me to spy on him for you? I can follow them around with my yellow bucket and keep notes on the wife.'

Summer looked suddenly serious. 'I hate you doing this. You don't need to. I can take care of you.'

'I doubt that. You can't take care of yourself.' She pointed to Summer's eye.

'How did you end up cleaning anyway? No offence but it's kind of incredibly beneath you.'

'Don't knock manual labour. One day you may have to work for a living.' She sliced the thick rind of the lemon on the chopping board.

'When you were with your husband –'

'Do we have to talk about –'

'Fine, if you don't want to we won't.'

Hannah wondered how much to admit about Aidan. 'You really want the truth?'

'Bring it on.'

Perhaps it was time to tell her, she decided. 'We'd been married four months and I stopped having sex with him.'

'Why?'

'Because it felt all wrong.'

Watching Summer trying to prise open a bottle with the end of a knife, she took it away from her before she could damage herself.

'Aidan taught geography. He didn't know how to hide his laptop's browsing history or his passwords. He had a file of websites about young girls, younger than you. What I did wasn't very brave. I forwarded it to his head teacher. I wanted to make sure he was taken out of the system.'

Summer watched as Hannah measured the spirits.

'The next night the doorbell rang. We'd just sat down for our evening meal. I thought it couldn't be anyone we knew because they would have called first, so I pushed my plate away and headed along the hall. I remember I could see two figures through the glass, but I knew at once what they were because I heard a headset crackle. I opened the door to a man and a woman, both short and broad, in these lemon jackets covered with reflective panels. The woman barely bothered to look at me. She said, "Does Aidan Reynolds live here?" They walked past me, straight into the kitchen. I caught sight of Aidan's face. He looked – unsurprised. The man said he was under arrest on charges pertaining to the distribution of corrupting materials and the sexual grooming of minors.'

She dropped ice into the blender. She could not look at Summer as she talked.

'They'd already spoken to the school staff and found reason to arrest him. One of them took his laptop. I said I would go with them to the station but Aidan wouldn't let me. He collected his coat and his glasses and went off between the two of them. He never said a word, didn't even look back. He knew there was more for them to find. I didn't have a lawyer, didn't know what to do or who to call, so I just waited there. I got a phone call to say that they were holding him overnight, and that I was not to touch anything in the flat. That night Aidan hanged himself in his cell. They'd taken away his belt but hadn't checked all of his pockets. He had a length of nylon curtain cord on him. Who carries nylon cord around?'

'Holy shit,' said Summer. 'No wonder you wanted to get away from there.' She reached out to touch Hannah's hair. 'You know it wasn't your fault.'

'Of course it was. He would still be alive if I hadn't sent the folder.'

'Yeah, and he'd be molesting kids. He knew what they were going to find, otherwise he'd never have kept the cord.'

Hannah rubbed at her eye. 'I went to a restaurant to see a friend. I knew we shouldn't have met there because it was too close to where I lived. The place was half full. My friend was at the table, reading the menu. She said neighbours were asking after me. They'd heard – well, of course they'd heard all sorts of things. I hadn't spoken to them. I didn't want to have those conversations.'

She rattled the shaker and drained the mix into the glasses.

'She poured me a glass of wine. I explained that I'd had some online abuse. I didn't go out much after Aidan died. People were posting stuff asking me how I could have done it. I replied to a couple, told them it wasn't a choice. I remember the restaurant door behind us opened and closed. I had the sensation of someone standing by the table. I turned and saw that it was Aidan's sister. Before I could say anything she picked up my wineglass and threw it in my face, called me a fucking bitch and walked out. I had red wine running from my chin. I tried to clean myself up but everyone was staring. The wine had an earthy, leathery smell that stayed with me for days. A week later I booked a flight and left.'

Summer held her hands. 'You're here now, and that's all that matters.'

She gave Hannah a hug that turned into a kiss.

Hannah did not even realise that she was crying.

12.

Friday evening. The sun's warming orange glow had faded behind the deep green dales, but not before backlighting the scene with a luminous farewell, a curtain dropped onto the performance of the day.

Night sounds had started rasping through the open patio doors. They sat side by side, their hips and arms touching, calmed by each other's company.

'We don't like the Russian wife,' said Hannah. 'She's spoiled and blames the cleaners for everything she damages. I'm helping Daniela remove these long black streaks from the floors where she drags her boots over them.'

Summer stirred her drink with her finger. 'Maybe you should tell her what you think of her.'

'I told you, I don't talk to any of the other clients. I'd lose my job.'

'But you'd be free.'

'I guess no one's ever told you that freedom is expensive.

Anyway, if you like freedom so much why did you get involved with a married man?'

Summer ran her finger around the rim of her glass. 'He's so transparent. A wolf in wolf's clothing. His tongue virtually rolls out of his mouth every time he looks at me. I honestly thought I was in control of the situation. Can't believe I was so stupid.' She slapped Hannah's thigh with the back of her hand. 'Enough morbidity. Let's toast the goddess of the night.'

The star realm reached down to the line of the pine trees, sparkling like rock salt. Some of the glimmers were so faint that they could only be seen by looking to one side.

'I used to know all their names.' Summer daintily sipped her drink. 'That's Cassiopeia and that's – I think – Cepheus.'

They turned off the pool lights to see the sky more clearly.

Hannah swung out of her seat and straightened her T-shirt. 'His wife is probably really sweet and hasn't a clue what goes on behind her back.' She cut a lemon in half and squeezed it into fresh glasses, adding the maraschino liqueur. 'I think you're going to have sex with him.' She passed over the fresh cocktail.

Summer accepted it in mock shock. 'Would you be jealous if I did?'

'God, no. He sounds reptilian.'

'*Reptilian.*' Summer laughed. 'He has very blue eyes and wears the whitest shirts you've ever seen. Part of me wants to be here when he shows up, just so I can tell him what I think of him.'

'Then you'd be creating a bad situation.' She looked around the room. 'This place is a mess. Good job you have a maid.'

She took a sip of her cocktail and coughed, holding her palm to her chest. 'Fuck, that's strong. Thank you for your advice, grandma. Being so much older definitely makes you the expert.'

'So what are you going to do?'

'Honestly?' She looked away to the pool. The white cat was crouched low, lapping water. 'What's that?' She peered into the ultramarine water of the deep end.

'What's what?'

'I thought I saw something.'

'What do you mean? What sort of thing?'

'It's gone now. Are you coming in tomorrow?'

'Why?'

'You can talk me out of it, stop me from giving in to temptation.'

'I think you know your own mind, Summer,' she answered primly.

They drank more cocktails and baked cardboard-tasting pizzas and covered the floor with giant orange scatter cushions and tried to get the ridiculously complex TV system to work. Hannah felt a warm buzz from the liquor.

'You can stay tonight if you want,' Summer said, rolling onto her back. 'It's not like we're short of room. Although I warn you, I am seriously perky first thing in the morning. There will be showtunes, and bacon and eggs. Except there's no bacon.'

'I can't. Julia's adding another villa to my schedule tomorrow. I'm supposed to come before your alpha male arrives.'

Summer laughed. 'He's just a cheesy middle-aged guy trying to reassure himself that he's still got it. But I'll have to be careful.'

'Why?'

'He's a lot bigger than me. I think he's used to getting his own way.'

'Then don't be here for him. Seriously. Not if you think he could get weird.'

Summer drained her glass and settled further back in the cushions. 'It sounded glamorous being whisked here, but it's boring after you've got a tan. Imagine being stuck in this house all the time.'

'I can break you out,' Hannah said, sitting forward. 'I can wait just up the road, and you can signal if you need me to intervene.'

'No, I can handle it.' For a moment the night and the cicadas closed back in, filling the ensuing silence.

Hannah watched Summer as she sank contentedly into the cushions with the base of her empty cocktail glass resting on her bare stomach. 'It's all so easy for you, isn't it?'

'What do you mean?'

'There's nothing about you that's like a normal teenager. You do realise that? Summer, what are you going to do with your life?'

Summer turned and smiled her secret smile. 'I'll be the Keeper of Secrets. I'm the one person you can tell everything to. You know why?'

'No, why?'

She leaned forward and whispered. 'Because I don't exist.

Nobody knows me. Even my online avatar isn't me. It's some girl I found in a magazine. That way nobody can ever own me. They can't find me unless I want them to.' She bounced up onto her feet. 'So tell me something about you. I don't even know if you can sing.'

Hannah was thrown for a moment, then laughed. 'No, I don't sing. I have a voice like a foghorn.'

'But you dance.'

'*Everybody* dances.'

'No, they don't. Come and dance.'

Hannah folded her arms. 'You are too used to getting your own way.'

Summer grabbed at her. 'Dance for me?'

'You're spoiled. Another spoiled pretty girl. I really should clean up your mess and go.'

'You're not cleaning up anything. This is how I like it. Come on.'

Pulling Hannah to her feet, Summer thumbed a track on her playlist. An Ibiza anthem burst out, its bass thumping from two speakers tucked into the corners of the patio. She turned up the volume until it shook the windows and echoed across the valley.

Hannah tried to keep pace with Summer but the other girl was too fast, too frenzied. She whirled and twisted, dropped and jumped, her hair whipping across her face, her hands passing in front of each other. Seizing Hannah, she pulled her into her orbit until they were moving together.

That was how Hannah would always remember her friend, on this violet night, with the windows open and the song flooding out, and a cool breeze blowing in from the indigo hillside.

As her bus descended, creeping around the hairpin bends, the coastline gradually appeared. The low sun fractured the sea, hurting her eyes. Gold light bathed the pink breast-shaped cone of the Hotel Negresco, turning the Promenade des Anglais into a shimmering ribbon.

On Cap Ferrat there were prickles of light that might have been flashbulbs from some celebrity event taking place in another world where nobody had to think about bleach or polish or vacuum cleaner bags. Down there, the partygoers pretended not to see the silent people who kept it all running, the Eastern European maids who stood by with champagne and canapé trays, the Filipina girls who waited with dustpans and brushes, the black boys who ran to bring out the Ferraris. If the rich ever noticed them, it was to covertly envy their youth and strength.

We choose to be invisible because we don't want to be a part of your world, Hannah thought. *Keep your private clubs and invitation-only dinners, I've just had cocktails with the most beautiful girl in existence.*

13.

On Saturday Steve arrived at Nice Côte d'Azur on the 7:10 a.m. Gatwick flight, picked up a taxi and headed for the agency. As the driver loaded the address into his navigation system, he sat back and let the day ahead unfold before his eyes.

The logistics were simple. Summer's flight was at six so she needed to leave the villa by half three. He'd managed to get Jennifer and Jamie onto a 4:30 p.m. flight, which with the hour's time difference meant that the earliest they could be here was after eight. Giles and his wife were coming out a few minutes earlier from Heathrow, Jennifer and Jamie from Gatwick. There was absolutely no danger that his wife would find out anything about Summer, although he could see why Giles was so mesmerised by the arrangement.

When he closed his eyes he saw Summer drifting golden and naked through the rooms, still dripping from the pool. After they had fucked, her damp impression would remain upon the bedsheets. Her ghost image would linger after she left, her perfume discernible to a sensitive nose, her shower-wet footprints still visible on the tiles. The thought of Jennifer obliviously passing through the girl's traces excited him beyond reason. In some ways the anticipation was better than the act.

On the Promenade des Anglais there was not a breath of cool air to be had. The town was listless in the heat, its grand hotels as becalmed as ocean liners caught in the Sargasso. The local residents had vanished into cool dining rooms. Only the British were desperate enough to sit in the exposed *plein soleil* of the grey pebbled beaches.

In the office of *Vacances Paradis* Julia Martinez fanned herself with a brochure even though the air conditioning was up high. The arrangements at the Villa Lavardin were not her concern. The Englishman's *putain* was bored and bad-tempered. Later the wife would arrive, and as long as Hannah did her work well, she would never know that her husband had installed another female there.

Steve checked the address. The agency proved to be a hole in a wall. Julia was waiting for him in a sunshine-yellow trouser-suit made from the kind of fibre that looked like it would go up in a sheet of flame if she smoked carelessly. She waved him to the only spare seat, her charm bracelet chattering, and pushed a bunch of keys at him.

'So. This is your set. The young lady said she would leave hers and close the front door when she goes. But you will see her first I think, yes?'

He'd tried to get hold of Summer all morning but she hadn't picked up. It sounded as if this absurd woman already knew too much of his business, but he had to ask. 'If the young lady called you to say she was leaving the keys, is she not planning to stay until I get there?'

'That I cannot say. It's not a matter for me, but I think she is maybe too much by herself and wants to be somewhere more – lively.'

He tried to maintain his smile, as if Summer's decision had always been the intended outcome. 'Very well. We'll be checking out next Saturday. I suppose you'll need to come to the villa before we go.'

'Just for the formalities. Your maid will be with you tomorrow. She can prepare breakfast and if you have a party she can serve drinks for you by special arrangement, with me, not her or you know, money disappears *pouf*. So here is your contract, Mr Else-berry.'

Julia did not like this man in his expensive blue suit and open-neck white shirt, trying to look like he had a home in Monaco. The English came here on business but they still brought their white hats with them because it was the Riviera and they thought they were being sophisticated, but they were being old-fashioned and ridiculous. The world was passing the English by now, only they could not see it. She was thinking of having the brochures printed in Mandarin next year.

'Please, use my pen.' She pulled a biro out of her hair with some difficulty.

Steve accepted the agency's introductory package, a folder filled with ads for casino shows featuring semi-naked girls in white ostrich feathers. It might have been printed in the 1970s. He signed a single page and returned it.

Julia gave him her broadest smile. 'Thank you, Mr Else-berry. I hope you will have a very successful *business* trip.' Her emphasis.

At the car-hire office a few doors along it took almost an hour to find a car and fill in the new forms. He was finally given a small silver Mercedes hatchback, which was not what he had ordered. He added the villa's address to the satnav. As he turned onto the Haute Corniche he considered the Summer question. His ego told him she would be at the villa, but what if she had decided to take off? Who knew what she might tell other people? He would not be able to control her, and that could be a problem.

As the kilometres passed beneath him and the car passed from light to dark, flashing through the hillside tunnels, he convinced himself that she would still be there waiting. He knew her well enough to be sure that when the time came to leave she wouldn't make a fuss. She was too smart for that.

Yes, he thought, keeping an eye on his GPS system, what had at first appeared to be a risk was actually no risk at all. He and Summer shared too many secrets. If one broke the rules, so could the other.

She would be there, down by the pool, waiting for his touch. If he was a gambling man he'd have put money on it.

14.

Summer was still by the pool.

She thought it would be interesting to wait for Steve and give him a piece of her mind, just to watch his face drop as he realised that sex was not on the menu. She thought of his wife and child turning up with their luggage a few hours later, the embraces and intimacies and private family jokes that would instantly wipe out the memory of her existence. She felt like giving him something to remember, but not what he'd expected.

Her thoughts turned to Hannah, as cautious as a fox, who thought before she spoke but reacted with her heart. She wished she could be like that. Instead she told everyone everything and left them to sort out what was true. She was sure of one thing: she wanted to see Hannah more than she wanted to see Steve.

Rising up on one arm, she turned her head and listened. For a moment it sounded as if Hannah was at the upstairs gate but no, it was just the wind lifting and clattering the bamboo chimes.

Her drink – the third of the morning – fell off the end of the lounger and smashed. *Crème de violette* flooded over the warm stones, staining them. She picked up the curved shards of glass and absently placed them in a flowerpot. Feeling a sharp little sting in her foot, she checked her sole and pulled out a crystal sliver. *Like Sleeping Beauty*, she thought, *pricking herself on the needle.*

The tops of the pines were moving. Something black and sinuous skittered between the branches, leaping from tree to tree. The pool glimmered as breezes crossed its surface. More pine needles and dead leaves blew in to choke the filter, a sign that the long parched summer was coming to an end. The water level had fallen an inch or so. A fine line of dirt marked its old height on the ultramarine tiles.

The pool boy had been due to appear early this morning but had failed to turn up. The house was in bright sunlight but somehow looked threatening, like a great cat motionlessly watching a trapped bird.

She texted Hannah and got no answer. She said Julia had given her an extra villa to clean, and maybe that was for the best. She had the feeling that Hannah might have taken this week all too much to heart. She needed to lighten up a little more. Who knew what could happen in a day, an hour, a minute?

Hannah over Steve. It wasn't much of a contest. With that, Summer reached a decision.

This was one mistake she no longer intended to make. She told herself she had nothing to apologise for. Steve had chased her for weeks and pushed her into making the trip. She decided to text him and explain.

No, it would be better *not* to text and make him sweat. Perhaps he would think twice about seducing innocent young girls. Not her, obviously, but future ones. It felt cowardly leaving before his arrival, but the idea of a sexual sparring match at the villa had completely lost its appeal. Looking at photos of Jihane on her phone made her realise how big the age gap was between her and Steve. How could he remember what it was like to be a teenager? It was a miracle she had survived the intense unsureness of her earlier years, the making of so many mistakes. In three months' time she would be nineteen, but she felt as old as the rocks.

She texted Jihane and asked if he could pick her up. He texted back and warned her that it would take him a couple of hours to get there because he'd only just got the house back and needed to clear it up a bit first.

There was a shriek and a rustle in the bushes. She looked about herself and listened, but the fight stopped as quickly as it started.

She put on more oil. Still no sign of Hannah. She'd cracked a coral nail. A piece had come off. The stuff was supposed to be chip-proof and now it needed repairing. Life was a *total* pain.

She listened. For a moment it sounded as if there was someone else here. Then nothing.

The sunflower sun glowed out, unfolding light and warmth across the patio and the pool as if granting heavenly approval. She turned to face it, closing her eyes, feeling the heat on her skin.

She had really been hoping to see Hannah before she left. She checked the time on her phone. A final half an hour by the pool, then she would pack her bag and get ready to leave.

As a civilised gesture she should tidy up the villa for Steve and his family because it looked as though Hannah wasn't going to come, and Summer didn't want her getting into trouble.

She looked over to her red bikini on the railing behind the outdoor shower and made a mental note not to forget it. She should have sunbathed naked from the start instead of getting these little white patches. Maybe Jihane had a roof terrace where she could get an all-over tan. Naked above the city, seen by everyone and no one, how cool would that be?

Holding a hand to her eyes, she searched the treetops and saw the coiled black things jumping again. Something about them bothered her. It was like lifting a pretty stone and finding centipedes underneath.

Thirty minutes, she thought, lying before a pool like a thousand glittering mirrors, beneath a sun bombarding her with benign irradiance, stilling her mind, leaving her to draw in the diurnal heat like a motionless lizard.

Thirty minutes more and she would be gone.

TWO:
THE GUESTS

15.

Steve checked his watch: 12:57 p.m. He was later than he'd expected to be, thanks to the hire place and the traffic backed up all the way from the coast, but there was still some time left before Summer had to leave for the airport.

He was thinking of himself, of course, something he did best alone and at length. Selfishness was a survival instinct that came to him as naturally as breathing. He was already prepared to discover that Summer had taken off, such being the way of mercurial young girls. His biggest fear was not of guilt or discovery but that he would always be like this, looking over his wife's shoulder at the next girl passing by. He blamed his father, whose roving eye had eventually destroyed their family.

The thought of keeping Summer with him in the villa until the very last minute aroused him again. He had been meticulously working his way through the fantasy; following a bout of rowdy, sweat-soaked lovemaking the naked girl, now anxious and upset, clutches her clothes to her as the doorbell repeatedly rings. She frantically looks for a way to escape. He shows her a secret door leading to the hidden back garden and tells her to hurry or she'll be caught. Tearful and grateful for release, she rushes out. He closes the door behind her and turns to greet the new arrival, still tumescent and scented with sex.

But it wasn't really about sex, he acknowledged with a certain amount of regret. It was power, the pleasure of the middle-aged man. He had always been a risk taker. It was the only way to separate yourself from the herd. If you suggested that something desirable could happen, you created the desire in others to make it happen. In business he concentrated on building up so much goodwill that clients overlooked their most fundamental problems.

It was not a strategy that could work forever; eventually the golden boy always tarnished. The trick was to get out before it happened. He had set himself the target of retiring at fifty. Jamie would be in his mid-twenties by then and might have finally put down his headphones and chosen a career. He and Jennifer could buy a home in Europe – not France, Italy perhaps – and find a kind of peace together. An Englishman's home was his castle, preferably somewhere other than England.

Carefully making his way down the dirt track, he parked in the shaded carport and unloaded his case. For a moment he thought he saw someone from the corner of his eye, but the bushes behind him stilled.

There was no sign of Summer rushing out to greet him but he sensed she was there. She was happy to let him know that she couldn't be bothered. For someone so young she was cheerfully louche and amoral; it was one of the things he liked best about her. When he walked out onto the patio she would be sitting by the pool, languidly smoking and affecting disinterest.

The front door was shut but the key only needed turning once. He unlocked it and pushed it open. Bamboo wind-chimes rattled somewhere on the patio. It was surprisingly dark inside. He saw shiny beige tiles, amber sofas and armchairs, enough pastel furniture to fill a rest home. The stippled white walls were covered with the kind of cheap landscapes found on sale in any artisanal French market.

He knew at once that she had not left. The air smelled of lavender air freshener, cigarettes and her oddly bitter jasmine perfume. The fractious phone calls that had passed between them would be quickly forgotten. Setting down his bag, he picked up another of Julia's brochures from the coffee table. *S'il vous plaît respecter notre belle villa!*

He knew she would be beside the pool but wanted to prolong the moment of anticipation, so he made his way upstairs with his bag. The narrow staircase turned tightly, the hall opening to three bedrooms. In the master bedroom a pair of girl's jeans lay crumpled on the floor. He opened the wardrobe. Only two compartments held clothes. Four T-shirts, a pair of Adidas trainers, red knickers, a sports bra. In the bathroom was makeup, mosquito spray, some kind of hair control product called Ultra-Maximizer and lots of little sample pots. A female *in absentia*.

He looked down from the window. Beside the pool, one lounger had been moved close to the water's edge. Some kind of see-through floral top was trapped by its back leg. *She's still around,* he thought, pleased to be proven correct. Of course she would want to make an entrance; she fostered an aura of surprise. He vaguely recalled her story about backpacking through Europe last year and how she wouldn't learn to drive until all cars become electric. She was a fantasist, of course, because of her age. Dreaming was a pastime for the young.

He had taken a chance arranging the trip like this but it had been worth it just to see the look on Giles's face. He needed his manager to see what was expected of him. Giles never took chances, so he had to be loyal to the man who did. Giles could make contact with all the people Steve couldn't reach because he had the confidence of privilege, whereas Steve was self-made, a phrase he hated because it implied that he was a shopkeeper who had taught himself to read. It had taken Steve a while to realise that a good education had little to do with intelligence. Despite going to a decent grammar school he had never managed to rid himself of a trace of accent that was redolent of terraced houses.

As he bounced back downstairs, he realised how incredibly untidy she was. It looked as if she'd had a party. This couldn't be the mess of one person, surely? The kitchen was a maelstrom of half-eaten toast, spilled booze and pieces of fruit. Now he had to factor in the clearing-up time.

He checked the fridge. On its shelves he found a half-litre bottle of Gordon's gin, some beers, a couple of weird liqueur bottles and two packets of cheese strings. What had she been living on? Alcohol and cigarettes, probably; so much for the healthy lifestyles of the young.

There were pizza boxes in the wastebin, two sun-dried

tomato and pepperonis. Either she was a secret binge-eater or she'd had her boyfriend over. He had been taken for a ride, paying through the nose so that she could catch up with some flat-stomached barman she'd enticed on her last little jaunt.

He opened the patio doors and inspected the pool area more closely. Patches of oil on the sun lounger formed a ghost image of where she had been lying. The pages of a fashion magazine flapped over in the rising breeze. The pool rippled forlornly. Walking to the patio edge, he looked out into the scrubby field below where a lone goat disconsolately chewed on a tuft of thistles.

The more he thought about it the angrier he became. She was probably out with the boy right now and would come back with some cock-and-bull story about the bus being cancelled, so late that she accidentally-on-purpose clashed with Jennifer, Jamie and the others arriving. It was hard to remember the last time he was this angry with a woman. But of course she was not a woman, just a wayward, spoilt little cocktease. He'd been screwed around long enough. *If she wants a fight,* he thought, *I'll give her one.* But even this thought was tinged with desire.

When he yelled out her name she surprised him by answering. She was inside, calling for him. He ran back toward the house. His anger vanished. Suddenly there was everything to play for again.

16.

Jihane brought the battered blue Renault to the track turn-off and was about to sound his horn, but as soon as he glimpsed the red rooftops through the pines he decided to text Summer from the road instead.

The villa was much grander than he'd expected. He hadn't fully grasped the situation, partly because Summer didn't explain how or why she was staying in such a place, and because he hadn't thought to ask her. All he knew was that she'd had some kind of falling out with a friend or lover and wanted to leave so badly that she needed to come and stay with him.

He imagined her leaving brawlers in her wake. She had no impulse control or common sense, but most of his friends were like that anyway. He'd liked her from the moment they'd met in the club and had somehow ended up in a bar where the sea spray came over the walls onto the dance floor and it had been 5:00 a.m. and neither of them could stop laughing. He wasn't sexually interested in girls but she had an aura that raised her above the crowd. She drew attention from everyone, and any girl who could do that with such casual disdain was cool with him.

When there was no reply to his text he knew he would have to go up to the front door. The sky looked troubled. The air was still. There were no birds singing.

Something stopped him. He decided to text instead: *You want this lift or not?*

He waited. No reply.

She couldn't still be asleep, not on the day she was due to leave the villa. He knew she drank too much; maybe she was out for the count. Stepping back, he tried to see if there was any movement inside the rooms, but they looked dead and empty. He cocked his head and listened.

A sudden high cry came from somewhere below, behind walls, hard to tell if it was human or animal. It sounded as if it was in pain.

He crossed to the right-hand side of the villa and listened again.

A wood pigeon burst out of the foliage with a shriek, flapping past him, its wings sounding like thrown books.

He held his breath.

This time her voice was unmistakable. She emitted a series of yelps, or was possibly laughing somewhere deep within the house. He considered waiting a little longer but decided against it. She was clearly in there but whatever she was doing was monopolising her attention. Perhaps she was singing along to her headphones down by the pool. But that meant his call would have cut in and she had chosen to ignore it.

With a snort of exasperation, he decided that she could sort out her own problems. He returned to his own vehicle and started the engine.

He had to head past the village, which was called St Martin-Sous-Roches, presumably because it was wedged under the umber rocks that had tumbled this way from the Massif Central like a great tray of dropped brioches. It was one of the few seriously unpicturesque villages he'd come across in the Alps Maritimes. A few rows of stained stone houses, a flyblown boulangerie, a run-down restaurant called Auberge Eric and a bar where a handful of raspberry-nosed old drinkers probably started hammering the Ricard at ten every morning.

At its centre stood the green-tiled spire of L'église de St Saturnia. The village of St Martin-Sous-Roches was a planetary system that still revolved – just – around the sun of belief.

The Chinese family's cars were too flashy and fragile for daily use, so Jihane was insured for their runabout. The Renault had a taped-up back bumper, three hubcaps and a dozen car-park dings, so it fitted perfectly at the kerb outside Chez Dany.

Afterwards he realised it was a mistake returning to the same bar in daylight. It looked even more disgusting than he'd remembered, and the air was thick with brandy fumes.

One of the regulars recognised him and sarcastically asked if he'd come to get into another fight, camply mimicking the way he'd fought back. The barman with the birthmark on his face reminded them that it had been the local lad's fault for starting it.

They must have remembered the young girl he'd brought with him that night, but there was no common consensus as to whether she'd been in this morning. Some pretty hikers had asked for directions, and there had been someone else, hadn't there? When they fell to arguing about that, he explained that he was looking for Summer Farrow. Their responses were predictable. They made fun of her name and his accent and pretended not to understand what he was saying. One of them asked if he was going to kidnap this girl and take her back to his tent.

It wasn't until Jihane got outside that he even realised their joke was connected to his Arabic colouring. Sometimes it was pretty hard getting into the mindset of provincial prejudice. A pretty little girl of about nine or ten stood beside the kerb watching him. The intensity of her blank gaze pulled him up short.

'Hello. Are you waiting for someone?' he asked in French.

She pointed back into the bar.

He crouched a little. 'What's your name?'

'Clémence.' She reached out to touch his hair.

'Clémence, have you seen—?'

He stopped and rose. There was no point in even asking. But something wasn't right. He walked back to the car. He had been thinking to head along the corniche toward Nice, but found himself driving toward the villa once more.

He tried calling Summer again, but her phone continually went to voicemail. He asked himself how well he really knew her, and the answer came back: hardly at all. She seemed to drift on the tide of life, going wherever it took her, but he couldn't imagine her wanting to stay on here. The villa was isolated, and there certainly weren't any wild Saturday night parties planned in the village. Perhaps she had grown impatient and gone ahead to Nice.

He figured she would call him again as soon as she wanted something. He'd thought there must be a level-headed side to Summer under the crazy teenage stuff, but maybe he'd misjudged her and she was just another rich little wild child who would drift off into drugs and parties, never to be seen again.

He parked the Renault by the side of the road and walked up the grassy drive. A silver Mercedes Hatchback was now sitting in the driveway, its engine ticking. So she had a man with her now. She could at least have answered his text, if only to put him off.

He was about to ring the doorbell when he heard a series of small, rhythmic cries from the garden beyond the back gate. The thought suddenly occurred to him that she was having sex. Unwrapping a piece of gum, he moved to the gate and pressed his face against the planks, trying to see in.

There was a sudden dark movement across the gap. Somebody else was just on the other side.

17.

Hannah checked the time and began to fret. She was still stuck at the Villa Champs D'Or, trying to move an enormous steel-framed bed away from a wall, and wondered if Summer was annoyed with her for not turning up.

Julia had called early and asked them to reverse their usual schedule because the rich and famous Russians – Hannah almost heard her spit when she named them – had been screaming at her on the phone about the mess they'd made and were unable or unwilling to clear up. Could they go there first, Julia pleaded, and make things nice so that *Vacances Paradis* didn't get into any more trouble because God forbid another lawsuit?

Daniela was downstairs sorting out the mess around the pool. They wouldn't be able to leave until they had put the place back to normal. The Russians had thrown a party last night, during which the guests had hurled food into the hot tub and left broken glass all over the patio. The chaos extended to the rooms upstairs. Trays of canapés had become ammunition in some kind of war game, and one of their children had shoved a leaking litre bottle of Coke behind the headboard of his bed.

She wished she had taken the morning off to rescue Summer. For all her bravado she'd sounded apprehensive. It was impossible to know what the girl really thought. One moment she talked about sexual experimentation, the next she seemed horrified by the idea. As Hannah tried to shift the bed again, she realised that one thing had been constant from the moment they'd met: Summer's loyalty toward her had been unwavering. She felt a little annoyed for having her heart so casually and unexpectedly exposed.

The bed pulled free – its back legs had become glued to the floor with cola. Along with the bottle she also found a diamond ring stuck to the floor with spilled sugar drink. It looked expensive; the central stone was surrounded by amethysts in a setting of fluted gold arches. Carefully unsticking it, she placed it on a table where it would be easily found. This, she decided, was another reason why Julia was so keen to prevent her staff from talking to guests. The situations in which they found themselves were fraught with potential misunderstandings.

She wondered how much more Daniela had left to do. Perhaps she could still get down to the villa before Summer left?

That hope was dashed when Daniela appeared in the doorway with a fresh bucket of soapy water, complaining that she had just found lasagne trodden into the stair carpets. It looked as if they would be another hour.

But there was a bicycle in the garage. She could head down

there now and be back in just a few minutes. Daniela wouldn't even notice she had gone.

Hannah had a sudden sense of what she might lose; Summer was the kind of girl who would swear lifelong allegiance, then vanish overnight. People like her didn't need anyone. They cut a path through their lives unaided, barely noticing those who fell in their wake. They needed to be fought for.

The cycle ride was downhill, following the switchback trail through cliffsides studded with pale green agaves and cactuses. She made good time, spokes spinning, gliding around the hills, her legs stuck out straight, sliding to a stop in front of the turn-off to the villa, where she dismounted.

Tucking the bike behind a bush, she went up to the back gate. There was no sound from the pool. Summer usually had music playing. She heard the wind in the trees, nothing else. Either she had already gone or she was inside packing. *No*, she thought, *she's not gone yet. I can smell her scent.*

Hannah looked down. There was a silver gum wrapper on the step. Someone else had been here.

She reached through and opened the metal latch, pushing back the gate by a foot or so. The strangeness of the villa struck her once more. Here in the hills there was always a sensation of height. Nothing was level. Even the roads were cambered. Sometimes, after staring up at the sky, she had to stop and rebalance. The villa was perched, its patio, pool and gardens built on ledges at the mercy of the landscape. It felt curiously impermanent, as if a slip of one degree would fling everything down into the valley.

How did the guests pass their days? Did they simply unplug

their brains and rotate their loungers to follow the parabola of the sun like flowers? Did they check their phones, waiting for the hour when it was acceptable to start drinking? Too much leisure was a dangerous luxury. In this place of scheduled indolence an apocalyptic event might pass unnoticed. She might look up at the dark ridge of pines and see oily black smoke rising above the treetops, the only sign of some dire catastrophe.

She looked out across the fields to the adjoining gardens on the other side of the valley. The parcels of land were chaotic and irregular, attached to each other by snaking paths. A neighbouring villa was hemmed with manicured olive trees. Terraces were stepped into the hillside and eventually led up to an odd green-tiled house barely visible through the bushes. Hannah wondered why she hadn't noticed it before.

The cicadas fell silent with shocking suddenness. She heard a car approaching. Turning around, she saw the Mercedes bump onto the grassy track and head toward her. She pulled the gate shut and slipped behind the bushes to reach her bike but it was too late; the tall tanned man who adroitly parked and climbed out could only be Steve Elsbury.

He matched Summer's description perfectly; there was something of a menswear store mannequin about him, stiff, sturdy and posed, his hair blue-black and glossed. He raised his vintage green and gold sunglasses and looked up at the villa.

She thought of going over and casually introducing herself: *Hi, I was just passing, I'm your maid, I'll be here later.* As if that wouldn't make him suspicious. Besides, she had already broken the no-speaking rule once and was not about to do it again.

She had missed her chance to see Summer alone. Perhaps

it was for the best. Summer had got herself into this situation. It was time she learned a little responsibility. Hannah could not afford to wait around while this creep prowled the villa, sniffing after her. She was needed back at the Champs D'Or.

Steve took his luggage from the boot of the Mercedes. She waited until she heard the thump of the lid shutting and the trundle of his case, then pushed back into the bushes and slipped past him to the hidden bicycle.

By the time she had cycled up to the Champs D'Or she had regained her composure, if not her breath. It was tempting to ring and disrupt whatever was happening between them.

Put it out of your mind, she decided. *If you play it by the book from now on you might manage to keep your job.* She would go to the Villa Lavardin later, when Julia's schedule required her to be there.

For now, she concentrated on the problem of removing Coca-Cola stains from behind the bed.

18.

'A hundred and fifty euros? That's outrageous.' Giles opted for a look of theatrical shock. The taxi driver didn't bother turning around but stared straight ahead and tapped the meter, pointing to the implacable proof.

'Darling, you were the one who voted Leave,' said Melissa. 'The pound is an international embarrassment. We're "the sick man of Europe".'

'That was the Ottoman Empire.'

'Just pay the man.' She searched in her Vuitton bag for sunglasses, huge caramel-coloured squares of plastic that reduced her to semi-blindness but concealed laughter lines.

Giles felt for his wallet but continued to complain. 'It's probably not much more to take the helicopter, for God's sake.'

'But then you've got to come back on yourself from Monte Carlo to get here and *that* taxi would probably cost a fortune. Just give him the money, darling. And don't bring God into it, not in the South of France.'

'Where is this bloody house, anyway?' Giles peered from

the passenger window but saw only rocks and pine trees. 'Can't you take us up to the door?' He spoke over-enunciated French, adopting the tone of the Englishman abroad as if dealing with someone who was partially deaf.

The driver pointed to the rubble-strewn track ahead. 'The road is bad for the car.'

Giles reluctantly counted out the notes. 'This is a Mercedes. It can survive a mortar attack.'

'We should have waited for Steve's family,' said Melissa. 'They'll have to pay the same amount. We could have saved them some money.'

'I couldn't remember what time her flight was.' Giles waited for change that was clearly not forthcoming.

'I should have called her, seeing as we've met properly now,' Melissa said. 'I do hate Heathrow. You taxi for such a long time it feels like the pilot has decided to drive all the way there. Of course she was EasyJet and going from Gatwick, which means being surrounded by people who all appear to be moving house.'

Giles watched as his wife slithered awkwardly off the leather seat and stood by the rear of the vehicle, waiting for the driver to unlock the boot.

Framed by olivine larches and pines, against the buzzing of cicadas and an oppressively hyper-real sky, they stood apart, looking like ride-sharing strangers rather than husband and wife.

Melissa had the upright bearing of a former dancer, her oaken tan one shade above melanoma. Today she was dressed in a swirling orange and white Mary Quant sixties original dress and strappy heels.

Giles had married in a frenzy, anxious to be absolved of his first wife, but now regretted acting in haste. His wife was a tyrant. He had not yet admitted it to himself, but he now regarded Melissa as something to be endured for an unspecified period of time, like a pulmonary infection.

The track of puddled caramel-coloured earth was less than a hundred yards long; the villa had tucked itself beyond the bend of the highway. It had rained overnight. The air smelled of lavender, honeysuckle and goat dung.

Giles sniffed the air and pulled a face. He set about dragging his Samsonite suitcase but it came off the path and gravel jammed the wheels, so that he was forced to lift it. Melissa left her case where it was.

'Can't you bring that?' asked Giles irritably. He could already feel sweat starting to bead in his thinning hair.

'You can come back for it.' Unconcerned, Melissa looked up at the windows then headed toward the villa, all pinkish-amber plasterwork and white bordered windows shrouded in purple bougainvillea, vivid colours one never found in Farrow & Ball. The green wooden shutters on the upper floor were all closed. The downstairs rooms looked locked and dark. The villa was picturesque without being pretty, in that it conformed to expectations without displaying any actual personality.

There was a car in the driveway. Melissa had gone the wrong way and had to clamber around the side of it, her heels sinking into the grass.

She tapped her foot on the tiled step. Something was out of place here. She had taken a feng shui course once and this felt all wrong.

'What if we're the first ones?' she asked. 'This car could be the maid's.'

'A Mercedes,' muttered Giles, 'I don't think so.'

'Why didn't you arrange to pick up the keys in case Steve's flight was delayed as well?'

'He should have landed ages ago.' Giles set down their cases on the orange tiled patio. It wasn't entirely a lie. He knew exactly when his boss had landed and why, but it was not something he could discuss with his wife.

He pressed a white bell set in a fluted plastic box above an old nameplate that read: M *Lavardin*. The cicadas stopped for a moment, then resumed. He listened at the door. It was safe to be here now. Even taking into account the fact that they were early, the girl would have gone to the airport by now.

'Why isn't he answering?' Melissa called. The delay was long enough to make her wander away and check her messages. Anything that made her wait for more than a few seconds was enough to draw forth her phone. She prayed the villa had fast broadband; she was not prepared to go back to a world without connectivity, even for a holiday.

Giles rang again, then pressed his ear to the door. 'There's definitely someone moving about in there.'

Melissa searched for her cigarettes. 'Why don't you go to the back of the house?'

'I'm not going to creep around in the bushes,' said Giles indignantly. 'It's not my villa. That would be trespassing.'

Melissa gave a special sigh, the one she reserved exclusively for her husband. 'Steve rented it for the four of us –'

'Five, his son's coming.'

'– so presumably you're down as one of the guests.'

'How do you know that?'

'Because he probably had to put everyone's names on the rental agreement in order to get the keys. That's how agencies like – what was it called?'

'*Vacances Paradis.*'

'That's how they work, the same as Airbnb. More upmarket, obviously, although you can stay in the smartest French places and find light bulbs held in place with sticky tape. How they ever got a reputation for being chic I'll never know. I think I can see someone. Off you go, go on, the back gate's ajar, I can see it from here. Have a look, just don't stand on any of the plants.'

I talk to him as if he was a dog, she thought, returning to her phone. *I need to, it's the only way he hears me. Ideally I'd have a whistle.* One bar, barely a signal. Putting the phone away, she rapped impatiently on the door. A startled yellow grasshopper landed on the orange floor tiles and sprang away.

Now that Giles had gone she was stuck here in the porch and nobody was making their way to the front door, and it all felt vaguely sinister. There was nothing for it but to follow her husband through the gate and past a perfectly trimmed barrier of japonica. The gardens were separated into sections with frail bamboo walls. She could smell rosemary, mint and, inevitably, more lavender. The villa was spread over three levels on a hillside that looked like a someone had taken a great scoop out of the land, leaving a shaded green valley beyond it.

As she followed the path downward she realised that the rear wall dropped, revealing a floor below with full-length windows that folded back onto the pool. Shadow bisected the water so that one elongated panel glittered with blue diamonds while the remaining section was an inky ultramarine. The shadows beneath the striped yellow sun loungers were so sharply delineated that they might have been painted on the ground. The beds had been set in a regimented row but one had been drawn out and moved diagonally to face the sun, its front feet almost over the lip of the pool. Something as iridescent as dragonfly wings lay underneath it.

She looked up, instinctively aware that Giles was being annoying. He was pressed against the patio window with one hand cupped around his eyes, tapping rapidly on the glass.

He recoiled suddenly. 'Jesus! Someone just ran across the lounge. Actually *ran*. Why don't they come to the door?'

This wasn't right. He squinted up at the sun, as if finding its glare a personal affront. Giles burned easily, especially in the long dog-days of summer. He fancied his skin was already tightening. He'd seen a dark blur of movement inside, flitting between the armchairs, but it had gone now.

Melissa stopped on the patio and waited. It was typical of her husband to stand helplessly at a window complaining to no one in particular. She examined the back of the villa, counting the windows. 'All these rooms. How many does this sleep?'

'Eight or ten, I think.' He tapped and waved at the glass without effect. 'Steve says he got a very good deal. It'll be nice to have the extra space.'

'It seems –' she sought the right word, '– excessive.'

'Why, because we're not inviting half a dozen homeless

people to come and stay with us as well? I refuse to feel guilty for enjoying the fruits of my labour, God knows the government takes more than its fair share. We've got a maid for the week, so you can feel guilty about that as well. Wait, I can see him. It *is* Steve. He's in there. Why isn't he letting us in?'

Melissa stood against the end door and drew hard on her cigarette. Removing it, she breathed out and inhaled, replacing the smoke with air so fresh that it tasted of chlorophyll. It was now extraordinarily quiet, as if the surrounding trees were absorbing all the noise. It was the first time she had not heard traffic in months. She longed to be left alone for the week, to close her eyes and imagine everyone gone.

There was something black and sinuous moving across the tops of the trees, disturbing the branches, like a large black rat or –

'What *is* that?' she asked.

The door beside her suddenly opened, catching her in mid-turn on the steps. 'Oh,' she exclaimed in surprise, 'you *are* in.'

Steve was dressed in a white Le Coq Sportif shirt with sweat stains darkening the armpits, pressed navy shorts, white socks and new Adidas trainers. He had a black plastic bag in one hand and a tennis racket in the other. His hair was out of place. Beads of perspiration glistened on his forehead. He stared at her dumbly.

'You've been caught red-handed,' she joked.

They had met once before at the Ivy Club, just after Steve had offered Giles the position as his second-in-command. She had forgotten how tall, wide-shouldered and cartoonishly attractive he was. Now she saw he had muscled thighs too. Apparently he had once competed in some surfing championships. A bit of an adrenalin junkie. Good-looking older men appealed to her more than wispily handsome youths, not that she had much of a chance with either.

'Is anything wrong?' she asked.

Steve returned to his surroundings. 'Forgive me – Melissa.' He fought to recall her name. 'I wasn't expecting you until later. I, ah – fell asleep. I probably got the time wrong.' He pushed the door back wide with his elbow. 'Please, come in.'

'Giles told me he'd ping you our flight details. Did he not do that? It would be just like him.' She screwed her cigarette butt into one of the patio pots and stepped inside.

'He did but he told me you would be here at six.'

'It took a while to find a cab – the French don't seem to understand the concept of queueing, but... oh, I see, no, we caught the earlier flight. I don't need to tell you what unearthly hour we were up at this morning. Giles panics if he's not at the airport a full two hours ahead of time, but I suppose you know that. God, then we *are* early. I'm so sorry, I hope it won't inconvenience you.'

Steve searched for somewhere to deposit the bag and headed for the kitchen. He left an acrid trail of sweat and alcohol that seemed out of character. 'Let me just get rid of – where is he?'

'Giles? He went around the other side of the villa looking for you.' She looked about, wondering who else was here. 'When I last spoke to your wife she thought they might be a bit delayed.'

Steve searched the floor distractedly, as if wondering what

other surprises were lying in wait for him. 'That's annoying. Did they say why?'

'Well, Gatwick, it hardly matters, does it? There's always something.'

She stopped, unsure of where to go. Steve was clearly not ready for them. He stooped to pick up something, furtively shoving it into the bag. 'I should track Jennifer's flight,' he said absently.

'So when did you arrive?'

'Me – oh, just an hour or so ago.'

It certainly didn't look as if he'd arrived an hour ago; the room was in disarray. There were cigarette ends piled in an ashtray but she couldn't imagine that Steve smoked.

He continued to look about himself, barely concentrating on her. 'I mean I got to France earlier, but I needed to arrange a few meetings in Nice and sort out the keys for the villa, that kind of thing. They have an agent who looks after the property and organises the cleaning services. They can arrange for a chef to come and cook for us if we want.'

'I can imagine what that would cost up here.' As her husband had not returned and Steve had his hands full, Melissa was forced to go back and bring her own bag inside.

'I guess the maid didn't come yet.' She set down her suitcase. The ashtray had been hastily emptied, she noted. 'It's like hotels, I hate it when the rooms aren't ready and they leave you sitting in the foyer with a fruit drink. I'm sure Giles can give you a hand.'

'It's fine,' Steve assured her. 'I can manage. Let's go and find you a bedroom.'

She checked the furniture appraisingly. 'Very nineties, almost back in fashion. I haven't seen this many pastels since we threw out my mother's things. At least it's lovely and cool in here.'

'Thick walls. They keep the sunlight out.' Steve wiped his hands and stepped forward to take her bag.

'No, really, leave it for Giles to do,' she instructed. 'He needs the exercise.'

As Steve went ahead she glanced back at the disturbed room and felt positive that something nefarious had been going on here. *What have you been up to?* She permitted herself a private smile. *Secrets don't last long around me, darling.*

19.

By the time Steve woke up, sore-eyed and dehydrated, indigo shadows had already started to drop over the far corner of the swimming pool. An empty whisky glass stood on the table beside him that he did not remember drinking from. He'd dreamt that a cat had fallen into the pool and he had fought about it with Summer. The dream must have been vivid because he had lashed out and scratched the knuckle of his right fist on the corner of the coffee table. He checked his watch. 3:51 p.m.

Smoothing down his hair, he wandered into the kitchen.

A total fucking disaster.

His foot kicked a bottle of nail polish across the floor. He opened the back door. The first dead leaves crackled across the patio. An emerald lizard was so bright and still that it might have been stencilled onto the remaining sunlit wall. A plastic chocolate wrapper as shiny as a beetle's carapace scuttled across the stones.

He knew he shouldn't leave the tidying up until the last minute but was stricken with a rare bout of indecision. A level of healthy risk was one thing, but he was not prepared to countenance chaos.

It's fine, he told himself, *I'll deal with this.* He tried one of the cheese strings and spat it out, mixed himself a strong gin and tonic – there were lemons all over the counter – and was about to start clearing up when somebody rang the doorbell.

He had been planning to change – he was still in his navy shorts and his white shirt – but there was no time now. As the bell rang again he bent low and looked at the shadow beneath the door. He could hear a woman's voice, someone he didn't recognise. She spoke clear, loud English to someone who did not reply.

The doorbell rang again, longer this time. He began grabbing at the magazines, makeup pads, pop socks and empty plastic bottles that lay across the floor. Summer appeared to have spent her days walking around shedding beauty products and bits of tissue. Was the ability to spontaneously produce all this stuff one of the perks of being a teenaged girl?

He needed to answer the door, but not before he'd dispensed with the most obvious signs of female occupation. He could clear the ground floor, see who it was, head upstairs and quickly return the bedroom to normal.

He heard the woman say: 'I don't know why you didn't arrange to pick up the keys in case Steve's flight was delayed as well.' She sounded as if she was training a dog.

He followed her silhouette as it moved around the side of the house to the terrace. She peered in through the sliding glass doors, staring right at him. It took him a moment to realise that she couldn't see him clearly.

'I think I can see someone,' he heard her call. It dawned on him that this was Giles's wife, Melissa – but they weren't due to arrive for ages yet.

Summer was bound to have left more stuff in the pool house and on the patio. Either she was still around or she had departed in a hurry. A narrow stone staircase took him to the rear of the lower building, where he let himself in and found towels, a hairdryer, yellow knee socks and some kind of glittery top on the back of a chair. An empty Sainsbury's bag lay on the cord rug. He bundled everything into it. *Fucking hell*, he thought, *there's more of her shit on the patio.*

Giles put in a sudden appearance, bounding onto the terrace like a entertainer popping up to surprise children. He cupped his hands around his eyes and pressed against the window, peering and muttering, tapping the glass, being his usual ineffectual self. Giles already knew far too much for comfort. Now he'd think the setup wasn't so slickly professional after all.

Being diminished in the eyes of an employee spurred him on more than anything else. Steve found himself holding a plastic bag full of her crap plus a tennis racquet, but it would look weird to hide them now. He ran back upstairs and answered the front door, aware that he was sweating.

'Oh,' said Melissa, 'you *are* in.'

She came back up the steps to peer at him through immense sunglasses. She was wearing a chignon in multiple shades of blonde and a complex arrangement of day jewellery. She looked as expensive to maintain as a baroque church.

'Forgive me – Melissa. I wasn't expecting you until later.

I fell asleep.' He pushed the door back wide with his elbow. 'Please, come in.'

'I think my husband went around the other side of the villa.'

Stepping inside, she stalked about scrutinising the décor, talking all the way. He needed to lure her upstairs so that he could continue clearing up without her noticing. He tried to listen but only picked up every other sentence.

'– my hopeless husband obviously neglected to warn you that the flight was earlier than expected. He only told me at the very last minute. He says he moved it forward deliberately but he always tries to claim that his mistakes are deliberate, as I'm sure you've discovered by now. You can never assume anything with Giles, especially when it comes to travel arrangements because of course he's utterly terrified of flying, which in this day and age is simply bizarre.'

'He didn't mention anything about moving the flight.' Steve really wanted to get rid of the carrier bag and the tennis racquet but could not afford to look even more suspicious.

'There you are, you see. I'm sorry if you were trying to grab some shuteye.'

'No, not really, I just dozed off for a moment.'

'If you just point me to our bedroom I'll have Giles deal with our cases.'

'Of course.' He led the way to the staircase. 'I didn't sort out the room situation so if you just –'

They heard sharp knocking coming from downstairs. 'That'll be him.' Melissa shook her head in apology. 'Hopeless.'

'It's okay, stay here, I'll let him in.'

Steve ran downstairs, shedding the bag and racquet behind the living room sofa, then took the staircase down to the pool house. Apart from the items he'd discarded the rest of the place seemed – on the surface, at least – to be clear of all evidence of occupation. Apparently Summer had not managed to spread her spore this far. He opened the patio door to Giles and welcomed him.

'Sorry about the surprise,' said Giles. 'She didn't tell me until the last bloody minute that we'd somehow ballsed up the booking. How anyone can mistake a.m. for p.m. using a twenty-four-hour clock is beyond me.'

'No problem, Giles. Well, we'd better get you settled in,' he said with fake cheer. 'I'm in the master bedroom and Jamie's going to have the one next to us, but there are three other bedrooms already made up so please, choose whichever one you want.'

As he prepared to guide Giles back upstairs, he spotted a folded A4 sheet of paper lying on one of the dining chairs: Summer's EasyJet ticket, Nice to London. *Christ*, he thought, *I assumed she had the boarding code on her phone. Maybe she had both.* Quartering the page, he slipped it into his back pocket.

Giles had stopped on the first step and was looking back at him strangely. 'Is something wrong?' he asked over-emphatically.

'Nothing at all.' He gave his best smile. 'Up you go, let's take a look at the rooms.' As he waited for Giles to negotiate the turn in the staircase, he glanced back in the direction of the pool and saw a young woman in a bright yellow T-shirt walking around its edge.

Who the hell is that? he asked himself.

20.

As Daniela's car lurched away, Hannah let herself in through the unlocked side gate and crossed the top patio.

Looking into the rooms she caught sight of herself; she was still wearing shorts and a yellow T-shirt instead of her black-and-white maid's uniform. Daniela had warned her to change outfits as soon as she arrived in occupied villas because Julia had a habit of turning up unannounced. But what was the point of wearing a uniform in an empty house?

She checked her phone. There was no message from Summer so everything was presumably okay. At the bottom of the lower staircase she stopped and took another look around, checking the pool house, glancing into each room in turn. There were voices coming from the upper building. A snippet of conversation reached her, something about the stowing of suitcases.

She walked around the edge of the pool to a store room that stood between the main building and the guest wing. It was where all the flammable cleaning products were kept, somewhere she could change without being disturbed. The uniform crackled with static as she put it on. Outside, she smoothed the skirt down.

The shadows on the pool made it appear bottomless. Its flagstone surround had stairs that descended into a semi-cultivated wilderness of wild saffron and hibiscus. One path ran parallel to the patio directly beneath it, past the wall of thorny bougainvillea, while the other became a winding walkway leading to a rugged, stony field below. In the distance goat bells clattered.

She would have to go and introduce herself to the new guests and try not to stare at the legendary Steve. A moment ago she thought she had caught him looking out at her from one of the upstairs windows.

There were people coming. She crossed to the shallow end of the pool, where the shower stood against a wall of rough grey slate. Leaning into the cool shadows behind it, she waited and listened.

'I've never been so embarrassed in my life,' the tall woman said. 'I mean, it's obvious he's had a party here or something. Did you see the mess? Are we supposed to not notice? There are beer bottles behind the sofa, for God's sake. I thought he only arrived this morning?'

'Melissa, even if he had someone here it's none of our business,' replied a male with a soft, wheedling voice. 'But how could he? Think about it logically. He was on the seven o'clock flight, then he had to wait for a hired car and get the keys for this place. He's hardly been here. Maybe the maid didn't come in.'

'Giles, even you can't be this clueless. He's had a woman over. A man that good looking always has a girl stashed somewhere. I know the signs.'

'How do you know them?'

Melissa did not reply. She stopped before the sun lounger. Caught around one of its legs was a strip of transparent coral-coloured material studded with tiny crystals. Summer's beautiful wrap, her favourite item of clothing. Hannah had never seen her without it. Surely the woman had to notice?

'So is he going to brief us about what to say in front of his wife or do we have to pretend that everything's normal?' Melissa bent over and for a moment Hannah thought she was going to untangle the wrap, but instead she adjusted the strap of her shoe.

'You don't have to do anything, it's not your business,' Giles replied. 'There's probably a very simple explanation. Steve is usually very organised but he's been distracted lately. The clients are being difficult. I imagine he just kicked off his shoes when he got in and –'

'– ate two pizzas and drank four beers, a scotch and a bottle of gin before playing a game of tennis? Sometimes I wonder about you, Giles, I really do.' Melissa straightened and walked on. 'I know you were born with a silver spoon in your mouth but the nurse didn't have to hit you over the head with it.'

Giles did not reply. He was used to insults.

'Oh my God, you know something about this,' said the strident woman. 'He's told you to keep your mouth shut, hasn't he?'

'It's nothing like that, it's just –'

'Just what? Giles, does he tell you what to say?'

Hannah stayed and listened; she could hardly do anything else. A strong citrus perfume eclipsed Summer's scent, something for an older woman, Chanel-ish. She checked her own wrist: Daisy by Marc Jacobs, courtesy of the Russians.

She sprayed it to ward off the smell of cleaning chemicals. At last the couple's argument fragmented and became indistinct as they moved back inside the villa.

Hannah was about to move from the shower wall when she noticed a streak of fire-alarm red on a rail beside her. Summer had hung her miniscule bikini there. How could she have forgotten it?

It weighed nothing. Rolling the pieces together in her hand, she slipped them into her pocket. She needed to go in and start cleaning, but her stomach was in a knot. She felt as if she shouldn't be here at all.

Walking to the edge of the field, she sat down on the bottom step and listened to the birds. She scratched at the mosquito bites on her ankles, thinking. This was not how she had expected Summer to leave. It looked more like she had fled in panic.

There was no sound from the villa now. It was probably safe to go in and start work. She pressed her palms flat on the sun-warmed stone. Summer's footprints were here. Did she run away before Steve arrived or wait to confront him? Did he frighten her, tell her to get out?

As she passed the pool she knelt beside the sun lounger and picked up the wrap, running it through her fingers. It smelled of Summer's scent, jasmine mixed with something sharp and herbal.

I love it, it's called 'Dangerous' and comes in these huge cheap-looking bottles. You could use it to track people.

Summer's sunglasses lay in the flower bed nearest to the sun lounger, presumably shifted there by the wind. She always wore them outside.

When Hannah looked at the ground more closely, she spotted several small pieces of glass and a violet blot from a spilled drink. The glass had obviously fallen from the arm of the lounger. Beside the stain was what appeared to be a drop of blood, dry and dark. About eighteen inches away she found another, this one larger and oddly shaped. It was part of a bloody footprint; she could even see the little gap left by Summer's toe-ring, as clear as if it had been deliberately printed onto the stone.

Something shone in a runnel between the tiles. Digging her fingers into the gap, she pulled out the slender gold neck-chain. On it was a plate inscribed with Summer's name. The clasp was still intact. One of the links had been broken open.

She had waited for Steve, not to have sex with him but to tell him exactly why she had changed her mind. She'd done it even though she was scared of him.

Hannah recalled seeing the Mercedes arrive outside the house at around one thirty. That meant he had been here for nearly three hours. In her mind's eye she saw Summer getting a little drunk, impatiently pacing and growing angrier, waiting to cause a scene when he arrived.

Someone came charging down the staircase and belly-flopped into the pool with a rebel yell, making her start. The water slopped from the pool and flooded over the tiles, washing over the scarlet prints.

Hannah went to introduce herself to the guests, the neck-chain, the glasses, the red bikini and the diaphanous shoulder wrap bundled in her bag. It was all evidence that might be needed later, although she was not sure why.

21.

Jennifer's headache did not ease at Nice Côte d'Azur airport, where delayed flights filled the terminal with holidaymakers who looked as exhausted as refugees.

She took two Nurofen but a slender needling pain persisted through the taxi ride. The car was icily air-conditioned but the driver refused to allow her to open a window. He cited trouble with customers who left without paying, as if she was likely to clamber out and run off in her heels. Jamie was slumped next to her, his Bluetooth headphones fixed over the white cotton hood of his sports top, a uniform look he adopted wherever he went, whatever the temperature.

From the aircraft window the villas of the Cote D'Azur shone like trays of expensive confectionary, perfect little packages of peach, apricot and meringue. From the taxi you could see behind the promenade's rhinestone shops to the backstage areas. Here, if visitors cared enough to look, was the mundane mechanism of the resort, the garages, plumbing suppliers, junk food outlets and sex shops.

Passing beyond a band of graffiti that encircled the town like a tidemark, their taxi climbed into the green and amber mountainside, where the villas looked like ornate presents strung around a gigantic Christmas tree.

According to Jennifer's phone it was 25°C. Dense spiky greenery rolled past the car on both sides but fell away every few kilometres to reveal rock outcrops, vertiginous drops and hairpin bends looping around the landscape. The Haute Corniche clung to the hills like a black ribbon tied around the pines.

Jennifer reached over and lifted one earpiece. 'Jamie, can you take them off now? We're nearly there.'

Jamie removed the headphones but kept his hood firmly in place. 'I'm not having the smallest bedroom. I'm not sharing.'

'Then you have to assert yourself.'

She felt guilty for making Jamie come with them but he was hardly ever around these days, and it would do them good to spend time together, maybe even allow them to rediscover themselves as a family. They certainly had some making up to do. Jamie's life existed almost entirely online. He no longer felt comfortable talking face to face with anyone. She worried that he would never find friends of his own age with whom he could physically socialise.

'I'm sure it won't be as boring as you think. We'll all get on well together. Wait and see.' She heard herself saying the words but did not believe them for a second. The taxi braked sharply as a coach appeared from around the next bend. 'It'll all be very English and polite,' she added redundantly.

'Can't wait.' Jamie dug himself further down, the knees of his torn black jeans raised against the seat in front.

'You haven't met the Sutherlands. You never know, you might get on. I don't want you just staring at your phone, slumped forward the whole week looking like you've been tranquillised. Perhaps you could lay off the tweeting, or whatever it is you do now.'

'I'm staving off boredom. Teenagers can literally die of boredom. It's true. I read about it.'

'You're staving off thinking. You have a good brain, I wonder that you don't try using it.' She peered out of the rear window. It seemed an awfully long way. 'I meant to call Melissa back. I can't remember when she said they were leaving. Ah – it looks like we might be here.'

'Where?' Jamie made a half-hearted attempt to look for the villa.

'There, just beyond the trees.'

'Jesus, it's in the middle of fucking nowhere.'

'That's the point. And don't swear in front of the others. They may not be so easy-going.'

'Giles works for Dad. Who calls their son *Giles*?'

'Old money, apparently. Giles was supposed to go into Parliament. I imagine Melissa can be a bit full-on. She smokes like a chimney.'

'Olds are so gross.'

Jennifer ignored his comment. 'I'm not sure what she does. Your father did try to explain it to me. If they get too much he's hiring a car so we can just head off somewhere. There's supposed to be a village that's walkable.'

'What's there?'

'Probably a patisserie, a smelly old bar and a bunch of elderly men playing *pétanque*. It's France. I don't know, Jamie, you have to make your own amusement. Talk to people, make some friends.'

'Yeah, right.'

She undertipped the driver while Jamie unloaded the bags. The villa was surrounded by spindly pine trees. Their trunks cast hard black shadows on the road and striped the earthen track that led to the front door.

Jamie stopped and crouched before a small emerald lizard that balanced motionlessly on an upturned rock. The sight gave Jennifer hope. Her son was taking an interest in something.

Steve came out to meet them.

Sometimes she saw him not as her husband but as strangers did, tall and strikingly different, with a special kind of saturnine masculinity, as still and dark as a lake. It was annoying; she grew older but he seemed to stay exactly the same.

What did others think the first time they faced him? Did he make them feel tongue-tied and inadequate? Did he encourage deference and put them on their best behaviour? Overtly handsome men knew precisely what effect they had on people and how to exploit it in a thousand subtle ways.

Today he was wearing a freshly ironed short-sleeved white shirt, pressed blue shorts and white trainers. He might just have come from a tennis green. After giving her the faintest graze on the cheek he took the bags from Jamie.

'Come and have a look at the place, tell me what you think. It's classically French, by which I mean there are bowls of plastic flowers everywhere, along with those awful lavender air fresheners, but there's tons of room.'

She stepped inside and took it in. Amber tiled floors, honey-coloured wood, faded pink and apricot fabrics, lots of twisting steps and narrow doors, a terrace that looked across the valley, the sea hidden somewhere far beyond.

Steve whispered conspiratorially, 'Giles and Melissa arrived here a while ago. Melissa is unhappy that I've taken the largest bedroom for us.'

'But you booked the place and sorted everything out. You get first choice. That's how it works. Can Jamie have his own room?'

Steve's smile was broad and unnervingly white. 'Jamie can have a whole building if he wants it. The place is huge.'

Jennifer looked around. The villa seemed not at all how a maid would leave it. There was something odd that she couldn't quite put her finger on. It reminded her of Steve's man-cave in their London house.

Giles sauntered in from outside, beaming. He had already changed into baggy orange Hawaiian shorts that revealed his laughable knees and a too-tight pale green Gant shirt that did the same for his nipples. 'Jennifer, you got here, how lovely you look. The South of France suits you.'

'Giles.' She allowed him to reach up and air-kiss her. 'Where's your wife?'

'A good question.' Giles gave a shrug. 'She was here a moment ago. Normally you just have to listen for a few moments to locate her.'

'Jamie's the opposite,' Jennifer told him. 'As silent as the grave. He was here a minute ago. He'll choose a room and stay there with his headphones glued over his ears, appearing at mealtimes and finally turning up for the taxi back to the airport. At that age.'

'Looking forward to meeting him. It's a pity we didn't bring a child, but Melissa forgot to have any.' Giles barked out laughter and beamed around. 'Well, now we are five, all here safe and sound. It's Saturday night so let's party.'

Pulling off his shirt he galloped downstairs and executed a noisy, splashy belly flop into the pool.

22.

Steve's brow furrowed when he saw Melissa and Giles. They could not have made it more obvious that they'd been arguing. They entered the living room with false frozen smiles, like a pair of flight attendants about to impart bad news from the pilot.

'Steve, this place is the most marvellous find,' Melissa enthused. 'Thank you so much for letting me come and stay.'

'She'll be able to keep your wife company while we work,' Giles added. 'They can go shopping together.' Melissa shot him a sour look.

Steve barely heard them. He wanted to know who that woman was he had seen wandering around in shorts by the pool. He needed to find out what the hell she was playing at. What if she was a friend of Summer's? Just what he needed right now, more trouble.

He turned back to Giles and Melissa. 'I saw a supermarket on the way in. Shall we go and get some provisions?' His head hurt. He needed some ibuprufen. In all the stuff Summer had managed to spread around the villa he had found no headache tablets.

'I want to get some cigarettes anyway,' Melissa said. 'They're so cheap here I should be able to get lung cancer before the end of the week.'

When the doorbell rang again, Steve began to feel as if he had stepped into a French farce, albeit one with potentially catastrophic consequences. He approached the front door with trepidation, trying to make out the figures through its dimpled glass panels.

His wife and son were standing on the pathway. He went out to meet them. He could feel sweat trickling between his shoulder blades. *Deep breath*, he told himself, *you need to look relaxed.*

'You got here quicker than we expected,' he said cheerfully. 'Giles and Melissa are already here. They changed their flight. Come and have a look at the place, tell me what you think.' Pecking at her cheek, he led them inside.

Giles put in an appearance, a dry towel around his neck, and launched into an anecdote about a school trip to France that ended with him in hospital, but he had a way of describing experiences that rendered them as dull as Victorian sermons. Melissa ground another cigarette into a patio plant pot, spat out the last of her smoke and cut her husband short. 'I'm so sorry, we should have called you, we could have waited for you. You must think us dreadful.'

'It was no problem,' said Jennifer. 'We were delayed but made up the time. Then we managed to get a cab straight away.'

'We're heading to the supermarket and need your input,' Giles explained. 'We're going to barbeque – what was it?

Sardines with fennel, and we'll make an absolutely mental salad full of healthy stuff, and get cakes and pick up lots of good plonk, obviously. But I'm sure you'll come up with a more sensible list.'

I guess I've been pegged as the one with boring common sense, Jennifer thought with a sigh.

Rooms were chosen and a shopping list was drawn up. Unspoken rules concerning territory and responsibility had come into operation; the large indoor kitchen established itself as a gathering point.

Calling failed to produce Jamie, who was settling into his room and staying as far away from everyone else as possible, so they left him and drove off to the enormous Carrefour they had passed on the way in. Steve was relieved to be out of the house. He glanced in his rear-view mirror to find that Giles was watching him intently. He should have known that taking Giles into his confidence could potentially prove disastrous. From now on he would have to watch his step very carefully.

Hannah watched the guests drive off. She had been waiting for a chance to catch Steve alone but it had not arisen. She had yet to get a close-up look at him. His aftershave lingered. Tom Ford, inevitably; he had drenched himself in the stuff, Tobacco Vanille, judging by the musky richness of it. She had once worked in a department store, and the scents had lingered so heavily on her that she was unable to sleep at night.

She needed to think. As soon as she was sure that they had gone she returned to the pool patio, but when she searched for any lingering sign of Summer's bloody footprint she found nothing. Giles's belly flop had completely dissolved the proof of her presence.

As she set about tidying the villa she wondered what else Summer had left behind. It seemed that someone had hastily cleared up ahead of her. Rubbish had been stuffed into a Sainsbury's bag and left behind a sofa.

The floorboards creaked above her head. Someone was still here. She made her way upstairs and along the corridor. Only one door was open. Inside the bedroom she glimpsed a thin figure in a white hooded jacket and headphones moving around. It had to be the son.

The villa felt different with Summer gone and new guests in it, as though it had been usurped by invaders. Pushing the thought from her mind, she set off to find sponges and fill her bucket. She told herself that she would feel more settled once she had spoken to Summer.

Despite the bloody footprint and the broken wineglass, Hannah was not overly worried. Either Summer had left like a petulant teenager before Steve's arrival or she had made trouble and stormed out. She had used him to buy her airfare and lend her a villa, then had called her friend in Nice to line up another stay. The pair of them were probably having a good laugh at Steve's expense.

She checked her phone again but found no more missed calls or texts. *She's probably already at the coast*, she thought, *not remotely concerned about either of us.*

Julia had instructed them to keep their phones switched off in the villas, but before putting hers in silent mode she walked along the stone path that ran beneath the pool patio, past the wall of thorny red bougainvillea, and tried Summer's number once more.

This time she heard something new. An echo of the ring, a faint trilling, very close by.

She held her phone away from her ear and listened. The sound was coming from the base of the bougainvillea. Ignoring the thorns that pricked at her arms, she felt around in the leaves. The phone lying was at the edge of the stone path, its screen split diagonally. The patio wall was directly overhead. It was the spot where Summer had left the bloody footprint.

The phone had fallen from above and landed on its corner. It still lit up when she touched it, revealing a screenshot of a tropical beach, but was code-protected. She needed to work out a way of opening it.

I keep my entire life on my phone, Summer had told her.

Hannah was sure of one thing: the phone had hardly ever left her hand. Whatever else she'd left behind, Summer would never have gone anywhere without it.

'I always forget how much better the food is in Mediterranean supermarkets.' Giles had taken control of their trolley and was pushing it with childish delight. Clearly, buying groceries was a new experience for him. 'All this fresh fish. I've never seen a sea bass that big. Birds with their feathers on, no idea what that one is. I suppose they pluck them while you wait?'

'You can get everything done here,' said Melissa. 'Ask someone in Waitrose to spatchcock a chicken and all you'll get is a blank look. The English prefer to watch baking programmes and eat junk food.'

'Wow, whole octopus.' Giles waves the vacuum-packed creature at his wife. 'I thought they were intelligent. Didn't see this coming, did they? Shall we get one?'

'For God's sake, Giles, put it down.' She waved him away.

'Hey, let's get something here.' Giles pointed to a section labelled, embarrassingly, *British Cuisine*. A Union Jack had been attached to the shelf, just small enough to be humiliating. 'Heinz Baked Beans. You can't make a full English breakfast without them. What else have they got?'

'Chicken tikka masala, PG Tips and Marmite,' said Melissa. 'The sum total of our national pantry. Steve, what do you think Jennifer and Jamie will want to eat?'

'We'll lay on a buffet and let them choose,' he told her.

Whenever Giles steered their trolley toward tins and packets his wife gently guided him in the direction of the fresh vegetables. Tomatoes and peppers were being sprayed with water droplets by a young woman in a striped store apron, as if preparing them for a camera close-up.

'Eight types of tomato,' Giles pointed out. 'We can fry the green ones, like in the film.' As the first bout of politeness between them faded, the choosing became a courteous battle of wills, and by extension, lifestyles.

'I think we should try and eat healthily this week,' said Jennifer, meaning well but sounding prissy.

'What's the point of black-leaved lettuces covered in dirt?' Giles asked, pushing on past them.

'You put the stalks in water and they stay fresh for days,'

Jennifer explained, placing one in the trolley. 'If you leave the mushrooms in the sun for an hour it puts back their vitamin D.'

'I take a supplement,' said Giles, alarmed by the thought of actually having to cook. 'We don't need to do anything too complicated tonight. I mean, we'll be eating out quite a bit, won't we?'

Melissa studied her husband much as an anthropologist might monitor a newly discovered simian species that had turned out to be less interesting than expected. Presumably Steve had given Giles a job because Giles's father was politically infamous and knew the right people. As a consequence, Giles had inherited his friendships by osmosis. The higher end of the hospitality industry was notoriously clubbable, as much about where you had been to school as what you drank. Hearty, unscholarly men like Giles were always welcomed. Melissa grudgingly cared for him because he was unprotected, a vulnerable ecosystem supported by wincing clichés, cheerful honesty and unfashionable ideas.

'Ah, the booze, finally. I'd rather have a bottle in front of me than a frontal lobotomy, eh?' Giles rubbed his hands with glee as they entered the wine aisles.

Steve felt his usual self-possession returning. Away from the villa and Summer's cloying perfume he could think more clearly. He kept a watchful eye on the Sutherlands as they bickered and dithered around the shelves. He did not judge or take sides but listened and offered the occasional practical suggestion. He spoke just often enough to make sure that they fell silent when he did. It was important to him that Giles and Melissa considered and heeded his decisions. They worked against each other, so somebody with a stronger will needed to take charge.

He held out his hand and splayed his fingers. They shook a little, then became steady. He smiled to himself. Everything was going to be all right after all.

23.

Jamie heard the car returning to the villa.

In a few moments the peace would be broken and the long evening would be filled with bad music, raucous laughter, offensive jokes, a smoky barbeque and too much wine. With a grunt of annoyance he headed back to his room and looked for a T-shirt that would upset his mother.

A few minutes later he readjusted his headphones and went outside. Through the charcoal smoke he saw foil-wrapped packages lined up next to the glowing brick barbeque. Giles had been given something to do to keep him out of the way, and was haphazardly chopping a fat ridged tomato in the outdoor kitchen.

Jamie headed downstairs by the side steps, planning his route so that he would not have to make conversation with the others. The swimming pool was a window to a stranger world. Kneeling, he dappled his hand in the water.

He tilted his head and listened. A house with so many occupants had to be full of ghosts. For a moment he imagined he heard a splash, as if a phantom diver had sprung from a board and plunged into the deep end.

He leaned over the side of the patio and listened to the field beyond. The wind was rising. Somewhere off to his left a branch crunched and fell. The trees made noises all the time, even when the air was still. They creaked and squealed, their leaves sounding like static, as if they were trying to home in on a clear signal.

For once his mother left him alone. Usually she crowded in with endless plans and suggestions. He did not like being told what to do. The other couple talked all the time and said nothing, their pointless chatter rubbing away at his own thoughts until they become smudged and unreadable.

Why was it that married people fired conversational bullets at each other? Why did they ignore each other's answers? His father went his own way, barely listening to his mother, and when he did so, it was only out of politeness. He always looked as if he was waiting for her to finish so that he could leave the room. His mother had probably been interesting once but now she was stuck in a kind of time warp.

As for Giles and Melissa – he had trouble taking their names seriously – during the two brief moments when they tried to speak to him they became nervous and patronising, going on about him being so young and having so much time ahead of him, as if the length of a life was all that mattered. Did they have any idea how much being young sucked now? People like Giles and Melissa had ruined the world. Having eaten up all the good times, shat all over the planet and stolen his future, boomers could hardly be surprised when he ignored them.

This year Jamie had been trying to make sense of himself. He had stopped taking advice from others and started concentrating on his own plans, which did not include university or working in an office full of screens and cubicles and Friday cakes. He was not prepared to be emasculated by the failing capitalist system. Whatever he said to his parents horrified them, so he had learned to keep his mouth shut.

He knew that the week ahead would mainly consist of avoidance. There weren't too many role models for him here. Giles barely seemed to have a gender and was content to let his wife peck at him like a seagull on a corpse. There should probably be a Euthanasia Act, he thought, providing lethal injections for anyone who had outlived their usefulness by their thirtieth birthday. They could be given a test, and if they passed it they would be allowed to live for another year. Hardly any of the adults he knew would pass. Only his father would manage it. Steve played the system while everyone else was still trying to figure out how it worked.

Jamie remembered his father taking him to the edge of London on his tenth birthday. Steve had refused to let his mother come because he said Jennifer was smothering the boy and making him soft, so father and son headed out by themselves. Steve explained that she would never have approved of what he was about to do. With that, he stepped away from Jamie and left him alone in the middle of Epping Forest.

He remembered standing alone in disbelief, the dripping oak trees all around him, the cavernous greenery, the haze of grey mist over the ferns, the damp seeping into his sweater. He called out to his father's retreating back but there was no reply.

There he remained in the same circle of trampled bracken for almost an hour, assuming his father would return. Then the cold clouds descended to the tops of the oaks and it began to pelt with rain.

He had cried a little, then angrily set off, marching in a straight line because he understood that the danger lay in walking aimlessly. He retraced their steps to the outer edge of the forest, where he found his father waiting for him. Understanding dawned and the lesson was learned. But he never forgot and he never forgave, not entirely.

He wondered about his father. Whatever Steve's business (and there had been many) he usually ended up being away for half of every month, much to his mother's dismay. It didn't matter to Jamie because he understood Steve. Neither of them wanted to be left with Jennifer, who always looked disappointed and forever tried to limit their optimism with words of caution.

Jamie rose to his feet and made a reconnaissance of the property. The villa looked as if its component parts had been added like Minecraft pieces. Birds had nested beneath the rafters. Centipedes and lizards raced between rocks and sturdy brown ants with long shiny bodies trooped over the patio flagstones. There was another world beneath his feet. The ants scurried across a makeshift bridge to the next stone, linking themselves in chains. They co-operated seamlessly, while the humans above them could not even decide how best to make dinner. In a post-apocalyptic world it would not take long for the villa to be reclaimed by nature. *Bring it on*, he thought.

A movement in the air caused him to lift his head and search the sky. The branches of a pine tree crackled and fluttered. Rising from within them came a bird with an immense wingspan, brown-bodied, six feathers like talons sprouting at the end of each wing. The creature passed overhead, moving with the silent stateliness of a passenger jet, and disappeared behind the villa's roof, as if it had spotted the English invaders and wanted to be as far away from them as he did.

The wind dropped suddenly, and for a small moment there was absolute silence. He looked up at the light-filled villa and the jagged dark treeline. Something had just changed, he was sure of that. He smelled pine and earth and something unpleasant burning. He closed his mouth to keep it out. The palms of his hands started to tingle.

Putting up his hood and fixing his headphones over it, he sat back on one of the poolside loungers and cleared his mind of harmful thoughts, losing himself in the beats.

24.

Melissa walked to the pool edge, shook loose her sandal and lowered a silver-painted toe into the water. It was cooler than the surrounding stonework. She started a ripple that fanned out across the pool, lifting dead wasps and clumps of pine needles. The sun lay low on the treeline, cutting shafts of light through the pine branches. She could smell the barbeque, a bonfire, lavender, fresh-cut grass.

'Someone else has been here,' she said too softly for the others to hear.

Something was definitely going on, and she wanted to know what it was. Steve had been inside the whole time they were ringing and knocking, and when they were finally granted entry he looked as if he'd just run a marathon. The living room a mess, the air disturbed. She had not seen or heard anyone go out, but it felt as if he had been caught with someone when they arrived. *The maid*, she decided. *Oh my God, he's schtupping the staff.*

Then there was the way he kept checking his phone and the other rooms, glancing about when he thought no one was looking, searching for anything out of place. It felt as if a plan had gone wrong. Melissa was alive to such nuances; among her friends she was the premium source of scandalous rumour.

It was their first night in the villa, Saturday night, party night, everyone feeling the first flush of sunshine and wine. Even Jamie had been prised away from his phone and ordered to help with dinner. He did so by drifting about with inappropriate kitchen implements – at the moment, barbecue tongs – and leaving them in the wrong places.

Apart from the boy, who was perversely wearing black leggings and a T-shirt featuring a Vietnamese prisoner being shot in the head, the others were dressed in white and cream and pale blue cotton and were milling around in the kitchen area, trying not to get in each other's way. They bustled back and forth with bowls, cutlery and vegetables, but it was really only Steve who did anything. He was the motor around which everyone else turned. He had chosen and purchased the meat, and selected the best vegetables, an unrepentant alpha male whose determination and appearance of rectitude forced everyone else to fall back feeling vaguely inadequate. His time was coming to an end, Melissa felt, but not quite yet. The likelihood of infidelity made him terribly attractive.

The buffet was laid out on the canopied dining table on the patio. The dishes were artistically surrounded with purple bougainvillea petals, Melissa's contribution.

'Bacon,' said Giles, setting down a stack of plates. 'How could we have got the wrong bacon for tomorrow's breakfast? I mean proper thin rashers, not that thick stuff with the chewy rind.'

'Basically you're your mother, aren't you?' Melissa emptied out the last of the shopping bags. 'Look at the stuff you picked up. Teabags, Ritz crackers, Shredded Wheat, baked beans, then we go back to London and listen to you wax lyrical about the Mediterranean diet.'

She knew she shouldn't be so spiky but he brought it on himself. Giles resented her for rolling up her sleeves and showing the can-do aptitude he lacked. He denigrated her job despite the fact that for the last three years she had been the main provider. He was not Machiavellian enough for the Foreign Office, not ruthless enough for senior management. As they'd started to slide into debt, Steve's offer had arrived like a hurled lifebelt.

Jennifer sorted through the bundles of fresh vegetables and listened to the banter, wondering why she and Steve never sounded like that. Her husband rarely spoke at all. At mealtimes he read the news headlines on his iPad. She daily lost count of the number of times she waited for an answer, staring at him while he stared at his screen. Technology had created secondary infections, forcing others to wait for replies or endlessly repeat questions. She had not expected marriage to leave her lonely. Aloud she said, 'Does anyone have any allergies?'

'Giles won't eat wild mushrooms,' Melissa said, 'something to do with dogs peeing against trees.' Her offer of helping in the kitchen consisted of moving cutlery from one counter to another and back again. 'So how did Priorat go, Steve?'

Steve looked up from the chopping board. 'Fine, why?'

'Giles said you had to deal with an awkward client.'

'Something like that, yes.' He sliced the stalk off a lettuce and expertly separated its leaves.

'But you managed to sort it out.' Melissa waited. She was used to getting answers. Giles shot her a filthy look, which only confused her more.

'That depends.'

'On what?'

'On how much you know about wine.'

'I'll let you know if you start mansplaining too much.'

Steve set down his knife on the chopping board. 'Last year was a good harvest for a limited-batch wine called *Las Dos Hermanas,* so its value was pushed beyond our usual reserve. They're trying to peg the price against projections for this year but I'm not prepared to take the vineyard's word about their ability to increase output.'

'So does that mean...' said Melissa, keen to understand. Jennifer tuned out of the conversation. She had heard enough about wine to last several lifetimes. She took the largest ceramic salad bowl to the patio table and set it down. Someone was burning wood in the distance.

Giles searched underneath the barbecue grille. 'I can't tell if this bloody thing is lit or not.'

'Let me.' Jennifer liberally sprayed a washing-up bottle of lighter fluid onto the blackened grate, which exploded into bright yellow flame.

Moving him gently aside, she laid out five large *camerones* and brushed them with olive oil as Giles watched her. The boyish curiosity on his features suggested that he was witnessing an act of unimaginably alien complexity. 'I'm hopeless at barbies,' he admitted.

Checking that the wood was hot, she set the shellfish out across the iron staves of the grille.

'I thought Steve did all the cooking.'

'It doesn't mean I can't cook, Giles,' Jennifer replied.

'Who's not having one?'

'Jamie doesn't eat shellfish. He says they're sea lice.' She produced a steak from a separate wrapper and handed it to her husband.

'It's not easy having a kid, is it?' Giles said with sudden force. 'We tried for so long, I can't tell you how long. It cost a bloody fortune and did neither of us any good.'

'It wasn't easy conceiving Jamie.' She paused for a sip of wine. 'Or raising him. He was always difficult. Now everything we do embarrasses him. Steve says he can always see what Jamie's thinking. I can't. I have no idea what's going on behind those headphones. When he hit puberty the shutters came down on me. I'm the less popular parent. He has a natural affinity with his father.'

Giles kicked at something on the ground, trying to think of an appropriate response. 'You must be very proud of your husband.'

'Oh yes, we all try to measure up to him.'

She took the plates to the table. Of the four adults here she was conscious of being the only one who did not have a full-time job. The bookshop had failed through no fault of her own. She was still paying off Steve's debts from the money her mother had given her. The fact that he was grateful and tactfully never mentioned her lack of employment only made her feel worse. Everyone looked up to him. He could do no wrong.

He was, she knew from experience, very good at covering things up.

'Yes, he's a very clever man, your husband,' Giles added, determined to worry the subject to death.

Jennifer enjoyed watching her husband prepare food. He had taken carvery courses, adding them to his manly skills in a way that felt peculiarly selfish, as if by learning them he took those abilities from her. She felt the same sensation of being robbed when he ordered the main course she was about to choose in a restaurant.

Steve possessed a gliding charm, the fluidity of movement one usually associated with gay men. As he wiped the blood from the fat-marbled steak and flensed some more varicose crayfish, he worked with good-natured efficiency while the others tried not to stand back and marvel. Jamie hovered nearby, secretly studying his father at work; hero-worship became uncool if it was noticeable.

'Your husband,' Melissa said admiringly as Jennifer passed, 'he's extremely confident in the kitchen.' Somehow she made almost every comment sound sexual.

Jennifer sat down beside her at the marble-topped counter. She was wearing too much white. It made her look washed out. 'My husband likes order,' she confided. 'You should see his tool shed. He likes his possessions labelled and correctly displayed. He can only function efficiently if everyone else follows his rules. I argued at first but now I just go with it.'

Melissa was puzzled. 'What if it's something you don't agree with?'

'Then I drop my objection. I find it's best that way.'

'It makes you sound terribly downtrodden.'

'I'm not, not really. I have all the things I want.'

'That's not the same.' Melissa reached across to dip a spoon in the salad dressing. 'It's about the terms under which you get them.' She tasted the spoon thoughtfully. 'I used to be in corporate law. I'm wary of men who set their own rules. Do you and Steve ever have proper talks? Giles and I don't seem to anymore.'

'Steve tells me a bit about his trips. He has this way of explaining that doesn't really tell me anything. "We went to a restaurant where the chef would only cook steaks *saignant*," or, "We sat on the runway for ninety minutes." I can't say he ever gives me the sense of a journey experienced or enjoyed.'

'Men don't though, do they? When my father was in a hospice all he and Giles talked about was motorway junctions.' She smiled indulgently at Jennifer, who looked as nervous as a rabbit, ready to dart away at any moment. She wanted to understand what kind of woman could marry Steve, about whom Giles spoke in terms usually reserved for Hollywood legends.

'How is my husband working out?' she asked. 'I hope he's not annoying your husband as much as he annoys me.'

'I think it's going very well.'

Melissa touched her arm. 'I hope you didn't mind me coming along. I haven't had a break since the beginning of the year.' She watched Jennifer moon over her wineglass and felt sorry for her. She looked like someone who kept her weight down for her husband. 'I'm looking forward to just sitting by the pool and doing nothing.'

'To be honest I was surprised when Steve asked *me* to join him,' Jennifer admitted. 'It was very unexpected.'

'I'll get the full story from Giles and report back to you,' Melissa laughed. 'I'm sure if they're thinking of getting up to mischief we can beat them at their own game.'

'I don't want to upset Steve. This trip is very important to him.' Jennifer picked up her wineglass and went to the open kitchen. She stood closely behind her husband, who kept his back to her. She knew if she wasn't in his sightline he would never think of looking for her.

Giles had found a dinner bell and rang it to call everyone to the table. The smoke from the barbecue drifted over the hibiscus bushes. Steve found the switches for the outside lights. The pool shone blue and yellow. They sat beneath a pergola laced with sticky blue flowers.

With a few bottles of red wine emptied everyone finally started to relax, although Jamie only briefly removed his headphones and lowered his white hood to eat. Now he sat folded up in a way that only the young could manage, listening to his phone beside the illuminated pool.

'Aw, pussycat!' Giles pointed to a small white cat that had appeared from somewhere in the bushes. It wore a makeshift collar of knotted blue ribbon around its neck, so it must have strayed from a neighbour's house, although it appeared that hardly anyone else was living between here and Saint-Martin, so completely were the villas buried in their hillside dugouts.

As Giles fumbled after the creature it avoided him, disappearing under the dinner table, rubbing its ribs along their legs and brushing them with its tail, imitating amicability while searching for fallen scraps of fish.

Melissa was soon quite drunk, not slurring or offensive, just blunt enough to make the others wary of certain conversational topics.

'I thought I saw the maid earlier,' said Steve, opening a bottle of *Picpoul de Pinet*.

'Was she here?' Melissa asked. 'Me, me.' She held up her empty glass. 'You'd think she'd come and introduce herself.'

'She doesn't officially start until tomorrow morning.' They sipped and sat back. 'How far do you think the sound carries across there?' Steve pointed into the valley. 'I can see some houses. Do you think they can hear us?'

'We can hear their goats,' Jennifer pointed out. 'Why don't we go to a market tomorrow morning? There should be one around on a Sunday.' She scuffed the cat's ears, waiting for a response that didn't come. The cat had alarming bumps under its fur so she took her hand away.

The dishwasher beeped and Steve rose to empty it. Melissa noticed that he dropped the knives and forks neatly into their rightful places, as if he had been doing it for years. 'You soon found your way around,' she called.

He stared at her with blank blue eyes. 'Hm?'

'The cutlery.'

'Oh. Kitchens make sense to me. They're workshops. I can see where everything goes. I used to love Airfix kits when I was a kid.'

'Giles can't boil an egg.' Melissa swilled her glass. 'He minces about in the kitchen in a pinny but he's really quite helpless.

We eat out most of the time. It's a good job you took him on, Steve. He'd never have found another job.'

'I'm good with the customers,' said Giles defensively. He had not been able to catch Steve's eye since they arrived. The evening felt tainted somehow, the four adults play-acting as if they were in some bucolic French film, the red-and-white chequered tablecloth, the lowering mulberry trees, bowls of fresh fruit, emptied bottles, the mute hooded boy lurking in a corner, the wife getting drunk, the presence of a poorly hidden secret. All they needed now was Charles Trenet on the speakers.

Giles wished he didn't know about the girl who had been here. 'I'll have another glass too,' he suggested.

Jennifer rubbed more bite cream on her elbows and wrists. There were already angry red welts all over her legs. She walked across to the pool and sat beside her son. Jamie looked up at her with a weary impatience that suggested he was counting down the seconds until she left.

'Darling, I wish you wouldn't wear that T-shirt, it's horrible. You've got a bite on your neck. I have some cream for that.'

She went to touch it but he swatted her hand away. 'I don't want it. It smells.'

She rocked back on her heels with a sigh. 'You know, you could go into town without me tomorrow.'

Sensing a trick, Jamie slowly removed his headphones.

She nodded back in the direction of the dinner table. 'I don't think Melissa wants to go to the market. I can't say I blame her. She and I will just be left standing around watching the men haggle over prawns. Perhaps you could keep them under control.'

'I don't like being told what to do.'

Jennifer sighed again. 'I only want what's –'

'I want to spend more time with Dad.'

'Maybe I can persuade your father not to work too hard while he's here,' she said, rising. 'Come and have a glass of wine with us.'

'You know I don't do alcohol.'

'Okay, then something else to eat.' He never responded to the enticement of food. 'Oh come on, Jamie. Try to have fun, just for me? Where's my ickle boy?' She tugged at his hood until he angrily pulled it back into place. It always had to be a certain way.

'You're the one who feels the need to socialise, not me,' he pointed out.

'If you're going to be mean I'll leave you alone for a while.'

As she reached the foot of the staircase she looked over at him and wondered if she would ever get her son back.

The selection of fine wines on the kitchen counter beckoned. She refilled her glass before deciding to take the bottle with her. Tonight Jennifer felt like exceeding all warnings to drink responsibly.

They moved to the big outdoor sofa by the pool, underlit by wavering blue reflections. Melissa's wineglass seemed to be emptying itself. 'So he's going through the terrible teens?' she asked, upending a pack of cigarettes and tipping out the last one. 'I'm smoking like a chimney.'

'It's funny –' Jennifer had been going to say that her husband had started smelling of cigarettes lately, but thought better of it. 'Jamie was diagnosed with ADD. He used to be on methylphenidate but stopped taking it. He doesn't know what he wants to do with his life. I suppose he'll live at home with us until he's thirty then go off with someone we hate. He's not at all like his father. He has no confidence.'

Melissa looked across the open kitchen's counter to where Giles and Steve were belatedly making a whipped-cream fruit dessert. Giles tried to split a pomegranate into segments without covering himself in scarlet juice and failed spectacularly. He looked like he had just been beaten up.

'Break it open in a bowl of water,' Melissa called, shaking her head. 'My husband has a good heart but he's not the greatest thinker. I keep hoping he'll reveal hidden shallows. He takes people at face value. Sometimes he hugs me until I can't breathe. I'm grateful that Steve saw something in him he could use.' She ignited and inhaled as if her life depended on it. 'It's good to get away. This year I'm going to four days a week. I've qualified as a meditation therapist, so I want to make more time for that.'

Jennifer could not imagine a less likely meditation practitioner. Just being near Melissa made her tense. She moved her chair back a little to avoid her haze. 'What is it you do?'

'I run role-playing events that encourage prickly resentful managers to be more proactive. Mainly I just frighten them. I have a great resting bitch face.' She ran her hands over her face and turned to Jennifer, who could not help but laugh. 'I have to work. I couldn't stay home, no offence. God, I feel a bit pissed.'

'We get through a lot of wine, as you can imagine.' Jennifer looked out toward the smoky blue hills. 'Steve always says, "Just try this one for me." He can be very persuasive.' She fell silent for a moment. 'He once had an affair, in case you're wondering.'

'Oh God, I didn't –'

'It was on your face. Men like him always have affairs. Girls are his blind spot. They rob him of reason. I let him know that I knew about it.' She nodded a little, reassuring herself. 'He never saw her again. But it makes one wary.'

'I suppose these things tend to go away by themselves if everyone keeps their heads.' Melissa spoke without conviction. The most comforting thing about Giles was his fidelity. He hardly had sex with her, let alone with complete strangers.

'Steve's not…' Jennifer began but detected a histrionic note in her voice and started again. 'He's not how he seems.'

'How does he seem?'

'You know. Like the kind of schoolboy who always did his laces in a double knot. That's just the outside. He's more vulnerable than anyone realises.'

'I certainly don't see that.'

'There was a time – he had a sort of breakdown. His old company folded. I think for the first time in his life he felt helpless. He couldn't remember where he'd been or what he'd done. Stress. God, don't tell him I said anything.'

'Giles has had his fair share of problems.' Melissa topped up her glass. 'He used to drink quite heavily but he cut right back. My worry now is that he's in a job that involves downing alcohol on a daily basis.'

'I hadn't thought of that.' She glanced back at Steve and Giles drinking in the kitchen. 'During his breakdown Steve just slept. He virtually stopped eating, wouldn't see a doctor. Stubborn, like his father. Stress still makes him fall asleep.'

'How long did it last?'

'Not long, about six weeks. Then one day he went back to normal. Erased it all and started over. It's complicated.'

'At least I can never accuse Giles of being that. He has the kind of follow-you-around loyalty you usually only find in baby penguins. Actually, can we talk about something other than the men?'

'With pleasure,' said Jennifer.

Directly below them, at the bottom of the stairs leading to the wild fields, Jamie sat with his headphones off, listening to the night.

25.

That evening Hannah stood on the tiny terrace of her flat looking down at the striped awnings of the *Vieux Marché*. In her right hand she held Summer's smashed phone.

She set off into the narrow backstreets, passing countless stores selling the same souvenirs in slight variation, past the T-shirts and pool floats, the kind of items Summer would have gleefully bought. The French shopkeepers were still smiling; *be nice, the tourists will be gone soon.*

A dozen chaotic little shops around the bus station offered phone unlocking services for a few euros. It didn't take long to get the thing open.

The first thing she found was a selfie Summer had taken by the pool at 1:27 p.m. on Saturday. She was naked on the lounger with one arm behind her head, twisted into a mocking pose copied from an old glamour magazine. The colours chromatically shimmered beneath the shattered screen, gold tinged with crimson and blue.

Hannah went to her recent messages. Summer hardly ever

called anyone but sent endless emoji-laden texts. She quickly found the thread she was looking for, exclamation-pointed exchanges between her and Jihane that confirmed their plans. Going through the address book she found only half a dozen numbers. There was no list of favourites but one contact was marked with a star.

The call went to a recording: 'The centre is now closed. Opening hours are 9 a.m. until 6 p.m. Mondays to Fridays. Please leave your name and number –'

She cut the line, then searched the contacts again. Jihane seemed to have no last name. She tried his number.

'Yup.' North African chillout music played in the background.

'Hey, is this Jihane?'

'Depends. Who are you?'

'I'm a friend of Summer's.'

'Are you Hannah?'

Relief flooded over her. 'Yes. I was up at the villa with her.'

'Yeah, she mentioned you.'

'Is she with you?'

'No, man. What's happening? I was supposed to give her a lift. I came by to drive her back to the coast on Saturday but I think she was with some guy. I checked again later but she'd gone.'

'Do you have any idea where she went?'

'That's the problem. She said she'd be ready to come with me but never showed. Maybe someone else picked her up?'

'I don't think she knew anyone else. She left her phone and some other stuff at the villa. I thought she might need it.'

'She can be flaky. She leaves stuff everywhere.'

'So what happened when you got there?'

'I just rang the doorbell.'

'There's a side door with just a latch on it. She might have been down by the pool.'

'She was expecting me. Did she tell you about the fight? We got into a punching session with one of the inbreds in her neighbourhood bar. He didn't like her hanging out with me.'

'I saw her bruised eye.' She tried to decide how much to tell him. 'She said she'd changed her mind about hooking up with the guy who rented the villa. I thought she was going to stay with you for a few days.'

'That was the plan, but I guess it's off the table now. There's not much I can do until she gets in touch.'

'She met you in Ibiza last year?'

'Yeah, we had fun but I don't really know her that well.'

'You have my number now. Could you call me if you hear anything? If my phone's off it means I'm working at the villa.'

'I don't know. Seems like people are always looking for her. There was a guy in Ibiza. She disappeared on him. This feels like a repeat performance.'

'If I find out anything else I'll be in touch,' she told him and rang off.

She found what she was looking for in the back of a jewellery outlet. The old man was seated half-asleep at a device that mechanically inscribed nameplates. It only took him a moment to fix the neck-chain so she could open it by the clasp, but she was about to pay when she had an idea and asked him to inscribe her own name on the back of the plate.

He used the same typeface, cleaned it and slipped it on her

neck. She felt closer to Summer wearing it. When she looked in the mirror and flipped the plate back and forth, *Summer-Hannah-Summer-Hannah,* it seemed as if the two names merged into one.

The chain felt like armour plating around her neck, as if it somehow protected her. She walked through the warm back-streets until the restaurants ushered out the last of their diners.

The evening had been measured in emptied wine bottles. After the crustaceans had been disembowelled and the salads ravaged, Steve took his place on the top terrace of the Villa Lavardin and smoked a Cuban cigar. The mock-antique lamps leaked golden light into the hibiscus bushes. It didn't take long for Giles to come puffing up the stairs and find him.

'Bloody fantastic place, Steve. You really know how to pick them. I'd be hopeless. It's a good idea about going to the village in the morning. I read something about a Sunday market. It'll probably just be jams and those awful yellow ceramic cicadas: I think they're napkin rings. Who has napkin rings these days apart from my mother? But we might find some top scoff. May I?' He pointed at a low wicker armchair.

'You don't need my permission to sit down, Giles.'

'I started watching the news on my iPad but it was too depressing. We're living in divisive times.'

'They're not divisive if you make a choice and stick to it.' The end of his cigar shone orange in the blue darkness. 'William Blake said that active evil is better than passive good.'

'I went to school with a chap called Blake. He stole my pocket money for years. Became the ambassador to Ghana of all things.' Giles rolled his wineglass in his palms. 'I've been meaning to say thank you. For giving me a chance.'

'It's early days.'

'I've been watching you with clients,' Giles remarked. 'You take the most incredible risks, telling them things that haven't happened yet.'

'Because I know I can make them happen. You have to look at something from every angle before you act.'

'Not me, I go by gut instinct, that's good enough for me. I won't let you down.'

'We'll see.'

The brandy warming in his palm prompted him to ask, 'I know we said we wouldn't talk about it, but what happened to...' He baulked at her name, as if using it made him complicit.

'Summer Farrow.' Steve exhaled loudly. 'I decided not to get involved.'

'Look, don't touch, eh?' Giles's toothy smirk could be seen by lantern light. 'Good move.'

Steve drew on his cigar, tasting peppery earth. 'I thought about her and realised she simply wasn't worth the trouble.'

'But when we had lunch you seemed keen to have her come and stay.'

Giles seemed incapable of working anything out for himself, so Steve helped him. 'It never went further than a fantasy.'

'Probably for the best. You have to be careful nowadays. Inappropriate this-and-that.'

'It made me think about my work-life balance. I haven't been away with the family in ages. Jennifer and Jamie usually go somewhere at Christmas. I never go with them.'

Giles shifted his chair a little closer. He looked even redder and shinier than usual. 'So you haven't spoken to her since, this girl.'

'For fuck's sake, Giles.'

'Fair enough. I mean it's none of my business, but a thing like that could ruin a jolly good marriage.'

'You're right.' Steve savoured his cigar. 'It's none of your business.'

Somewhere out in the fields an animal emitted a thin, high shriek. It sounded as if it was in pain.

After the emptying of bottles and the weary goodnights, as Jennifer removed her makeup and Steve stood in his shorts brushing his teeth, she said, 'He's an amiable imbecile. You can see that, can't you? Is that why you hired him? So that he wouldn't be a threat?'

Steve spat into the sink. 'It's a job only suited to certain temperaments. All the travelling and socialising. He's tenacious, I'll give him that. I'll feel better about him once he's got me the right introductions.'

She closed the lid of her night-cream pot and examined the results. 'I suppose he must know a lot of people. Melissa says his father's on the board of some big government think-tank. I guess the old school tie still opens doors.'

'He's inviting me to some social events this week, dinners and drinks with British vintners living on the Cote D'Azur, so we'll see.'

She sat back and watched him, frustrated. 'You'd tell me if there was something wrong, wouldn't you?'

He turned off his toothbrush. 'What are you worrying about?'

'You seem a bit distracted, that's all. I just like to check in with you.'

'Everything's fine. Really.' He turned to face her. 'I watched you at dinner, so serious, busy making sure that everyone else was enjoying themselves. You have to stop overthinking everything. Concentrate on yourself for a while and let them get on with it.'

With that, she realised that another conversation had been shunted onto a branch line and closed down. He appeared to have no idea how infuriating he could be.

'What happened today?' she asked.

'What do you mean?'

'I couldn't get hold of you earlier.'

'When?'

'I tried you several times from Gatwick.'

'Are you checking up on me?'

'No, but your phone was dead for a couple of hours, like it was turned off. I was worried, that's all.'

'I was probably just out of range for a while. I told you I fell asleep. I didn't hear anything until Giles and Melissa started hammering at the door.'

'You should be more careful. You've cut your hand.'

He examined his knuckle. 'The wineglasses are very thin. I broke one.'

She searched for her book, Graham Greene's *The End of the Affair*. She was on the last chapter and turned away from him in bed to finish it beneath the inadequate lamplight.

Outside, the night was as silent as a cemetery. The pool had stars in it.

26.

On Sunday morning Hannah set her alarm for 7:00 a.m. As soon as it buzzed she slipped into shorts and a T-shirt, packed her maid's bag and pulled up the bus schedule on her phone. Daniela wasn't working today, so she had to allow extra time. They had agreed to take turns with Sundays. Julia would have had them both working seven days a week but couldn't find a way around the employment laws.

She caught the bus early so that she could take a look around the villa without getting in anyone's way. Her curiosity had been aroused. Summer was incapable of rinsing a glass or emptying an ashtray, which meant that Steve had hastily tidied. He'd been in such a rush that he'd missed the bikini, the sunglasses and the wrap.

The more she thought about it the more convinced she became that they'd had a fight. Steve must have got rid of her quickly before the others arrived, but how?

She felt uncomfortable about meeting Steve. Down in the store room she donned her itchy nylon maid's outfit. The bottom bedroom had been furnished as cheaply as possible with white Ikea flatpack cupboards and a single bed that felt damp. Looking for towels, she stood on a chair and checked the cupboard shelves above the clothing rail.

She could see a bright fabric case of some kind, pushed right to the back. She stretched on tiptoe and tried to reach it. Her fingers brushed a strap, so she pulled.

The sunshine-yellow backpack had a pink Hello Kitty mascot attached to it. As Hannah drew it out a paperback landed on the floor. She picked it up and riffled the pages. *The Labyrinth of Shadows*, bookmarked at page 17.

Setting the backpack down on the bed, she unzipped the main compartment. A bottle of pills, some kind of prescription medication. A couple of cheap T-shirts, a pair of trainers, a yellow Superdry top that smelled of Summer's scent, bitter and hippyish. A pair of torn jeans, some underwear.

In the side pocket she found a plastic wallet of credit cards and a set of house keys. Her stomach sank. From the keyring hung a plastic-framed photograph, taken when Summer was a year or two younger. Anyone seeing this and knowing that she had stayed here at Steve's expense would peg him as a paedophile.

There was a matching pocket on the other side of the bag. Digging into it, she felt something thin and rectangular, and yanked it out.

Summer's passport.

Leaving the villa without her phone could have been a mistake, but this? How could she have gone anywhere minus her credit cards and passport? The bag had been hastily hidden.

A pitch-black thought began to spread. Summer hadn't

just gone. Something terrible had happened to her. What other explanation could there be?

The room suddenly felt unbearably hot. Her skin was prickling. She went outside and breathed deep, rubbing at her arms, staring up at the sky.

In the distance a barking dog was suddenly silenced. She heard Summer calling out to her in a strange high voice, begging for her help. The cry resolved itself into quarrelling pigeons, thrashing about in the branches of a nearby tree.

She made her way to the upstairs kitchen to await the guests. First to appear was Giles, dressed in a non-runner's idea of what a runner might wear. He had chosen baggy white shorts over black leggings, lemon-coloured trainers and a matching lemon top with a Nike swoosh.

'Hullo, the new girl, er, excellent –' He looked around, desperate for help, before asking very slowly and loudly, 'So, what should we call you?'

'Hannah,' said Hannah.

'Oh, right, English, very good.'

'Hannah Carreras.'

'Oh – well, anyway.' He took another furtive look around. 'Well there's not much to do, I think we're making our own breakfasts and if there's anything specific I'm sure Steve – Mr Elsbury – will tell you.' He smiled and raised his eyebrows, much as distant colleagues did when they passed each other in corridors. 'Well, er –' He patted his hands on his thighs and looked to the door. 'Off for a run.' And with that he escaped.

Melissa came down in a blue silk dressing gown, wearing her hangover with bad grace. She did not bother with small talk.

When Jamie fiddled with the kitchen radio and found some kind of angry rap station she silenced it by removing the plug from the wall. Hannah found herself in an empty kitchen again, so she washed up, unsure how available she should make her services.

'You're the maid. Hannah, yes?'

She looked up from the sink.

Steve was perfectly dressed in navy shorts and a shirt the colour of expensive notepaper. A silver Rolex, a simple gold wedding ring. He was still and deliberate, not a man to be messed with. She started to have a sense of what she might be up against.

'I imagine your duties will be light. We may want you to do a dinner one evening. Julia said you can arrange that, yes?'

'Yes.' She cleared her throat. 'Yes. You can arrange it with me or through the agency.'

'Good. There shouldn't be much for you to do today.' He smiled broadly, revealing white, white teeth. 'Actually there's one thing you can do.' He led her outside to the terrace and indicated a wide, heavy wooden chair. 'I think this will be my corner.'

'Nice and sunny,' she said.

'I can see everything from here. Help me position it?'

It was extraordinarily heavy to lift. He caught her eye and kept it raised a trifle too long. They shifted it to an angle.

He smiled again. 'Thanks.' And she was dismissed.

I can see why Summer saw him as a challenge, Hannah thought as she headed across the terrace. Even if she found a way to mention her she would have to explain how they knew each other, and would probably make a mess of it.

There's a simple logical explanation for everything. I doubt I'll even need to speak to him, she told herself as she went down to clean the outside kitchen.

The guests finally took off in the hatchback. The Sunday market they'd read about consisted of some vegetable stalls, a hot dog truck and an old man selling weird-looking gardening tools. As the shops were shut and everyone else in the village appeared to have gone to church, they returned to the villa to sunbathe and read. They pottered about, fastidiously arranging and tidying, acting like owners rather than temporary custodians of the villa.

Hannah sat on the steps and made notes in her pocket diary, but came to no conclusions. She wished she had photographed the bloody footprint on the pool patio. She checked the bus times. On Sundays the service was intermittent. The sky clouded over and everyone went inside. She needed to do *something*. Perhaps she could get a reaction. Slipping back to the pool house, she climbed on a chair and took out the yellow backpack once more. What if she left it out somewhere?

Carrying it up to the terrace, she stowed it in the corner beside some palm pots that surrounded Steve's heavy chair. He would be bound to see it when he came back to sit there. For good measure, she returned Summer's crimson bikini to the towel rail of the outdoor shower. *Now let's see what happens,* she thought.

THREE:
THE PROOF

27.

By 7:30 a.m. on Monday the terrace balustrade connecting the rooms at the Villa Lavardin was already hot to the touch. The main kitchen was flooded with sunlight so Jennifer lowered the blinds. She needed something to dispel the familiar fuzzy ache of a half-hangover, so she headed down to the pool.

The water was still in shade, the deep end dark and mysterious. Nobody else was up yet. Stripping to her one-piece swimsuit, she slipped into a cool green world. Wasps took turns to dip down to the pool's surface. A nest of leaves and pine needles had blocked the overflow, so she pulled the tangle clear and allowed the water to circulate once more.

She swam with long unbroken strokes, dipping and turning at the end, keeping a steady pace. After twenty lengths a sense of calm had formed about her like a carapace. Ascending, she washed in the open-air shower with the slate tiles.

When she removed her wet costume and went to hang it, she found the rail already occupied by another bikini, a trashy little thing of strings and tiny triangles. There was no one here who could wear it. She held it up against herself. It couldn't belong to the maid; she was too well constructed to get into it. Perhaps the pool person was a girl or it belonged to a previous guest. But that made no sense because Steve had booked out the villa for the week before. Unsure of what to do with it, she wrapped it in her towel. She knew she was being paranoid. It was probably nothing.

Jennifer's suspicions had proven justified in the past but not lately, not for a long time now. These days her husband was preoccupied and distant. He needed to get his new company making money. She saw a similar distance growing in her son. If they kept this up, at some point she would start questioning her own existence and begin to fade from view. She thought: *All it takes for a woman to vanish is a loss of confidence.*

She looked up at the bedrooms. How much did husbands hide from their wives? She could deal with Steve's vanity because she understood his need for it, but he was becoming unknowable, and the same traits were appearing in Jamie. Did all fathers have this effect on their sons? The boy had none of his father's grace.

The quirks of the villa's guests had started to reveal themselves. Steve and his son were obsessively neat. The boy had brought hardly any clothes with him but had a backpack full of electronic gadgetry. Giles clipped wiry ginger hairs from somewhere and left them scattered around the sink top. His wife was incapable of replacing a lid on anything.

Hannah remained hidden in the background but watched them all carefully, like a naturist studying an insect colony. She had already learned how to stay invisible. As she walked down the side steps, she covertly glanced at the shaded spot where she had left Summer's backpack.

It was no longer there.

The clearest view of the villa was from the rear door of the pool house. The valley was so quiet that she could hear any conversations that took place in the opened front rooms. Only the bedrooms and bathrooms were beyond range. She pulled out a kitchen chair and sat in the shadows, watching.

By now the guests had formed routines. The table positions were established, the sunbeds chosen, the rituals of laying out and clearing away designated according to ability and availability. Jamie clearly didn't do breakfast, therefore had no role in its preparation, and Giles looked incapable of drying a glass without cracking it, so was excused from this duty.

The outdoor kitchen was an accumulation of cereal boxes, fruit peel, toast and jams. Steve was unshaven. He looked as if he had not slept well. When the bell rang he flinched and set off to be first to the front door.

Julia Martinez was wearing a white skirt and jacket with a matching patent leather handbag and heels. The skirt had the telltale lateral creases of an outfit that no longer fitted. She did not wait to be invited in. Steve looked as if he was afraid of her.

Hannah sat and watched the play unfolding above her as it moved from room to room.

'So there, your friends have arrived,' Julia said, noting a pair of suitcases that Melissa had placed by the doors to the living room. 'Samsonite, nice, is good quality, no rubbish.' She pulled a fold of paper from her bag. 'Mr Steve, I am so sorry, the form is wrong, you didn't sign. If my boss sees this he goes yadda yadda Julia in my ear and I am in trouble, so you must do this. And now there is more of you do you need more keys because – if I can have a word –' She led Steve to the patio, past the others. Seeing them looking, Julia ostentatiously slid the door shut behind her and lowered her voice.

Hannah had to creep forward to hear. Luckily, Julia specialised in stage whispers. 'The girl, I gave her a set of keys and now she is gone so I hope you have them. I hear from Raphael who runs the bar in the village that there was a fight.'

'What kind of a fight?'

'Oh a bad one, furniture smashed, bad.' Julia's spider-lashes moved further apart. 'She didn't tell you? She and her boyfriend, they drank a lot and he hit one of the local men smack bang like that. The girl, she broke a table and promised to come back and pay for it – there are fights in there all the time, is no special thing maybe – but she did not come back and Raphael is embarrassed because I let her have the villa, so he tells me this.'

'How did he connect her to me?' Steve asked, glancing back at the villa.

'That is my fault.' Julia patted her heart. 'I was dropping something off for his wife and he ask me who is staying at *La Terrasse* – this is the old name Madame Lavardin had for this villa, when her husband was still alive, God rest his soul – and I tell him you. Is not a secret, no?'

'No, it's not a secret,' Steve replied carefully, 'but I don't want everyone knowing my business.'

'Then there is no harm done,' the agent assured him. 'But if you could see Raphael and maybe pay him for the table, is not much money and better to keep everyone happy here. I hope your friend got away on time.' Julia's lipstick smile was so wide and false that Hannah wondered if she was planning to blackmail him.

'Fine, I'll go and sort it out with him,' he assured her. 'My wife and our friends are all here now for a week of peace and quiet, you have your form and I will drop off all the keys to you when I return to the airport on Saturday afternoon. Unless you would rather I left them here.' Making sure that she recognised the tone of finality in his voice, he left her alone on the patio.

Jennifer watched the proceedings from the kitchen window, clearly suspicious. Hannah stayed in the shadow of the pool patio and tried Summer again, but as usual the call went directly to voicemail. She watched Julia walk to the end of the terrace and light a cigarette. Feeling sure that her boss had come to check on her, she went upstairs.

Julia waved out a match and flicked it into a bush. 'Hannah, good you are here, how were the Russians?'

'We got the place straightened out but there are still some marks on the walls where the children drew with pens.'

'Don't care, not your fault, they will pay, take photos. What is happening here?' She jabbed a scarlet claw at Hannah's opened shirt. 'Why am I seeing these buttons undone?'

'The uniform cuts under my arms.'

'So eat less. I hope you are looking after these people.'

'They don't want me to do much.'

'You could make some business for me.'

'I could make them cocktails. They drink a lot.'

'Typical English.' Julia pursed her lips in disapproval. She lowered her voice. 'You saw the young girl? Last week?'

'She left on Saturday.'

'You don't speak to her, no?'

'No, of course not. But she went without telling anyone –'

'Good, no talking to the guests, yes? Keep things clean. Do a good job. Use bleach.' She stopped on the step. 'There is no pool boy this week – he walked out, broke his parole, you don't want to know, I'm trying to find another one. Do you know how to check the pool?' She raised a hand. 'Better not, it's chemicals, you could go blind God forbid. I'll find someone. No more lawsuits, I couldn't stand it. The gardener will be in but don't talk to him either, he is a crazy man.'

Hannah gathered her equipment and headed into the main house. She smiled and nodded to the guests, who saw her carrying a yellow plastic bucket and look awkward in the way only the British did about staff arrangements.

Giles broke rank by studying her with friendly appraisal. 'How long are you here for?' he asked as if talking to someone through a sheet of glass. She tapped her watch and held up two fingers.

'Ah. Right. Jolly good. If you, ah, need anything –' Confused, he let the sentence peter out and made a quick retreat. Julia was right; silence worked best and allowed her to get on with her job.

With everyone downstairs and the beds due to be made, she had a reason for searching upstairs. Summer's scent was strongest in the main bathroom. As Hannah put soap and tissues back in their correct places she thought of her skewed smile, her flat stomach, the turn of her wrist, her lazily raised eyes. Doubts started to set in. Was it possible that she had simply forgotten the time and left in a rush to avoid Steve?

She opened the windows to air the rooms and watched as the guests decamped to the poolside, staking their territorial claims with suncream bottles, towels and paperbacks.

As she made the beds, she strained to hear the conversations. The big blonde woman, Melissa, pretended to read a Jo Nesbo thriller. Steve had a copy of *The Twelve Caesars* by his sunbed. His chest hair was sculpted and he had a surprisingly narrow waist. No sign of a dad-bod there. His disappointed-looking wife had not tried to compete with this level of gym fitness and wore a black one-piece swimsuit. She had found a dogeared copy of Daphne du Maurier's *Rebecca*.

Melissa's husband looked more than ever like a jolly infant that had somehow found itself clutching the sports section of Saturday's *Times*. The son avoided them all and sat fully clothed by himself at the edge of the pool with his headphones firmly in place. Occasionally he nodded along or glanced back at the house. For a moment she caught him looking at her, but he quickly turned away.

When Giles decided to inflate a giant pink *Simpsons* doughnut and sit wedged inside it like a baby waiting to be washed, Jamie disgustedly rose from his cross-legged position and headed off. With his hands in his pockets and one final glance back at the others he disappeared among the bougainvillea bushes. Torn between group sociability and his solitary aural world, he always chose the latter. *So would I,* Hannah thought, grabbing the corner of a duvet and giving it a good shake.

She still had Summer's sunglasses in her pocket. She went to the bathroom and left them on prominent display, then returned to her post at the rear of the pool house. From the end bedroom she could see into the sunbathing area where the couples were seated. The red bikini had vanished from the rail. One of the guests must have removed it. If she had paid more attention she would have known which one.

'Hey.'

She looked up to find Jamie, his face a ghostly white, standing in the pool house doorway. He removed his headphones and pulled down his hood. She was surprised to find that he had a shock of red hair as bright as an emergency sign. So that was why he kept the hood up; he burned.

She gave him an acknowledging smile.

'I heard what she said.' Jamie pointed back at the terrace. 'Your boss. You're not supposed to talk to us.' Something in his manner bothered her. Jamie had his father's way of standing, as if he had been appointed to assess the security of the house. 'I'm not like them – the others. They won't even notice you. If you want a cigarette or a drink or want to take a walk, come and find me. But not in front of them. They don't have to see. I'll keep a look out for you. Is that okay?'

She nodded. For a fraction of a second she saw his loneliness.

'Good.' He smiled awkwardly then raised his hood once more, letting her pass. Refitting his headphones, he watched her go.

Hannah took two plastic sacks up to the side gate, ready for collection. She was just about to leave when a sun-burnished, unshaven elderly man pulled up against the bushes in a red flatbed truck.

'You are the new girl?' He had a strong Niçoise accent. He climbed down with difficulty and glanced furtively around. 'I take care of the gardens. They say, "Matthias, everything's getting overgrown." I tell them heat and rain is a perfect combination, but more work for me. It's a microclimate. Perfect for growing figs and clementines.' He hitched up mud-stained trousers. 'Don't touch any of the plant beds, you understand? I'm responsible for them.'

She nodded. 'Okay.'

'The other girl, she's gone?'

Hannah nodded.

'She should put her clothes on when there's an old man walking about. My heart is not so strong.' His chuckle turned into a cough. 'You are friends?'

Oh, because we're both English, she realised. 'Yes, but she's probably gone back to London now.'

Matthias pulled a bottle of water from his back pocket and took a slug. 'I don't think so.'

'What do you mean?'

'Her friend was taking her to Nice.'

'Are you sure?'

He made his way to the back of the truck and started unpacking tools. 'That's what she told me. She talked to me a little. She was sunbathing and I was trying to work. She was completely naked. She said her friend was coming to pick her up, and did I want a free flight to London. I think she was joking but I told her no thanks, not with your English weather! A strange thing to say, eh? She was very funny. Completely naked, did I mention that?'

'I've been trying to get hold of her.'

'Young people,' Matthias sighed, dragging a bag of soil from the back of the truck. 'You have all these amazing devices and you still can't talk to each other.'

As Hannah said goodbye, she saw him take something wrapped in a plastic bag out of the glove box. She recognised the smell immediately; it was impossible not to notice the dense odour of super skunk. From the size of the bag it looked like the friendly old gardener was also the area's local drug dealer.

28.

Jennifer gave up and closed the paperback. It was impossible to concentrate. Something felt wrong. She was struggling with Giles. He talked about wine with the enthusiasm of a drinker rather than a winemaker, and apparently enjoyed watching sport. Beyond that he was a blank. He had no internal life. Every thought in his head came out of his mouth. Melissa had all the personality; she was sharp-tongued and attractive, if a little flashy, a compensation for her husband's absent charisma. Her charms didn't appear to work on Steve or Jamie though; so far they had barely spoken to her. She was above their age threshold.

As for Jamie, he had apparently had his vocal cords cut, and was probably happier being completely ignored until he emerged from his post-puberty cocoon. So much for the fantasy she'd had of reconnecting this week.

She went to the edge of the pool and lowered her legs into the warm water. It was easy to forget how to make friends. At Christmas parties she watched Steve work his way around the room, smoothing a path between people who had nothing in common, breaking the ice by making them laugh and eagerly concur. His ability to combine business and geniality mystified her. Of course he played poker well too, which meant that he was a good liar.

She turned and found his lounger empty. Where had he disappeared to?

Steve stood in the living room of the main house, looking down in horror at the yellow backpack. He had smuggled it from the poolside without anyone seeing. Whoever had left it behind his sun lounger had done so intending him to find it.

Kneeling, he unzipped the top and peered inside. He thought he had got rid of it, but couldn't remember what he had thrown out on Saturday afternoon when Melissa and Giles arrived – he'd had a drink and everything had happened so fast.

A feeling of doom descended upon him. Fucking hell, her passport was here. He removed it and zipped the bag shut.

'What are you doing?' Jennifer stood in the doorway with fresh towels in her arms.

He stepped in front of the backpack, raising his hands, misdirecting her. 'You don't need to get your own towels. We have a maid to do that.'

'Really, Steve, I'm not infirm. I like to do things. The idea of having a maid at all is a bit – well, you know.'

He tried to think fast but his usual acuity deserted him. 'It's the same as having hotel staff make the beds, isn't it?' He walked her out of the room and closed the door behind him. 'Stop tidying up. The maid's here to work. There's nothing for you to do. Breakfast is cleared away, just go and chill out for a while. Enjoy the sunshine.'

'What are you going to do?' Jennifer knew he disliked sunbathing and was always happier getting on with something.

'I need to make some calls and confirm our appointments,' he said. 'Giles's leads haven't come back to us.'

She laid a hand on his arm, concerned. 'Are you worried about the company?'

'Not the company – the loan. It's all going to be about timing, and I need to get it exactly right. I'll be more settled after we've secured the orders.'

'Melissa was telling me that Giles lost a lot of money a couple of years back. Did he tell you that?'

'I knew about it, yes.' Giles had said nothing about losing anyone's money. He would raise the subject with him later. Right now he needed to get Jennifer away from the living room.

She refused to move. 'So is he coming up with the goods?'

'Not yet, but there's still time.' It was the wrong time to have this conversation. 'Maybe I'll take a walk into the village.'

'Would you like me to come with you?'

'I just need to do some thinking and clear my head.'

'Okay.'

'We can go for a walk later if you like.'

He smiled reassuringly and moved to kiss her on the forehead, but she raised the stack of folded towels between them. 'I'd better put these somewhere.'

As she headed off upstairs he started to wonder if she knew

anything about Summer, but dismissed the idea as absurd. He had been especially careful. He needed to believe his own narrative. Nothing had happened, therefore there was nothing to know. Yet someone wanted him to know that *they* knew.

Wait, he thought, *wait. There are people in and out of the place all the time, the maid, the gardener, a pool boy presumably. Anyone might have innocently moved it.* Giles knew about Summer too, but his loyalty was not in question. He needed the job too badly.

He tried to think what to do with the backpack. If he put it in the outside bin someone else might find it.

He had noticed a pile of leaves and dry branches smouldering in a rusted incinerator at the bottom of the garden. Wedging the bag tightly under his arm, he left by the side steps and headed there. The old man he had seen armed with a rake earlier had disappeared. Now might be the only chance he'd get.

He decided he would burn everything except the passport, but he had a terrible feeling that it wouldn't stop here. If someone really wanted to take him down they would have to do better than trying to scare him.

Next time, he told himself, he would be ready.

From behind the banana leaves that shielded the rear of the pool house, Hannah watched Steve feed the backpack into the incinerator, holding it down with a stick until it caught alight. A thin, oily thread of smoke rose above it.

He took the credit cards out of their plastic wallet and flicked them into the fire one by one. Then he glanced back at the villa, checking that he had not been seen, and stood over the flames until they died down.

Afterwards he stirred the ashes with the stick, then shook out a clean white handkerchief and carefully wiped his hands.

As soon as he had gone back upstairs, Hannah made her way over to the incinerator and looked inside it. There was nothing left of the backpack except some grey ash and two metal buckles. The cards had shrivelled to tiny black blobs. She realised now that she should have kept the bag. The evidence had been obliterated.

Glancing up at the villa, she saw one of the bedroom curtains move. She could not afford to be seen down here. Leaving the cover of the banana trees, she made her way back toward the house.

She was sure of one thing. Summer was dead, and Steve had killed her.

What could he have done with her body? It wasn't inside the villa, even though that was the sort of thing murderers did, hastily burying their victims under floorboards, in cellars and attics; she'd read enough true crime paperbacks to know that. The villa had no cellar or attic. It was not a set from a horror film, even though it now felt haunted.

What if he hadn't killed her but just knocked her unconscious? He would have had to take her outside and find a temporary hiding place, leaving her where no one would see or hear her.

Beyond the end of the garden was the plant nursery, presumably managed by Matthias. It seemed a promising place to start looking, as it had a shed and was filled with several mounds of freshly dug earth. He could have dropped her into one of the holes and quickly covered it over, maybe moving her after dark in the car. Unfortunately, the plant beds could be seen from the villa. If she wanted to examine them, she would have to wait until the guests had gone out.

What about further out in the valley, beyond the property boundary? Could he have dumped her there? A stone path led to the edge of the wild land. Summer was small and light. He could have carried her down without anyone seeing him and taken her far out into the woodlands. She could be lying there now, tucked up in the scrubby underbrush, virtually invisible.

It was no use; she couldn't cover the whole of the valley. It would take a team of police officers to conduct such a search.

The police. She hadn't seen any gendarmes in the village, but presumably they were there. She could talk to one of them and get some advice. What if they wanted to come here and question the guests? Steve would report back to Julia and at the very least she would be out of a job.

What had happened on the night Summer had headed into the village to see Jihane? It wasn't a long walk to Chez Dany. *Summer, whatever happens I'm doing this for you,* she reminded herself, setting off.

She passed the outlying houses and entered the village square. The grinning pig in the chef's hat outside Auberge Eric was life-sized and made of fibreglass. In one fat trotter it held a plate of pork sausages, in the other a large fork, ready to serve itself up. The menu was old-school French café food at its grimmest: gizzards, giblets and guts served with sludgy brown ratatouille, or a Salade Niçoise topped with tuna still bearing the mould of its tin can. The only other place to eat was a pizzeria, Bellissimo, which was anything but.

Hannah squeezed past a pair of grizzled Australian hikers arguing over an ancient Ordnance Survey map outside Chez Dany. Removing her sunglasses, she stepped into the gloom.

At the counter the owner, Raphael, was hunched over the sports pages of *Nice-Matin*. The maroon birthmark across the upper left side of his great leonine head gave him a carnivalesque air. At the end of the counter a handful of customers drank bitter coffee with cognac chasers. It had only just gone eleven, a time that marked the border between aperitifs and alcoholism.

A slender-hipped young waiter with a tattoo plaster on his neck listlessly wiped crumbs onto the tiled floor. One of the tables was missing its glass top and had been moved to a corner. As in every French café-bar, a stack of plastic folding chairs stood against one wall.

Deciding that it would be better if she didn't let them know she spoke French just yet, she seated herself at the counter and ordered a coffee in English.

'The girl who came in,' she said, 'I heard there was a fight?'

Raphael looked like a man who always poured a calvados into his coffee before touching it. He turned from the espresso machine and examined the newcomer. 'Good morning,' he said with reproof.

She had forgotten to start with formalities, a sign that she was more nervous than she'd realised. 'Good morning. What coffee do you have?'

'We have café. The machine is not working.' Sluicing it

from a glass jug into a tiny white cup, he left it on his side of the counter just to give the waiter something to do. 'Who told you about this fight?'

'Julia Martinez, the letting agent from *Vacances Paradis*. She said there was some trouble the other night.' Hannah pointed at the damaged table.

'Yes, the girl, of course there was trouble.' He eyed her with suspicion. 'If you're her friend, you need to tell her to keep herself under control.'

'What was the problem?'

'There is only ever one problem with a girl like that. Boys. She was with an Arab.'

One of the other customers muttered something unintelligible.

'Did they argue with each other?' Hannah asked.

'We saw the Arab waiting for her outside,' said Raphael. 'They came in and had a few drinks. Jacob was at the bar. He's just a farmhand, he doesn't like Algerians. I have to keep an eye on him because, well, he's not so clever. We've all told him he can't just touch women. The Arab got upset and there was an argument. The table went over. Sixty euros to repair.'

'I'll make sure someone comes up from the villa to pay you for the table,' she lied. 'Who was the boy? Did you get his name?'

'*Quelqu'un a-t-il entendu son nom?*' Raphael asked the whole bar. The drinkers looked at him with the blankness of sheep. 'He said he was sorry for what happened. He was protecting her. We are not prejudiced up here, it's just some of the locals – well, they don't go to town much.'

'Did you hear anything they said?' She tried to sound as if she was casually picking up gossip.

'No, they were quiet up until the fight. Behaving themselves. I have to look after Jacob. He's been in jail a few times. He can't go back there again because there's no one to take care of his mother. Look, I don't want anyone to get in trouble.' Raphael lowered his voice. 'These things happen from time to time. I wouldn't ask too many questions around here. They don't like it, especially from visitors.'

Hannah glanced at the other drinkers, who were watching her.

'It's okay, they don't speak English.' Raphael leant forward. 'Everyone is interested in this girl because – well, who wouldn't be, the way she looks? If she comes back, I'll tell her you're looking for her. You're at La Terrasse, yes? Madame Lavardin's old place? Give me your mobile number.'

'It's okay,' she said. 'I'll come by again.'

'Sorry I couldn't be more helpful,' Raphael apologised with a Gallic shrug. He didn't charge her for the coffee.

Taking her coffee to a table, she tried the contact number Summer had starred on her phone. Her call was answered on the second ring.

'Can I speak to Summer Farrow?' she asked, not sure what to say next.

'You're calling from her phone.' The speaker was female, older and guarded.

'She left it with me by mistake. I just wondered –'

'Summer Farrow.'

'That's right.'

There was no reply.

'My name's Hannah Carreras. I just want to get this back to her.'

'I haven't seen or heard from her in –' The woman stopped.

'How long?'

'I think – a little over two years.'

Hannah digested this news. 'Are you her aunt?'

'No, her carer. Just while she was in recovery.'

'What was she recovering from?'

'This is the Yardley Fairfield Centre. What's your connection with her?'

'I'm her best friend. The last time I saw her she forgot her bag and I need to return it. I couldn't find a number for her parents.'

'You won't. If you're her best friend, you'll know they're both dead. I don't have any other contact numbers for her.'

'Why was she there?'

'You'll need to take that up with her. Patients' records are confidential.'

'Please, I can't find her and I don't know where else to look. I think something has happened to her.'

'I'm sorry, I can't help you. Miss Farrow was discharged from here after she became a danger to herself and others. This is a voluntary admission clinic.'

Panicked, Hannah rang off. She ran a search for the Yardley Fairfield Centre. Its website described it as a private health facility designed up to help teenagers with behavioural problems.

I'll find you, Summer, she thought, setting the phone on the table before her. *If people don't search for each other, what happens when they're in trouble?*

She needed a proper plan. Leaving things around for Steve to find had proven to be a disastrous strategy. As she drank her coffee she tried to work out who to trust at the villa. She chewed her thumb, thinking.

The wife, she decided. She was the one who should know.

She could write a note and leave it where only Jennifer Elsbury would find it. Tearing a page from her notebook, she wrote in block capitals so that it didn't look like her handwriting.

ASK YOUR HUSBAND ABOUT THE 18-YEAR-OLD GIRL WHO STAYED HERE LAST WEEK. SHE HAS GONE MISSING. HE KNOWS WHAT HAPPENED TO HER.

She wished she could talk about it with someone – Daniela, perhaps – but she knew her friend would be horrified. She couldn't accuse anyone outright.

The wife had to put everything together by herself.

29.

Steve's shirt smelled of bonfires. He went up to the bedroom and changed, then checked his emails for replies to Giles's requests for meetings. As he was coming down the stairs Giles met him. He had the furtive air of a spy on his first mission.

'Ah, Steve, glad I found you,' he said. 'Can I have a quick word?' He guided Steve outside and around the corner of the villa.

'And I need to talk to you,' said Steve irritably as he followed Giles. 'I've heard nothing from your leads. I told you to copy me in on the appointments.'

'I found these.' Giles turned and opened his right fist. The crimson bikini unfolded like a crushed flower. 'They belong to her, I imagine.'

'How would I know, Giles?' Steve snapped. 'Why on earth would they belong to her?'

Giles turned the bottom half around. 'Look at them. I mean, bless our lady wives but neither of them would fit these. It would be disgusting.'

'So what? She must have left them behind. Where were they?'

'Well that's the thing. They were on top of a towel in the kitchen. I think your wife must have left them there. She was doing something with the towels earlier.'

'Why didn't you just get rid of them?'

'I thought when you see your girlfriend in London –'

'She's not my fucking girlfriend and I'm never going to see her again,' he explained with exaggerated impatience. 'You were right, Giles, it was a terrible idea.'

'No, I said it was immoral. I know we're only human but we don't always have to act on our impulses. I'm a practising Christian and I simply don't think it's right. I mean if that girl –'

'Can we just not talk about "that girl" anymore?' He raised his voice more than he intended. 'She's gone, okay? Forget about her. All you saw was a girl in a bar. You didn't see a girl here. You saw nothing.'

'If you say so, but it's not easy when there are things like this.' Giles looked down at the skimpy red bikini bottom in his hand. 'I was only trying to help. I'll get rid of it.' He sounded reluctant, as if he knew the discovery could give him an advantage.

'Concentrate on what you're supposed to be doing. You need to sort out tomorrow's meeting schedule. None of your contacts have been in touch to confirm. You were meant to be in charge of this. I can't start cold-calling them.'

'I'll get on it,' Giles raising his hand in a promise, a gesture that would have had more gravitas had he not been holding a bikini bottom.

If he hadn't been so sure that Giles was too slow-witted to be Machiavellian, Steve might have begun to wonder if his associate was planning to blackmail him. Giles went up to the terrace and when he returned was all smiles again. He headed for the pool with a cheery wave intended to show that he had nothing in his hands. Had he simply thrown her bikini in the rubbish where anyone could find it? Or had he decided to retain it?

From beneath the edge of his hood, Jamie watched his father's new second-in-command sink himself bottom-first into the giant doughnut and push off from the shallow end. Giles patted the water with his palms and waggled his legs delightedly, a forty-year-old man returned to infancy by listening to 'Dancing Queen' on his phone.

With a grunt of disgust Jamie buried himself deeper inside his sweatshirt and returned his concentration to his playlist.

'Hey,' said Melissa, wandering over. Today she had chosen a lurid orange one-piece, Lolita sunglasses and cork-soled sandals that made her look like an extra from a 1960s movie. She raised her glasses, glaring at him until he took off his headphones. 'There are ice lollies in the freezer. The last person here must have left them behind. Do you want one?'

'No,' he said quickly, adding, 'thanks. I don't do sugar.'

She looked at him sitting cross-legged in his skinny black jeans and baggy sweatshirt, like a denim-clad Elizabethan courtier. 'You keep yourself pretty well covered. Those jeans must be hot.'

'I don't do sun.'

She crouched down beside him. 'So, what *do* you do?'

He chose not to reply.

'Come on, there must be something you like.'

'Lizards.'

'They can't be the only things. You like those.' She indicated his headphones. 'What are you listening to?'

'You wouldn't like it.'

'You're right,' she admitted. 'I don't have kids. I know you need space to figure out who you are, and these questions are probably annoying. What do you want to be?'

'A Shaolin monk.'

'You do understand that would involve learning Mandarin and becoming a disciple for a decade?' She tried to see his eyes. 'I think that's the answer of a kid trying to fob off an adult.'

'I'm not good at this –' He waved his hand dismissively at the swimming pool. In the background, Giles began singing along to his phone in a series of falsetto yelps.

'I know what you mean. If my husband's irritating you I can have him neutralised.' Melissa removed Giles from her sight by lowering her sunglasses. 'I imagine he's put you off older people for life. Believe it or not, he means well.'

She rested her hand on the arm of his chair. 'It must be weird for you, Jamie, going away with strangers. Americans have a chance to get used to it because they're packed off to summer camps when they're young. God knows I don't contribute much. The only thing I know about fine wines is how to drink them. And teenagers are a mystery.'

'I'm not a teenager, I'm Gen Z.'

'Whatever you call it, darling, it's the same thing. You're self-obsessed, insecure and angry with everyone over twenty, like Lord Byron and Caligula. I don't even remember being your age. I'm always amazed by people who can recall everything about their formative years. Actually I find the whole of life to be one big fucking mystery. Sorry, I should set an example. But fuck it.' She tapped out a cigarette and looked about for a lighter. 'The way I see it, we're adorable from age three to nine, then we behave like total arseholes until we're twenty-one, then we're unutterably boring while we let work suck everything out of us, and after fifty-five we either relax or go completely off the rails. You don't drink.'

'No, I don't like it. I prefer to feel in control.'

She made a study of his face. 'Whereas I don't. Funny, it used to be the other way around. The students were wild and the adults were appalled. Do you have a light? Oh come on, don't pretend you don't.'

'I don't smoke, Melissa. I don't drink coffee, either. I don't do stimulants.'

'Darling, I think you need to find something that stimulates you, fast.' On the far side of the pool Steve was watching something through a pair of binoculars. She rose to her feet. 'Well, have fun with your technology.'

She left a trail of blue smoke behind her.

Steve saw them springing between the branches, undulating dark creatures with thick coats, too long and glossy to be rats.

'What are you watching?' Melissa tried to keep her smoke away from him but it always made a beeline for non-smokers.

He handed her the binoculars. 'In the tops of the pines, just over there.'

She watched for a minute, then reacted. 'They're black. What are they, minks?'

'Squirrels.'

'Pity. They'd make a nice coat.'

'It's because we're in this valley. They have no contact with other drays. They're a genetic mutation. According to our gardener they're cut off here so they breed inwards, and it changes their coding.'

'When did you meet the gardener? Is he cute? You *are* a dark one.' She gave back the binoculars. 'Human beings always change when they become isolated. Me, I'm a great believer in mingling species.' She held onto the binoculars for a fraction too long.

Steve turned to look at her. With Giles under suspicion right now, her timing was terrible. His pale eyes remained as impassive as an animal's. 'Do you always flirt in front of your husband?'

'Who says I'm flirting? I can't help being like this. The Cruella de Vil act is a survival instinct, nothing to feel threatened about.'

'I just thought –'

'Don't backtrack, it's unbecoming. After two husbands, two abortions and three miscarriages I'm immune to embarrassment. I don't care what others think, although I imagine you do. Aren't you meant to be working today?'

'I need your husband to finalise the appointments.'

'Yes, I heard he promised you access to his famous little black book.' She glanced back at Giles splashing about in the pool. She wished he would stop behaving like a child in front of his new boss. 'He's not as strong as you. He's been through a lot lately.'

'I heard he lost some money.'

'He trusted the wrong people. He'll work until he falls, trying to make everything right, so he's easy to pick on. He's like the last gnu at the back of the herd, the one the hyenas tear to bits. Giles was raised to believe in the gentleman's agreement, the handshake, the unspoken understanding. I'm afraid the real world came as rather a shock to him. The people he considers to be his old friends are nothing of the kind.' She suddenly realised she was trying to warn him that Giles might let him down. 'I wonder, we barely know each other but may I ask you to promise me something?'

He leaned on the railing, looking back at the jagged treeline. 'That depends on what it is.'

'Promise me you won't dump him as soon as you've got what you want.'

Steve thought it best not to reply.

'Please, Steve. It's the only thing I'll ever ask of you, I promise.'

He kept his eyes averted. 'I'll do my best to make sure he's kept on, Melissa. It's up to him now. I need those leads to work. He has to appreciate what's at stake. Talk to him. Make him act. Scare him if you have to. He'll listen to you.'

'What's it worth?' Melissa asked with a sly smile.

30.

Hannah felt increasingly disoriented. There were snakes in this Eden, but identifying them was far from easy. She was comforted by the conviction that Summer was watching over her, influencing events. She was still considering this when her ride home arrived.

'Are you okay?' Daniela asked as she climbed into the Fiat. 'I thought perhaps, well – *il y a quelque chose qui cloche*.' Something's not right. For once she had hit the nail on the head. The car jerked forward just as Hannah was trying to get in. Daniela panicked, apologised and threw on the handbrake.

'Julia was at the villa today, checking up on the new guests,' Hannah told her.

'Already? She usually only does that when she thinks there is a problem. It's so we don't have to get involved.' Daniela crunched gears and tore away down the hill. 'If you start talking to the guests you'll get caught up in all their troubles.'

Hannah could feel the letter burning in her pocket. She

needed to find an envelope for it, to make sure that it reached the right person. 'Is it true she has a gun?'

'I wouldn't be surprised. You know there are stories about her, right?'

'What kind of stories?'

'They say she used to run a call-girl ring in Nice but the police put pressure on her to get out of the business.'

'You don't think –'

'It still goes on? I hope not. Of course, you can never be a hundred per cent sure. People here know how to keep secrets.' She held Hannah's gaze a little too long before having to right the steering.

Steve asked his wife if they could cook the dinner together. Right now it felt as if he needed to keep her on his side. Besides, it would stop Melissa getting too close to him. He would have to be on his guard all the time.

Having spent the afternoon secretively texting gamers on the other side of the world, Jamie suddenly decided to go into the village, so the two couples ate together in the open kitchen by the pool. Melissa took over the task of mixing cocktails. 'There's something called *crème de violette* in the cupboard that smells like bath cubes,' she told the others. 'Let's stick to gin.'

The dinner, chicken legs with grapes and white wine, was light and swiftly consumed. Plates and glasses were scattered over the tables. Steve had arranged to have a selection of wines delivered from his clients. Cheeses came out, along with some kind of chocolatey shop-bought dessert that Giles contributed.

The starlit sky was lighter than the black valley below. Candle flames rose without a flicker in the warm, still air. The day had been hot. Jennifer's skin tingled.

Everything should have been perfect.

Jennifer touched the diamante sunglasses in her pocket. She had found them on top of a box of tissues in their bathroom. She would have to ask the maid if they were hers, but they looked as if they belonged to a teenaged girl. As the villa had been empty the previous week, how did they get there? And the bikini she had found and left on her towel, it had vanished. It felt as if there was someone backstage moving props about.

Giles and Steve punctuated the conversation with endless phone texts. Every couple of minutes rectangles of hard white light shone at the edges of the table. Finally Melissa had had enough. Taking a rope basket from the counter, she set it down on the dining table. 'All right, put them in,' she instructed. 'All the phones. We're trying to have a grown-up conversation here. Come on.'

'Don't be ridiculous,' said Giles. 'This is a work week for us.'

'Yes, but you've done nothing today and it's nearly midnight.' She raised the basket. 'Just for tonight. I've put mine in. You'll get them back when we go to bed.'

It suddenly seemed like a very good idea to Jennifer, who agreed. 'Yes, come on, let's have one night without the damned things. Everybody in.'

Steve was about to protest but realised how it would look. Reluctantly he surrendered his phone. Giles guiltily handed over his. Melissa set the basket down beside the table. 'Glory be, an evening of behaving like adults for once.'

Giles and Melissa discussed their respective parents. 'His mother's awful,' Melissa declared. 'She bullies people into submission. It came as no surprise to me when I heard that her husband was having an affair.'

'Steve's father was a serial womaniser,' Jennifer said rather too loudly, surprising herself.

'Oh really?' Melissa's interest rose as she upended another bottle. 'How did you find that out?'

The table fell silent.

'Well, his mother was very timid,' Jennifer began. 'She didn't like to admit –'

'You couldn't help but know.' Steve cut across her. 'Women calling the house at all hours, phones that suddenly went dead, endless excuses and lies. My father was always away on business so the time zones – well, it was harder to get hold of people in those days. For years my mother never said a thing, not a single fucking word ever came out of her mouth until –'

There was an awkward silence. 'We don't have to talk about it,' said Giles, anxious to keep the evening on an even keel.

'It's fine,' Steve told him, 'I'm fine. The crazy thing was that I adored him. He was full of life and energy. And I hated her for not standing up to him.' He raised his eyebrows as he rotated the glass in his hands. 'Try and make some sense out of that.'

'I guess you found him exciting,' said Melissa. 'Little boys always do.'

Steve barely heard her. 'He told me the world was my oyster, and she told me I couldn't have it. He always said yes, she always said no.'

Another silent moment passed while Jennifer opened a

new bottle of red and set out fresh glasses. 'Families poison you without meaning to,' she said with an air of finality. 'He's gone now.'

'What happened?' Melissa asked.

Steve looked uncomfortable. 'He left her. She found out he was having an affair with a girl from the office, and when she confronted him he walked out on her. He drove to a hotel, checked himself in and died that night in his bed. Alone. Natural causes.'

'My God, the guilt, how awful.' Melissa was genuinely shocked.

'This wine's corked,' said Giles, pulling a face. 'Don't drink that.' He reached out to put a hand over Melissa's glass, then fought to save it from toppling over. His chair slid back with a screech. There was an ominous splash.

They turned to see the rope basket slowly settling into the deep end of the pool. Melissa's mouth fell open. 'Was that…?' she began.

Everyone jumped up. It was Steve who stripped down to his shorts and dived in.

'He's had an awful lot to drink,' Melissa warned. 'I made those gin cocktails very strong. Can somebody put the pool lights back on? The remote is around here somewhere.'

Steve swam straight down, kicking his legs back. The water was warmer than the night air. The pool seemed deeper after dark. He kicked hard again and reached the edge of the rope basket with his fingertips. He could feel one phone, then another, but ran out of air. Bursting up to the surface, he deposited Melissa's Samsung and Giles's iPhone on the pool edge.

'Why don't you give him a hand?' said Melissa, pushing her husband. 'For God's sake, what do you want, an invitation?'

'There's no point in both of us…' Giles began lamely. 'I can't find the remote for the lights.'

Steve swam down again. A high-pitched buzz filled his ears as the weight of water pressed in on him. The pool looked deeper than ever. He could see nothing ahead but felt the basket once more, and touched another phone, Jennifer's. Again he started to run out of air and surfaced. Surely he used to be able to hold his breath longer than this?

'They're absolutely ruined,' said Melissa angrily. 'Giles, what is *wrong* with you?'

Steve set the phone on the lip of the pool and dived again. This time his descent was messy and disoriented, and he struggled to reach the floor of the pool. He needed to find his own phone but it wasn't in the basket. He could see the rope coils beneath his fingers, then the tiled floor and finally a face, upturned, pale green and female.

He put his outstretched fingers into its open mouth, felt cold lips and teeth brush him, eyelashes, an open eye, fine trails of hair drifting around his arm.

He yelled, releasing silvered gobbets of air, and kicked up fast. But he had gone in the wrong direction, across the deep end instead of upwards. He drew in more water, gagging. There was a burst of noise above him and someone's hands reached down to pull at his shoulders.

Melissa towed him to the shallow end. He felt the tiles sliding beneath his feet as she hauled him upright. Then he was out and bent over, heaving. He was violently, copiously sick over the drain. He fell back against the patio wall and wiped his mouth.

'Are you okay?' asked Melissa. 'It looked like you lost consciousness for a moment.'

'My phone,' he tried to say, 'my phone's still down there,' but nobody was concerned with phones now. They fussed around him, being unbearably solicitous while still finding time to disagree with each other. He needed to be away from them, otherwise he would tell them what he saw. But even before he looked back into the water he knew there was nothing to see.

Wrapped in a bathrobe, pushing all help aside, he made his way up to the bedroom alone feeling foolish and ashamed. The water felt sticky and chemical. No matter how hard he tried to dry himself it seemed to cling to his skin. His mouth was metallic with chlorine and something else, something earthier and even more unpleasant. Mouthwash didn't help. When he closed his eyes he saw her face, pale and accusing, and did not know if it was real or not.

31.

Hannah arrived early on Tuesday morning, anxious to plant the letter where Mrs Elsbury would find it. Dressed in her maid's uniform, she stood at her post in the kitchen, the coffee on, ready to offer a breakfast service. She had slept badly and felt barely awake. No sound came from upstairs, so she went outside and settled in a wicker armchair to await their arrival. She had taken a blank envelope from a kitchen drawer and written *Mrs Jennifer Elsbury* on it. The letter was pressed flat inside her Agatha Christie, doubling as a bookmark.

Presumably the bikini and the sunglasses had been found by now. She wondered what the reaction had been. They had not been thrown away; she had checked the bins and found nothing. Had they been quietly disposed of elsewhere? It hardly mattered; by themselves they provided no conclusive proof of misdeeds. She needed to provoke a bigger response.

She had given back too many pieces of evidence. Before

surrendering the backpack she should have taken out Summer's passport. She had seen Steve pocket it, but where had he put it? In the car, perhaps?

There was something missing. Lapsed time, disappeared minutes, like a momentarily dropped broadband signal. She was too close to see the full picture. When she looked out at the wild woodlands beyond the villa and the white clouds above the treeline where a lone eagle coasted on the rising winds, she remembered something Daniela had told her.

There's a camera in the porch, so they know when everyone comes and goes.

She ran back up to the front of the villa and checked under the eaves. There it was under the wooden beams, a tiny modular lens like a shiny black egg, trained on the front door. Presumably it was recording anyone who arrived or left.

Reaching on tiptoe, she was just able to feel around it with the tips of her fingers. A thick black cable was screwed into its back. She followed it down and across the brickwork, where it had been stapled into place. It folded back around the corner of the house and ran behind some agapanthus plants before going into a wall.

She could see the break from where she was standing. Kneeling to get a closer view, it was obvious that the cable had been cut at an angle with gardener's secateurs or something similarly sharp, like the lethally edged chef's scissors she had found in the dishwasher.

———

Upstairs in the villa, Jennifer was the first one awake. Steve hugged the edge of the bed, too far away for her to reach. She decided it would be best to leave him asleep.

She looked in on Jamie. Her son slept in a way only teenagers could manage, spread-eagled face-down with one arm in an impossible position. She could smell alcohol and socks. Part of her was perversely pleased that his ascetism had proven to be imperfect. It made him a little more fallible and human, like those girls who swore to be virgins until they married, only to fall secretly pregnant.

It was another beautiful day. She had to stop herself from being so surprised by sunshine, such a British habit. Going downstairs and opening all the doors, she greeted Hannah and allowed her to prepare toast, eggs and bacon – to hell with the extra expense. There would even be baked beans for Giles. She knew that the smell would bring someone to the table. Hannah slipped out of the kitchen as soon as Jennifer released her, but sat quietly outside below the window, listening and writing in her notebook.

Giles was the next to appear. His face was red and puffy, and there were bites all over his arms. 'They've made a meal of me,' he said sorrowfully. 'I just had a look at the pool. Steve's phone is still on the bottom. I feel absolutely awful. Did anyone else's dry out enough to start working again?'

'Mine hasn't.' Jennifer passed him bacon and eggs from the warmer. 'Not that I get many calls. Are you hungry?'

'Starving. Beans, wow. But I don't like them touching my eggs. What can I do to help?'

'The maid's done it all. Although you could butter some more toast.'

'Sure. Where's the –'

'Just look around, Giles.' She was already growing impatient with him. He poked about in the recycling bin and looked in the microwave. She turned away, busying herself with plates so that there was no time to think about how unbearable he was. No wonder Melissa drank.

Giles took a slice of toast and nibbled at a corner. 'How's Steve? Only I arranged a meeting for us in Grasse this morning.'

'He's still asleep. What time is your meeting?'

'Not until eleven-thirty. It'll take us about an hour to get there.'

'I'll make sure he's up in time,' she said briskly.

'I, er – perhaps – yes.' Giles wandered outside, leaving the rest of the toast unbuttered.

It was Melissa who got the last phone out of the pool. She set it down on the kitchen counter and watched in dismay as water drained from the keys. 'There's a house phone but it doesn't seem to work,' she announced. 'What if there was an emergency?'

'I grew up in a house without a phone, I'm sure I can manage now.' Jennifer set out plates for fresh fruit. 'I thought a good breakfast might bring Steve and Jamie down. They were sleeping very soundly.'

'My father used to fall asleep at Formula One events so he found it quite easy to ignore my mother,' Melissa said. 'Giles is the same. It's as if he dies at bedtime. I like to think it's caused by a clear conscience, but it could be simply because his mind's completely blank.'

'Steve shouts in the night,' Jennifer said. 'Sometimes he wakes up as if he's just had the most terrible fright.' It was against her character to discuss such intimacies, but after their alcoholic conversation the night before any topic seemed open for discussion – anyway, Melissa had no sense of privacy.

Melissa ground out her cigarette. 'Can I do anything?'

'Keep an eye on the toast for a moment?'

Jennifer went upstairs to their bedroom. Steve was still folded over at the edge of the bed. He turned and blearily opened his eyes, looking creased and dream-haunted. 'What time is it?'

'Nearly nine. Giles has a meeting fixed for you. It's okay, you have time to get there but you need to get up. There's a cooked breakfast going downstairs if you fancy it.'

He raised himself with a wince. 'I'd love to but –' He suddenly pushed off the bed and scuttled to the bathroom. She heard him vomit into the basin, then spit. He returned with wings of black hair dangling over his ashen face.

She put a hand on his shoulder. 'Are you all right?'

'Stomach cramps.'

'Change of diet. I have something for that. Come downstairs and I'll get it for you.'

They applauded him at the table. Even Jamie turned up to see what the fuss was about. Steve seated himself with great delicacy.

'That was quite a night,' said Giles. 'Of course, we're all without phones now, thanks to me. I'm so horribly embarrassed. When we go into Nice I'll buy a couple, unless anyone has any better ideas. I hope we're all insured.'

The group relaxed and ate. Steve picked at some dry toast. 'I've got my phone,' Jamie pointed out.

'Five people can't share it,' said Jennifer. 'I'll be fine for a few days. I don't really want to throw money away on another one before putting in a claim.'

'What are you going to say, that my husband drop-kicked it into the pool?' Melissa helped herself to bacon. 'Is this pancetta?'

Jamie amazed everyone by loading his plate. 'What happened?' he asked his father.

'I tried to save the phones,' Steve explained. 'The pool lights were off.'

Jennifer passed Jamie toast. 'We couldn't find the remote. He got turned around in the dark and drank some chlorine.'

'I didn't. I was fine,' Steve snapped. 'I got most of them up.'

'Are you sure you're all right?' asked Melissa. 'You look awfully pale.'

'I'll be fine so long as everyone stops making a fuss.' He shoved back his chair and headed for the door. 'Giles, come with me, I want to go over something with you before I get ready.'

He grabbed Giles's arm in the hall. 'What did you do with the bikini?'

Giles dropped his frown. 'Oh, don't worry about that. I got rid of it. Why are you so worried? I thought you were the one who advocated guilt-free sex. It's not as if anything happened –' A cloud crossed his features.

'What?'

'Forget it, it's none of my business.'

'She was gone before I arrived, Giles. I keep fucking telling you and will continue to tell you until you repeat it back. Your imagination is working overtime. You think there was a girl but there was no girl.'

'You see I know that's not true,' Giles persisted. 'It isn't just the bikini. I'm sure I saw something else of hers when I went down to the pool patio, some kind of orangey red see-through thing, but it's gone now.'

'Then you imagined it,' he hissed.

'You know me, I can't lie. If somebody asked me –'

'Are you trying to get a hold over me, Giles? Is that it?'

'No, of course not.' Giles looked horrified.

'Then concentrate on what we have to do today. If we don't come back with at least a verbal agreement, you're going to be calling every single one of your old college chums and getting them on board even if it takes you all night.'

'I'm not sure I can do that,' said Giles uncertainly. 'These kind of people – well, they don't like to be pushed.'

Steve brought himself close. 'I'm relying on you to push very hard indeed. You're no use to me if you don't. I brought you for your address book, not your negotiation skills.'

Giles's defeated silence was the most eloquent statement he had yet made on the trip.

In her seat beneath the kitchen window, Hannah scribbled out snippets of conversation. Later she would decide where to leave the butterfly-wing wrap, but first she had to get the letter of accusation to Jennifer.

She went in to clear up the breakfast things.

32.

The Elsburys and the Sutherlands went to separate parts of the villa, creating an invisible demarcation that preserved their privacy. Hannah filled the dishwasher and cleaned the counters, and was about to make the beds and tidy the rooms when she heard a car horn outside. Daniela was going to pick up some bathroom supplies at the discount store and wanted her along to help.

As they drove toward St Martin-sous-Roches, Hannah looked out at the empty grey streets and the gravelled main square with its pollarded ash trees. In winter the town was only just below the snow-line. When the spring thaw came, the flood-gutters that criss-crossed the village would become inundated, forcing the shops to close for days at a time. How isolated did the women become, especially those trapped in bad marriages?

Her phone made her jump.

When she was in her car Julia always shouted on the phone because she drove with it mounted on the dashboard and had the windows open, and tackled the hairpin bends of the Haute Corniche at speeds Lewis Hamilton would have thought twice about.

'Is Tuesday,' she bellowed. 'I always check with my girls on a Tuesday, is nothing to worry about. Was everything okay at Madame Lavardin's villa? They are happy, yes? You tell me, it will save me calling them: I don't like him.'

'I haven't spoken to them,' Hannah promised. 'You said not to.'

'I know but you have eyes. No complaints yes? Because Mr Steve is up to no good. This I know from Beausoleil. Is another agency. Often he stayed in one of their flats on his trips. Marie-Thérèse has a big mouth and tells me everything. So is important to make him happy but not too happy.'

'What do you mean?'

'Marie-Thérèse put a red star next to his name. For being too friendly with the girls, you understand my meaning. She had to talk to him about it.' An oncoming coach took the bend wide in front of her. She blasted her horn but refused to slow down for him. '*Quel gentilhomme! Connard!* She says I must be careful who I send to look after him, not too sexy, no offence to you.'

'He hasn't stayed at the villa before, has he?' Hannah asked.

'No, is too big, usually he takes one of Marie-Thérèse's apartments in the old town but this time he is with his family. You will tell me if you see anything strange yes?'

As Hannah hung up, she wondered if Julia had seen something that had made her suspicious.

'I need caffeine first,' Daniela warned her, looking for a

parking space. 'I want to kill the new guest in the Champs D'Or.'

'Why?' Hannah asked.

'She's this executive-type who won't let me use the coffee machine and swore at me for spilling water in the kitchen. Water! I felt like slapping her and to hell with it. What else would I do though, work for Amazon? At least I have some control here.'

'Daniela, if you saw something bad happen in one of the villas, would you do anything about it?' Hannah asked as they pulled into a space.

'I think you know the answer to this. We're not guests, just cleaners. Besides, who would you tell? Not Julia.'

'I don't know – the police.'

'That would be the fastest way to lose your job.'

Hannah looked out of the window and watched as a police car crawled past. Talking to gendarmes would carry more weight if she had Summer's passport with her, but they would probably just take it and thank her for handing it in. Besides, Steve wasn't likely to leave it lying around.

She ordered two tiny espressos which they drank standing at the counter. Daniela talked about her son, who needed expensive dental work that his father refused to pay for. Hannah was unable to follow her convoluted story.

'You're not listening.' Daniela drained her coffee and zipped her jacket. 'Come on, after we've been to the store I'll run you back.'

Half an hour later she crunched the battered Fiat to a stop outside the villa. '*Tu t'en sors?* Are you *sure* you're okay?'

'I'm fine, really.' She knew Daniela was suspicious but did not have time to worry about it.

She stood outside the house for a moment, steeling her nerves, then let herself in via the front door, closing it quietly behind her. The hatchback had gone. Presumably Steve and Giles had left for their meeting.

She could hear indistinct voices somewhere below. The wives were making the most of the sunshine. Unsettled weather had been forecast for later in the week. They were at the back of the villa. Now was the time to do it.

Slipping off her trainers, she ran up the stairs with the envelope held tightly in her hand. Where was the best place to leave it? Steve would never think of looking in his wife's toiletries. She had left the sunglasses there and they had disappeared.

Hannah headed for the master bathroom, where she wrapped the letter in Summer's scented transparent shawl and slipped it into Jennifer's makeup bag. She was about to vacate the room when she heard someone outside the door. Holding her breath, she flattened herself against the wall.

Someone was standing very still in the corridor. She inclined her head forward an inch and looked.

'I know you're there.'

Jamie was watching her intently, his headphones around his neck. She had no idea how long he'd been standing there. 'There's nothing worth stealing,' he said airily. 'The other woman has some jewellery that looks expensive, but I suppose you already know that.'

He lowered his white hooded top and once again she was struck by how thin and pale he was, like a skinned fish, his alien appearance augmented by his shocking red hair. He wore black leather wristbands that looked as though they might slip off his skinny arms.

'What are you doing?' he asked, curious.

She backed up against the bathroom counter, watching him.

'It's okay, I don't bite.' He stared her down. Unshrouded, his eyes had youthful intensity.

'I have to clean the sinks.' Her fingers closed over the bag.

He stepped further into the room. She moved around him, keeping her fist out of his sight-line.

'You don't miss much, do you? I've seen you. You're always watching us, especially my dad.'

'He's paying for the villa.'

'So you have to keep him happy. He has to sign a piece of paper saying that you've satisfied all his needs.'

Why is he talking to me? He barely opens his mouth to anyone else. 'The agency tells me what to do,' she said.

Jamie walked softly forward, moving in like a predatory cat. 'But if he had a specific request, like making you clean the shower while he watched you, just to make sure you did a good job, you would have to do it.'

'Yes.'

'And if I asked you?'

'I'd say no because you're not in charge. You have no power over me.'

As he stepped forward she nimbly moved back, wielding her phone in her free hand. 'I have to film this, to show my boss I've done a good job.'

'You're just a servant.'

She turned from him, keeping the phone raised like a pointed pistol. 'And you're just a boy.'

She was anxious to leave but he reached out as she passed and brushed her wrist with his fingertips. He studied her eyes intently. She moved her arm away but his hand followed it down. He stared deeper into her pupils. She tried to look blank.

Jamie ushered her out. 'Go on then, get back to work – but I'll be watching you.' He waved her away.

He's protecting Steve, she thought as she left the bathroom and moved off along the hall. *He suspects his father did something bad. Maybe he even has proof. And he's frightened I'll find out the truth.*

She walked away as calmly as possible. None of this was working out right. She should have acted immediately instead of having to rely on an anonymous note. The most important thing now was to get Jennifer Elsbury to read it.

When she looked down from the living room window she saw Melissa slathered in sun oil, stretched out beside the pool. It was amazing she didn't slide right off her lounger and vanish into the bushes. Jennifer was in the water, moving through it like a professional swimmer. Her clothes were lying on a wicker chair beside the pool shower. Hannah ran downstairs and passed through the pool house, slipping out of its end door. Staying in the shadow of the slate wall near the shower taps, she placed the makeup bag on top of Jennifer's folded jeans.

From his upstairs window, Jamie looked down at the sunbathers on the pool patio. He could not see exactly what the maid had done, but knew she was up to something. She kept checking on the others while she fished around behind the shower, then moved back into the green shadows. He watched a while longer but failed to find her again. She couldn't have left, because he would have seen her on the staircase.

She was out to cause trouble. Was she really a maid, or was she working for one of his father's creditors, gathering information and sending it back to his enemies? He had thought she was pretty at first but it turned out she was just like the rest: self-interested and disrespectful.

He needed to keep a close eye on her from now on.

Hannah stayed near the bag. She had forgotten to zip it shut. It was lying on its side and looked as if its contents might slide out.

She got on with her duties, wiping down the kitchen and emptying the recycling bin, watching the wives from the windows. Jennifer showed no sign of vacating the pool.

As she made the beds, Hannah considered the problem. She had to be careful; Jamie was still lurking around somewhere. From what Julia had told her, it sounded as if Steve had a history of arranging to meet girls in the apartments he'd booked, which meant he had plenty to hide. Confronting him would get her nowhere. Her opinions carried no weight and he would simply dismiss any accusations she made.

She went downstairs to clean around the outside shower area, surreptitiously listening to the women's conversation, but there was only so much time she could spend wiping the taps. She was about to pack up her equipment when she heard Jennifer say, 'The whole thing seems wrong.'

Melissa glanced up and noticed Hannah. 'I say, are you going to be much longer over there?'

Hannah mutely returned her gaze and then left, taking her bucket with her. She ascended to the stone half-landing, where there was a tap for the garden hose, and turned it to a trickle, pretending to fill the bucket.

Jennifer got out of the water and wrapped a towel around herself. She went to the chair holding her clothes and refolded her jeans. As she did so, the wrap and its note fell from the makeup bag and landed on the tiles. The envelope had slipped out of the material and lay on the terracotta tiles in plain view.

'Do you want some sparkling water?' asked Melissa. She searched around for her towel, then wandered over to the shower. Jennifer checked her sun lounger, making sure she had left nothing underneath it.

Look behind you, Hannah willed her silently. God, they were slow. Melissa was almost standing on the note.

As Jennifer turned, she spotted the wrap and the folded page and went toward them, but Melissa got there first.

'Are these things yours?' She held up the wrap and sniffed it. 'I keep smelling the same scent all around the place.'

Jennifer took the wrap from her and examined it. 'I think this was on one of the loungers when we arrived.'

Melissa looked at the envelope in her hand. She had to see that it was not addressed to her.

Not you, Hannah screamed silently, *the other one! Show it to her!*

Melissa held the envelope back for a moment, then tucked it away in a pocket.

'I'm going to make some coffee,' said Jennifer. 'If you want one.'

There was no way of following them inside. Had Melissa guessed the contents of the letter? If she shared it, would Jennifer summon up the courage to confront her husband, or dismiss it and protect him?

That's the worst part of being a maid, Hannah thought. *You only get half the story.* The good part was that they barely noticed her. She had no more villas this afternoon so she decided to stay around for a while. Julia was off entertaining clients somewhere.

She sat at the rear of the pool house and read the same page over and over, thinking about Summer. As she dozed in the afternoon heat, Summer slipped into the events in the book, exploring the house where a murderer dwelled, failing to notice as he came up behind her with the gardener's ripsaw in his hand –

Summer cried out.

Hannah awoke. For a moment she was lost, trapped between fantasy and reality. She had heard Summer, of that she was sure. But the girl had gone now, replaced by a sussurance of foliage. She sensed no further presence here. It was as if her spirit had cried out a farewell as she departed.

There was no point in staying any longer. She packed her bag and was about to leave when Jennifer came down the staircase with a look of panic on her face.

33.

When Steve and Giles finally returned it was clear that they had been drinking. They looked far from happy. Giles resembled a flush-faced schoolboy caught without his sixth-form tie. Steve had a red wine stain on his pressed white shirt. They drifted into the open kitchen and headed straight for the fridge. When men went out together, thought Jennifer, why did they never eat?

'Something to celebrate?' she asked, taking plates to the table.

'They've given the entire fucking order to someone else,' said Steve. 'After everything they promised.'

She stopped. 'So why were you drinking?'

'We needed to talk through what happened,' said Steve. 'The fuckers.'

'We bought a pair of cheap pay-as-you-go phones because we need them for work,' said Giles. 'I'm going to set them up now.'

'What are we supposed to do?' asked Melissa, entering in time to catch the conversation.

'I'm waiting for people to call back.' Giles looked baffled. 'Do you really need a phone?'

'Giles, don't be a dick.'

He turned to Jennifer but his usual amiability had faded. 'She says that because she's jealous that I had a better education, and I'm still in contact with my old college chums.'

'You had a more expensive education,' Melissa conceded. 'I imagine you were bullied at school. Certainly not remembered. In case you haven't noticed, your "chums" only deal with their peers now. And nobody says "chums" anymore, for Christ's sake.'

A crash in the living room made everyone start.

They turned toward the opened doors and saw something large and dark moving about inside. 'What the hell is that?' Giles cried.

Something else fell over. Glass broke.

Steve was the first to move, heading toward the doors as the others followed behind him. Grabbing the broom Hannah had left beside the door, he brandished it before him like a broadsword. There was another crash and a peculiar strangled moan. Steve froze and turned.

'It's a goat,' he said. 'A fucking *goat*.'

'Jesus.' Giles backed away.

The animal had a shaggy black coat and disturbing yellow eyes. It bleated and shook its foolish long head, ringing its bell dully. It had been trying to eat some plastic lavender from a vase.

'Somebody get it out of there before it shits everywhere,' Melissa commanded. 'It stinks.'

'You're so good at giving orders, why don't you get it out?' Giles countered.

'Fine.' Melissa ran into the living room, waving her arms and bellowing. Startled, the goat discharged a faecal torrent and bolted further into the room, where it span around, smashing into a coffee table before hopping and prancing out of the door.

'It takes a woman to do a man's job,' said Melissa. 'He's evacuated his bowels on the rug. Someone else can clean that up.'

Steve drew Jennifer out onto the terrace. 'I'm late because he and I needed to talk,' he explained, trying not to be overheard. 'Giles drinks. I mean he *really* drinks. I've not seen him like this before. He's not going to be any good. These people he knows – they don't want anything to do with him. The friendships he has with them, they might have been there once but they're all in his head now.'

'Then he's of no use to you. I warned you about this.'

'Oh, he'll still be useful,' Steve replied mysteriously.

On the far side of the terrace, from somewhere inside the heliconias, the goat released a long, melancholy fart.

'That's all this trip needed, a distressed goat with IBS,' Jennifer said. 'Someone had better clean up the living room. Is the maid still here? We'll have to pay her extra.'

She headed off to find Hannah.

Goat shit, thought Hannah. *This wasn't in my job description.*

'I'm really sorry about this.' Jennifer watched her guiltily, but stayed well back.

At least it kept her near them, even though they were more guarded when she was around. As Hannah mopped the floor, she tried to imagine what more she could do to provoke the situation. Steve was either incredibly lucky or smart enough to surround himself with allies. Summer's clothes, her backpack, the letter – why weren't they all arguing among themselves? Maybe they simply didn't care. Nothing definitive had come to light and they were completely preoccupied with their own lives. Everything now hinged on Melissa sharing the note.

'There's some more under here,' said Jennifer, pointing to a reeking green puddle beneath the coffee table.

If tensions were rising in the Villa Lavardin, they did not reveal themselves from outside. As always, everything appeared tranquil. The house sat absorbing the warmth of the late afternoon sun and the trees gently spread themselves. The hibiscus bushes were sunk in shadow, their crimson petals preparing to twist shut for the night.

And just below the crumbling planes of the russet mountain that dominated this particular corner of the Alpes-Maritimes, a blank-eyed girl called Clémence was sitting in a field.

Clémence did not go to school with other children of her age; her mother had been granted a special dispensation to keep her back at their farm. She did not know that anyone was out looking for her.

She had been playing inside her favourite bushes down near the main road. Now she was tired and hungry. Most of all she was annoyed with her cat Pitou, because he had gone missing again and last time he had returned to her with his snowy white coat full of fleas and burrs after chasing rats through the bushes in the gardens of the Villa Lavardin.

At least this time she knew where to look for him.

34.

Melissa stood at the village's lookout point with the note in her hand. She had opened the envelope and read its contents the night before, but had not absorbed its implications. It was obviously from the maid. Who else could have written it? The girl bothered her, always watching from the corner of her eye, always writing in her notebook.

She did not need to reread the note. Everyone would suffer in the fallout. The best thing would be to tear it up, but she could not bring herself to do so. Information, she reminded herself, was currency.

She looked out at the view. Not very Instagram-friendly. A factory and some kind of gravel pit ruined the shot, not that she had a phone to take it with. She had a fleeting idea that Steve had somehow engineered the loss of his phone. Perhaps he had photos of the girl on it.

Overthinking, her curse.

She had borrowed the car and driven to the village with all the windows open, blasting the cool morning air through her hair, trying to clear her head. The sun was just about to appear over the hills, banishing the long blue shadows that striated the square. The patisserie wasn't open yet and she needed coffee, so she returned to the villa. While she was deciding what to do she glimpsed two police vehicles, parked and silent, their blue lights spinning, gendarmes standing by. Moments later they were lost behind trees.

She came in through the back door and made coffee. Sunlight washed over the kitchen, polishing everything. The air had snap and brilliance. Over the warbling of wood pigeons came a harder sound, someone barking an angry reply. *Please don't let it be Jennifer and Steve having another argument,* she thought, looking for Nespresso capsules. They should never have smoked dope last night. It had altered everyone's perceptions. Now the gardener, who apparently supplied the entire neighbourhood with dope, was their dealer because Giles had cheerfully made a purchase from him.

She was sipping her coffee and about to light a cigarette when Giles come puffing across the terrace. As far as Melissa was aware, he had never been for a run before this week.

'What on earth have you got on?' she called, her lighter poised in mid-air.

'It's what all the professionals wear.' He came to a stop and dropped his hands to his thighs.

'Yes but not all at once, surely. You look like a children's TV presenter. I don't think you should wear tights with your legs.'

'At least I made the effort. You weren't there when I woke up.'

'I couldn't sleep.'

She didn't need to elaborate. Giles was barely listening.

'I ran for ages, right to the edge of the town. I've got a stitch now. I'll need to take it easy for a while.'

Whenever Giles did something out of character, alarm bells rang. 'What are you up to?' she asked.

'It's okay, everything's back under control,' he replied, sniffing himself. 'I need a shower. There was a bit of a commotion going on. Police cars, cops redirecting traffic, people standing around.'

'Did you find out what it was?'

'Some woman was crying and carrying on outside her house, making a dreadful fuss about something. A gendarme was trying to calm her down.'

'You wouldn't think there'd be much excitement in a place like this.' She checked the toaster. 'It's good to know other people are miserable. Are you ready for breakfast?'

'Let me freshen up first.' He headed for the stairs as if he had stilts for legs.

Melissa sat down at the counter and glanced back at the pool. Sunlight glinted on the aluminium steps. After last night's drama the pool looked uninviting. She supposed they could go to the coast but nobody went to the beach in Nice.

She returned to the door, listening out for the maid.

Upstairs in the master bathroom, Jennifer turned the diamante sunglasses over in her hand. It seemed absurd to suspect Steve of being unfaithful again, although he was certainly acting as if he was guilty. But then there was the physical impossibility of it; he had only arrived at the villa a short time before her. How was he supposed to have committed this act?

'It's a pity they made you take the place for a fortnight,' she called to the bedroom. 'Having to leave it empty like that for the first week.'

'There was nothing I could do.' Steve's voice was muffled; he was twisted up in the sheets.

She came in. 'Are you all right?'

'My stomach's still hurting.'

'Melissa said it's stress. She can make you a smoothie that might help. She cut some herbs from the garden.'

'No thanks.' Steve winced. 'She might try to poison me.'

'Did you know she's a meditation therapist? She says it's made her a much nicer person. I can't imagine what she was like before.'

'It feels like a knife –'

'You work too hard. You need to –'

'What I need is an account the size of the fucking Bandol contract and I'm running out of ideas.'

'But you're not in trouble.'

He tried to raise himself and fell back with a grunt. 'Not one of Giles's amazing contacts has come through. He walks into meetings acting like a colonial landlord. He says things like, "Don't worry, the British are here," as if anyone in the room could give a flying fuck. It's humiliating. He doesn't have a clue how serious this is.'

'Try to get some rest.'

She put the sunglasses back in her pocket and went to look in on Jamie. Much to her surprise he was up and dressed in black shorts, a black T-shirt and a matching baseball cap.

'You look nice,' she said. 'Give me the white hoodie and I'll wash it.'

'Yeah, right. Everything you wash comes out pink. I'll do it. I'm off.'

'Where are you going?'

'The village. I don't want to sit by the pool listening to Giles singing all day. His songs are shit, he's completely flat and he doesn't even know the words. The weather's supposed to break tonight.'

'How do you know?'

'I didn't chuck my phone in the pool.' He held up his iPhone.

'You know, maybe Giles did us a favour. I haven't missed mine at all. Hardly, anyway. Can you bring back some milk and anything else you fancy? Cake or something. I'll give you the money.'

'It's okay, I have some. I found out where all the lizards are. They're bright green and they bite, one hung onto my finger, I've got a bruise, see, but they're not poisonous. They live under the rocks by the goat field. Milk, cakes, anti-Giles earplugs. See you later.' And he left.

Well, she thought, *virtually a whole conversation. Wonders will never cease.*

35.

In the kitchen Melissa clattered crockery in the sink as Giles returned in his awful grey suit. 'Giles, why didn't you say anything to me?' she asked.

'About what?'

'Your deal with the gardener.'

'I thought you'd tell me off if you knew.'

'How on earth did the subject come up?'

'I saw him working in the plant nursery and we chatted.'

'What, "the azaleas are lovely, do you sell super skunk?" Really?'

'He had them on him. He suggested it, not me.'

'No shit. Where's Steve?'

Giles pointed up at the bedroom. 'He's not feeling very well. Stomach.'

'Too much alcohol and rich food.'

'You've had the same, plus a thousand cigarettes.'

'There's something else –' She stopped herself, changed tack. 'He's angry with you.'

'They say you always learn about people's odd habits when you go on holiday with them.' He rolled his eyes comically.

'Darling, could you just stop being such a caricature for five minutes?' She laid a hand on his arm. 'You have to come through for him. You know that, don't you? Otherwise you're going to lose your job.'

Giles looked genuinely surprised. 'He couldn't just fire me.'

'He won't need to if the company's gone. It's in debt. I heard them talking. Steve's taken out a loan to tide him over until you come up with the goods. Do you understand the danger you're in?'

She felt a presence behind her and turned to find Steve in the doorway knotting a blue silk tie over a fresh white cotton shirt. He had a way of silently appearing that could be most disconcerting.

'Let's get this over with.' He beckoned to Giles, unsmiling. 'You, now. I'll be in the car.'

Giles meekly followed him out of the house.

The villa felt as marooned as a disabled ship. It was so quiet that the sound of a magazine page turning was enough to break the silence. The mysterious envelope had been trying to burn its way out of Melissa's bag. As soon as she spotted Hannah crossing the patio on her way to the pool house, she followed her down.

Hannah was just setting out her cleaning equipment when Melissa walked in, making her jump.

'You and I need to talk about this.' She took the envelope from her bag and removed the note. 'I know you left it. You were the only one who could have. You were hanging around by the pool and it wasn't on the chair before you came down. I'm not going to do anything that will get you into trouble. I just want some answers.'

Hannah took back the note as if it might sting her. 'I wrote it,' she said softly.

'It's a good job I found it before Mrs Elsbury did. You could get into a lot of trouble. Why do you think her husband has something to do with this girl?'

'I was here last week preparing the villa,' Hannah explained. 'I met her. She was staying here. She told me he paid for her trip out from London.'

'He – you mean Steve? Why would he do that?'

'They had an arrangement.'

'What kind of arrangement? You're talking about sex, I assume?'

Hannah tried to keep the strength in her voice. 'He was meant to come out and be with her toward the end of the week, but he couldn't leave London in time. He said he would still be able to see her on Saturday when he arrived, but she changed her mind. She didn't want to go through with it. She was going to have a fight with him.'

'And you know all this because –'

'She told me. Her name is Summer Farrow.'

'But Hannah – may I call you Hannah? – your note implies that he had something to do with her going missing, either by forcing her to run away or, well –'

'She never left the villa, she couldn't have, everything she owned is here.' Hannah tried to remain calm but her fears rose.

'I found her bloody footprint and broken glass beside the pool, like they'd had a fight. It wasn't there the night before.'

'Well, I admit that's strange –'

'And this was around her neck. It was broken but I had the link repaired.' She held the gold chain away from her throat.

'That has your name on it,' Melissa pointed out.

Hannah ignored her. 'I should really go to the police. Before you got here it was just the two of them. I'm sure she was still here when he arrived. I saw his car pull up.'

'We turned up early,' Melissa said dully, almost to herself. 'He was out of breath, clearing something away.'

'Summer was staying in the main house. He hid her bag down here, where nobody would find it.'

'Where is it now?'

'I saw him burn it in the incinerator. There's nothing left.'

'Why didn't you…? Oh, of course you can't say anything.' Melissa studied her face. 'What do you think happened?'

'He wanted to have sex with her before his wife arrived. She told me she wouldn't go through with it. She was worried that he might become violent. She's eighteen, Mrs Sutherland. He's a physically intimidating man. I think he killed her.'

Melissa's cigarette took a while to light.

'I think that by the time you and your husband turned up he'd managed to hide her body. He took her out there later.' Hannah pointed out to the valley spread below them. 'There are several mounds of earth over where the olive trees start. It's where the gardener gets his soil for the plant nursery. I think if I tell the police to dig them up they might find her.'

Melissa looked around and spotted the paperback of Agatha

Christie's *Five Little Pigs* on the chair. 'Read a lot of murder mysteries, do you? What is this girl to you?'

'She's – a friend.'

Melissa waved smoke away. 'How much of a friend? Okay, Hannah, let me tell you what probably happened. Mr Elsbury arranged to see this girl, they had an argument as you say and she stormed off. No one's been butchered and stuck under a tree, because that is not what civilised people do. If Mr Elsbury acted without propriety in any way, I'll take care of it. I won't mention this just yet.' She held up the letter. 'You're not the only one who's keeping an eye on things around here. If your friend turns up, make sure you let me know. My phone got damaged but this has my email address.' She handed Hannah her business card. 'You've done your part, but you're very lucky not to be fired. Do we have an understanding?'

Hannah nodded dumbly and pocketed the card.

'Good. No more notes.'

As she left Hannah behind in the pool house, Melissa felt vindicated. She had known all along that he was up to no good. The maid knew it too, but she was over-imaginative and anyway, who would believe her?

Melissa headed up the staircase toward the main house. Her husband was about to lose his job but information was power, and now she was in charge.

36.

After her confrontation with Melissa, Hannah found herself panicked and unable to settle. There was something calculating going on behind that woman's eyes. She was not to be trusted.

Hannah called the only person who saw her as a human being. Daniela picked her up on the way to get coffee in St Martin-sous-Roches.

As the Fiat entered the main square they passed an old man pinning a sheet of A4 paper to the patchwork bark of a pollarded tree. 'Qu'est-ce que c'est?' Daniela asked.

The photograph showed a sullen-looking girl in a hand-me-down dress covered in red flowers. She was nine or ten years of age, sun-darkened and slack-jawed. Her eyes were lost in shadow. There was something about her that did not look right. Underneath the photo was written: *Avez vous vue elle?* There followed a brief description of the child and a telephone number.

Daniela stopped to chat with the old man, so Hannah went ahead and ordered their coffees. When her co-worker finally came in she was so bursting with news that she could barely get the words out. 'I just got questioned by a gendarme! He wanted to search my car. *Enfin, il y a pas de lézard.*'

There is no lizard, Hannah thought, *and I have no idea what you're on about.*

'They're looking for a child. She went missing yesterday. Stolen, right out of the village! She's at risk from strangers because she's – I don't know the word for this.' Daniela tapped the side of her head. 'A bad brain. Something happened when she was small. Her father hit her when she was about four years old and she was never the same again. He went to jail. The village was divided because some of them took his side.'

'You got a lot of information quickly.' Hannah sipped her cooling latté. 'Where did she go missing from?'

'Right here in the village, taken off the street. Can you believe such a thing? The trouble is, her father's out of jail and living with a new woman, some tramp he dragged here from Marseille, so the police are very interested in him. She goes around complaining to everyone. She says he hits her. I was told that part the other day while I was buying croissants. Of course, they know me. They would never tell you.'

'I thought nothing much happened in these small villages.'

'Don't believe it. You can't imagine what goes on during the dark months, after the tourists have gone home. There are a lot of mothers and not many fathers, if you know what I mean. You have to be careful. If a little girl can just disappear who knows what else might happen?'

After their coffee, Daniela dropped her off at the Villa Lavardin. They arranged to meet later at the Champs D'Or.

As Hannah watched her drive away, she approached the house with a sense of dread. The villa appeared calm and silent. The Mercedes hatchback was outside, its engine ticking down, the bonnet still warm. Unfortunately the door was locked.

She thought at first that some kind of ripe red fruit had been squashed under the offside rear tyre. She dropped down and took a closer look. Her fingers came away from the rubber with a smear of rank-smelling blood on them. The tread was still wet and pulpy.

She dug a twig into the tread and removed more coagulated gore. It was roadkill, a squirrel or a fox, but it unsettled her. She tried to see if there was any soil on the driver's-side floor of the Mercedes. Giles and Jamie didn't drive, so it had to be one of the others. What if Steve had gone out early to move the body before anyone else had risen and had hit something on the way back?

What more could she do to force out the truth?

Later, while she waited for the spin dryer to finish, she checked Summer's Instagram account again. There had been nothing new posted since the middle of last week. Searching through the previous year's selfies she came across a shot of Jihane, bearded and pretty, French-Algerian, described as *totalement déboussolé,* which she thought meant disoriented, although perhaps it was slang.

She called him again. It was hard to explain how she felt without sounding paranoid. 'How well do you know Summer?' she asked when he answered. 'All she told me was that you met last year.'

'It's nine o'clock in the fucking morning,' said Jihane, groaning.

'Please, just tell me and I'll let you go back to sleep.'

'I was working in this crazy bar. She was trying to get away from someone. I felt sorry for her.'

'Why?'

'Hang on. Dry mouth.' She heard him heave himself upright and take a drink. 'She's one of those girls creeps always hang around, thinking they've got a chance if they flash the cash. She wasn't interested in their money. Her family is loaded. Poor little rich girl, right?'

'I'm not so sure about that,' said Hannah. 'But she knows her own mind. She wouldn't let anyone tell her what to do.'

'She told me she was bisexual, only she hadn't done it with a guy yet. I'm like Too Much Information, not interested, you know? I guess you still haven't heard anything. That's what, three and a half days now? Where are you?'

'I'm at the villa.' She lowered her voice. 'I found Summer's backpack hidden in a wardrobe.'

'What do you mean, hidden? You sure she didn't just leave it behind?'

'The man she was meeting burned it when he thought no one was looking.'

'Wait, wait – I'm kind of confused, did she leave the villa or didn't she?' Jihane sounded as if he was about to fall back to sleep. 'If her stuff is still there –'

'She never left the place alive, Jihane, don't you get it? She couldn't have gone anywhere. He took her passport, even burned her credit cards. There are fresh piles of earth in the garden but I can't do it alone.'

'Do what alone?'

'Dig them up! What if she's under there? Maybe he's moved her somewhere else, I just don't know. He could have buried her alive.'

'Sounds like you've really thought this through.'

'I know, it sounds crazy, but I'm not crazy.'

Jihane yawned. 'I'm out of my depth here. What do you want to do about it?'

'That's the question, isn't it? I don't know anymore. I can't just go up to someone and accuse them of murder.'

'You know there's a chance that Summer may just be fucking with you. With all of us.'

'I really hope not.'

'Honey, you have to face the fact that she might have gone off with another lover. Are you sure she didn't just have a fight with the married dude and walk out on him? I've seen what her temper's like. Now she can't come back until he's gone. Why don't you just ask him?'

'I can't afford to lose this job, which will happen if I ask the client whether he murdered his girlfriend.'

He stifled another yawn. 'They just found the body of a local working girl down here in the Old Town. She'd been stabbed like fifteen times or something. It happens all the time and you never get the full story from anyone. It's worse up in the hills because there's so much money laundering going on. How do you think they pay for all those great big villas? Everyone knows you don't fuck with the Russians or you end up becoming part of the landscape. Maybe she got friendly with someone in the village and did something she shouldn't have. You could ask around.'

'Why does everyone think it's her and not him? She's the victim! If I start asking questions it'll get back. They all know each other. You have to help me, Jihane.'

'Okay, I'll give it some thought but not until I'm awake, which will be much later.' He put the phone down on her.

The spin dryer beeped and began to slow. Once it had come to a complete stop the villa fell silent but she could still hear something, a high, keening wail that tailed away, caught in the tree breezes. But it was just a kite, hovering in the air currents.

She could no longer hear Summer calling to her.

37.

Every year the fiesta was held in dedication to Saint Saturnia, who had been raped and decapitated by a Saxon lord, after which she carried her own head into the church and swore to protect the women of the town from harm, although these days she was best remembered for scaring some wolves out of the apse when she was twelve.

A stone frieze showed a wild-haired child shooing the snarling creatures away, as if getting rid of the neighbourhood's stray cats. It was set in the wall of L'église de St Saturnia, the unornamented little church where these events supposedly took place, and had been garlanded with blue and yellow flowers and spotlit for the occasion. Stalls had been erected all around the village square, but tonight customers were thin on the ground.

The Elsburys and the Sutherlands walked there at Melissa's suggestion, because the idea of watching Giles marinade himself in red wine was every bit as boring in the Alps Maritimes as it was in London. Jamie had wisely elected to stay away. As he had not yet learned to drive he was stuck at the villa, but at least the place was quiet now. *I'm starting to see his point of view,* Jennifer thought. *Watching your parents drink to excess and buy overpriced tea towels isn't the most enticing prospect.*

The square was always draped in bunting and bordered with stalls during saints' days, but such events had lost their meaning and were now too frequent to excite much interest. They remained an excuse for the locals to catch up with gossip and sell trinkets to tourists, although a few of the village's oldest women still preferred to kneel and pray in the cold church.

'Look at these.' Jennifer took a pair of blue ceramic anchors from a stall and held them up. 'What do you think? Are they napkin rings or earrings?'

'I don't know but they suit you,' said Melissa vaguely. 'These table mats are made in China. Anyone for a raffia wine server? I thought raffia was invented to give mental patients something to do.'

They passed food stalls that tested the commonly held British faith in the Mediterranean diet: plastic gingham counters offering sugared dough balls, fried chicken and burgers. Falafel was the healthiest option available. In the corners of the square fathers lurked with baby buggies, furtively smoking while their wives ran the stalls and sat in little groups away from the men.

'They've got a pop-up bar,' said Giles cheerily. '*Le Chat Noir.* That's original.' He crossed through pools of light cast by the church lamps, making a beeline for its plywood serving counter. The church itself, Jennifer noticed, kept its main doors firmly closed against the event.

Giles was already ordering drinks as the others arrived. The bar consisted of several trestle tables and upright metal beer kegs, but the wine was heavy and local. 'Not much of a party atmosphere,' he complained. 'Look at them all, faces as long as Lent.'

It's true, Jennifer thought, *there's not much merriment to be had here.* A band due to appear tonight had apparently been cancelled.

'Not even any music.' Giles nudged the man next to him. 'No dancing tonight, eh?' He did a little jig. The man shot him a filthy look and moved off.

Jennifer could sense the hostility in the square. A few angry-looking farmhands stood in one corner with their arms folded, as if waiting for a fight to kick off. In the street behind the church most of the stalls were closing. It felt as if someone had tried to cancel the festivities and failed. She was suddenly sure that they were disrupting an unspoken privacy. *We shouldn't be here*, she suddenly felt, heading toward the makeshift bar where the others stood drinking.

One of the buggy-pushing young mothers looked friendly enough to speak to. 'Did something happen?' she asked in stiff Anglo-French.

'One of the children from the Dufayel farm is missing,' the woman told her. 'She's just ten years old.'

'That's awful.'

'She doesn't speak. She can only say her name. Everybody knows her. They wanted to cancel tonight's event.'

'I can understand why.'

'We don't have a special school here so her mother teaches

her at home. The police have asked everyone to look for her. They've taken the father and his girlfriend into custody.'

'Why, do the police think they had something to do with it?'

'There's a lot of talk, but then –' she shrugged, '– there's always talk.'

'What's the girl's name?'

'Clémence. The Dufayels are not much liked but tonight many are out helping the mother to look in the fields. Clémence knows the hills well – it's not possible she got lost. Maybe they will find her.'

'Well I hope they do,' said Jennifer. 'We're staying in the villa belonging to Madame Lavardin. Is there any way we can help?'

The lady shook her head. 'Clémence understands enough to stay around here. The police know the area they must search, they just haven't found her yet.'

'Thank you for letting me know. I hope they find her in good health.'

'God be with her.' The woman touched her heart.

Jennifer reached the bar just as Giles loudly announced, 'Come on, let's cheer these miserable buggers up.' He began singing along to a radio that was softly playing in one of the windows behind the counter.

She tried to stop him but it was too late. One of the other drinkers turned and told him to shut up. Giles pulled a face and waved him away, and a moment later came stumbling back with blood dripping from his nose.

'The bastard punched me!' he cried, shocked.

'Go home, stupid fucking *rosbif*,' shouted his attacker, turning away.

Steve grabbed Giles before he could come back, swinging him away from the counter. 'Come on, let's get you out of here.' He grabbed a tissue from the bar. 'Wipe your face.'

As they walked off, the man checked his knuckles while his friends gathered around him and glared back at them.

'I'm surprised that doesn't happen more often,' said Melissa, shakily lighting a cigarette as they walked into the darkened streets away from the town square. 'Are you all right?'

Giles wiped at his face but a thin rope of blood continued to form. 'Of course I'm not all right. I don't know what's got into them.'

'Do you ever stop to think how we seem to them?' She drew so hard on the cigarette that the paper crackled. 'We used to come to Europe and laugh at the provincials. Now it's the other way around. Sweet revenge.' It began to patter with rain. 'Wonderful, the perfect way to end the evening. What else could happen?'

'A woman who has a farm just up the hill from here has lost her little girl,' Jennifer said. 'She's been missing for over twenty-four hours. They think she's out in the woods somewhere. Everyone's wound up about it. I imagine that's why the village was full of police.'

'Remember how I lost Jamie in Epping Forest once?' said Steve. He turned to the others. 'He must have been about ten years old. After searching for ages and going out of my mind with worry I found him back at the car. He'd got lost and walked back without me.' Sensing that sympathy was not with him, he shut up.

Giles tried to tilt his head back as he walked. 'It feels like it's broken,' he mumbled miserably. Blood had spattered the front of his shirt and dripped onto his trousers. 'I wasn't to know, was I? He had no right to attack me like that.'

'It's not broken, it just looks worse than it is,' said Melissa, feeling the bridge of his nose as he yelped. 'You always make such a fuss about cuts and bruises.'

'I was assaulted without provocation,' Giles complained, glancing back nervously.

'That's a matter of opinion,' said Steve. 'If it's broken we'll have to reset it.'

Giles's eyes widened. 'How do you do that?'

'Break it the other way.'

They argued all the way back to the villa. The locals watched them go, making obscene gestures behind their backs.

38.

That night the rain was apocalyptic.

Water sluiced down the hills and cascaded across the roads, turning them into rushing brown rivers. Lost in his sonic world, Jamie had failed to shut any of the doors or windows. Jennifer came stamping inside, her light summer jacket transparent and stuck to her skin. They set about closing the villa against the weather.

'For God's sake, Jamie, didn't you even see there was rain coming in? Look at the floors!' The boy had curled up on one of the sofas surrounded by plates and mugs, hood up, headphones still in place. When Jennifer snatched them from his head he reacted as if she had thrown boiling water over him. 'Did you hear me? What's wrong with you?'

Melissa gave her arm a gentle touch. 'He's being a teenager.'

'He's my son,' Jennifer reminded her. 'I know how to deal with him.'

When the thunder rolled overhead it sounded as if the surrounding cliffs were tumbling down. Always happier when she was doing something, Jennifer made coffee for everyone. Giles took every opportunity to vocalise his suffering. He lay with his head back on a cushion, surrounded by tissues which he tried to get as bloody as possible, making a fuss about not making a fuss.

Jamie studied him as if looking at a lizard, but was not curious enough to ask what had happened. Jennifer's suggestion of a game of Scrabble was pointedly ignored. Steve flicked the pool lights on with the remote and stood at the window.

Runoff from the hill behind the villa flooded across the stone patio, striating the water's surface with streaks of reddish brown. For a moment he thought he saw a small hunched figure, dark and indistinct, standing by the rain-flattened hibiscus bushes. When he looked again all he could see was a stack of logs.

Jennifer made toasted sandwiches and hot drinks that nobody wanted, but her anger refused to abate. In her bedroom she opened the wardrobe drawer where she'd placed the gaudy sunglasses. They smelled of the same cheap scent she'd detected elsewhere in the house.

Thunder echoed over the roof once more, flickering the lamps. A circuit overloaded with a soft pop, and the pool lights went out. It took Steve a while to find the fuse box. When he returned, Melissa was waiting for him on the terrace with a pair of large scotches. She handed one to him.

'I thought you might need this as we're the last ones left up. The others weren't too keen about sitting around in the dark. Well, that was quite a night.'

'Agreed.' He raised his glass to hers.

'There's something I need to talk to you about.'

'Please, not Giles again, not tonight.'

'This is rather more serious. It turns out that our maid is a friend of the girl you brought out.'

Steve kept his poker face and sipped his whisky in silence.

'She's threatening to go to the police.' She watched him set down his drink with great deliberation. 'I'm telling you this as a friend.'

'Hannah,' he said, as if struggling to place the name. 'I spoke to her yesterday. Why didn't she say something?'

'Put yourself in her position. She's intimidated by you.'

He shook his head in wonderment. 'I have no idea why she would make up something like this.'

'Hannah was here last week. She *met* her, Steve.' Melissa tried again. 'She feels very uncomfortable about it and doesn't want to lose her job. Her friend hasn't been seen since Saturday. Was anyone else here when you arrived?'

Steve looked out across the pool. It took him a minute to answer. 'This is getting out of hand. What exactly am I being accused of?'

'Evidently there *was* a girl,' Melissa said carefully, placing a hand on his chest. 'I'm sure you didn't do anything bad and I can understand why you don't want to talk about it, but she left a letter for your wife to find. Just hearsay of course, but it's lucky I got to it first.'

'A letter? I can have her fired.'

'Then you'll give her a reason to take it further. Let me deal with it. I think she's just got a little confused. There's been a mix-up, that's all, but an accusation can still stick even if it's wrong.'

He looked hard into her eyes. 'Listen to me. No girl will turn up because I did not meet her here.'

'But you met –'

'In London, yes, I talked to a girl, that's all, but not here. Someone has an overheated imagination. The maid probably made this whole thing up. The others need to understand that.'

'I can help you there. But you can do something for me.'

He looked down at her hand resting on his chest.

'I know you're angry. I know Giles has screwed up but don't abandon him. He looks up to you. Let him go if you have to, but do it on good terms. He's been through a lot. If you do that, I'll take care of this for you.'

'You know his leads are no good, Melissa.'

'He isn't trying to deceive you. He hasn't seen those people for years. He honestly thinks they remember him.'

'Let me see what the note says.'

She unfolded the page and held it up for him to read. When he moved to take it from her she placed it back inside her shirt. 'So do we have a deal? I'll sort out your problem if you look after Giles.'

'That's blackmail.'

'No, Steve, it's insurance.' She patted him on the shoulder and headed to the gardens.

Steve had always been fearless, ready to set an example to others. Now he felt a weight of dread descending upon him, and no amount of lying could set him free. Two years ago Jennifer had discovered some messages he had been sent from a waitress in Manchester. He flinchingly recalled the texts, sent without any understanding that their meeting was a one-off, a momentary lapse of judgement on his part.

He had deleted them and sworn his faithfulness, but after that Jennifer no longer trusted him. Overnight he became a model husband, a perfect father. He stayed home because it was expected of him, and began to think of his watchful wife as someone in a permanently bad mood.

Looking back, he knew he should have shown self-restraint, but then there would have been no risk. That was where the real pleasure lay. The modern world was risk-averse.

He needed to feel alive. That was what women didn't understand.

39.

The wind punched down from the hills into the streets of Nice. A muddy crimson dawn broke and Hannah dragged herself from damp, tangled bedsheets to get ready for work. She had barely slept. Images of Summer had been rolling over in her head like a loop of film, but now they had become muddled with the disappearance of Clémence.

In her mind's eye she saw Giles talked into buying dope from the gardener, taking the car to get cash from the ATM in the village. On the way back he hit a little girl as she darted out across the road. He had alcohol in his system and was carrying drugs. Knowing he could go to jail, he jumped out and looked for a place to hide her. He panicked, laying her in a ditch that subsequently filled with water. It was nearly the plot of a paperback she had filched from the Russian villa.

Daniela was waiting for her on their designated street corner shortly after nine. The journey up to St Martin-sous-Roches took longer than usual because Hannah had to keep climbing out of the car to move rocks. Several times she needed to guide Daniela around heavy falls of red earth. The air was rich and loamy, as if the hillside had ruptured into open wounds.

'Sometimes so many stones come down that the maintenance crews just paint new yellow lines around them,' said Daniela. 'God makes this landscape beautiful and every now and again he destroys it. I keep thinking of that poor little girl, out in the storm. The police are going from house to house, but everyone knows what happened.'

'They do?' Hannah tried not to look at the crevasses racing past the car.

'This isn't the first time Clémence has been lost. She wanders off all the time. She's never been properly cared for.'

Suddenly Summer's disappearance had been pushed into second place by this phantom child. Hannah almost resented her for claiming the spotlight.

'The family has already started to mourn, that's how much hope they hold out,' said Daniela, reliably gloomy.

'You don't think someone deliberately abducted her?'

'Why? Her parents aren't rich. Maybe it was the father's girlfriend, the crazy *putain*. You hear all sorts of rumours.' Daniela crunched over a small rockfall, momentarily losing control of the Fiat. 'They say her father isn't her father, that he looks after Clémence for someone who was unfit to raise her. The girl's existence is an embarrassment. Maybe the police know more than they say, what do I know? She's been out in this weather for forty-eight hours. Last night I prayed and lit a candle for her. She knows the land. There are many small caves and hiding places. She plays in all of them.'

'Perhaps she was hit by a car that didn't stop. Perhaps she's still lying by the side of the road somewhere.'

'I'm sure that was they first thing they checked.' Daniela ground the gears and screeched the Fiat to a halt. 'I don't know, maybe somebody did take her. There are godless people who are prepared to take revenge by hurting an innocent child. Her father has quite a few enemies.'

'How much longer do you think they'll keep looking?'

Daniela shrugged. 'Until there is no chance that she can still be alive. Once there was a farmer's boy up here who lived on the land for nearly a month. He knew what to eat and where to find water. This was a long time ago. Children nowadays, I'm not so sure. Clémence knows the fields better than she knows people. She is not a likeable child, more like an animal. They arrested the father but they're always arresting him, it doesn't mean anything.'

'You seem sure of that,' Hannah replied.

'I know her mother. *Les chiens ne font pas des chats.*'

Hannah assumed she meant that the apple didn't fall far from the tree. She alighted from the car and took a deep breath. The air was scrubbed clean, the sun so bright and hard that it felt as if the ground would start steaming.

'Don't be fooled,' Daniela said. 'There are thunderstorms forecast for the next few days.' Her phone rang. 'This will be Julia, wanting me to explain why we're running late.'

'How does she know?'

'She tracks me on GPS.'

'You're kidding. Is she allowed to do that?'

Daniela rolled her eyes. 'Do you think she would care? You've met her, haven't you?'

Hannah thanked her and let herself into the villa via the back gate.

The patio was a mess. The area around the pool was covered in tidemarks of earth, so she hosed down the stones. It felt as if she was washing away the past. The trail had gone cold.

She was just setting the loungers back in a line when Melissa came and found her. She was wearing a striped black and yellow dress and looked like a wasp. Stopping before her, she lit a cigarette. 'You always seem to be here. Your other clients must be getting jealous.'

'It's a big house. I have a long list of things to do.'

'I should tell you I decided to show Steve the note. He's absolutely positive he hasn't seen the girl since he got here.'

'If he didn't see her why would he burn her things?' Hannah set down a chair and rose to face her. 'He's lying to keep the truth from getting out. He can't just deny her existence.'

'I want to help you, Hannah, but do you have any evidence? Real evidence, not just items of clothing?'

'No,' said Hannah vehemently, 'but he does. He still has her passport. I saw him put it in his pocket.'

'Are you sure about that?' asked Melissa. 'Nobody else saw her.'

Hot blood suffused her cheeks. 'That's not true! Jihane, the boy she met on holiday, he was there when she got into a fight at the local bar. Raphael, the owner, he saw her, and so did the men who drink there. The gardener, Matthias – and my boss, who gave her the house keys! And me, and Steve, about a dozen people in all.'

'So it's "Steve" now? Let me play devil's advocate for a

minute.' Melissa waved a curl of smoke away and rested her right elbow on the left hand. 'Are you sure you all saw the same person?'

'Of course. I'd recognise Summer anywhere.'

'One pretty young girl is very much like the next. Think carefully. Could they have been different people?'

The idea was absurd. The way Summer looked, everybody noticed her. 'No, it's not possible,' she said, shaking her head.

Melissa crushed out her cigarette on the stucco wall and flicked it into the flowers. 'I must admit I didn't expect Steve to deny meeting up with her. You've got me believing she exists.'

Hannah was lost for words.

'You…' Melissa began. 'You haven't had any – problems – in the past, have you?'

'What do you mean? You think I just go around making things up?'

'Well, it all seems to come from you.'

She was horrified by the idea. 'I've never had any problems, I'm perfectly fine. I didn't know what else to do.'

'You need someone to back up your story,' Melissa suggested. 'I think you should hold off doing anything until after we've gone. It would be better for everyone.'

Hannah was exasperated. 'Why won't you believe me?'

'Because you're telling me that he murdered his secret girlfriend and hid her somewhere out there in the fields,' said Melissa. 'I need proof.'

'Then help me find her body.'

'Fine, I'll meet you at midnight armed with a lantern and a shovel and we'll go digging up the hillside, shall we?'

'Wait, I have her phone. I found it on the path below the patio.' She pulled it from her pocket and showed Summer's nude selfie to Melissa.

'Good lord. Not shy, is she? Well, it's *somebody's* phone.'

'You can see it was taken right beside the pool.'

'Is there anything that explicitly mentions Steve?'

'I think she avoided texting him in case his wife found the messages. Or she erased them.'

'Then find me the passport,' Melissa said, 'and I'll go with you to the police.'

As Melissa left, Hannah remained in the middle of the patio, unsure what to do. Finally she straightened her uniform and went up to the main house.

The other guests nodded to her as she passed through them, accepting her as a silent presence, someone they did not have to befriend. In the English manner of avoiding embarrassment there was no acknowledgement of their conversations. It made things less awkward for everyone.

Yet nothing was normal about the scene. Steve was making an anxious phone call on the terrace. Giles had a swollen nose and a puffy violet smudge below his left eye. Jennifer had taken a book out to one of the overstuffed sofas under the villa's eaves and was ostentatiously pretending to read it. Melissa had gone into the kitchen. Hannah watched as she poured what looked suspiciously like vodka into her glass of orange juice.

Her phone suddenly lit up; Jihane had sent a text.

Near you in St Martin-sous-Roches around lunchtime! Want to meet up?

The café in the square, she texted back. *I can get there by 1pm.*

She needed to locate the passport. If she could find it and give it to Jihane he could take it to the police. She didn't trust Melissa to help her. How many places were there to look?

She made her way to the first-floor bedroom corridor and listened. It sounded as if everyone was downstairs. She checked the drawers in Steve's half of the wardrobe, but found nothing. His trouser pockets were empty. Where would he keep his valuables? This wasn't a hotel; there was no safe.

Beside his bed a side table held cufflinks, some small change and his copy of *The Twelve Caesars*. When she picked up the book, the passport fell out.

Stunned that he could leave it there in plain sight of his wife, she slipped it inside her shirt.

Steve walked in. He looked surprised to see her.

'Everything okay up here?' he asked, leaning against the door. As usual he wore a freshly pressed white shirt and navy slacks, as impeccable as a magazine advertisement. She kept her distance. Now that he knew about the note he had the air of a shark scenting blood in the water.

'I saw you talking to Melissa,' he said with an air of false apology. 'I hope she wasn't being an awkward guest.'

'No, she just wanted me to take in some dry-cleaning for her,' she said.

'She didn't have any in her arms.'

'In her room.' Hannah cleared her throat. 'It's in her room.'

'You and I haven't really had a chance to talk.' He smiled warmly, the indulgent host. 'I hope we're not too messy for you. There must be a lot for you to do because you're always here.'

He walked to the window and looked out. 'There's a smell of drains. They probably got blocked in last night's storm. Can you call someone?'

'I'll tell the manager.' She moved toward the door, careful to let him see that she had nothing in her hands.

'So – Hannah, if you need anything, make sure you come and talk to me, yes?' Another smile, open and inviting. 'The villa's booking is in my name. I'm the only person you need to deal with, so I'll probably be able to help you best.' He paused for a moment, as if struck by a sudden thought. 'Were you cleaning here last week?'

'Yes.'

'You came in once, twice? More than twice?'

'Several times.'

'Hm. Well, that's good to know.' He drummed his fingers on the door frame and suddenly stopped, as if reaching a decision. 'Remember, if you have any problems, talk to me first. And if anything else occurs to me don't worry – I can always come and find you. I know where you are.'

For the first time it crossed her mind that her own life might be in danger.

FOUR:
THE BLAME

40.

If a giraffe wandered into the café he'd get fewer looks, Hannah thought. Jihane appeared incredibly out of place. The boy was long necked, slight and slender, with ridiculously large brown eyes. The sides of his head were shaved, leaving a mop of bleached hair that stood up like a feather duster when he removed his crash helmet. He looked as if a light breeze might blow him over the next hill. He sat opposite Hannah and drank his espresso in one gulp, a bundle of nervous energy.

'I had to pick up some plants for Mrs Chen. There's a big garden centre at the top of the hill.' He looked over his shoulder. 'I hate it up here. They don't like Algerians.'

'That fight,' said Hannah. 'What actually happened?'

He leaned forward, lowering his voice. 'Summer was wearing this tiny rah-rah skirt covered in sequins. I don't know what she was thinking. The guys had their tongues hanging out.'

'Was she flirting with them?'

'No – just being herself. There was a guy called Jacob who looked like he'd been kicked in the head by a horse, he couldn't take his eyes off her and put his hand under her skirt, just reached over and grabbed. We tried to keep things cool but he wouldn't take no for an answer and there was a scuffle, and he caught Summer in the face by mistake.'

'And she was okay about it?'

'I thought she'd throw a fit but ten seconds later she'd already forgotten it happened. Look, I don't want you to think I don't care about her but I can't afford to get involved in this. People come and go all the time around here.'

She took out Summer's passport and put it on the table between them. 'It's him, Jihane. The man she arranged to see killed her.'

Jihane picked up the passport and examined it. He shifted uneasily. 'I think you've got yourself into something you can't handle.'

'I know, I should have done what was expected of me and stayed out of trouble, but it's too late for that. Would you take it to the police?'

Jihane closed the passport and slid it back across the table to her. 'I can't. I've had enough trouble with them. I'm sure she'll turn up at some point with a random boy or girl in tow.'

'You think it's her, don't you?' Hannah was disappointed in him. 'You think she planned it all and vanished without taking her stuff so she could mess with his head. I called the airline and got nowhere with them. They couldn't let her board without a passport but they wouldn't even tell me that. Apparently they can only inform a family member. It must be possible to find out what he did with her.'

Jihane ran a hand through a clump of hair. 'She used this

guy to get out here, then left her old life behind. She probably used you too, and dumped you when a better offer came up.'

Hannah felt like yelling. Everyone seemed determined to frustrate her. 'Everyone keeps telling me that people go missing in places like this. I'm going to find her, Jihane. Would you help me dig up the garden?'

'Whoa, whoa.' He pushed back from the table. 'Summer's pretty messed up. Damaged people drag others down with them.'

'I know she had behavioural problems, she was in care for a while. It means she was vulnerable.'

'It's not my job to look out for her.'

'It's okay,' said Hannah, 'you don't have to make excuses.'

'It's different for me.'

'Why?'

'I'm not the one who's in love with her, Hannah.'

Jihane stood and picked up his crash helmet. She watched as he started his motorbike and roared off down the hill.

A steamy jungle heat was rising from the garden greenery. Hannah stood beside the thorny wall of bougainvillea below the deep end of the pool and listened intently to the conversation taking place above her.

'What's the matter?' Jennifer asked her husband.

Hannah moved over to the staircase and peered above the edge of the patio. Brown stains had spread across the tiled floor of the deep end of the pool. As Steve swam through the murky water they were lifted into tendrils that dissipated, settling again as he passed. Reaching the shallow end, he was unable to find the steps.

'Let me help you.' Jennifer waded in and held out her arms. Gripping his wrists, she gently guided him in and hauled him upwards.

'My eye,' he complained. 'It's burning.'

'Let me see.'

He turned to her and opened his left eye wide. 'I think I've got something in it.'

Jennifer could see it was edged in crimson. 'You've had some kind of allergic reaction. I'm not surprised with all that earth in the water.'

'You look like someone poked you with a stick,' said Giles. 'You can't go into meetings looking like that, old chap.'

'Well I can't let you take them for me, can I?' Steve rubbed at his eyelid. 'Not with a black eye and a broken nose.'

'You said it wasn't broken.' Giles indignantly touched his face.

Melissa ignored her husband. 'I have something that will take the redness out. They're just eyedrops but I use them all the time. I'll get them.' She headed back to her room.

Giles watched her go. 'She runs around after you, but not me,' he said jealously.

Jennifer studied Steve's eyes. 'A lot of sediment got washed into the pool from the terraces last night, and you don't know what kind of chemicals the gardener uses. Better stay out of the pool until it's been cleaned. You should complain to that woman in the loud jacket: you're paying her enough.'

Hannah made her move, keeping low as she reached the base of the far staircase.

Melissa took an age to find the eye drops. When she returned, she handed them to Jennifer, who read the label on the bottle.

'It says for tired eyes. At least it's antiseptic.'

Steve put in the drops and laid back on the lounger. The sun started to disappear behind a bank of rising grey clouds.

'I think that's the end of the good weather,' said Giles. 'Just as well. It's nearly time for our meeting in Nice. Any chance of some scoff to take with us?'

'There's a fridge,' said Melissa. 'Why don't you stick your head in it?'

'Giles, I can make a sandwich if you'd like that,' Jennifer offered.

'Thanks Jen, but I fancy a bit of red meat,' said Giles. 'Steve, what if we go in a little earlier and check out the special in that café, Auberge Fred or something, get ourselves a couple of steaks?'

Steve didn't answer. He was sick of Giles and his endless trivialities, the false bonhomie he sprayed over everyone like a toxic crop chemical. Everyone could see he had made a huge mistake inviting Giles into the company. The old school 'chums' in his legendary address book treated him with poorly concealed contempt. One referred to him throughout their meeting as 'Piggy', jovially adding that it was what everyone had called him, after the character in *Lord of the Flies*.

The drops didn't seem to be helping. Something was irritating the corner of his left eye. He rolled a tissue into a point and dabbed the paper spear into his tear duct. After some fishing and wiping he was able to find the source of problem, a tiny crescent of what looked like red plastic. He flicked it away with a grimace of disgust. In shadow the place felt haunted, as if Summer had deliberately chosen to stay around and unsettle him. The patio had darkened. A distant rumble sounded.

The first fat drop of rain was the size of a two-pound coin and splattered onto the tiles, leaving a mark like a paintball bullet. Steve opened his sore eyes and rose from the lounger, gathering up his belongings. They headed back into the villa just as the clouds rolled down toward the rooftops.

Hannah raised her head above the edge of the patio wall and looked for the spot where Steve had flicked the speck in his eye. She needed to find it before the rain washed it away. After looking for a minute she found a tiny crescent of coral nail polish. Summer had complained that her nail varnish was chipping. *If I was Summer*, she thought, *next time I'd do something much worse than just hurt his eye.*

She sat hunched in the corner of the side staircase and chewed her thumbnail. She needed a way of proving Steve's guilt. How long would it be before he realised that she had taken the passport?

She could think of no further reason to remain lurking around the villa this afternoon. The snippets of conversation she had overheard amounted to nothing. She was deciding what to do when Daniela called to say she had finished her villa and was going to the village. It would be a relief to get out of the house.

As she left she saw Steve watching her, anxiously moving from window to window, keeping her in his sight until she was lost behind the trees.

41.

The day had dawned as dark as night. Hannah showered, dressed and caught the bus to the villa. She needed to surrender one last piece of evidence. After mailing the nude selfie to herself, she placed Summer's phone in a spot where only Mrs Elsbury would find it.

Clipping shut her clear plastic cagoule, she set off for the village. Her weather app was forecasting light rain, not this. A dense blue-black wall of cloud had risen above the cliff-tops like castle ramparts, and began flickering with distant fire. The wind was rising through the firs. No cars passed her by. Fast-flowing streams punched pathways across the road.

The village appeared derelict. The houses on the eastern side of the square had shuttered their windows against the coming storm. A threadbare mongrel sat nuzzling its balls at the side of the road.

In Chez Dany the drinkers were lined up at the bar as if they had been appointed to protect the bottles. Raphael watched Hannah come in and started to make a coffee, which politeness dictated she would have to drink. For some strange reason he had taken a liking to her.

'You'll need more than that when the rain starts.' He indicated her cagoule. 'Do you want something to eat?'

'I'm waiting for Daniela.' She had experienced his desiccated sandwiches. 'Any news about the Dufayel girl?'

'There's going to be a service for Clémence today. That's all the old ones do around here, hold services and pray.'

'But are the police still searching for her? There has to be a simple answer. She must have got lost while she was playing.'

Raphael placed a burnt-smelling coffee before her. 'My dear Hannah, you are not from here. The countryside is not for children to play in. If you leave the road you can't walk anywhere in one direction for very long. There are cracks in the rocks big enough to fit your leg into. You can hear water rushing underneath, but you can't see it. Sometimes the run-off pumps out of the cliff in jets that can throw a clod of earth into the air. I've seen the mountain swallow a goat.'

One of the other drinkers snorted with laughter. 'You're full of shit, Raphael. You've been drinking your own calvados again.'

Raphael smelled of brandy and the parma violets he ate to make his wife think he didn't drink before noon. Today he wore a collarless shirt that revealed a deep scar on his neck. Together with the port-wine patch it lent him the air of a mythological beast that had fought many wars. 'I think she's down one of those crevasses with her leg broken, unconscious or dead,' he said gloomily. 'What nobody understands is why.'

'What do you mean?'

'The girl grew up in these hills. She knows you stay on the road. People are saying her mother was drunk again.'

Hannah thought about the sparse road traffic. 'There could have been a car. Would she have got in if someone had driven past her and stopped?'

'She's been told not to, but I don't know if she understands. How are the *rosbifs*? I hear one of them got punched in the face.' Someone in the back of the bar laughed.

'I think it was a misunderstanding. He didn't know about Clémence.'

'He should be more respectful. I guess they won't be coming back. The English are cheap but at least they're polite.'

She peered out at the blackened sky. Daniela pulled up, thumping her front tyre into the kerb.

'You'll have to go back to the Lavardin this afternoon for the linen van,' she said, sliding into the opposite seat and signalling for a coffee. 'The driver won't deliver to the Champs D'Or because he says nobody hears the front doorbell. Call me when it arrives and I'll collect it from you. I hope the driver hangs around because he's big and cute. And Julia may need you to do one of the harbour flats so you'd better leave your phone on, just for today. When the storms come the buses stop so it's difficult to get about.'

'I don't want to get stuck at the villa,' Hannah said, emptying sugar into her coffee to alleviate its bitterness. 'It's giving me the creeps.' She looked out across the empty square. Leaves and litter were being blasted across the cobbles.

'They used to call it the Villa Loco,' Daniela told her. 'There was always trouble up there. Julia found it hard to get maids for Madame Lavardin.'

'Now you tell me,' said Hannah. 'You mean the house is bad?'

'No, of course not, but people are bad and they leave their mark. There are happy houses and unhappy ones, that's all,' Daniela replied gloomily. 'You know the house on the other side of the valley?'

'The one with the green tiles?'

'Madame Lavardin lives up there by herself. She moved out of La Terrasse the day after her husband died, but could never quite bear to be out of sight of her old home. Her husband Emil used to beat her like a gong.'

Hannah was agog. 'How do you know?'

Daniela leaned forward. 'Everybody knows. He was in the money-moving business. Matthias the gardener worked for him, and the chief of police would bring his cronies over. Then one day, out of the blue, Emil is put in a closed casket. We all know what really happened. It certainly wasn't suicide. Nobody shoots themselves with a hunting rifle, except in the foot. And it wasn't old Lavardin. She couldn't even lift such a weapon.'

'So what did happen?'

'Someone from the village shot him. Probably from the gendarmerie, so of course no one was ever charged.'

'Why didn't you tell me this before?' Hannah asked.

Daniela gave a shrug. 'You're a stranger. There are people living up here for the last twenty years who are still called newcomers.' She checked her phone. 'The linen van won't arrive for a couple of hours. I'm afraid you have some time to kill.'

'How do you get to Madame Lavardin's house from here?'
Hannah asked.

'If you go by car it's longer, but you can walk there easily
enough.'

'Would you show me?'

'I can draw you a map.' Daniela took out a felt-tip pen and
drew on a napkin. 'Be careful if you're planning to talk to her.
She's as prickly as a cactus.'

'Perhaps I should take her some patisserie.'

'She doesn't eat, only drinks.' She threaded her arm through
her coat. 'I have to come back later to collect my son. I usually
let him have a pizza on Thursdays. Would you like to meet
him after you finish?'

Not particularly, Hannah thought, but agreed to come back.

Raphael impersonated a gentleman by holding the door of
Chez Dany open for Daniela. 'I think she spends more time here
than at home,' he said, watching her go.

'So do all of them.' She moved to a counter stool, nodding
in the direction of the career drinkers who clustered around
the far end of the bar.

'That's different, they're men,' Raphael said, as if his answer
was obvious.

She wasn't sure why he was so nice to her, but she was
grateful even though his coffee tasted the way an ironing board
scorch smelled.

'Your boss was up here looking at a new property the other
day. She always asks about you. She doesn't trust you.'

'Julia doesn't trust anybody,' Hannah told him. 'What have
I done wrong?'

'You haven't done anything wrong. She doesn't like her clients.'

'Why not?'

'You don't think they choose to live up here because of the scenery, do you? They don't want to be found, and it's best not to ask why. There are many secrets in these hills.'

'What kind of secrets?'

'They still talk about a Russian near here who so lived in fear of his business partners that he installed a foolproof security system in his house locking all the door and windows. Soon after he was burned to death by the only person he trusted, his butler, who set fire to the villa and left him inside. True story. You pass the ruins of the house near the turn-off to the Haute Corniche. The police left it there as a warning.' He set a glass of coffee before her.

'Daniela told me there's still no sign of the little girl.' She sipped at the coffee tentatively.

'One of the farmhands was working among the olive trees in the lower fields. He told the police that he saw Clémence walking with someone on Tuesday afternoon, but she was too far away for him to see clearly. He drinks, of course, but if it was her it's the last time she was spotted.'

'But you don't think it was an abduction.'

'I didn't say that. But if somebody did take her maybe he drove past her on the way to the Villa Lavardin. There's nothing else on that road until you reach it.'

'I'm at the house every day. I clean it from top to bottom. I've met all the guests – it's not possible.'

Raphael shrugged. 'All I'm saying is it's more likely to be

an outsider, someone on the road who stopped to give a little girl a lift.'

Or someone who accidentally hit her, she thought, remembering the hatchback's tyre rimed in animal blood.

42.

Madame Lavardin's house proved almost impossible to find from the main road.

Hannah passed a blockade of police cars. So the search was still being taken seriously. Officers were walking across the fields to the right of the road. They were bent over, moving with precise equal paces, fanning out in a line that headed north. The ground was steep and pitted. Agaves and thorny bracken sprouted between the olive trees, slowing down the search.

The road beyond looked impassable. Some of the sandy cliffs had calved and crumbled across the tarmac. The municipality had sent workmen to clear a lane, but they had not made much headway.

The drawing Daniela had made for Hannah on a napkin proved to be impressionistic rather than accurate. Where she had placed a turn-off from the corniche there were only boulders and fir trees. She turned the napkin around but it made no more sense the other way up.

Then it dawned on her; what she had taken to be a river

was in fact the stone path indicated on Daniela's map. A bore of sepia water gushed across the path, buffeted by the grass banks that had turned it into a watercourse. By clambering onto the highest mound she was able to follow the diagram. Rainwater dripped down her chest from the hood of her cagoule. She needed to get under shelter.

A spur of pine trees curtained the green-tiled house from its access. Daniela had told her that the old lady lived alone. At this altitude the steep path must be icy in winter. How did she manage to get out?

The house was drab, modern and surprisingly modest, a rectangular box that squatted in a patch of cleared woodland in deliberate defiance of the region's more romantic notions. It had a green-painted front door, small unadorned windows and sensors that flashed crimson in the grass as she approached.

The door was half open before she reached the front step. A woman in her mid-seventies stared out, heavily made-up, clothes shapeless and black, her black hair white at the roots and tied back.

'Who are you?' She had a strong Niçoise accent.

'My name is Hannah. I work for Julia Martinez at *Vacances Paradis*. I'm looking after your old villa. I wonder if you could spare a minute?'

For a moment Madame Céline Lavardin appeared not to have heard. However, she opened the door a fraction wider.

The rooms were dark and heavy with furniture, as if the contents of a larger house had been forced into storage here. The old lady picked her way through the armchairs, between overloaded occasional tables. No amount of floral perfume

could mask the smell of boiled vegetables and rooms kept too
long shut.

'You say you're "looking after" the villa. I assume that means
you're cleaning it.' She touched the jade necklace at her throat.

'Yes, I am.' Hannah followed her back and was ordered to
a lumpy sofa covered in quilted irises. 'I love the villa – who
wouldn't? You lived there for so long –'

'So you knock on my door because you just happened to
be passing. Nobody passes. They come for a purpose, usually
to get money out of me.' Madame Lavardin's face might have
been carved from the cliffs themselves. Her dense makeup
formed a thick protective mask.

Just be honest, Hannah decided. *She'll see right through you if
you're not.* 'There's an atmosphere in the rooms. It's hard to
explain. I thought if I met you –'

'We built it.' Madame Lavardin cut across her. 'We had
many houses then, long before you were born. My husband
Emil never wanted to be tied to one place or one woman. If you
knew how he did business you would understand. I never
knew who might be going to call.'

'What line was he in?'

Madame Lavardin's throaty laugh turned into a cough.
Her hand rested on the edge of a mantelpiece lined with small
monochrome photographs, a carefully curated timeline of
memories. 'Buying, selling, what do you want me to say?
The people who came to the villa for dinner, little men
who thought they were big, and their ridiculous wives. I
didn't know what they did and never understood what they
talked about.'

'I didn't mean to pry,' Hannah said hastily. 'It's none of my business.'

'And yet you came here, so listen to me. I'm too old to keep secrets.' Madame Lavardin hunted down a cigarette and lit it with a dry brown hand. 'It was always about money, where to keep it, when to move it, how to hide it. The chief of police would sit in the kitchen drinking brandy. It felt as if everyone knew what was going on except me. Emil always said stay in the kitchen, it's safer that way. I suppose they told you I shot him?'

'There was some talk about it in the village.'

'There would be. They know a thing or two about scandal. They cheat on their wives to get their cousins pregnant, then take sides and don't speak to each other for generations.'

She flicked her cigarette over a piece of scalloped white porcelain with deliberate carelessness.

'Emil lived in fear of his enemies coming to the house, and did everything he could to protect himself. Someone he trusted let themselves in. I was there when it happened, and because my husband was friends with the police chief there was no investigation. Emil was tired of running. Men tire easily. Women endure.'

Madame Lavardin had the bluntness of extreme age. 'Emil brought money into St Martin-sous-Roches. Everyone knew it, and everyone pretended they didn't know how he got it. They never asked questions while they were getting rich.' She moved around the sofa, holding onto its back. 'This is how it once was. Look, look.'

The painting above the sideboard showed the Villa Lavardin from the pool patio. Five doors, four chimneys, rows of windows in sharp sunlight, the surrounding trees in full spring greenery. It was truly amateurish.

'When did you paint it?' Hannah asked.

'Sometime in the early 1970s, I forget when exactly.'

'You didn't want to stay on after he died?'

She set her cigarette in the scalloped dish, leaving fierce red lipstick on the filter. 'Emil never gave me children. It was quiet when we lived there, the house full of men making plans, working into the night, but it was a lot quieter after his death. No, I didn't want to stay there. My husband brought darkness into our home.'

'But you can still see the villa from here.'

'Yes, I can still see it. But from a distance.'

Hannah's arms felt cold. She rubbed their backs. 'There's a feeling I get when the sun goes behind the trees, as if someone is out there –'

The old lady's laugh turned into a phlegmy cough. 'Why do you think I'm here? That feeling never goes away. You can't just paint the walls and change the furniture. This place is only seven years old, so there are no ghosts.'

'You don't mind people thinking you killed him?'

'They can talk about me all they like. It's a very small village; there's not much else to do. Let them think I did it. I quite enjoy my role as a murderess. It gets me faster service at the boulangerie.'

'What do you think happened?'

'Emil hid himself behind locked doors. I knew he was going to be punished by someone in the village. I don't know who, and it hardly matters. After he died there were no more visits

to the house from unpleasant men. The police stayed away.
When there's no reason to look for an answer, answers aren't
found. That's how it works around here. I don't go out anymore,
certainly not to La Terrasse.'

Hannah hesitated. 'I think something bad has happened
there again.'

Mme Lavardin's smile had something of the grave about
it. 'I'm not surprised. But it's no concern of mine anymore.'
Her smile faded. 'Oh, I see. You're sensitive to these things.
Something happened to you.'

Hannah didn't know how to explain. 'My husband…' she
began.

The old lady regarded her. 'Hm. We should drink.'

Hannah realised that the little silver-plated trolley beside
the sofa had some of Raphael's home-made calvados on it. 'I'm
working today,' she said.

Madame Lavardin deftly poured two glasses and raised hers
in a toast. 'You can drink and work, you're in France.'

Hannah had not meant to talk about herself, but once she
started she could not stop. Aidan's death, Summer's appearance
– everything came out. She stayed longer than she had
intended.

Madame Lavardin was clearly enjoying herself. She knocked
back the remains of her sizeable brandy. 'Women get used to
living with such feelings,' she said. 'We know what pain feels
like.' She uncorked the bottle once more. 'I think we'd better
have another one, don't you?'

'But I don't know what to do,' Hannah said, offering her glass.

'I think you do,' said Madame Lavardin. 'When no one else

believes you, you have to take matters into your own hands. You English are all so reticent. There's no point in accusing the man. Men shut down when they are accused. You must tell the wife. We're the ones who always have to take action.'

Hannah slipped her hand into the pocket of her jacket. Her fingers brushed the edge of Summer's passport. 'I think I know what to do,' she said.

43.

When Jennifer opened her handbag to look for a tissue she found a red corner sticking up. Lifting out the passport, she turned to its photograph and found herself looking at a girl with straight blonde hair and frank blue eyes. She looked like a Woodstock-era hippy chick or a Manson acolyte.

Jennifer had only left the bag unattended on the kitchen counter for three or four minutes. Locking herself in the bathroom, she breathed out very slowly and studied her face in the mirror. The creases in her forehead had lately become permanent. She felt quite calm and composed. What shocked her most was that she did not find herself questioning the evidence at all. It condensed her worst suspicions into a single unifying truth.

There had always been shadows within Steve that made his behaviour hard to fathom. When he had told her about the two-week booking he had made it sound like an oversight. Now his real intentions were apparent. He had brought the girl to the same spot where he was bringing his wife because the idea excited him.

She ticked off the points on her fingers. His jumpiness, her belongings, his guilty looks; everything suddenly made sense. Before the trip she had heard him making hushed, urgent phone calls in his study. The blankness inside him made him capable of more than just womanising. His ego was his weak spot. If the girl had made fun of him he would have responded in anger. He had a temper she had glimpsed too many times.

An immense bang of thunder made her jump. As she went to the window the valley disappeared behind veils of rain and a hail of droplets vibrated the glass. The pool was misted and mysterious, its green depths concealed, the terrace instantly awash. Water seemed to be pouring from a thousand channels.

On the far side of the pool the trees thrashed back and forth. The swirling air was full of pine needles. She found a cardigan and wrapped herself in it. The villa felt cut off from the world. She thought of going over to the other wing and talking to Melissa. Could she be trusted? It was in her interests to make sure that Giles clung on to his job.

The passport must have been placed in her handbag by the maid. She was the only outsider, always standing back to let them pass, always aloof and unsmiling. There was something unbalanced about her, the way she covertly watched them all.

Jennifer felt a migraine starting.

She thought back to two years ago, when she had accused Steve of having an affair. He had refuted it absolutely, but when the awkward evening phone calls suddenly stopped she hated him for the vehemence of his denial. She studied the passport once more. It felt like an item returned to a family in mourning. The girl in the photograph was appallingly young and looked like easy prey.

In the darkest corner of her heart Jennifer knew that her husband had done something terrible. If she went to the police everything would start to come apart.

Her thoughts darkened further, for there was the little girl from the village to consider. Suppose he had seen Clémence walking along and had taken his anger out on her? His girlfriend was dead, his business was collapsing, who knew what he was capable of doing? His rational exterior could conceal a screaming mass of terror.

She was trapped here. Water spouted from the gutters, turning the villa into a monsoon palace. Terrifying thoughts cascaded; it was the start of an unravelling neither she nor anyone else would be able to stop. She foresaw her own losses, her marriage, her son, her home.

Dazed, she stepped out onto the terrace and let the rain wash through her. With the door open, water flooded into the living room until it looked as though the pool had overflowed into the villa.

She had no idea how long she stayed in the downpour, but when she re-entered the living room she was chilled to the bone and shaking violently. She grabbed a towel and tried to dry her hair.

Her phone beeped with a text. The big meeting Giles had arranged had been cancelled. The husbands were on their way back.

Wait, she thought, *if the girl was staying here by herself how did she get into the villa? Steve was in London.*

She needed to find the number of the leasing agent, Julia somebody. When she searched for the name of the rental agency there was only one member of staff listed.

She called Julia Martinez.

44.

In Nice, the torrential rain blocked the drains, disgorging sewage across the Promenade des Anglais. McDonald's wrappers, polystyrene boxes and pulpy grey masses of cardboard swirled past the smart cafés as if deliberately trying to embarrass them. The mock-deco awnings of the bars had been drawn in before they could tear and collapse. The city looked forlorn, as if it had closed up and gone into mourning for the loss of the sun.

Julia ran the agency alone most of the time, reporting once a week to her boss in Madrid. The stupid boy she had hired to take care of the phones had complained about his salary cut and walked out on her. Now she sat in the front office watching the rainwater flood under the glass door and listening to the dripping bucket in the hall. *Vacances Paradis* was meant to look glitzy and Riviera-like from the outside, but behind the photographs of pink stucco mansions was her poky little office with its photocopier and broken coffee machine.

She looked out of the steamed-patched window. The

promenade was deserted. The palms bowed under the onslaught of rain. This was too early, October weather. It would wash out the end of the season.

The phone startled her. She listened to the voice on the other end, but unusually it was a while before she had a chance to get a word in.

'I'm afraid we don't give out information about our clients,' she said finally, scrutinising her nails.

'But I'm his wife,' Mme Elsbury told her. 'I know there was a problem with the booking because my husband explained that he had to take the villa for two weeks. I need to know who was staying here during the first week because I found some things of hers and want to return them.'

Julia had dealt with problems like this before. Only last month one of her bookings turned out to be for a young Russian lady entertaining men in her rented villa for €2,000 a night, which would have been acceptable, this being the South of France, if there had been a decent cut set aside for *Vacances Paradis*.

The current situation was tricky, though. Her mind flashed through the consequences. If she admitted giving the keys to someone else and Mr Elsbury denied it, as Julia imagined he would, they could make trouble for her. If she said she handed them to a young girl who was waiting for Mrs Elsbury's husband, her client would become an even bigger problem. Mr Elsbury was footing the bill. If she did him a favour and denied handing out the keys, she could make sure he showed her some financial gratitude.

In a situation like this, you always followed the money.

For a moment she waited with her hand over the phone.

'It is true that there was a requirement to rent the villa for a minimum of two weeks, madame. I saw Mr Else-berry on Saturday morning, when he came here. I gave him the keys for the villa then.'

'I know her name,' said Jennifer. 'It's Summer Farrow. She's eighteen years old, for God's sake, blonde and very pretty. Are you sure you haven't seen or heard of anyone by that name?'

Julia pretended to think. 'Not that I can recall.'

'Eighteen,' she repeated. 'Can she even rent a villa at that age.'

Julia hardened. 'I did not rent it to her, Mrs Else-berry, I rented it to your husband. Perhaps you should speak to him. I don't know, maybe he can help you with this problem. I am not responsible for the private arrangements of the guests.'

That's shut her up, she thought, thanking the angry wife for the call and ringing off. Then, *What if she talks to the maid?*

She searched for Hannah's number and called her.

'Hannah – where are you?'

'Hi Julia, I haven't left the Bellevige apartments yet. I'm waiting for the rain to ease up. I can't get anywhere else while it's like this.'

'No, of course not,' Julia said with impatience. 'You haven't spoken to the family at Villa Lavardin, have you?'

'No, I did exactly as you instructed.' She sounded as if she was telling the truth, but the English always did with those china teacup accents going clippety-clip.

'Good, because they are going through some problems at the moment, is very important that you do *not* speak with them. I don't want you drawn into anything unpleasant. The wife may try to make conversation with the yap yap yap to you. Don't allow that to happen. If she says anything, ignore her. She does not pay you, I do. Report the matter to me and I'll take care of it.'

Holiday people, Julia thought as she ended the call, *worrying about their little domestic dramas while some of us are trying to earn a decent living.*

As lightning flashed outside, she set about thinking up ways to extort additional payment out of Mr Elsbury.

45.

It was only after Jennifer had pulled everything out of the wardrobe that she found the phone with the shattered screen. It had been placed on top of her underwear.

It lit up when she touched it. She opened *Messages* and went to *Recent*. At the top she found a series of texts between Summer and someone called Jihane.

Steve is desperate to get with me Saturday afternoon

Can't believe you gonna stay there & wait for him to jump you he's 40 ffs!!!

I may say no haven't decided

Don't do it you don't need the trouble

He can be very persuasive he scares me a bit

Then get out of there girlfriend!!!

I want to see the look on his face when I turn him down

Trust me it's not a good idea to cut your eyes at a man expecting sex

And later:

Why aren't you answering your phone?

Are you OK?

Did you have a fight with him?

Please answer just to say everything fine

Can't wait any longer call me when you can

Tell me you're all right

If you in trouble tell me

Fuck u summer where the hell are you

A timeline of increasingly fraught messages, with every minute and second recorded. She was standing in the middle of the bedroom floor, still holding the phone. On the bed lay the passport. She listened. Keys landed in a china bowl. Her husband's shoes clumped up the stairs.

'Jennifer? Are you up here?'

'Hi, give me a minute, will you?'

Recalling the yoga exercises that could control her breathing and make her at least appear calm, she raised a shaking right hand flat in front of her and stilled it. She tried to think of somewhere to hide everything.

Grabbing her cloth shoe bag from her case, she dropped the incriminating items into it and threw it into the wardrobe.

Checking herself in the mirror, she pushed her hair back into place and patted a streak of dust from her shirt. Steve was standing in front of the door as she opened it, waiting for her. As usual, he looked as if he had just been unboxed. There was a blankness in his face that he had long ago learned to substitute for anger.

'How did it go?' she asked.

'Giles barely said a fucking word. He'd had a drink somewhere, I don't know how, I was with him nearly the whole time. I should have frisked him for a hip flask. He can't even share the driving with me because it turns out he's lost his licence. I'll give you one guess why.'

'Didn't he drive in Priorat?' She stepped away toward the windows.

'The ban hadn't started then. He neglected to mention that he had a fucking court case pending. He's supposed to be besties with the guy we were seeing today, but it was obvious from the outset that nobody knew who he was.' He held up his forefinger. 'Not true, one guy looked really pissed off about us being there at all. There was somebody new running the company, a young woman, and the old boys act did *not* wash with her. The second meeting was called off because of the storm.'

'You still have a few more to go, don't you?'

'Not at the same level, nothing as important, and it's not going to get any better. This was the one Giles said couldn't go wrong. We're working our way down the client list now. The big hitters have all passed. I have to get rid of him.'

Is that why you want to get rid of him? she thought. *Or is it because he knows what you did?* 'Then you'd better speak to him.'

Steve seemed suddenly hesitant. A fresh squall of rain hit the windows, making them both turn. 'A couple of cars have been washed across the road,' he said absently. 'There's more rain coming in tomorrow. Maybe we should leave early. Where's Jamie?'

'No idea. Maybe he'll answer if you call. He doesn't bother with me.' With her head turned she couldn't be sure where he was standing. She thought she might scream if he touched her, so she carried on moving away from him. 'Perhaps I should mix you a drink.'

'I need to change my shirt first,' he said, slipping around her to the wardrobe. 'I got soaked just getting from the car to the front door. Giles looks like he fell in the pool. What's for dinner?'

'Chicken, I think. We've enough food for tonight but we'll need to find a shop in the morning.' *How easy it is to fake normality,* she thought bitterly. *I've had years of practice.*

'Friday – there'll be a market on.' He opened the wardrobe door and took out a long-sleeved T-shirt. 'For fuck's sake, this was supposed to have been washed and ironed. Look at the state of it.'

'Wear the blue sweater, it'll be warmer.' She snatched it from the bed and threw it at him. Ignoring his protests, she pulled the sweater over his wet hair. 'There you are. Actually, pour me a gin, would you? I think I'd like one.'

'It's a little early to –'

'I'm gasping for a drink, go on.'

She shoved him out into the hall and stepped back inside the bedroom. She needed to confront him in a way that would leave no doubt between either of them. If the case against him wasn't airtight he would find a way to wriggle out. Who else was on his side? Giles had every reason to support his boss. Mrs Macbeth was clearly determined to keep her husband employed. Jamie would never hear a bad word against his father. Even the rental agent was covering for him. The maid was only interested in finding her friend.

She was alone.

She stood at the landing window with her hands against the cool glass, trying to stay calm.

As she went downstairs, she heard a door open and close. The kitchen lights flickered and a dull roar rebounded from the hillside. Rain was coming in from the terrace. Rivulets followed the indentations in the tiles, sending tributaries into the room, insidiously invading it. Terrible things were going on behind her back. She wished she was home where her world was dull and safe and she could be lied to without consequence.

Someone had been in the kitchen. She could smell the odd jasmine perfume again. Steve was standing under the eaves at the far end of the terrace. He had not mixed her a drink, so she poured herself a glass of Shiraz and downed it in two long gulps. Her resolve grew firmer. *Let others be dazzled by my charming husband*, she thought, *I see the skull beneath the skin.*

The wine started to raise her body temperature. She returned to the counter and refilled the glass to the top.

When he came back inside, she would be ready for him.

Outside, Hannah stood beneath her clear plastic umbrella just below the edge of the pool patio, looking up at the kitchen. She had a valid reason for being here: she was waiting for the linen van. They didn't need to know that the driver had called her to move the delivery back to tomorrow because of the roads. If Jennifer accused her of leaving the passport and phone she would admit the truth. The police would be called, Julia would be told, and Steve would be forced to defend himself against a charge of murder. She had read that the guilty could be convicted even without the victim's body being found.

She felt as if Summer was standing at her side, holding her

shoulders, lacing her fingers, filling her with the strength she would need to see this through. *Together,* she thought, *we can survive this.*

Ten minutes passed but the kitchen door remained closed. It appeared that Jennifer was planning to stay inside.

Hannah checked her watch. She was due to meet Daniela and her son. As she passed by the kitchen on her way to the side gate she took one more look in, but now the room was bright and empty.

46.

Jamie sat cross-legged under the canopy that covered the outdoor kitchen. Turning off his phone, he removed his headphones and rubbed at his ears. The pool was spattering like hot fat.

When he squinted back at the villa through the shimmering rain, he saw his father pacing at the end of the terrace, as if trying to reach a decision on a matter of great import. His mother was in the kitchen, looking apprehensive. It was the layout of a videogame: coop the adults up in a glamorous cage and make them drive each other insane. But if it was a game, his father would always win. While others did nothing until it was too late, Steve always took action. Once they had hit a fox on a country road, and his father shocked them all by stamping on its head and kicking it into the holly bushes.

Jamie had asked why they couldn't have put it to sleep somehow. Steve had knelt beside the boy. 'It was going to die, Jamie. It's better not to prolong the suffering.'

He came to regard his father as different from other men.

Unsentimental, practical, sure of what was right for himself and his family. His voice commanded. His smiles had purpose. He appeared larger, as if he had been slightly magnified. When he spoke others listened.

Jamie drew up his legs and studied the illuminated windows through the rainfall. Melissa was moving about waving her arms, arguing with her husband. Giles was arguing back, trying to look reasonable, scrunching up his fat, bruised little face as if pleading for his life. In order to make sure that he didn't lose his wife he had turned himself into a human apology.

They all thought he saw nothing, but he saw their flaws as if they were breaks in an electrical circuit. If this was adulthood he wanted nothing to do with it. He settled his headphones back over his ears and closed his eyes to their world. As the heat-death of the planet engulfed them the adults would still be arguing about what to wear for dinner. To hell with them all.

Steve stepped back through the doors, leaving fresh trails of water. Jennifer stood awkwardly before the dining table with her hands at her sides, as if ready for anything. She had tied her hair back and changed into a black sweater he had never seen before. The change felt ominous.

'I was just talking to Giles and Melissa, thought I could take us out to dinner tonight, cheer things up a bit.' Steve brushed rainwater from his trousers. 'We'd get in anywhere with the weather like this, although I imagine a lot of places won't open so maybe we could go down into Nice or something.'

No reply. He glanced over at her.

She pushed a white plastic shopping bag at him. He peered in the top and saw a battered phone, a bikini, some kind of transparent orange wrap, a keyring, sunglasses.

'I think you'd better sit down,' she said, indicating the chair opposite.

There was a dangerous quaver in her voice. He had only heard this tone once before. 'Jennifer –' he began.

She raised her palm. 'You don't get to talk. You can talk your way out of anything. Not this time. I want to know what happened. If you start lying to me I will go to the police. Why were her belongings left behind?'

His gaze held steady. 'Where are you going with this?'

'Two years ago a girl came to the house and showed me a bruise on her neck which she said you put there. She said it was an accident but you had hurt her. It was late, you were away, I'd never seen or heard of her before and I thought she was crazy. She said you were rough with her.'

'She came to see you?'

'You always had girls hanging around you. I said I didn't believe her and sent her away. Just after that I found the texts and you stopped making your secret phone calls.' She picked out Summer's bikini and turned it over in her fingers. 'Summer Farrow turned you down. Did you punish her as well?'

He stared at his wife, his mouth firmly shut.

'Did you do more than just hurt her?'

He remained as motionless as the shop window mannequin he so often resembled, unable to form the words.

'She never left here. Her calls stopped at 1:32 p.m. There was someone waiting for her outside the house.'

'Jennifer, you have to believe me when I say –'

She shook her head violently. 'That's one thing I will never do again. You know, I actually don't care what you did. If she was stupid enough to fall for you she deserved whatever she got. I've spent the whole of our life together protecting you. I was frightened – not of losing you, because I guess I lost you a long time ago, but of losing my security. Just out of curiosity, how did you do it?'

'Will you just listen to yourself?' He tried to laugh.

She held up Summer's phone. 'If you don't tell me the truth I'm going to call the police right now. How's that for listening to myself?'

There was no way out. He could not bring himself to look at her.

'When did you meet her?'

He cleared his throat. 'About five weeks ago. She did all the chasing, not me. I'm telling you, I did not go anywhere near that girl.'

'But you wanted to. Why didn't you?'

'I liked the fantasy of it, who wouldn't? It's a guy thing. Nothing happened.'

'So everything fell into place, with you coming out here and having to book the villa for a fortnight? Or did you plan that part as well?'

'I let her take the villa for the first week while it was empty on the condition that she left before any of you arrived. By the time I opened the front door she was long gone. She had a friend in Nice and went to stay with him.' He was thinking on his feet, trying to calm the situation down, but the ground was shifting. 'You know, I think you're the only one having trouble processing this. You seem obsessed with the idea that I'll go off with someone. Have you ever thought that it might just be in your mind?'

'In my mind.' She drew out Summer's passport. 'She left without taking this.'

'Maybe it's an old one.'

'It's her current passport, Steve.'

He was pouring sweat. 'I can't explain that.' For the first time he had no idea what he would say or do next. 'She can't come back and get it while we're here.'

'She hasn't even tried to call you? Not even rung her own phone? I called the agency and spoke to Julia. She flatly denied giving this girl the key to the villa, so how did she get in?'

He could feel the rainwater turning to ice between his shoulder blades. 'Julia's covering herself. I'm the client, I'm the one paying her. She gave Summer the keys. She told me she did. I don't know why she would lie to you.'

'While you try to work it out, Steven, I'll decide what I'm going to do. Stay and finish your business here. It's up to you how you handle Giles and Melissa.'

'Giles – *he* knows about her. He could have planned all this.'

'Setting aside the fact that he's not smart enough to rearrange a cutlery drawer, what would be the point?'

'He didn't approve of me seeing her but he's been taking an unnatural interest in her ever since he found out. They're in it together, trying to cut me down. They both know I'm about to fire him.'

'What's Giles going to do, take over the company behind

your back? It's obvious to anyone that he couldn't run a sandwich shop.'

He rubbed a hand across the back of his broad wet neck. 'I don't know what to think anymore. What are you going to do?'

She held his gaze. 'I need to get away from you because you are toxic. You always were. I was just too in love with you to see it.'

She left the room without looking back.

He did not understand. Throughout their marriage Jennifer had always deferred to him. This was entirely out of character. He felt a reckless fury growing inside him. He'd almost had everyone convinced that he had never touched Summer, but it felt as if Summer was still pulling the strings.

You have to act fast, he told himself, *and bring this to an end right now.*

47.

Daniela was sitting in the window in Chez Dany with her little boy. He had long, darkly lustrous hair and sat before a white cardboard pizza box almost as big as himself. 'This is Theo,' Daniela said. 'He's six so he's allowed to bring his pizza in while Mummy has a glass of wine to stop herself from going crazy. Say hello, Theo.'

The boy pulled out a pizza slice and waved it at her, then smeared tomato paste down his blue sweatshirt. As Daniela wiped his hands Hannah bent down to him. 'Hello, Theo. I don't want to interrupt your meal.'

'His new favourite word is "fries". He's going to grow up speaking American and all his teachers will beat him. He's a good little Niçois, aren't you, Theo? So you managed to get away?'

'I don't want to go back there until they've gone. I don't suppose they want to see me either.'

'Is this about the girl who was staying there?'

'Daniela, do you believe in ghosts?'

'In spirits, perhaps, and the Holy Ghost.'

'Then it's her spirit that's haunting the place. It feels like she's still watching me, thrilled by all the chaos she's caused. I think I'm going crazy. I hear her in my head. How can anyone believe in such things?'

'In times of great stress, of course you can,' said Daniela fervently. 'My brother had visions of the Blessed Virgin all the time. Of course, he was a priest, so he had to see them for work.'

'I keep thinking she's going walk right back in. But I know what he's done –' wary of Theo she lowered her voice, '– he buried her in the grounds and may have killed this other girl as well, the one from the village.'

'*Tu décroche le pompon, vraiment.*' Daniela rolled her eyes.

'I unhook the pompom?' said Hannah. 'Seriously?'

'A strange feeling is one thing, but I think you're making up these stories in your head. You're working in a strange house, your mind plays tricks.' She saw how upset Hannah was and relented. 'I daresay you have good reason to believe all this is true, but perhaps you've just connected things wrongly.'

'It's not just a belief, I *know*.'

'You also know that if you talk to the police Julia will find out. She finds out everything.' She dabbed at Theo's cheese-covered chin with a wet wipe. 'Your friend is not going to turn up and you will never know what happened. The same with the Dufayel girl. This is the reality of such things.'

'But their loved ones must look for them.'

'Not if they believe there was no crime involved. I'm not sure anyone will look for your friend. As for the little girl, well, it will suit her family if she never comes back.' Daniela gave

her a very Gallic look, as if to say, *this is the way of the world now*.
'Of course, the authorities will need to look into such matters.
Theo and I just saw the cops. It's strange that they haven't come
to your villa yet.'

'Why would they?' Hannah asked.

'They think Clémence might have taken shelter in a barn
on one of the rental properties. There are only three other big
houses on the hill.'

'I don't think there's a barn,' Hannah said. 'I found a
woodshed but it's completely stacked with logs.'

The morose young farmhands who sat steadily drinking
brandies in the corner of the bar knew what they were talking
about. Jacob skulked with them, openly glaring over at the
two women.

Raphael stopped at the table. 'They think it was someone
from the Villa Lavardin,' he said, surreptitiously indicating
behind him. 'Jacob wants to get a group together and go up
to the house.'

Hannah tried not to return their gaze. 'Can he do that?'

'They've lost one of their own, they're entitled to an answer.
If the police don't go there, they will.'

Hannah checked over Raphael's shoulder and saw Jacob
raise his chin at her in defiance. 'Can you at least stop Jacob from
going with them?'

'I'll try but he's a sly one. If he goes, I can't stop him. I can't
leave the bar.'

Daniela started to pack up her bag. 'Let me give you a lift
back to Nice. You don't want to be stuck here with this randy
old goat.'

'He seems to have taken a shine to me,' Hannah admitted.

Daniela lifted Theo from his chair and set him upright, dusting him down. 'No disrespect to you, my dear, but he takes a shine to every female because he cannot tell their features apart. He suffers from agnosia; face blindness. It's a genetic disorder not uncommon up here, where the gene pool is a little on the shrunken side. After his stroke it got worse.'

'You're telling me I'm looking for proof that a girl existed in a town full of face-blind people?'

'Take my advice. Just do what you usually do. Tomorrow is your guests' last day. They're leaving first thing on Saturday. Keep your mouth shut and hang onto your job. Then there'll be nothing to worry about. I have to get this one home. He's about to get an energy rush from the pizza so I need to wear him out a little.'

She reached out a hand to Hannah. Her palm was rough and warm. 'I'm a very straightforward person, Hannah, but I'm not stupid. I can sense that you became close to this girl, probably closer than anyone else. If you don't know what happened to her then maybe no one ever will. You understand why, don't you? Because she doesn't want you to know, and perhaps neither does God.' She lifted Theo into her arms, cradling him tenderly. 'You don't know the plan He has for everyone.'

'Maybe I'm just a lousy judge of character,' Hannah admitted. 'Did you know that Matthias the gardener is a drug dealer?'

Daniela patted at Theo's mouth. 'That's old news. He's been doing it for years. I can tell you where he keeps it, too. In your back garden, in the nursery. It's not just marijuana either. He plants lots of little plastic bags that never grow, even though they're covered in soil and watered. All the lads here know about them but Raphael stops them from stealing because he feels sorry for Matthias.'

'Why does he feel sorry for Matthias?'

Daniela neatly folded her used napkins. 'He lost everything when Emil Lavardin died. I warned you, this is what happens when you start to get involved. You become a part of the story.'

'Thanks for the advice. I'm coming with you.'

Something cracked against the glass door. At first Hannah thought it was a stone but it was a hard white peppermint, thrown at her with some zeal by Jacob.

She stepped outside. There were dozens of deep little puddles in the pale gravel of the village square. At least the rain had stopped, although the clouds were as sharp as wire wool and still held inner darkness. Daniela stopped Theo from attempting to splash through a miniature lake.

When she looked back at the bar, she saw the farmhands through the window, watching her intently.

48.

The atmosphere in the villa was becoming more uncomfortable with each passing minute.

The table had been laid for a buffet that no one wanted to eat. Jamie remained hunched in a corner of the furthest sofa, his hood pulled over his eyes, trying to avoid the sight of his mother, who was furiously wiping the kitchen counter. It was obvious to him that something really fucked-up had happened but he tried not to think about it. Let the adults accuse each other and rant all they like, just so long as he didn't have to be a part of it. His teachers were always telling him to 'get involved', but why would you? He closed his eyes and imagined the others standing on the deck of a ship that was thankfully sailing away from him.

Giles peered myopically at the rainswept pool. 'Are we on a generator here?'

'How would you know what a generator looks like?' Melissa moved him out of the way so that she could get to the bar. Steve skulked in a corner of the living room.

'There are no flights out tonight. I checked.' Jennifer continued to scrub at the counter.

'The storms will pass in a few hours,' said Melissa, 'we'll be fine.'

'I want to go home early.'

'She needs to go back,' Steve announced without looking up at them.

'There are too many of us here.' Jennifer scraped away at an imagined stain. In the awkward silence that followed, Melissa shot her husband a look of puzzlement. The swelling around Giles's nose had subsided but the bruise was now a blackish yellow. He appeared about to burst, as if in some mental anguish.

The lights flickered again. Everyone glanced up except Jamie. Giles winced. Melissa had seen this look on her husband's face before, usually when he was about to put his foot in it. She used to find his guileless honesty refreshing. 'Giles, you're supposed to be working. I don't see many deals being done.'

'Oh, we're laying the groundwork,' Steve cut in sarcastically, 'building client relationships, aren't we, Giles? Giles is introducing me to all the key players. Unfortunately none of them remember who Giles is except the one who called him Piggy.'

'That's not my fault, old chap,' Giles cried. 'It was my nickname. Everybody gets a nickname at school.'

'Not if they don't want one,' said Steve. 'Not if they're named after the character who gets killed.'

'Jennifer, you can't go,' Melissa pleaded. 'Don't leave me with these two children.'

Like a pupil desperate to use a toilet, Giles raised his hand. 'Look, I know for a fact that she wasn't even here.'

The silence that followed was horrible.

'Who?' Melissa asked slowly.

'The girl, she left before Steve got here, I know because she was a smoker and when we arrived he was clearing away her stuff and I could still smell her cigarettes, and Melissa found her wrap by the pool. I found a pair of panties too, only I got rid of them, at least I thought I did. The girl had gone, honestly. Probably in a taxi or something.'

'Then you must have seen her leave,' Jennifer snapped.

'No, I –'

'Well you were coming up the only road, Giles. You would have seen her leave either by car or walking because there's only one way down and the road up goes nowhere.'

'No, I wasn't –'

'So she vanished into thin air.' She moved in on Giles. 'If she isn't dead then where is she, this girl Summer, who has no clothes, no money and no passport and who never left the villa? Where is she, the girl my husband was planning to fuck in our bed?'

With theatrical timing, the lights went out.

Steve collected a torch and a knife from the kitchen. He knew there was a metal fuse box at the end of the hall. At first he could not find the cause of the problem, but it appeared that a surge had tripped the master switch, so he flipped it back. He closed the box door and headed back into the living room, walking into an escalating argument.

Jamie had pulled down his hood and removed his headphones. 'You never take his side, you never think about what he has to go through with you.'

'I don't know why you always have to defend him.'

'I have to because *you* never do.'

Jennifer was clearly trying not to lose her temper but her eyes had filled even though she was determined not to cry. 'Right from when you were a little boy you've made excuses for him. Why? He never did a thing for you, Jamie. I raised you, clothed and fed you, taught you at home while he was out trying to sell another of his hare-brained ideas.'

Jamie tried to speak but she thrust a warning hand at him. 'My parents helped to fund every one of his businesses, and all I got back from you was hatred. Because the man who spends most of his time trying not to look at you these days always has to be the hero in your eyes, so *I* have to be the villain. He tries to tell me it's all in my mind and you're still looking for a reason to defend him. What does he have to do to lose your respect, beat someone to death right in front of you?'

'I don't have to listen to this –'

'Do you know how often he used to threaten me in the early days, how he'd promise it would never happen again and beg me to take him back? Instead of walking out I paid the bills and kept my mouth shut, and he's got you under the same spell. Your father is dangerous, do you understand? No, just block out the world and hide under your headphones. Do what I did all those years and see where it leaves you.'

She broke off when she saw Steve standing in the doorway. His hands were by his sides, unmoving.

'I think you need to calm down,' Melissa suggested. 'Think about what you're saying. He's your husband.'

'A husband is the last person you can ever trust.'

Melissa searched around for her cigarettes. 'I think you're projecting your marital problems onto this business with the girl.'

'Really? Is that what I'm doing? Thank you, Melissa, for your valuable insight. Maybe I should have been more like you and pushed my husband all the way back into nursery school.'

'I think you're being very nasty.' She located her lighter. 'It isn't like you.'

'That's right,' Jennifer agreed, looking around wildly, 'I'm meant to be the nice one who puts up with all the lies.'

'At least think about it logically,' Melissa suggested, playing devil's advocate. 'Steve has been with my husband during the day and with us every night.'

'That's not strictly true,' said Giles slowly. Everyone turned to look at him. 'Steve hasn't been with me. He's only been to a few of the meetings. I've been handling loads of them by myself. He said we shouldn't overpower the clients by going in heavy-handed, that it would be more useful for me to learn how to deal with them alone. He told me not to mention it. I don't know where he's been.'

For a moment nobody registered what had happened. Giles was suddenly on his knees, then keeled over, crimson gushing from his nose and lip. Steve stepped back and shook out his fist.

Melissa dropped down beside Giles. She looked up at Steve in disgust. 'You fucking maniac, what the hell is wrong with you? After all he's done for you.'

'He's done nothing for me.' Steve examined his knuckles. 'Thanks to him the company's screwed.'

'You can't blame him for your errors of judgement.' She shuffled forward on the floor and lifted her husband's head.

'The only error of judgement I made was hiring him.'

Jennifer turned to their son. 'Jamie, give me your phone.'

Jamie stared at her furiously. 'Why?'

'Just do it.'

He dug the phone from the pocket of his jeans and reluctantly handed it over. Melissa swung around at them. 'One of you get a doctor, he's really hurt. Are you calling one?'

'No, I'm getting a taxi,' Jennifer said. 'I'm not staying here a minute longer. He's not going to die from a little slap, Melissa. If you hang around my husband you have to get used to those. I'm sorry, Jamie. I know right now you hate me. This shouldn't have happened in front of you but maybe you'll finally understand.'

'I'm not a child,' Jamie muttered.

Giles appeared unconscious. His head lolled to one side, leaking blood. 'You could have killed him.' Melissa crushed Giles's head to her breasts in anguish. Blood dripped dramatically onto her white cardigan.

Jennifer punched out a number, waited, tried another. Steve remained still and silent, his right fist dripping on the tiles.

'I think his nose is really broken this time, Dad,' Jamie said.

Giles groaned and tried to get away from Melissa by rolling over on his side. He coughed, blasting a fine crimson spray across the floor.

'No, baby, stay there,' Melissa intruded, stroking and hugging, enveloping him in smoke because she had still not put down her cigarette. 'I knew something bad would happen. All the messes you had to clear up, all the dirty work. I thought I could fix it.'

'Recorded message,' said Jennifer, more to herself than to anyone else. 'There aren't any taxis tonight. They can't get up here until tomorrow morning.' She placed Jamie's phone beside him.

Steve left them huddled in the villa. Closing the glass door behind him, he walked down the curving staircase and stood at the edge of the pool. The water had an oily, lapidary surface that shimmered in the rain. Dropping down onto the concrete lip, he rinsed his right hand in the pool, watching his blood disperse in the iridescent ripples.

The rain fell so hard that it took him a minute to realise that he was crying. He was suffused with a darkness he could neither comprehend nor control. A rage of humiliation swept through him. He was not even capable of failing grandly, but had instead attacked a weak acolyte. Everything that had happened was Summer's fault.

The pool invited him into its murky, olivine depths. He collapsed beside it, dragging his fists back and forth across the concrete edge until they bled again. Then he whispered his secrets into the water.

49.

Friday dawned muggy and foetid. A faint grey fog hung over the road and the Villa Lavardin. As Hannah got out of Daniela's car she saw that spills of amber rock had spattered across the tarmac. The air was thick with the smell of earth and rain-washed lavender. The red roof of the villa peeped out between the misted fir trees. Somewhere a bird called plaintively to a missing mate.

This is the last time I'll see these people, she thought. *Take Daniela's advice. Smile and keep your mouth shut.*

But she couldn't stop herself from thinking, *Matthias's nursery bed. I should at least take a proper look at it.*

The atmosphere inside the villa was malevolent with last night's cigarette smoke and alcohol fumes. The blinds were still drawn, the shutters closed. The mess in the living room had not been cleared away. A party, Hannah thought at first. There were four emptied red wine bottles on the counter, a saucer contained cigarette ends and the remains of a smashed wine glass. Up until now the guests had been conscientiously neat in the common areas.

Then she realised the disarray looked like the aftermath of a fight. Some of the furniture had been haphazardly shoved back. She opened the blinds, put everything straight, then filled her yellow bucket and washed the floor.

There were seven or eight blood spots on the tiles near the back wall of the living room. Puzzled, she crouched to examine them. They led to a long smear of dried blood by the skirting board. She thought of Summer's footprints and scrubbed away the stains with a vengeance, returning the room to its pristine state.

To air the room she opened the doors leading to the patio. The swimming pool was now impossible to use, and there was a reek of drains outside. Hillside soil had washed down and clogged the pipes.

While she swept and tidied she tried not to think about what might have happened, but images leaked into her mind. She imagined Summer slaughtered and buried on the property, her spirit trying to attract the attention of the living.

Now that the rains had eased she could properly investigate the plant nursery. Unfortunately it was in full view of the villa's living room windows. She thought about the problem while she returned to the main kitchen and set about loading the dishwasher.

A noise at her back made her turn. Jennifer was staring at her wildly. She seemed smaller and thinner somehow, more vulnerable.

'It was you, wasn't it?' she asked, her voice like knives. 'You left this for me.' In her right hand was the passport. 'I should have started by asking you. Because if you were here last week you must have met her.'

'Yes, ma'am,' Hannah admitted, her tongue finally freed. 'I did meet her.'

'And she told you she was having an affair with my husband?'

'She said they met in London.' Now that the moment she had been waiting for had arrived, Hannah felt unsure of what to say. 'He flew her out here. She was due to go home on Saturday afternoon but she never left.'

'So he killed her and disposed of her body? Do you understand how ludicrous that sounds? Why haven't you gone to the police?'

'I can't prove it.'

'And none of the more obvious explanations crossed your mind? That she walked out in anger or had an accident after she left?'

Hannah had not expected Jennifer to accept the truth about her husband. Perhaps she would stand by him no matter what the police discovered. It made her wonder what would have happened if she had remained silent about Aidan.

'You've caused us all a lot of pain with this. What we say or do has nothing at all to do with you. You had no right to interfere.'

'There was blood on the pool patio, Mrs Elsbury. I saw her footprints.'

'Oh? What happened to them?'

'They got washed off.'

'Why didn't you come and talk to me when you first had an inkling about all this?'

'You wouldn't have listened. A little girl in the village disappeared, and I think it's connected. People don't just vanish.'

'So my husband is responsible for both disappearances?' Jennifer had been trying to remain calm but was losing the battle. 'First he's an adulterer, now he's a serial killer? You're obviously mentally unbalanced. I need to talk to your employer. I think you had better leave this house.'

'I was not hired by you.'

'Then I'll make sure you're dismissed. For all I know this is entirely your fault. Have you caused this kind of trouble before? You need to go right now. Perhaps you should leave me the keys.'

'I can't do that,' said Hannah firmly. 'I have to return them to Mrs Martinez.'

Shivering with rage, Jennifer stood her ground and waited while Hannah packed up her cleaning equipment and let herself out through the patio door.

She was shut out now. Unwanted and no longer employed. She knew how Julia would react when she got the call. She would take the client's side without once thinking to defend her employee.

It was over. He had won.

FIVE:
THE TRUTH

50.

Stretching out his arm, Steve found his fingers touching the floorboards. He was in one of the unused bedrooms, lying in a child's bed with his feet hanging over the end. The knuckles of both hands were scraped and swollen, his right palm torn with lateral scratches. He tried to focus on his watch: 10:15 a.m. Why was the villa so silent?

When he sat up, a thunderous ache settled across his brain. There was a half-empty bottle of vodka lying next to him on the bed. His thoughts came slowly and thickly. He tried to recall how last night went down and only remembered punching Giles in the face. Well, that was the end of their working relationship. Giles would probably try to sue. Melissa certainly would. For all he knew the police might be on their way here to arrest him right now.

And it was all Summer's fault. Women were his passion and his downfall. He loved the sight, smell and taste of them. There was no woman he had ever met under the age of thirty in whom he could not find some attractive feature, yet a part of them stayed forever beyond his reach.

When he tried to stand up, the room tilted. There was a Rorschach blot of blood, starkly scarlet, on his new white shirt. Parts of the evening were completely lost from view. It had been a while since anything like this had happened.

Christ, he thought, *if I can't remember last night what else have I blanked out?*

He couldn't be sure of anything anymore. He drank from the sink tap and leaned against the wall to settle his balance before stepping out into the corridor. The door to the main bedroom was shut. Jamie's room was open and empty.

He caught sight of himself in the hall mirror. A sickly, dark-eyed face stared back, barely recognisable. He looked haunted.

Down in the kitchen the kettle was still hot but no breakfast had been prepared. He couldn't remember where he had left his phone or wallet. Although the rain had stopped, water still dripped everywhere. The pool was a jungle swamp. Swathes of red mud laced the patio in bloody tidemarks and scraps of mist hung in the trees like watching phantoms.

He made coffee but could find no milk except some kind of appalling plant-based substitute. Taking his bitter cup to the damp outdoor sofa under the eaves, he flopped down into it and tried to clear his head.

Perhaps Giles and Melissa had gone home, and his wife and son had given them a lift to Nice airport, leaving him to cool off. He had no idea whether the car was still here. The sheer unfairness of it galled him. He had always been kind to Jennifer, always supportive. Sometimes in any marriage lies had to be told, and sometimes the lies had to be large. It was a known factor, embedded in the reality of any sane working relationship. What was more valuable, peace or truth?

He had to ask himself: what did he want from his marriage, presuming it was still salvageable? Stability? Security? Comfort? It would be tricky to regain any of those qualities now.

It felt as if he had been taken apart and left unassembled. The police would most likely arrest him on suspicion of murder even though there was no body. His reputation would be left in tatters, his business and marriage destroyed. He needed a plan and had nothing.

Hannah needed a floor plan. There was a drawing of the house in the *Vacances Paradis* brochure, but it was sketched in pastel pencils and turned out to be spectacularly fanciful. Following the stone steps below the pool, she looked over into the plant nursery where young saplings sat in boxes beside troughs of herbs, fruit vines and vegetables. Behind them was a long ridge of freshly turned earth, darker than the surrounding soil.

What if I was wrong about everything? she thought. She imagined another scenario in which Summer found the gardener's drugs and enlisted Jihane to help sell them. That alone could have been grounds for murder. Violent death happened in these hills. Madame Lavardin's husband had been killed right here in the house.

Somewhere nearby the gendarmes were meticulously examining the woodlands for clues to the whereabouts of Clémence. They would soon arrive to comb the scrub surrounding the villa. Others would arrive too.

She sat down on the wet steps and hugged her knees. Suppose everything she'd believed to be true was false? Summer, not free-spirited and life-enhancing at all but calculating, mercenary, vengeful, malicious. Summer who had been taken away from her parents and placed in care, who changed her life story to suit her moods, who might have been insane for all she knew. How easily she had entrapped them all!

She dragged her fingers through her rain-damp hair. *Only consider the things you know to be true.*

There were two ways out of the villa: on foot to the village or in a vehicle, both taking the same route. It was clear that nobody in St Martin-sous-Roches had seen Summer since the night she and Jihane had fought in the bar. How would she have paid for a cab if her purse and cards were still here? She never had any cash. Every instinct told her that Jihane was not lying. He was as innocent in this as she was.

Everything led back to Steve. She needed to stay close to him now. He would never admit to anything. He would continue to lie long after any case against him was proven.

From her vantage point here she could see where they all were. Jennifer was talking to Melissa in the kitchen. Steve had gone up to the terrace. Jamie was in his bedroom. If they could just all stay away from each other in separate rooms until it was time to leave, Steve had a chance of getting away with murder.

She had to make sure he didn't.

In the corner of the staircase wall that overlooked the pool patio, a large amphora stood on a wrought-iron tripod. It was heavy but she was able to rock it back and forth, until she managed to topple it over the edge of the wall.

It exploded on the steps below like a cannon shot, scattering great amber shards everywhere, firing some pieces into the pool.

It was time to flush them all out.

51.

Steve's damp shirt stuck to his back. Mosquitos had left welts along his veins. He looked decidedly less perfect now. He felt changed somehow, as if a part of him had been cut out.

He sniffed the air. Something smelled rancid, as if an animal had died nearby. The rain might have killed an animal and washed its corpse onto the property.

He had cancelled the last of his meetings. There was no point in trying to hold them now. His torn palms had started to bleed again. The shocking scarlet grazes were like stigmata. How had it come to this?

From behind him came the sound of women talking. Melissa was saying something about today's flights being backed up from the storm. 'You might as well stick to your original plan and fly back tomorrow. You won't find anything earlier.'

'I'm not taking the same flight as him.' So the two wives were suddenly friendly? What the fuck was it with women? Why did the aggrieved one always seek out a commiserating sidekick? He strained to hear the rest of the conversation.

'Then stay on for a couple of days. Seriously, why wouldn't you? If you really don't want to see him, go down into Nice and find yourself a nice little Airbnb. Actually, damn the expense, stay at the Negresco. I would. You shouldn't be around him. He's obviously very troubled. And he doesn't know his own strength. Look at the way he laid into Giles, what more proof do you need?'

Melissa poured herself a strong black coffee from the cafetière. 'You said he's had affairs in the past. For God's sake, you're married to him, you must be able to see what he's like. So buttoned down, all those pressed white shirts, never a hair out of place, what do you think that pressure does to someone? Trust me, I've met men like him before. Maybe going to the police will be the best thing you can do. You know, shake him up a little. Put him in his place.'

Steve had heard enough. Christ, the woman was mad. He sank further into the cane armchair, going so low that he could not be seen.

'I'm not going to the police,' Jennifer decided. 'There must be another way. Steve once told me he had a puppy.'

Oh no, he thought, *she's going to tell the fucking puppy story. Holy fucking fuck.* Steve pushed himself further down into his seat. Right now there was nothing he could say or do that would change his wife's opinion of him. Everyone could trot out a never-to-be-repeated story told in confidence if they were feeling mean enough. It felt like a conspiracy of witches. It would be best to get away and let everything die down, wait for them to get back to their senses.

To get off the patio he was forced to crawl along the tiles

and hide behind some hibiscus bushes. On the way he branded
a stone pillar with a bloody handprint. It was then necessary
to climb through the bamboo fencing between the flower beds
in order to reach the walkway. Halfway through he snagged
his shirt and was unable to free himself. Thrashing his arm
against the bamboo in a fit of frustration, he put a six-inch rip
in the sleeve.

As he stood between the main house and the guest wing
wondering what on earth to do, he watched as a bloody great
pot threw itself from the staircase and exploded with a boom
on the patio. Frozen in mid-stride, it was impossible for him
to leave and impossible to remain. The others started looking
out to see what had happened. What he really wanted to do was
head upstairs, knowing that there was a half-litre bottle of vodka
stashed in the bathroom.

Instead he was confronted by a startled-looking Giles, who
was wearing an absurd Hawaiian shirt with pictures of hotels
all over it. His nose had turned into a reddish-black blob and
was twisted to the left. On top of it he had ineffectually stuck
a children's pirate plaster.

'Did you do that?' Giles asked, looking down at the shattered
mess on the patio.

'What, you think I'm responsible for every fucking thing
that happens around here now, is that it?'

Giles gave him a look of undiluted mistrust. 'They're going to
find her body sooner or later, you know, and then everything
will come out.'

'I didn't kill her, you fucking retard.' He raised a menacing
fist.

Giles flinched and backed away. 'Then where is she? Why do you keep lying to everyone?'

'God, I should never have hired you,' Steve sighed.

'Why did you?'

He looked up at the sky. *Rescue me from this fuckwittery.*

Giles pulled a pewter flask from his back pocket, unscrewed the cap and took a slug. He was thinking about offering it when Steve snatched it from him.

'Do you really want to know why?' He drank deep and coughed. Giles had filled it with the coarsest brandy he had ever tasted. 'I never went to university. I started work at eighteen. Most of the time it didn't matter but I just – couldn't – get any higher. Everyone's polite, everyone says we must get together for dinner or drinks but they *never ever* name a fucking date. I thought it would be good to have someone who could speak their language. Except you can't, can you? You're the right class but you're not smart enough for them. I thought giving you the job would make you loyal, and if the company went down you'd be the last one to leave the deck.' He rolled his eyes at Giles. 'Do you understand? I hired you to take the fall. Why else would anyone employ you? I thought you were my fail-safe. How ironic is that? In the meantime you fucked my marriage.'

'You couldn't go on treating people the way you do forever, Steve.'

'Everything was fine so long as nobody knew, you utter tool. Get out of my sight before I tear your nose right off.'

Giles was nothing if not dogged. Although he kept well out of Steve's reach he stuck around. 'So where is she? Do you have any idea? What really happened after you got here?'

'If I do this again are you going to fucking listen once and for all?' The brandy burned his throat less the second time around. Giles's hand opened to accept the flask but Steve hung onto it.

'She wasn't here but it felt like she hadn't left, like she was playing a game and hiding somewhere to watch my reaction. I went room by room, checking under beds and in cupboards, getting more and more angry. I thought I must have missed something. All these outhouses and sheds where the staff keep their equipment. I could smell that horrible cheap fucking perfume she always wore. Finally I gave up. I'd been drinking while I was looking and I fell asleep.' He stared Giles down. 'Okay? I know it's not very exciting but that's what happened.'

'And you don't know anything about the little French girl?'

'Of course I fucking don't, you plankton. You think because my date fell through I decided to go after a mentally-challenged child? That silly tart conspired with that clearly unstable maid to drop me in the shit, and the little French girl got lost and drowned and they haven't found her body yet. That's what any sane person would think.'

Giles backed away as Steve stormed past on his way to get the vodka from his room.

As Hannah headed up the side staircase it started to rain once more. Giles was standing just ahead with his back to her, motionless, getting soaked. She'd assumed they would all come out and see the smashed amphora, then start fighting again. Instead they had clearly decided to be English about it and pretend that nothing unusual had happened.

She found a dry spot under the mulberry trees below the pool and stayed there for a moment. This wasn't how life's mysteries were meant to be solved. She thought of Summer framed against the setting sun, the cauldron glow of the dying light touching the edges of her hair. She heard her delighted laugh, saw her eyes slowly closing in pleasure.

A sense of futility overcame her. How had she ended up like this? She couldn't manage a week of employment without risking everything, and for what? An infatuation with an irresponsible, emotionally damaged hippy-chick who had done nothing but play games with her.

My time is up, Summer, she thought. *I've got nothing to lose. I'll give it one last try. I'll dig up the plant nursery with my bare hands. I'll be the one who found you. But I swear to God, if you suddenly pop up in a new dress saying sorry you meant to call but you met someone gorgeous who took you to Monte Carlo for the week, I swear I will split your fucking skull with a shovel.*

I'm not doing it for you anymore. This is for me.

52.

Pushing her way through the garden's orange birds of paradise and blossoming hibiscus, she emerged from the side stairs onto the terrace. The outside kitchen and patio stood empty in wet shadows, bereft of their former glamour. The loss of sunshine had drained the villa of its colours. A broken drainpipe dribbled water onto the roof of the pool house.

'Doesn't look so good now, does it?'

Jamie was watching her from under a tree. He was folded up with his knees against his chin, his hood pulled low. She had never seen him in different clothes.

'Was that your little temper tantrum, the pot?' Jamie glanced down at the shattered amphora. He climbed to his feet by unbending without taking his hands from his pockets. 'Is it because they fired you?'

She turned to face him. 'Guests don't have the power to fire me. Tomorrow you'll all be gone and I'll still be here, getting ready for the next family.'

'Lucky you. Well, you've heard the truth now. My father didn't kill your girlfriend.'

She wondered how he could possibly know that about her. Maybe he was more perceptive than he looked. 'You can't be sure of that.'

'I think I know him better than you.' The rain fell harder. Jamie wiped his nose on the back of his sleeve. 'Why do you all want to blame him?'

'Who else should we blame?'

'None of you wants to believe the obvious answer. She framed my father. Her disappearance is fake news. She planned the whole thing and ran off with her friends. Not with you. She'd finished with you. You just didn't want to believe it.'

'You know nothing,' said Hannah.

'Yeah, well, you're just the hired help. That's why you can't leave. Without her you don't exist. You're hanging around this place like a ghost. Nobody even remembers who she was or what she looked like.' He gave an odd little laugh. 'Maybe you conjured her up. Maybe you killed her and forgot you did it.' He came closer and stared into her eyes. Without his sunglasses he looked as if he hadn't slept for days. 'We're kind of similar, you and I. Nobody notices me either but I see what goes on, just like you. Outsiders always do. My folks could do whatever they want, but instead they come here and spend the whole time destroying each other. I'd rather be dead than be like them. My father wanted to have sex with someone young and pretty because his dried-up wife only talks to him when she needs something, so what?'

'They're your *parents*.'

'If nobody knew, who would it hurt? Your girlfriend came out here for a married man. It's obvious she threw herself at him.'

Hannah felt the blood rise to her cheeks. 'You say you see what goes on. What have you seen, Jamie? You hide away like a shy seven-year-old because you can't handle adult conversations; you can't even take your headphones off, so what have you picked up in your role of observer?'

'I know what *he* did.' Jamie raised a bitten fingernail and pointed at the villa. Hannah turned and looked up. Giles was standing under the eaves of the terrace.

'What do you mean?'

'He's the betrayer,' Jamie said.

When Giles saw Hannah coming up the stairs toward him he nearly bolted back into the living room, then realised that it would look odd if he did so.

Hannah gave him a false smile. 'I came to say goodbye.' She held out her hand.

Giles looked as if he had been in a car crash. There were wads of crimson tissue wedged in his swollen nasal passages. 'You'll have to pay for that vase-thing you broke. I saw you do it.'

She raised a hand. 'I hope you enjoyed your stay. Please rate us on Tripadvisor. Have a good trip home.'

'You know where she is,' Giles said suddenly, with an air of desperation. 'You do, don't you?'

'I'm through trying to convince any of you. I'm going to go to the police. There are gendarmes in the village. There's enough evidence here to pull up a forensic team from Nice and rip the place apart.'

Giles glanced back at the villa apprehensively. 'You'll need her passport to prove anything. They won't listen to you otherwise. You haven't got it.'

Hannah was suspicious. 'You want to help me?'

'I can get it back for you. I know where it is. Wait here.' He slipped inside and closed the patio door.

She waited.

Giles slid open the patio door and handed Hannah the passport.

He needed to incriminate Steve. All his life he had been the sidekick, the spear carrier, the straight man, the warm-up act. Bullied into a state of serfdom at school, dismissed with faint ridicule at college. He had warded off harm by clinging to his dubious ancestry and his father's connections like Van Helsing clutching a crucifix. The same old prejudices he had endured in the education system soon surfaced in business; he had flailed from one unsustainable career to the next.

Being punched in the face by a boss who, it transpired, had hired him not to bring fine wines to the luncheon tables of London but to stand him in a police line-up when the auditors arrived was the final straw. Right now he would be happy to incriminate the smooth-talking fucker for every crime under the sun. If he was going down he was going to make damned sure that Steve went ahead of him.

If the police need any further circumstantial evidence, Giles was pretty sure there were a few London barmen who'd be able to recall the lovebirds snuggling together and engaging in PDAs.

As Hannah took the passport she noticed that Jamie had disappeared from his spot beneath the tree. He was probably disappointed that the confrontation hadn't ended in another fist fight.

'I didn't see Steve but he's still around somewhere,' Giles warned. 'You'd better be careful. I think he could be extremely dangerous.'

She thanked him but was not quite ready to leave. There was one more thing she had to do.

She made her way down to the plant nursery.

53.

The staircase to the fields was slippery with mud. One look inside the mounds of black earth, she told herself, then she would head to the village. It was just as Daniela had predicted: she would never see any of them again, and would never have any answers.

She didn't see him step out in front of her.

He simply appeared on the landing. He wore a freshly pressed white Gant shirt, navy slacks, brown loafers, one hand casually resting in his pocket. How did he pull off the fashion thing even now?

'Well, well,' he said with false geniality, 'fancy seeing you again.'

The relaxed tone of his voice made her flesh creep.

'You always seem to be lurking somewhere. Why is that? What are you doing out here?' Steve stretched his leg out against the wall, blocking her route to the nursery.

'I'm waiting for you all to leave,' she replied.

'For us all to leave.'

She nodded.

'You don't like me much, do you?'

'I don't know you, Mr Elsbury.'

He wagged his index finger at her. 'You know, something about you bothered me right from the start. You don't look like a maid. You're not the type, not with those neat little hands. Always acting as if you're about to be found out. Every time you were nearby and we were talking you paid too much attention. You girls.' Steve laughed and shook his head. 'I don't know why it took me so long to think of it. You planned this from the very beginning, didn't you?'

'What?'

He tapped a finger at the passport in her right hand. 'You and Summer. I was fooled because she mentioned a boyfriend. But there are no boys allowed here, eh? She forgot the bag in her rush to get out before I arrived, then tried to get you to pick it up behind my back. Was it just her idea or yours as well? It seems like something she'd come up with.'

'I don't know what you're talking about.' Should she bluster and push past him, she thought, or be forced to listen?

'Don't be naïve. This little honey trap. Not just to shame my family but to make it look as if I'd done something to her. She set me up and took off, you kept an eye on me to make sure I was truly fucked, then the pair of you will head off into the sunset together.'

'I never meant to interfere,' Hannah said. 'I just wanted to know the truth.'

'For her sake or yours? Could this just be about you, I wonder? Something bad happened in your past and now you want to do the right thing? Give me the passport.'

'The other gentleman got it for me.'

'Ah, Gentleman Giles. And why would he do that?'

'He wants to see you thrown in jail. Ask him if you don't believe me. I'd like to see that too, so I told him I'd take it.'

'Of course you did.' He came closer and held out his hand.

Her grip on the passport tightened. She tried not to sound panicked. 'I have a friend who knows I'm here. She's waiting for me. If I don't show up –'

He looked into the clouds. 'Tell me, am I in some kind of special hell where men are incessantly tormented by women? Is there a distant race memory of all the bad things we did across the centuries that makes you want to turn around now and fuck us up?'

As she turned to leave he lunged at her and span her around. Hannah released a yell and tried to fight him off, but his size and strength made it an unequal fight. Pulling down on her arm, he forced her to release it. 'I'll have to tell your employer about your habit of stealing.'

'Do what you like,' she said, trying to sound brave. 'I'll find another job.'

He waved the passport at her, happy to be in control again. 'You won't after I've finished with you.' He pulled out a lighter and touched its flame to the corner of the cover. It was slow to burn, the laminate releasing an oily black residue.

She took a step closer to show him that he didn't frighten her. 'I'm still going to the police.'

He walked away from her, the blackening passport in his hand. 'Do what you want. Just get out of here. If you know what's good for you, you'll stay away until we're clear of the place.'

54.

'What's going on out there?' Melissa asked, standing at the window with her hands on her hips. 'I thought you said you told the maid to leave? She's still hanging around. Quite a little firebrand.' She looked around for her coffee cup and added a little more brandy to it. 'You have to make a decision, Jennifer.'

Jennifer appeared not to have heard. She rubbed at a patch of nervous eczema that had appeared on her forehead. 'Jamie will be off our hands soon,' she murmured to herself. 'He was a happy child. Spoiled, of course, but smart and charming, like his father. All that ended with puberty. I thought I'd break through to him and we'd become friends, and it almost happened this week, I could feel it.'

'Sounds to me like you don't know what you want.' Melissa lit a fresh cigarette off the end of the last one, ignoring Jennifer's little cat-coughs. 'When I finally decided I wanted children I almost died trying to have one.' She opened the door and blew the smoke out in a token gesture. 'Well, you declared war. You should have done it a long time ago. Everything that's happened this week has been one big battle for control. I've seen what your husband does. He shuts you down every time you speak. He contradicts and controls and undermines you at every turn. You put the cutlery one way, he realigns it. He clears away any trace you leave behind.' She puffed pensively and like everything else she did, noisily. 'The sunbeds.'

Jennifer looked out at the pool. 'What about them?'

'When we arrived I didn't realise what I was seeing. The sunbeds were wrong.' She tapped the windowpane with a nail. 'You must have noticed. They were all arranged in a perfect line, but one of them had been dragged out and left at an awkward angle with clothing trapped underneath it. Your husband didn't do that, *she* did it. He hadn't got around to straightening it yet. He couldn't have because he would have seen the wrap and taken that as well. But by the time you arrived the loungers were all back in place. The signs were right in front of us and we didn't spot them. We have to alert the police before they find their way here.'

Jennifer knotted and unknotted her hands. 'If we do that who knows what else will come out?'

'You think there's more? The mind boggles.' Melissa tried to imagine such a possibility and gave up.

Jennifer was not listening. 'This will utterly destroy Jamie. He idolises his father.'

'Your husband is a violent, unstable man,' said Melissa. 'We need to act now.'

Jennifer went to the window and placed a hand on the glass. 'Perhaps I should let things take their natural course. Go away by myself for a few days and work through my options.'

Melissa was disgusted. 'You sound like you're ready to take him back.'

'People with money have choices. I don't have the luxury of deciding for myself. We're tied to each other financially.' Jennifer paced about the room, desperate for something to do. 'All my cash is locked up in his business.'

'I can give you the number of a very sympathetic divorce lawyer.'

Jennifer turned to her with a look of desperation. 'I don't want to lose Jamie.'

'Then you must decide what you value most.'

They stood beside each other looking out of the window as a fresh squall of rain hit the glass.

'Oh my God,' said Melissa, 'Steve's attacking the maid.'

55.

Steve waited until the remains of the passport were blackened glue, and took his leave, striding up the steps to disappear behind the manicured hedges of the terrace.

As she watched him go, Hannah realised she was shaking. When Steve's charm was switched off there was nothing beneath it but radiating malice. She stood beside the hibiscus bushes and looked down at the plant nursery. It was guarded by olive trees, urns, spades and a row of spiny cactuses lined against the low stone wall.

She tried to keep out of sight of the main windows by cutting across the flower bed, but missed her footing and landed on her knees, smearing glutinous mud across her jeans. Picking up a shovel, she headed for the first tamped-down mound of fresh earth and dug into it. The soil was soft and easy to remove, but there was nothing to be found. Trying the mound at the far end of the row, she doggedly removed chunks of soil.

It began to rain harder. She was covered in mud but could

not stop. The long trench where Daniela said Matthias buried his stash ran behind the mounds. She was not comfortable about disturbing it but knew it was where she had to look next.

About a foot down she uncovered a long grey metal screwdriver tray filled with small clear plastic bags. The one she balanced in her palm felt as if it was filled with icing sugar. She carefully put it back in place and was about to start returning the earth, hoping it would look as it did before, when she saw something red in the bottom of the pit. It was dark under the tree cover, so she pulled out her phone and ran its light over the piece of crimson cloth that stuck out of the dirt.

'Summer,' she said, reaching out a hand.

But as the phone light moved across the material she saw it was not Summer, just part of a towel Mattias had used and dropped into the hole. She tamped down the earth and rose.

There was no point in lurking around the grounds getting soaked. She was not going to start pulling the gardener's compost heaps apart. All this time she had been so sure that Summer could not have left because she couldn't accept that *she* had been left. The fault was all hers for reading something into their friendship that wasn't there.

So Summer broke a glass and cut her foot and caught her neck chain and was forced for some mundane reason to leave her belongings behind – the rest had been filled in by her over-active imagination in the way that the human brain compensated for a lack of visual input, and look at the chaos it had caused. Julia had been right all along: start talking to the guests and you quickly got yourself in a huge mess of trouble.

So much for her last attempt at uncovering the truth. It was time to admit defeat. She would walk to the village and call Daniela. Collecting her cagoule from the pool house, she climbed the side stairs and opened the back gate. The red earth path to the main road had turned into a river of mud. Stamping her feet on the tarmac, she rounded the next spur of land and saw the distant edge of the village.

Coming toward her was a gang of men in brown dungarees and orange waterproofs, the farm workers she always saw in Raphael's bar. She couldn't be sure that they were heading for the Villa Lavardin but there was nothing else up this way and they didn't look like they were going to work in the fields today. Some of them were quite obviously drunk. They were so busy talking among themselves that they hadn't seen her yet.

As she watched they stopped and moved to the side of the road, arguing heatedly with one another. Jacob threw aside his empty beer can and uncorked a bottle of calvados.

It was her fault they were here. She couldn't let them turn up at the villa without warning the guests, even after all that had happened. She turned and ran back before they could see her.

When Jennifer looked in on Jamie she found him buried under his blanket, asleep with his headphones on. The ability of the young to remain unconscious through everything always amazed her. She considered waking him but decided against it. It was best for her to go quickly and quietly.

Returning to her bedroom, she closed up her bag and carried it into the hall. A few minutes ago she had checked the EasyJet website. There were plenty of reasonably priced single seats available to Paris. She would book one on the way to the airport, find a good hotel and wait it out there, then decide what to do in her own time. She only had a light summer coat with her, nothing that could keep the rain out. She hadn't expected weather like this. She hadn't expected anything like this.

Jennifer was sure of one thing: even if Summer turned up on the doorstep this minute and swore that nothing had happened between her and Steve, her marriage was over. Her loyalty had been transmuted into something poisoned and foolish.

'It looks like you've finally made up your mind. Bravo.'

Steve stood in the doorway watching her. He moved about so silently that she was often startled by his sudden appearance. She had to be very careful now. She had no idea what state of mind he was in, or whether he was dangerous. He had been drinking, that much was certain.

'I need some time to think,' she said, checking for her handbag. 'I'll call you when I'm ready.'

'So you're not going home.'

'No, Steven, I'm not.' She set down her bag for a moment and studied his face, looking for any trace of emotion. 'Have you told me one true thing on this trip? Is it all just some game to you?'

Steve's dimple went up. He pursed his lips, thinking. 'I think everyone is overreacting.'

'Where were you while Giles took all those meetings? Or is that something else I'm not supposed to know about?'

He considered the question. 'I couldn't sit there listening to him bleat on in front of his inconvenienced contacts, humiliating himself, watching those tight little smiles from people desperate to get away. I waited in coffee shops and bars. I drove along the promenade in Nice, I drove around the hills up here, always trying to think how to save the company. Jennifer, I don't want you to go. Jamie's upset and I don't know how to deal with him.'

She regarded him with detachment. 'I spent enough time trying to help him when what he really needed was you. It's your turn now.'

Steve smacked a hand against the lintel. 'I can't believe this shit. I met a girl in London. I asked her to join me on a business trip. How do I even know she came out here? I spoke to her on the phone, she could have been in the UK, faking it. The maid is the one who's been leaving stuff all over the place, writing notes and making up stories. I mean, she's clearly frustrated and obsessed.'

'The agent told me –'

'The agent met somebody, certainly, but I never saw her. The barman in the village says he saw a pretty girl who could have been anyone. Without her the whole thing is just a fantasy.'

'But you admitted –'

'I admitted having thoughts about a girl. Nobody has been unfaithful. Nobody has been murdered. Nothing has happened.'

'What about the little girl from the village?'

He shook his head in disbelief. 'And she has nothing to do with this.'

'So it's just Summer who doesn't exist?'

She tried to push past him but he stopped her. 'You've got it all wrong, Jennifer. If you tell yourself that there never was a girl she will simply disappear. Everything can go back to normal. If you go now, I won't take you back.'

'Being with you is such a prize, isn't it?' She angrily shoved at his arm but it remained unmoved. 'Say goodbye to Jamie for me.'

'What are you going to say about me?' he asked.

'I can't imagine there are many people who'd be interested anymore,' she answered. 'Let me go, Steven.'

He looked confused. 'I can't do that. We have to sort this out, get our stories straight. I can't have people thinking –'

'– that you murdered a girl because she wouldn't have sex with you, no, I guess not. But I'm sure you'll come up with something to tell them because you always do. Only this time I'm around to give them the true version.'

His right hand came down on her before she realised what was happening.

Jennifer tried to lift herself from the floor but a spasm of pain seared across her right ear. She touched her index finger to her face and drew it back wet. All sounds shifted to her left side only.

'It's your fault. You shouldn't have pushed me.' He stared at his hand, appalled.

She rose in silence, brushed herself down with elaborate care, and checked herself in the dressing table mirror. His wedding ring had caught her ear and nicked it. A rivulet of blood striped her cheek. The cut looked more dramatic than it was.

'You did it, didn't you?' she said. 'You set her up as your mistress, and when she wouldn't do what you wanted you gave her one of your playful punches. But she stayed down. Where did you put her?'

'There is no girl,' Steve said with soft menace. 'There never was a girl. Nobody died. A girl like that is too perfect to exist. You're being irrational.'

'I feel very rational. Maybe for the first time.' She took out a tissue and dabbed at the cut. 'The police are going to take this place apart, and they'll keep going until they find her.'

'There's nothing to find because there is no Summer Farrow.' He sounded confident and calm now, as if he had reached his decision and was back in control of the narrative. He glanced along the corridor toward Jamie's room.

She made no further attempt to wipe away the blood but freshened her lipstick instead. She would wear the cut like a badge of honour. 'It's okay, Stephen, your son didn't see you. He never sees anything bad. You've always made sure of that. Stay away from me until I've gone.'

'I didn't mean to hurt you. I don't know what to do, Jennifer. Nobody believes me.'

'Enjoy the sensation. It must be new to you.' She stood her ground against him until he moved aside, then pulled up the handle of her bag with a sharp snap.

She glanced out of the staircase window.

Hannah was walking up to the side gate and trying the handle.

56.

Hannah stood on the other side of the gate attempting to raise the latch when suddenly it fell inwards and she looked up to find Jennifer staring through the gap at her. Her hair was a mess and she had blood running from her right ear.

'It's amazing how you always seem to be in the way,' Jennifer said. 'How everything always comes back to you.'

'Mrs Elsbury, are you okay?' Hannah asked, raising a hand. 'There are some men from the village on their way here. They're just up the road a bit. They've been drinking.'

'What kind of men?'

'They're farm workers, they're always hanging around the village bar. They want to ask you some questions. They think there's a barn on the property where the little girl might have ended up.'

'Christ. Can you keep them away from here? You know we're leaving first thing tomorrow. Call the police and report your friend missing if you want, but leave us out of it. Just say you never spoke to us.'

Hannah glanced back at the turn-off. She could hear them distantly arguing. 'I don't think they're going to be very reasonable.'

Realisation crossed Jennifer's face. 'This is because you've been in the village telling all and sundry about your friend, isn't it? They've put the two missing girls together and think it's us. You have to talk to them.'

'They'll come for your husband whether I talk to them or not.'

'This is absurd. I can't… I'm not going to do this.'

She slammed the garden gate shut and went back inside.

Hannah was amazed. What was the woman going to do when the men confronted her, keep the front door bolted and shout at them through the letterbox? Where did she think she was, in some rural part of England where people still argued over parking spaces? Pulling out her phone, she called Raphael at Chez Dany.

'I just saw some of your customers on their way here,' she told him. 'They're not sober and I think they're going to cause trouble. Why didn't you stop them?'

Raphael sounded upset. 'I couldn't, Hannah. They just want some answers.'

'Did you tell the gendarmes?'

'There's no point.'

'What are you talking about?'

'The police chief is happy to let them go. He can't walk onto private property and search it without a warrant. This means he can arrive there later with his boys and take away evidence. You understand? Evidence that Matthias may have.'

The penny dropped. They had been waiting for an

opportunity to take his drugs. They could destroy Matthias's relationship with his sellers and net themselves a haul that would never appear on the books. How long had the gendarmes been waiting for a chance like this to come along? They couldn't gain access to the Villa Lavardin and tear up the nursery without being reported, which meant they would have to log everything they took.

'Jacob is with them,' she told him. 'If he loses his temper again, someone could get seriously hurt this time.'

Raphael gave a deep sigh. 'What can you do? These things have to run their course. I told you that's how it works around here but you didn't listen. Hannah, you should get away as soon as you can. This is not about you or your guests.'

She ended the call. To get to the village she would have to pass the gang. She would be safer staying in the villa. She started to sympathise with Madame Lavardin, who had never been able to escape.

The old lady had said something odd about her husband. *Emil brought the darkness into our home.* He had kept dangerous company and failed to keep it out. Emil Lavardin had rebuilt the villa and his wife had painted a terrible picture of it…

She found herself looking at the photograph she had taken of Madame Lavardin's oil painting. The colours and proportions were hopelessly wrong.

She looked back up at the villa, then at the photograph of the painting once more.

It really was a terrible daub. Crooked lime-green pines and a fire-engine-red roof, five doors, four chimneys and three rows of windows, five, five and five.

The villa had five doors, four chimneys and three rows of windows. Five, five and six.

Madame Lavardin must have finished the painting before the remodelling was complete because in it the garden steps were only half-built and the doors were a different colour. In the building that stood before her, one extra window had appeared.

Hannah tried to imagine everything as Summer saw it on the afternoon she vanished.

The water stippling the surface of the pool. Barbeque tongs rocking slightly on the iron griddle. A breeze rustling the blue bushes along the terrace. The branches dipping in sequence as if a large hand was slowly brushing across them. A second wave of chill air followed, and a lesser third. They seemed to be guiding her eye in one direction.

Look up, said Summer.

Even from this proximity it took her a while to locate it. Glancing between her phone and the view it was now in plain sight, a small square indentation with four tiny panes that looked wrong. Why were they greyed out?

The window was fake.

It had to be in one of the squat buildings that stood between the main residence and the guest wing. There were still only five outer doors visible, all of which she had used, so the room with the false window could only be accessible from within the villa. She had searched all the communal areas and the various airless rooms that housed gardening tools, spare mattresses and sports equipment. This one had eluded her because there was no obvious way into it.

A hidden room. *Emil brought the darkness into our home.*

Less than a hundred yards along the road, six grim-faced men were getting closer to the villa. She heard voices strengthening, their boisterous confidence growing. The farmhands were trying to navigate the muddy path to the front door. Jacob stamped in a brown puddle and spattered one of the other men with mud. Moments later they were fighting.

Hannah ran inside, passing through the ground-floor rooms, checking each in turn. It was difficult matching the interior of the villa to the old painting. As she stopped and retreated to another corridor she wondered if everything had been rebuilt. It felt as if she was in a maze where walls and furniture rearranged themselves behind her back, drawing her in, preventing her from escape.

She should have left quickly and quietly without stopping, should have run away from the villa and never looked back, but it was too late for that. At the foot of the stairs she froze and listened for a moment.

The doorbell suddenly rang repeatedly and urgently. She went downstairs.

When she reached the kitchen she was amazed to see Giles wander past licking an ice lolly.

'Ah – er, still here,' he said redundantly. 'I got one of these out of the freezer to put on my nose but they're nicer if you eat them. I, er, imagine someone is sorting out a tip for you?' He sounded drunk. The doorbell rang again.

'Do you think we should answer that?' he wondered, setting the lolly down on the draining board. 'I thought it might be Jennifer's car but I'm sort of trying not to get involved. Perhaps you could –?'

She looked at him in dumbfounded amazement and headed out onto the rainy terrace.

57.

The nearest door was at least twenty feet away from the fake window, but she went there anyway. It was locked. She searched through her keys, trying each in turn.

The room was off the passageway connecting the two main buildings. Its interior was penumbral and smelled of damp, but was not as dark as she had expected. Dim daylight fell from the corner of the ceiling where a tile had come loose in the storm. A lethal-looking saguaro cactus awaited planting, its roots wrapped in a plastic bag. A green ping pong table stood folded in half, its net awaiting repair. Against the rear wall were dust-cloths, decorating equipment, a garden rake, an upright double mattress. The room seemed to serve no real purpose. There was nothing else to see.

Summer, are you here?

There was a faint clink of metal. She strained to hear.

Where are you?

She looked again at the back wall. The one item that seemed

out of place was the mattress. When she pushed against its edge, she realised that it was made of foam and moved easily.

'My husband lived in fear of them coming to the house,' Madame Lavardin had told her.

The low wooden door behind it was fitted flush to the plaster and had a rusted open lock. A black rubber wedge was pushed in at its base. Kicking it out, she pulled and the door grudgingly opened. She had to duck low to get through the entrance.

'Emil hid himself behind locked doors,' Madame Lavardin had said.

Locked doors.

Emil Lavardin had built himself a safe room, for all the good it did him, and had died because he'd let in a friend. In order to lead a secure and undisturbed life, Madame Lavardin had allowed the stories around his death to multiply. It didn't matter so long as no one realised the truth, that he had been hunted down by the local people he had trusted. It was the only way she could ensure her own future safety.

The grey chamber beyond the little door had absolutely no light, so she flicked on her phone's torch. There was an overpowering stench of faeces and unwashed flesh.

The safe room had metal shelving units along two walls, and was still filled with cans and jars of vegetables. Seen from this side it was obvious that the 'window' was nothing more than a painted and riveted steel cover set in peeling plaster. There were rudimentary washing facilities in one corner, just a drain and a tap, and an old-fashioned ceramic chain-flush toilet with no seat. She supposed it was possible to live in here for a while if you had to.

The girl was folded up on a filthy brown blanket on the floor, her left wrist tied with a thin rope attached to the base of a shelf unit. Her hair was sticky and matted with straw.

'My God. Summer.'

A half-eaten bread roll and an opened tin of sardines lay beside her right foot. Her red floral-print dress was stained and badly torn. She moaned and slowly turned her head.

Hannah took a step forward and reached out to touch her, raising her phone light in her other hand. As its glare moved across the captive girl she saw that it was not Summer.

Hannah whispered, 'Clémence, you have to wake up.'

The girl opened her eyes, then reacted as if she had been hit. She tried to scramble to her feet but the rope would not let her get further away. Twisting violently, she kicked out and released a volley of croaks, trying to free herself. She moved with the abandon of someone who did not care about injury.

Suddenly she stopped dead. Her eyes rolled up to their whites and she dropped, passing out. It looked as if she suffered from some form of epilepsy. She fell without hurting herself, an internal mechanism that prepared her for the familiar loss of consciousness. Her breathing became regular once more.

Hannah searched around for a way to remove her binding. She now saw that it was an old-fashioned skipping rope, much stronger than it first appeared. She ran back into the store room, searching for something that could cut through it, but in her panic all she found was a pair of rusted secateurs.

When she looked for the rope's end she realised that its painted wooden handle had simply been looped back on itself and tethered behind a heavy can of paint. It was enough to hold the girl in place because she did not have the ability to unravel it. Clémence began to stir.

'I can get you out of here,' Hannah promised, as much for her own sake as the girl's. She began to unwind the rope, trying to stay away from Clémence's limbs in case she started to flail again. It took a while to get the whole thing untangled, but now the girl would not stay still. She grunted and twisted and tipped her open mouth up at the ceiling, rolling her eyes back and forth. Hannah tried to contain her undirected energy but she flinched away, pushing further back from her in distress.

'It's all right, I'm not going to hurt you. *Je ne vais pas te faire de mal.* I want to get you out of here and take you home.'

She shone her phone torch into Clémence's flickering eyes. The girl released a knife-edge scream that hurt her ears. 'Please, calm down,' she begged, trying to show that she meant no harm. 'What happened to you?'

Under her coaxing, Clémence began to relax a little. Her breathing was an angry rasp, but steadier. Hannah undid the rope's last knot and cast it aside. She tried to get Clémence to stand, but her legs had trouble supporting her. She gave an odd bird shriek, a sound Hannah had heard before.

'You can do it, Clémence, you can stand. We can go home to see your mummy now.'

Clémence took a wavering step forward, then another, but Hannah knew it would be best if she carried her as soon as they got outside.

She ran to the door and pushed it back as hard as she could, and was about to return for the girl when she saw a figure on the stone path ahead of her. As it lumbered toward her she realised who it was.

'I heard that, I think the whole valley did,' said Giles. 'I didn't do anything.' He was shame-faced and miserable. 'I went out for a run but I got a stitch. She followed me back.'

She glanced at the safe room and saw that the girl had scuttled away into the shadows.

Hannah was determined to make Giles see that she was not afraid of him. When he spoke again, the sound of falling rain made him hard to hear.

'They always seek me out,' he explained. 'I think they must sense something. I'm ineffectual. You know, unthreatening.' It sounded so mundane, but she supposed the truth often was.

'She started crying so I gave her a big hug. You have to do that when something is hurting, you have to show love. When I stopped hugging her I realised she'd gone to sleep. I couldn't wake her. I didn't know what to do. The gardener had just been, so I rested her in the hole he'd made. He can't say anything because I know he cut the camera cables to keep his dope operation secret. I never meant it to happen. Who would? A man would have to be a monster. I didn't mean for you to find her. Poor little thing.'

As Hannah listened, it dawned on her that he was talking about the cat, not its owner. He had seen the holes she had dug in the gardener's nursery. Clémence was wearing a piece of blue ribbon around her left wrist, the other half of which had been around Pitou's neck.

'Such pretty white fur. She wouldn't have lived long,' Giles concluded sadly. 'She had tumours the size of golf balls under her little ribcage, so it was the kindest thing.'

58.

Before Hannah had a chance to reply, Clémence came running out of the store room at them with a scream. She swooped up the plastic bag that held the roots of the saguaro cactus and swung it over her head like a club.

Giles did not see what was coming toward him on the path. Clémence smashed the fat green spears of the plant into his face, where its spikes stuck fast, showering him in soil. Screaming, he tried to pull them from his flesh but only succeeded in filling his palms with pale needles. He fell back, stumbling out of the doorway.

Hannah watched in horror as Giles tottered about yowling like a crucified cat, the cactus firmly embedded in his face. At the top of the staircase he lost his footing and disappeared from view.

She ran down the steps, looking for Clémence, and spotted her hurtling off around the gardens like a fiery red Catherine wheel. When she dashed at the bamboo fence and slid straight through the only gap, Hannah realised just how well Clémence knew the layout of the house. Of course she did; she had always roamed through the area while her father worked in the fields.

Giles lay face down at the bottom of the staircase amid the shattered remains of the cactus and its soil. While trying to break his fall and prevent the cactus from being driven any further into his face, he had landed hard and snapped his wrist. His right hand was stuck at an impossible angle, the little finger twitching. As he tried to grasp with his left hand the spines that protruded from his eyes, cheeks and under his chin, he whimpered and squirmed, making the pain catastrophically worse.

Hannah looked up. The bushes rustled and stopped still. Clémence had gone. She knew she would never be able to catch up with the girl. The farmhands from Chez Dany were presumably milling about outside, trying to get in. If Clémence ran into them there was no telling what might happen.

There was nothing she could do to help Giles. Making her way up to the main building, she stopped by the double doors and checked that the living room was empty. She could understand why Giles had killed the cat but had no idea why he had taken the child. He must have spent much of his time with her, inside the villa but apart from it. A terrible pressure was building in her stomach, a feeling of something even worse to come.

When she patted the pocket of her jeans she realised she had left her phone in the safe room. She wasn't scared of Giles but curiosity possessed her. She ran past the front door, where the men were now bellowing and pounding their fists, and was about to head out through the patio.

Instead she stopped and listened.

A man had begun shouting loudly, as if through a megaphone,

his words echoing and indecipherable. The voice didn't belong to anyone she recognised. It was coming from the living room and had a tiresome hectoring timbre, as if someone filled with his own self-importance was making a speech.

The droning voice was coming from a portable speaker on the coffee table. It was speaking in German and nagged with the rhythmic repetition of a faulty flywheel. Suddenly an equally pompous English voice cut in to translate.

Hitler believed that Goethe and Shakespeare were worn-out and obsolete, that they produced nothing but filth…

Next to the speaker was an iPhone. She checked its illuminated screen. It read: *Part Two. The Strong Man is Strongest When He Acts Alone.* A podcast examination of *Mein Kampf.*

With a growing sense of dread she thumbed down the list of audiofiles on the phone. White supremacy. Serial killers. UFO cover-ups. Conspiracy theories.

Behind her Jamie stepped back into the room. She was still holding his phone. 'We need a doctor,' she said, trying to remain calm. 'Giles has had an accident.'

He snatched the phone from her and pocketed it. 'You can't use that one, I need it.' He reeked of super skunk and was having trouble standing up. 'There's a bunch of drunken yokels outside. I'm surprised they haven't got burning torches. Why isn't anybody dealing with them? Where's Giles?'

She pointed from the window. 'Down there.' He was writhing and crying at the bottom of the staircase, crawling about on the stones.

'What happened?' Jamie was suddenly interested.

'The girl got away.'

'What are you talking about?'

'I let her out. She's gone.'

'Show me.'

They headed across the patio and down the short staircase that led to the store room, although Jamie crashed through a couple of bushes on the way.

When he saw that the door was open and the chamber beyond it empty, the skipping rope lying across the floor, he roared, slapping at the wall. Without his hooded sweatshirt he appeared diminished and vulnerable, reduced to a skinny teenaged boy, a pale creature extracted from its armoured shell.

Hannah stayed beyond his reach. 'Why did you take her?' she asked as he bent over, breathing hard, his hands on his knees.

'Just tell me where she went.'

'She's gone home, Jamie.'

'Nobody knew she was here. *Nobody*.'

'I found the room. Giles saw the door open. He came in and she attacked him. She thought it was you coming back. Giles badly needs medical attention.'

'Let him die, who gives a fuck?'

'What did you do to her?'

Jamie trotted back and forth, uncoordinated and powerless.

'Did you assault her?'

'No, of course not.'

'Why did you take her?'

'I didn't. She was always hanging around at the bottom of the garden, looking for something. I couldn't fucking get rid of her.'

'So you tied her up with her own skipping rope.'

He seemed distracted, lost to his own thoughts. 'I fed her. She needed to understand.'

'Understand what? She's mentally subnormal, Jamie.'

'I was teaching her some respect. She got away earlier but I brought her back.'

'I heard her crying,' Hannah murmured. 'Were you just going to leave her here when the trip was over?'

'I was going to release her before I left.'

'Having power over someone like that is no power at all.'

'Everybody does what my father tells them to do.' As he looked around the store room she began to back away. He was searching for something in the stacked equipment. She realised that there was a rack of lethal-looking knives on the far wall but he ignored them.

'Summer didn't. What did you do to her?'

'Nothing. I never saw her. None of us did.' He reached in between the paint cans and rakes and rummaged around, pulling something loose. A shovel fell over with a clatter.

'You didn't know her,' said Hannah. 'She made a fool of your father. And you can't handle that. That's why you took the girl. You thought you were taking back control.'

'You can shut up now.' Jamie ignored her to concentrate on what was in his hands.

'You're not your father.' She had almost reached the door at her back. She talked knowing that if she stopped now he would see the vulnerability of her situation. 'Your little adventure into the world of men is already over, Jamie. The girl is on her way home and she'll bring the police here. Steve won't bail you out this time.'

He lashed at her with such speed and ferocity that she had no time to get out of the way. Falling back, she landed hard on the stone floor. He unlooped the blue nylon cord in his hands and pulled it over her head, dragging her across the ground in a single practised movement.

She tried to get her fingers under the cord but it was already too late. He was holding tight to the ends. He got as far as the doorway with her when she threw her legs wide, stopping him from going any further.

She could see the garden rake that had fallen to the floor and grabbed at it, but the pain at her throat was now so great that she could barely lift it.

He stepped down on her right thigh, then her left. When her limbs recoiled he was able to drag her out of the store room. His actions were workmanlike and mechanical, as if he had been tasked with removing sacks of soil.

As he pulled her toward the steps he slackened the rope for a second and she responded without thinking, lifting the rake by the end of its handle and swinging it behind her as hard as she could.

She almost missed. One of the tines caught the base of his neck, just above the collarbone, and hooked in when she twisted it. He was unable to move toward her without her pushing it deeper into his neck. She tried to slide out from beneath him but there was something wrong with her left ankle. Jamie shifted forward, still pinned in place, clawing at the rake head.

The sound of smashing glass came from somewhere above them, followed by shouts. Jamie pulled the rake tine from his neck and pressed his palm over the wound.

'They're inside,' Hannah said.

59.

The farmhands quickly became convinced that the guests were hiding something from them. The villa was obviously occupied but no one was prepared to answer. The arrogance of the British incensed them.

Jacob had acquired a machete from somewhere and hammered at the door with the end of its handle, but when that brought no response he picked up a rock and smashed a hole in the side window. The others started shouting at him – was he mad? Who would have to pay for the damage?

'Do you want to find the girl or not?' he bellowed back, putting his hand through the glass and trying to unlock the door. Instead he cut his arm and started hopping around, swearing and dripping blood on the path.

The argument among the others ended when one of them kicked the door open with his boot, splintering the lintel. They entered the kitchen to find a strange woman backed against the kitchen counter in a white towelling robe, a towel turreted on her head. Melissa unrolled the towel and took off her headphones – she had just had a bath in the guest annexe and had only come back for more wine. For a moment the incongruity of the situation stopped anyone from moving.

As soon as Steve entered, Jacob knew he had a target in his sights. He thrust the machete into the space between them and started furiously shouting in Steve's face. 'I've seen you making fun of us. Not so funny now, is it? What did you do with the girl?'

'How many times do I have to explain?' Steve shouted back at them. 'It's all in your minds. She never existed. There is no girl!'

'What the hell is going on?' Melissa asked, repulsed by the mud-streaked, drunken, red-faced farm worker whose right arm was streaked with blood. 'Who are these people? What on earth do they want?'

'These fucking inbreds think I killed Summer. Is there anyone left who doesn't believe I did it?'

When Melissa realised that Steve was the sole focus of their attention, she backed into the living room and smartly slipped out through the patio doors, taking a decent Shiraz with her. Jennifer was getting into her Nice-bound taxi, leaving them to deal with this ridiculous lynch mob – and where were the others?

Leaning over the terrace balustrade, she caught sight of Giles lying on his back at the bottom of the staircase that led off the property. The wine bottle smashed. She gave a cry and ran down the stairs, dropping to her knees beside him.

What on earth had he done to himself this time? What on earth had happened to his face? His flesh was a swollen mass of crimson ruptures, spikes grotesquely protruding from his eyes and cheeks, even his bloody gums.

———

Hannah and Jamie were frozen in place, their war overtaken by greater events. Hannah could smell the faintest trace of the perfume she had smelled every day in the villa, the scent of Summer that continued to linger around them all. She had brought this chaos down upon them like a goddess seeking vengeance for some perceived transgression.

Hannah looked back at the bewildered boy, his hand still clasped over the wound on his neck. He was checking to see if it had stopped bleeding when she punched the rake into his groin and rammed him into a plant bed filled with lethal-looking succulents.

As he fell onto his back she dropped the rake handle over his throat and lightly stood on it. She waited until his face had turned purple and he was started to lose consciousness before she raised her foot.

'You're not your father,' she said, walking away from him.

60.

Twenty-three minutes before she needed to go and get ready, Summer squeezed the rest of the oil onto her arms and massaged it in. She slathered her arms and legs, rubbing the rest into her chest and neck.

She raised her sunglasses and examined her domain. Everything about the villa reminded her of her father's place in Almeria. The first time she had gone there he had taken her onto the top terrace to watch the sunset, a spot of rickety wicker fences, joss sticks and rattan armchairs, and as the sky turned orange he told her she would never have to leave. She could come and live in the house with him, and would never need to return home. But when he remarried the offer was deferred and finally withdrawn amid apologies and excuses and wary little glances from his new young bride. When she got sick he didn't even bother to ring the clinic.

Summer raised herself onto one elbow. The first dying leaves had been shaken free by the recent winds and were now drifting into the water. Presumably Julia had garden staff who came in between rentals.

As she put down her foot she felt a sting in the sole. The curved sliver of broken glass came out cleanly, but blood ran under her toe ring and she left a dark print on the patio stones. She should have changed the cocktail glass for a plastic beaker. She imagined filling the pool with broken glass so that when Steve dived in he would emerge screaming, looking like a shark victim.

She started to think about making him suffer.

It would be so easy.

She tried another bloody footprint. This one was better. It was unmistakably hers because the toe ring left a gap in the print. She rubbed her thumb and index finger on the cut and left a bloody print on the arm of the sun lounger.

Given his track record, Steve would be so late arriving that he wouldn't have time to clear up before his wife and son got to the villa. The mischief grew in her. She thought: how else could she get him into trouble?

Running back up into the main house, she scattered her stuff in every room. Chocolate wrappers, packaging, tissues, bottles, clothes, magazines, a cheap bangle, anything she could think of. She hid makeup in the bedroom and pop socks in the bathroom.

She stood back and surveyed her work. It looked like a petulant teenager had thrown a tantrum, which wasn't the impression she wanted to leave at all. The mess would only cause him a slight inconvenience. Hiding her clothes about the place wasn't enough to make life difficult for him. What about something more obvious?

Her fingers touched the chain at her neck.

She had told Hannah a fanciful tale about it being given to her by her mother, as if her mother would ever have thought about anyone other than herself for a second. Summer had bought it in a street market last year, and the gold plate was already rubbing off. Yanking it from her neck, she dropped the chain near the scarlet footprint where it would be spotted.

Satisfied with her work, she returned to the lounger to enjoy her last few minutes of sunshine.

61.

On the staircase below the swimming pool a hysterical Giles clung uselessly to a stone pillar, attempting to haul himself upright. Melissa tried to lift him up the steps but he tumbled back down, dropping onto his knee with a shotgun crack and falling onto his face before she could stop him.

As the rain fell with renewed force, Melissa stepped back. 'I have to get help,' she explained. 'Just try to –' She stopped, unable to imagine what he should try to do. He shuddered violently and passed out. She needed to find her phone and call an ambulance. The rain battered routes through the canopy of branches, washing Giles's blood into the earth.

There was an eruption of glass up above as one of the patio windows lost its panes. The doors were thrown back with a great crash and Steve appeared like a chased fox, heading along the terrace.

The drunken farmhands yelled at him to stop but were still fighting among themselves. One had lost interest and was taking a piss against the birds of paradise. It was hard to tell if any of them meant to cause harm or whether they were merely enjoying themselves. One hurled a flowerpot at him but it went wide, smashing messily across the tiles. Steve headed down the stairs, closely pursued.

When Hannah stumbled from the staircase and raised her head above the parapet, she saw that the farmhands had cornered Steve by the shallow end of the pool, shouting and gesturing. They were demanding answers to their bellowed questions, but all he could do was shake his head in denial and confusion. Just when he should have shown some humility, he found himself unable to back down.

'He knows where she is, the fucking rapist,' Jacob shouted, but no one was listening.

Hannah was the passive observer of a tesseract of catastrophe that seemed to double in size each time it unfolded. Jacob pushed in front of his friends and speared the machete into Steve's already damaged shirt, tearing it wide, ripping the fine silk and sending pearlized buttons skittering over the wet tiles.

For a moment there was an impasse as each side regarded the other.

It could have stopped there, Hannah thought afterwards.

She ducked back down the steps and saw that Jamie had disappeared from the spot where he had fallen between the bushes. She checked on either side of the path. The rain was washing a streak of blood from the fat spiny leaves of an agave plant.

A lizard was staring at her from the sheltering darkness of the plant. She bent closer to see.

Jamie's outstretched hand, spider-like, seized her shirt, dragging her toward him. She fought to keep herself from falling into the agave's razor-leaves.

'Let go of me, Jamie,' she warned, but his grip tightened and she felt the soft soil sliding beneath her trainers as she was pulled forward. 'Listen to me. You didn't hurt the girl and you never met Summer. You haven't done anything. You said you didn't want to be like your parents. Now's your chance to prove it.'

The pressure eased for the briefest of moments. Swinging her arm wide she caught at a bamboo plant stick and tore it loose, ramming it into the shadowed space beneath the plant, where it struck something soft.

Jamie let out a yowl of pain. Her feet slid away in the mud and she dropped onto her back. Jamie half emerged, clawing at the branches, his white hoodie caught on the spines of the succulents. The more he struggled to free himself, the more entangled he became in their tenacious grip. He seemed about to cry.

She left him helplessly pinned in the bushes. A bright green lizard balanced splay-legged on a rain-streaked leaf, dispassionately watching his futile struggles.

She climbed back to the patio moments before the stand-off beside the pool broke down.

Steve was holding his ground. She did not hear what he said, but could tell he had struck the wrong tone. He pointed accusingly, he raised the flat of his hand; he was demanding that they leave. The farm workers roared at him and moved forward. Steve had nowhere else to go. The pool was at his back. Jacob shouted and raised his machete.

Steve took a hopelessly wide swing at Jacob, who shoved him hard with the heel of his free hand.

As Steve fell back, he slipped on the wet edge of the pool and went down. His skull hit the concrete lip with a crack that could be heard from where Hannah was standing. She saw a flash of scarlet burst out from his hairline. His hands went up to his face but this was no small cut to be stemmed with pressure. He suddenly convulsed, slithering down the pool steps. The side of his head looked like a seed-case that had split open.

Once in the water he thrashed briefly and sank stomach-down in the shallow end. The farmhands reacted in panic and started shouting at one another. Lost in the darkly clouding water, Steve ceased to move and slipped deeper.

One of the men tried to wade into the pool and retrieve the body, but only managed to push it further out of reach. His friend pulled him back and suddenly they were all in wild disarray, pushing, shouting and shoving, each desperate to be the first off the premises.

Transfixed, Hannah stepped onto the pool patio. Steve was spread-eagled under the water at the pool's deep end, his head lost in a maroon cloud. All the yelling ceased. Jacob and the rest of the farmhands had frozen into a tight group. They had stopped shouting at each other and were looking at a common enemy.

'Please,' Hannah said. 'Clémence has gone – she ran away from here. She's on her way home.'

'You,' said Jacob, pointing at her with the tip of the machete. 'You caused all this. You took my baby girl. You took my daughter.'

'She's not your daughter anymore, Jacob,' said one of the farmhands behind him. 'They wouldn't let you keep her.'

'She's still my blood. My Clémence.'

Slipping free from his companions he ran at her with a bellow of rage as blind and wild as the sky. Hannah saw his right arm rise up, saw him swing the machete blade toward her face, saw someone else arriving on the staircase in a lurid flash of purple, too late to distract him.

She lifted her hands and although she realised the terrible foolishness of this movement she found herself unable to prevent the action. She shut her eyes tight.

I'm sorry, Summer, she thought, *I failed you.*

The blade did not cut into her arms. There was a crack, like a branch being snapped.

With her palms still wide before her, she opened her eyes.

Jacob was lying on the ground clutching his right knee, which was pouring blood. The machete lay unmarked several feet away.

'You think you are some big shots but let me tell you, little boys, I am a better shot,' said a voice that owed its husky timbre to forty Gauloises and a bottle of red wine a day. Julia Martinez spotted her at once. 'Hannah, what have you done to my villa? Everything smash bang with the breakages, it looks like Pablo Escobar lives here.'

The other farmhands were being held at bay before her. Julia raised something silver in her right hand. 'See, Hannah, I told you I have a gun.'

'Julia?' She could see that her employer did indeed have a firearm, although it was the smallest gun she had ever seen. 'Why are you here?' she managed to ask.

Julia straightened her purple jacket. 'GPS. I told you I keep track. It's on your keyring. You're meant to be cleaning. Why did you have to talk to the guests?'

Jacob chose this moment of distraction to make his move and grab the machete to swing at her, so Julia shot him in the foot.

Hannah had to agree with Julia. The villa looked as if it had been caught in the middle of a gang war.

She needed to talk to the police but they were more interested in retrieving Steve from the pool. While they waited for someone more senior to arrive, two gendarmes covered the body in a yellow-striped sun awning, which seemed disrespectful.

When she tried to make her presence felt Hannah was told to vacate the villa at once, along with the remaining guests. Jacob was handcuffed by a gendarme who warned him to shut his mouth or have his jaw broken, although he was given a bandage for his bloody foot. The other farmhands were led off the premises while the police headed down to Matthias's nursery to dig up his flower beds. In the teeming rain they collected their haul and loaded it into seed trays which they took to their patrol cars. Nothing they found would ever be seen again.

Giles was taken to a hospital in Nice to be operated upon, attended by his wife. Nobody mentioned him much after that. Melissa insisted on taking Jamie with her. Hannah watched as he went meekly, without complaint. For a moment they looked like mother and son.

Hannah walked back to St Martin-sous-Roches and called

Daniela, but there was no answer from her. Raphael shrugged apologetically but refused to let her back into Chez Dany. She had proved him right; English girls were nothing but trouble. She caught the bus back to Nice.

Oddly Julia took it all in her stride, which suggested she was used to trouble, if perhaps not on this scale, and paid her for the month. She was certainly not angry, and seemed less surprised than relieved, as if a poisonous boil had been finally lanced. Even so, she billed Hannah for a shortfall in the inventory of cleaning products.

Shortly after this Matthias the gardener disappeared. Nobody said a word. The Villa Lavardin's gardens were dug up, then the property was locked and left alone, its terraces filling with dead leaves, its azure pool turning brown and stagnant.

It joined the ranks of hundreds of other villas in the South of France, deserted but for lizards, shut away with its secrets. The power was cut off. *No Trespassing* signs appeared. The walls became covered in graffiti, the pool drained itself dry and weeds grew between the patio stones. Children came to smash the windows, so boards went up.

Madame Lavardin no longer looked out on her old house. The shutters on her facing window remained firmly closed. She no longer cared about the place. They could pull it down and build flats; she would not be around long to see it.

The winter was severe and proved to be her last. Her death provoked a fresh round of gossip, and so life in the village of St Martin-sous-Roches continued to revolve around itself.

———

Out in the bay a red speedboat slashed a white line through an azure sea. The whine of its engine woke Hannah. She craned forward on the warm stone bench and looked down at the shoreline.

She had taken up her old position above the Baie des Anges. In front of her, an old lady donned plastic gloves to clear up after her terrier. Any minute now the senior *flaneurs* of the Côte D'Azur would arrive behind her, joining the nightly parade in their pleated skirts and blazers, their gold buttons and scarves.

There was nothing to do now but wait for the vermilion dusk and watch as the city went about its business, tethered to routines the tourists never noticed.

The last few days had been windy and overcast, but tonight the sky was clear. Hannah unscrewed her silver flask, pulled a cup from her bag and poured out a little of the violet cocktail. It had become part of her ritual, an invocation timed to the disappearance of the sun.

She took out her phone and found the last photograph Summer had taken: the selfie by the glittering pool. Her limbs gleamed with tanning oil, making metal of her flesh. She smiled into the light, smiling at no one because there was no one on the other side of the camera. She was entirely, eternally alone.

Hannah sipped her cocktail and sat back, folding her legs under her, trying not to hold her breath, waiting for the moment, wondering if it would come.

As the first orange streaks glowed in the sky a shape began to materialise, nothing more than a few wisps of high mist at first, but gradually they condensed into human form. A late ray of sunlight illuminated the girl who strode toward her naked, a golden cloud-phantom returned to flesh. She knelt down at the line between water and shore with her hands on her thighs and smiled up at Hannah.

The old lady with the dog followed Hannah's beatific gaze and saw only sea. Shaking her head, she led the dog away.

'Summer,' Hannah said aloud, rising to her feet and smiling in welcome. 'I always knew you would come back.'

62.

Summer took the selfie, naked and glamorous against the sparkling water, and was going to send it to Steve so that he would be forced to hide it from his wife, then changed her mind. Yawning and stretching, she wandered to the patio wall and set her phone down.

Every now and again a great gust of wind swept through the valley and whirled everything upwards. You could hear the turbulence approaching as if a giant was pushing apart the foliage. Dead leaves spiralled down into the water and drifted into the overflow. Her father's pool had exactly the same problem – all pools did. She didn't want to take her final swim through leaves.

As she descended the stone steps to the field below, she realised that Hannah would be able to tell her everything that happened here next week. The thought made her smile.

She studied the great curtain of scarlet bougainvillea that hid the side of the pool. It had to be here, hidden somewhere beneath the profusion of flowers, even though the owners had done a great job of covering it up. The grey metal door to the tank room was shielded by double-thorned branches. It was half the width of a normal door but much heavier, and proved difficult to open because it had dropped a little and was scratching a crescent-shaped scar in the ground.

After the bright sunlight it was pitch black inside. She pushed the door wide and let in the light. In front of her a white stone water tank took up the most of the room. Peering over its wall, she saw that the water level was half what it should have been. The blue nylon net fixed over the plastic pipe that came in from the ceiling was densely packed with pine needles and leaves. She tried to reach it, but it was too far away.

Sitting on the edge of the wall she swung her legs over, then lowered herself into the water. It felt warmer here, encased in sun-heated stone. The base of the tank was lower than the concrete floor in front of it, and made a nice pool by itself. Wading across, the water just over her hips, she unhooked the net and emptied the leaves over the side. Then she put her hand inside the pipe and unblocked it.

The torrent of water she released took her by surprise. *They pay people to do this,* she thought. *Maybe Hannah's right. She's onto a good thing looking after villas. I could become a pool girl for the summer. Nobody with a pool is poor. Not here, though. Mykonos or Ibiza.*

While the tank refilled she tried to float on her back, but had never been very good at it. Someone had written on the wall in black felt-tip: *Ne pas dépasser ce niveau!*

Enough. She needed to get back. Jihane was due to reach her in a few minutes. He had a very expensive bike. She wondered if he had another income separate to his earnings from the

Chinese family. Nobody ever told you the whole truth. Was there even such a thing?

The water gushing out of the tank pipe fell away to a trickle. She made her way to the side and went to climb out.

The top of the wall was only just above her shoulders. Reaching up and placing her palms on the top of the wall, she set the soles of her feet against the side and climbed, but slid back down.

She had covered herself in waterproof oil, and the tank's surfaces were slimy with leaf residue.

This is ridiculous, she thought, looking around. *Why aren't there any steps?*

But there were steps.

She could see them over by the door, a set of sturdy yellow plastic steps sitting next to a hooked steel pole and some chemical cannisters.

She heard a breeze rising in the trees. She tried to climb the wall again but her feet kept slipping. The wind caught the metal door and began to rattle it.

Bouncing up from the floor of the tank, she made a grab at the wall. She was only two or three inches short of being able to hook her arm over the edge but her hands slid off. *Idiot,* she thought, *idiot, all rush and no thinking. Take it slowly.*

But that didn't work either. As her arms grew tired her jumps lost height. A great gust of wind blew the door shut with a bang, leaving her in darkness.

The water started to feel cool on her bare skin. The door shook in the rising wind but refused to blow open again. She had no idea how long she had been in the stone chamber but it felt like ages. It was just so *stupid*. How could she not have realised that if she refilled the tank it would become too deep to climb out of?

She searched the ceiling to see if there was anything she could reach or hold onto. In the corner a blue nylon rope hung from an iron hook, the remains of some broken contraption the owner had once tried to rig. She grabbed the end, but then what? Swinging on it took her no nearer the wall.

Then it hit her.

The answer was so ridiculously obvious that she couldn't imagine how she had overlooked it. All she had to do was make the tank fill until it overflowed. Just stop the orange plastic ballcock-thing that prevented the water from overflowing and it would continue to rise. She would be able to float to the edge of the wall and slide over. She was five foot three, and there was still a lot of wall above the water-line. But there was nothing more coming out of the pipe.

The breeze. It had blown the door shut. It had blasted fresh bundles of pine needles and leaves into the pool. The pipe above her head must have become blocked again.

Stretching to her fullest height she could just about push her hand inside its opening, but felt nothing. The blockage was too far up to reach.

The top of the wall was only a little too high, but it might have been a castle's rampart. Furious with herself, she jumped for the side and slipped when she fell back. The chlorine stung her eyes. The water tasted foul. She tried to scrape the oil from her arms but only managed to split a nail and make it bleed.

She tried to calm herself and consider her choices.

People survive in the sea for days, she thought. *This is just a stupid sunken bathtub full of warm water. There has to be a way out.*

What if Jihane had already arrived? He could be looking for her. She started shouting but had no way of knowing what could be heard beyond the closed door. The pool was a long way back from the villa's drive. What if he had come by, waited and given up?

She carried on shouting until her voice faded to a croak. Coughed and ingested chlorine, which made her retch. Her throat was stinging. She wished she was taller. She wished Hannah would come and save her. She tried to shout again but only a rasp emerged.

Until this moment she had not considered that she might be in real danger. In the cooling stone chamber her muscles began to tremble uncontrollably. She needed to conserve her strength. Lying back with her arms and legs stretched wide, she tried to float but went under. She imagined being found dead in here, and what people would say about her. Nothing good, she was sure of that.

She was still glad she had come to the villa, because she had met Hannah. Perhaps she was not just a passing infatuation but someone you could spend your time with. More than ever, she wished Hannah was here because she would know exactly what to do.

The utilitarian simplicity of the tank's construction worked against her escape. There were no footholds because its builder had not considered that anyone would be stupid enough to climb inside it without bringing the steps with them, particularly if they were covered in a thick layer of oil.

She thought she heard someone moving about outside.

Footsteps, she was sure of it. Jihane was here – but no, he would never think of looking for the door. My God, what if it was Steve? She tried to call out but no sound emerged. Her throat was raw and burning. She splashed instead, but couldn't make enough noise. She was here, just here!

But the sounds retreated and her world shrank back to the size of her stone sarcophagus.

After that she heard no more footsteps. The light around the edge of the door faded and the temperature dropped. As time passed she started to drift out of consciousness. She was not in the tank but somewhere distant and starless. She could no longer feel any pain or cold, just numbness. There was no up or down. She existed in a dark limbo, like a lobster being chilled in a freezer before being pierced with a skewer.

And then it was morning and she was still alive, although hungry and exhausted. Her thoughts came to her more slowly. Holding out her hand in the direction of the wall, she carefully felt for its top. Beyond it lay the world she had sought to keep at bay. She was always running, always hiding, never engaging. Now that she was constricted by this prison she could see herself more clearly, sense the time she had already wasted. If she got out, she vowed never to make the same mistakes again.

There was a sudden burst of water from the pipe above her and for a moment she thought the blockage of leaves had cleared itself. The level rose, but to her horror she found that she was being forced to stand on tiptoe. The torrent returned to a trickle once more, then stopped.

If she propelled herself up, she could just about hook her

arms over the top of the wall. It seemed the smallest of steps from there to climbing out. She tried to imagine the look on their faces when a naked girl stepped back onto the garden path.

She tried to think, propelling herself around the edge of the tank, checking for anything that could help her. In the far corner was a dark amorphous blob floating just beneath the surface. Was it a rope, something she could use? Reaching out her hand, she tried to lift it but it slipped out of her grasp. As it did so it revealed matted fur and upturned teeth.

The rats had been dead for a long time and were knotted together, leaking a brown cloud into the water.

As she jolted back her numb foot slipped beneath her. She was caught by surprise and rolled under. The burst of chlorine that entered her lungs caused her body to spasm. Freed from the tether of gravity she turned over but connected with nothing. There was no floor, no ceiling, and she breathed in again thinking there would be air but there was just water. Lost in a directionless maze, she slowly revolved as if she had suddenly been released into deep space.

She lost all track of time. It was growing dark again and she could hear music coming from somewhere above. It sounded like Abba. *Please God,* she thought, *don't let me die to 'Dancing Queen'.*

She tried to call out but had no voice left, only the smallest rasp.

This should have been a near miss, a close call, one where she learned from her foolish mistake and was made stronger by the experience. But it wasn't like that at all. The shadows sneaked up on you slowly, and you didn't notice the lights were out until you couldn't see your hands. *Disaster catches everyone off-guard*, she thought. *I know that now because I can see with the clarity of approaching death.*

The shape of her life was suddenly clear to her, a grand eighteen-year span, which meant that at nine she should have been having her mid-life crisis. At that point her parents' marriage was already dying. Her father moved to Spain, her mother's drinking escalated and Summer enjoyed the first of her stays in the state care system. She skipped to the good part, her reinvention and independence. The thought made her smile in the dark.

She tried to summon up images of her parents but couldn't bring them into focus. The psychiatrist had tried to make her remember everything. It was better to remember nothing, to see nothing, to be nothing. *Mum*, she thought, *I wish we could have been friends. I wish you'd wanted me.*

Her body was tired. The music had stopped. It was dark outside and utterly silent. Gripped by a series of violent tremors it could not fight off, her body went into spasm and her head slipped under. Water splashed over the edge of the tank. Her foot struck the wall hard, again and again. The cessation of the seizure brought a sinister calm.

Hannah, I'm here, she thought. *You couldn't find me, so it looks like I'll have to come and find you. Don't give up. Wait for me.*

Naked and golden, she floated. Her limbs settled into the natural reflex of their musculature. Her knees bent, her hands trailing through the chlorine, her fingers lightly splayed. The upper part of her face broke the surface. A wasp alighted to drink from the corner of her left eye, then buzzed away. Her exposed tan-lines were shockingly white against the aquamarine of the water, her toenails an incongruously lurid pink.

She settled lower and started to sink. The filaments of her hair drifted across her face, obscuring her open mouth, her still wide eyes. Tiny jewel-like bubbles lay trapped in her thick lashes. The tranquillity of the pool invaded her heart, bringing a great calm. It removed her fears, because all fear was just a terror of the unknown and now she knew that her life stopped here, where it was warm and safe.

The chemical water gave her a strange radiance. She and it were perfectly still, blue and gold, pink and caramel, glimmering faintly. In selfies she always looked posed and unnatural, her body displayed for the benefit of others. Now, fully immersed, she was finally herself, youth and beauty in perpetual suspension.

Hannah. Her last word remained in the chamber like a distant echo. It dissolved into the dark water and was drawn through the tank and its pipes, to be released into the aquamarine swimming pool. It rose in steam from the surface of the water, into the jasmine-scented air and out into the velvet starlit sky above.

Acknowledgments

This book is a true story. Well, almost. An amalgam of several worst-case scenarios I developed in that very holiday villa. Avid readers may recognise the character of Julia from 'Nyctophobia', who was in turn based on a property agent I knew in the South of France. She really does speak like that. Darrell, Chris and Liisa, Mike and Sarah and Pete were all there but no characters in the novel were based on any of them, I hasten to add. I'd especially like to thank Paul Gill for bringing me into the Titan fold, which feels like I'm among old friends, and particularly my astute editor Cat Camacho. This is our first book together and I very much hope it won't be the last.

About the author

Christopher Fowler is the multi-award-winning author of 45 novels and short story collections, and the author of the Bryant & May mysteries. He has written comedy and drama for BBC radio, script, features and columns for national press, graphic novels, the play *Celebrity* and the *War of the Worlds* videogame for Paramount, starring Sir Patrick Stewart. His short story 'The Master Builder' became a feature film entitled *Through the Eyes of a Killer*, starring Tippi Hedren. Among his awards are the Edge Hill Prize for *Old Devil Moon*, the Last Laugh Award for *The Victoria Vanishes* and *The Burning Man*. He lives in London and tweets @Peculiar.

For more fantastic fiction, author events,
exclusive excerpts, competitions, limited editions and more

VISIT OUR WEBSITE
titanbooks.com

LIKE US ON FACEBOOK
facebook.com/titanbooks

FOLLOW US ON TWITTER AND INSTAGRAM
@TitanBooks

EMAIL US
readerfeedback@titanemail.com